The Amulet

The door opened slowly and there stood a
man. The dim light of the passageway
outlined his massive figure all too plainly. He
wore nothing but a loincloth and a glittering,
somewhat sinister gold mask that covered the
top part of his face. She saw the taut bulge of
his gentials and recognised the gleam of pure
sexual excitement in the dark eyes that
glittered behind the mask. Had he been
watching the beautiful dancers too? Or had he
been watching her, Catrina, as she furtively
stroked her own heated body. Perhaps, she
surmised wildly, he was some dark primeval
god who had come in answer to her surging
sexual need. Anything at all was possible in
this strange, exotically decadent household!

Other books by the author:

Elena's Conquest
Elena's Destiny
Nicole's Revenge
Nadya's Quest
Risky Business

The Amulet
Lisette Allen

BLACK LACE

Black Lace books contain sexual fantasies.
In real life, always practise safe sex.

This edition published in 2004 by
Black Lace
Thames Wharf Studios
Rainville Road
London W6 9HA

Originally published 1995

Printed and bound by Mackays of Chatham PLC

ISBN 0 352 33019 8

Chapter One

'*Great god of light, hear oh hear our prayer . . .*'
From the remote depths of the forest, the hushed
voices drifted in fervent unison up to the velvety, starlit
sky. As if in answer, a light summer breeze shivered
softly through the canopy of dark oaks, teasing the low
flames from the flickering ring of fires and twisting the
pungent smoke into swirling spirals. Somewhere beyond
the clearing an owl swept between the trees, its slow,
heavy wings beating against the warm night air like
some giant moth in the darkness.

The priest's handmaiden stood all alone in the ring of
firelight at the centre of the sacred grove. Around her in
the shadows, the people of the tribe knelt and watched
her, their eyes fixed hungrily on her slender, white-robed
form, while their lips moved together in the low, hypnotic murmur of the chant.

'*Oh, mighty Lugh, god of light, hear us, give us victory this
night!*'
The lonely figure of the girl in their midst gave no
sign of acknowledgement as their words lapped around
her. Everything about her was completely still, except
for the reflection of the firelight that flickered on the
smooth, silken tresses of her silver-blonde hair, and the

1

slight rise and fall of her high, small breasts beneath her thin woollen robe. Her hands were clasped tightly together, and her wideset eyes were pressed shut in the pale, dreamy oval of her face, as if she was in a trance.

But she could hear them. She could hear every word, and feel their hungry eyes, burning into her, waiting avidly; and with a sudden stab of despair, she pressed her hands to her aching eyes. It was no good. Her gift had deserted her. She could see nothing but the blackness, and spinning golden circles against her eyelids . . .

Then there were soft footsteps on the grass behind her, and she shivered as she heard the priest's urgent whisper in her ear. 'The amulet, Catrina – remember your amulet!'

Bowing her head in anguish, feeling the priest's hot breath on her neck, she clutched at the little silver talisman that hung on a chain around her neck. She felt the smooth coldness of it searing her fingers, and suddenly her mind seemed to empty itself into a dizzying void.

'It's working?' the priest hissed urgently into her ear. 'Quickly – can you see anything yet?'

'One moment,' she pleaded. 'One moment, lord Luad . . .'

Then, suddenly, she caught her breath in an agonised gasp, because her vision had returned.

He was there. The mist swirled down in the darkness of the distant valley, forming a rank, threatening miasma; but she squeezed her eyes shut even tighter until the mist slowly cleared, and he was there, riding out from the gates of the enemy city, the city of the Eagles. Torches blazed from the high stone walls, casting a garish orange light on the man's harsh profile as he lifted his face to the hills. Behind him, the flickering torchlight was reflected fiftyfold in the gleaming armour and crested bronze helmets of his cavalry.

Catrina took a deep, searing breath, her eyes still

tightly shut. In her mind she could even hear the steady drumming of the horses' hooves on the paved road that the Roman warriors had built so long ago. He was coming, the man of her dreams, up into the hills, riding blindly into the secret forests and bleak, moorland haunts of his enemies. *Into the trap* . . .

The shadows of her vision swirled around her, and the voices of the tribe penetrated her numbed hearing as the vision faded at last.

'Victory,' they were chanting more urgently now, *'give us victory this night!'*

Suddenly they seemed to press in on her, like an alien people, and the pungent smell of the dried herbs that the priest had scattered in the flames seemed to choke her, making her dizzy. In that moment Catrina felt helplessly trapped. She wanted to cry out and push them all aside, and run to the man in her vision and stop him riding into the terrible danger.

'Catrina.' The priest's strong hand gripped her shoulder warningly. 'Catrina, you must speak now. Everyone is waiting to hear your words.'

Opening her eyes dazedly, still trembling with fear, she saw that Luad the white-robed priest was still gazing down at her with his pale, anxious eyes. 'Tell the warriors that you dreamed of victory!' he urged in the same low voice that was meant only for her. 'Quickly – tell them what they want to hear, Catrina, before they grow restless and begin to doubt us!'

Catrina stared up at him wildly, her wide green eyes helplessly shadowed with what she had seen. She could feel the tribe's expectation reaching out to her in the sacred oak grove; could see the warriors' women standing waiting in the shadows, hungry to play their part in the coming sacrament. The warriors themselves knelt silently in the fire circle, their naked torsos gleaming with oil and blue war-paint as they waited to partake of the sacred ritual before riding out to battle with the red-crested Romans, mortal enemies of their people. *But the*

3

*man she had seen was a Roman, and he was riding straight
into their trap . . .*

With all the strength she possessed, Catrina forced
herself to look up into the hooded priest's compelling,
clean-shaven features and pushed the dream from her
mind, in case Luad should glimpse some remnant of her
vision. Leave me alone, priest, she thought rebelliously.
Leave me alone! Feeling for the familiar reassurance of
the silver talisman at her breast, her fingers tracing the
tiny outline of the goddess's head that was engraved on
its smooth surface, she said steadily, 'I see victory,
Luad.'

The tall, strongly built Druid continued to watch her,
just long enough for her to feel a shiver of fear as his
cold eyes assessed her. Then he nodded, apparently
satisfied, and turned to the hushed circle, to call out, 'So.
The goddess has spoken through her handmaiden,
Catrina. It is victory tonight, my people!'

A sigh like the night breeze rippled through the
clearing. The chanting began again, low and insistent. At
a nod from Luad, more herbs were strewn on the fires,
and the pungent smoke rose high in the air as the ornate
bronze chalice filled with mead passed round the circle.
A small drum began to beat lightly, hypnotically from
the edge of the clearing, filling the warm summer night
with the rhythmic resonance of bone on taut animal hide.
At its signal the waiting womenfolk glided forward into
the circle of fire and began to move to its hypnotic
sound, swaying in the smoke and shadows, their faces
rapt as their filmy gowns moved and clung to their half-
naked bodies. The kneeling warriors watched them hungrily, their senses inflamed with drink and the knowledge of what was to come.

Catrina stepped slowly back out of the ring of fire into
the darkness, her head bowed, feeling empty and
drained. Her part was over. She knew what would
happen next, and it wasn't for her. She knew that the
women of the tribe, their bodies bathed and scented in

homage to the mother goddess, would slowly weave their way closer to the warriors of their choice and then would disrobe to offer them their lithe, ripe bodies, driving their men into a frenzy of desire before pleasuring them and bringing them to exquisite release. Then the exultant band of warriors would ride away into the night to kill their enemies, the Romans.

Catrina stood apart as she always did; different, alone, separate from the rest of the women. Before tonight, she had never minded her isolation. Luad, her protector as well as her priest, had told her long ago that it was a precious gift to be marked out by the goddess as she was, to be favoured with her precious amulet. But now, she felt a strange, empty ache somewhere deep inside her as the other women joyfully filled the clearing with their dance, their sensuous bodies like swaying, golden-tipped flames, their lips reddened with *ruan* and their eyelashes stained with berry juice as they drifted on sweet clouds of incense and honeyed mead. One by one, they dropped to their knees before their chosen warrior, reaching out eagerly to caress the men's painted torsos with the priest's magic oil, running their delicate, lascivious fingers over the swelling chest muscles and stroking the strong, corded thighs of the warriors, preparing to make their own sweet sacrifice of the flesh.

Catrina suddenly turned her head away and pressed her burning cheek against the smooth, cool bark of a young tree. Never before had she felt so alone. Why – why was she different? She closed her eyes, but she could still hear it all; the murmuring words of the white-robed Druid, the throbbing beat of the little hide drum, stirring the kneeling warriors into a frenzy of excitement. She knew that the women would be dancing faster and faster now, would be brushing their proudly naked breasts against the warriors' mouths, hotly caressing the men's sturdy phalluses with their fingers until they stood strong and proud from their sinewed thighs, murmuring incantations to the mother goddess as they twined their suppliant bodies round the hot, eager men of the tribe and worshipped them.

Catrina would always be apart from them. Luad had told her so. 'My maiden of snow,' he had called her proudly only that afternoon, fingering and lifting her silky, moon-silver hair as she had worked to prepare the herbs for this night's ceremony. A snow maiden indeed, as untouched and pure as the icy streams that ran from the mountain in winter; she was part of their rituals yet separate, and Luad made sure that everyone knew it. Sometimes, Catrina was troubled by the warriors staring hotly at her slender yet womanly body, ravaging her high-breasted tenderness with greedy, disturbing eyes; but she knew that under the priest's protection, she was as remote from them as if she was in a silver cage. No one dared to cross the Druid priest by even thinking of touching his chosen one.

She was apart from these people; accepted by them, but not one of them. She didn't even look like the big, tawny women of this tribe, but was slender and start-lingly fair, with a small, delicate face and shadowy green eyes. And she had the gift of the sight. Taking a deep breath to steady her churning thoughts, she turned her gaze back to the clearing and watched them in the maelstrom of their ritual, as she'd watched them so many times before; the hooded priest, standing at the edge of the clearing as if in a trance, and the figures twining slowly, fervently, on the mossy floor of the firelit grove. Just a few feet away from her, a stalwart warrior was shuddering as one of the women reached to guide his heavy, throbbing phallus deep into the velvety soft-ness between her legs; they began to couple in silent passion, the woman offering her ripe breasts to her man's hungry lips as she wrapped her strong legs around his waist and writhed in primitive delight.

Catrina felt a strange tremor run through her own body as she watched from the shadows. She'd seen it all so often before, but tonight something was different. Her

6

blood pulsed hotly in her veins, in a way she'd never known before, and she knew she was not in control. She felt sick with apprehension, haunted by her searing vision of the Roman with the sea-blue eyes, and her body was in a helpless, sweet torment that she didn't understand.

She swallowed hard, her breathing shallow and unsteady, because the sight of the nearby warrior, triumphantly plunging his manhood deep within the gasping woman in a final explosion of fleshly homage, made her feel weak with a strange yearning. Her small, high breasts tingled and chafed against the white woollen tunic, as if longing for the hot wetness of a warrior's mouth; the secret flesh between her legs pulsed and trembled rebelliously, and she was conscious of a shameful, seeping moistness that oiled her thighs. Oh, what was happening to her? Crossing her hands across her breasts to try to assuage the sweet, painful ache that was gathering in her strangely stiffened nipples, she squeezed her eyes shut in anguish.

Then Catrina let out a low cry because Luad's hand rested on her shoulder again, and this time she saw with a heart-stopping jolt that his face was dark and dangerous beneath his enveloping white hood.

'You keep yourself too much apart, lady,' the Druid said softly. 'The warriors will think it a bad omen, on this of all nights.' His fingers rested heavily on her shoulders, teasing aside her long, silken hair; the tips of his forefingers and thumbs rested lightly on the little silver amulet, and she trembled as she felt his power burning through the precious metal. She fought down a shiver of fear. Why couldn't he leave her alone? She said quickly, 'I am tired, Luad, that is all. May I leave now?'

His fingers massaged her amulet slowly. 'Then you must fight your tiredness, must you not? You are special, Catrina, very special. You have the sacred gift from the gods, the power of seeing.' His hands slid back to her shoulders, and moved round to knead at the nape of her

7

neck. 'Do you still see the enemy, Catrina? Are the Romans still riding towards us?'

She closed her eyes, shivering as she felt the power surge through her, and in a low voice she replied, 'Yes, Luad. I see the enemy.' Then suddenly she remembered that in her vision there had been a man of their own tribe riding beside the Roman leader, and she blurted out, 'Where is Brant tonight? He is not among the warriors!'

Luad smiled thinly. 'Brant is doing his duty. He has gone to the stone city to tell the red-crested soldiers that a convoy of women and children, travelling south from a remote fort, is under attack from a neighbouring tribe. That is why the Romans ride out so speedily.'

'Then the story of the women and children is not true? It is a trap?' Catrina's voice was scarcely a whisper.

'Of course it is a trap.' Luad spoke scornfully. 'But how did you know of Brant's part in all this? Can you see him?'

Catrina shut her eyes again in an agony of suspense. Yes, there was the red-headed warrior Brant, on his shaggy mountain pony, riding at the Roman leader's side. Brant was smiling up at him, whispering his lies, and the Roman with the blue eyes was listening intently and not seeing Brant's duplicity. Catrina clenched her fists, trying to reach out to him, to fight through the bleak mists that separated her from him, but she'd almost lost him, and she was in despair.

Then, suddenly, her vision grew clear again, and he was there. The man of her dreams. He was gazing straight at her, and she waited breathlessly for him to recognise her, but somehow his eyes, his beautiful dark blue eyes, were sightless. Horrified, she realised that the man was *blind* . . .

With a cry of despairing pity, she reached out into the darkness to touch him, to help him. Deep within her trembling, vulnerable body she felt a fierce stab of something that was almost pain, only it wasn't a pain, more a sensation of incredible, tender longing that hurt her terribly, a feeling that she'd never experienced before, as if some secret, innermost part of her that had always been frozen in unawakedness was melting into warm, anguished life. No! He mustn't die! Sweet goddess, she prayed silently, touching her amulet, save him for me . . .

She dragged her eyes open, frightened at the sensation engulfing her. Numbly she saw the silent, intent figures still writhing in erotic ritual in the shadowy circle; saw the dancing flames gleam on the painted, rippling muscles of the big Celtic warrior Cernwi as he lifted a suppliant woman astride his hips, his eyes closing in rapt adoration as his partner lowered herself sighing on to his erect manhood and he was able to sheathe himself deep within her. The woman threw her head back, murmuring little crooning sounds of pleasure, and rubbed her pink-tipped breasts rapturously against the solid wall of his oiled chest, clasping her thighs fiercely round his thrusting loins and twining her fingers in his shaggy hair as she rode him into oblivion. They were like fire spirits as they mated so primitively in the fierce, sparking light of the flames. And the agonised Catrina, silently watching them, was aware again of the strange, pulsing moistness between her own slender thighs and thought suddenly, What would it be like? To feel a man like Cernwi holding me, worshipping me with his body – to feel that strong, magical shaft of flesh deep within my own forbidden places, jerking with hungry life . . .

Luad had moved behind her. He was watching Cernwi and his woman too; she heard the sharp intake of the Druid's breath as he watched the big warrior spurt out his seed. Then, suddenly, Catrina felt Luad's hands on her breasts. She stopped breathing, stunned with shock as his hands slid beneath the soft white wool of her robe, because he'd never touched her like this before. His palms were cool and questioning, and her stomach lurched at the unexpected tingling sensation. Then his fingers fastened, very gently, on her tender nipples, pulling and teasing at the rosy buds; and the colour rushed to her face as she felt the turgid flesh stiffen shamefully at his expert touch. She twisted her head to gaze up at the priest, not understanding. Then she saw the hot, hungry look in his eyes, and felt the rough ball of his thumb insistently circling her pouting nipples, and she sprang away from him, feeling somehow desperately betrayed.

She had travelled with Luad for many years now, amongst the tribespeople of the wild northern forests and hills. Luad was young for a priest, in the prime of his manhood, and she accepted it as quite natural that he always participated in the rites he'd initiated, joining with the women at the climax of the ceremony. Catrina had always assumed that he took his pleasure like a sacrament, condescending to bestow his virility on the eager womenfolk of the tribe with a kind of cool detachment. He was popular with them, too, because he was tall and strongly built, with long, flowing dark hair that emphasised the cold refinement of his cleanshaven face.

But now, she suddenly realised with a blaze of alarm that the Druid priest was hot and hungry for a particular kind of fulfilment. This time, his chosen woman was to be her, Catrina!

He was drawing closer again, even though she'd sprung away from him like a frightened woodland animal. His hands slid out to encompass her waist and pulled her close to him, so she could feel the hard heat of his body through her thin white robe. His breath was hot in her face as he took her helpless hand in his. Then, in a husky, unsteady voice, he whispered, 'Hold me, Catrina. Touch me. Feel the power in me.'

With a juddering shock, she realised that he was guiding her numb fingers between the parted folds of his robe to where the all-too masculine flesh stood out hard and proud from his body. As he pushed her trembling palm against the hot, velvety rod, she saw his

10

avid eyes light up and heard his shallow, excited breathing rasping through his lungs; he squeezed her fingers shut, forcing them to the throbbing tip of his phallus, and she gasped as she felt the quivering flesh of his manhood. He shuddered in delight at her touch, his eyes closing in rapture, and rubbed her imprisoned hand swiftly up and down his rampant, bone-hard erection; with a low cry of defiance, Catrina pulled herself free and sprang back away from him, her fists clenched, suddenly realising.

Luad the priest had been keeping her all this time for himself . . .

Again, the acute sense of betrayal washed over her, and she rubbed her palm rebelliously against the wool of her tunic as if his fiercely aroused flesh had scorched her. Her heart thudded painfully as she backed up against the gnarled trunk of a twisted oak, and she saw the Druid's face tighten as he let his garments fall back into place. He said slowly, 'You reject Luad the priest, Catrina?'

Catrina moistened her dry lips, knowing real fear. Then she tossed back her long, silky hair in a gesture of defiance. 'I have the sight, my lord Luad,' she said quickly. 'I have to keep myself apart, or my gift will be lost for ever. That is what you've always told me.'

The Druid's brows drew darkly together as he pondered this, and Catrina held her breath, tense and ready to run. Then he said reluctantly, 'That is true. But you may minister to my needs without violating yourself, because I am a priest. Let me show you how . . .'

Catrina braced herself against the tree, reaching behind her to grasp at the rough bark, her face white with unspoken resistance. Then there was a waft of musky perfume and Catrina saw Eda, one of the most beautiful of the tribe's women, gliding softly towards them from the firelit circle. Her tunic had slipped from her shoulders so that her full, heavy breasts were proudly bare, their nipples dark-crested and stiff as she swayed towards the watching priest. Shooting a look of contemptuous scorn at the slender, silvery-haired Catrina, Eda tossed back her mane of waist-length copper hair and lifted her hands to Luad's shoulders.

'My lord priest.' Her voice was low and seductive, and slightly slurred; Catrina realised that she had drunk deeply of the sweet, potent mead. 'The ceremony draws on, and I would claim my privilege.'

As her luscious breasts rubbed against the coarse fabric of the tall Druid's robe, Catrina saw him catch his breath, his eyes mesmerised by their fullness, and heard him grate out, 'What privilege would you ask, Eda?'

Eda sank gracefully to her knees before him, murmuring, 'I would honour you, my lord!' Without waiting for his reply, she carefully parted his heavy robe and gasped in delight when she saw that his heavy phallus was already erect and trembling with arousal. Shooting a glance of open scorn up at Catrina, she leaned forward to kiss the veined purple shaft, while stroking at the heavy, hair-roughened sac of his testicles with sharp, eager fingers. Luad hissed betwen his teeth with excitement, and Eda lifted her head to smile up at him. 'Is it your will, my lord, that I should pleasure you? I assure you, I can offer you more satisfaction by far than your little priestess. She would not know what to do, my lord, with a handsome, virile man such as you.' She turned a cold grin on Catrina. 'Would you?'

The colour flared to Catrina's face. 'It is true I lack your experience, Eda,' she said in a low voice. 'Can you remember the names of all the warriors you have coupled with tonight?'

For a moment Eda's face tightened in anger, then she smiled and said, 'Jealous, Catrina? Never mind. I think it's ice that runs in your veins, not blood. At least you will never know what you are missing.' Then she broke off, because the Druid's fingers were tightening in her thick, shimmering coppery hair, and he was saying hoarsely, 'Do your work, my fine Eda. Take me in your mouth – ah, yes. Do your work . . .'

With a slow, secret smile, Eda dipped her head to swirl her pointed tongue around the tip of his phallus. The priest shuddered, and his penis grew even thicker, the swollen glans prodding hungrily at Eda's voluptuous mouth. Eagerly the woman wrapped her velvety tongue round the taut, throbbing flesh and drew him deep between her hot, moist lips.

Catrina, frozen into immobility, saw Luad jerk and close his eyes as he braced his muscular, strong thighs firmly against Eda's delicious ministrations. He came within seconds, pumping himself with a groan of release into the redhead's eager mouth, while Eda sucked and licked, swallowing hard until the very last of his seed was spent.

Catrina didn't wait to see what happened next. Tearing herself away, she ran from the clearing and pushed her way through the woods towards the nearby stream, plunging her face blindly into its cool, clear water. Her blood surged dizzily through her veins and her small breasts tingled with shame.

Eda was right. She, Catrina, was the outsider. With her fair colouring and slender build, she didn't even look like the rest of the tribe. If only she knew more about herself and her past, then she might feel as if she belonged! But she had no memory at all of her childhood, of the empty years before Luad had claimed her; and no possession except her precious little silver amulet.

Luad had found her one cold spring day, crouching behind the rocks just above the moorland path along which he was travelling. It was the first of her memories, and she remembered every detail, every word of the encounter. The young priest had reined in his shaggy pony and said, 'What are you doing here all alone, child?'

She was shivering visibly as she whispered, 'The river

13

flooded my home, and swept me away. Now I have nowhere to go.'

Luad had nodded, frowning. There'd been heavy rain for weeks, and he'd heard the news that the great river that flowed down through the city of Eboracum to the sea had burst its banks, wreaking havoc on the lowland settlements. He'd asked gently, 'There are none of your people left?'

She had caught her breath and whispered, 'No. No one.'

Luad had gazed down at her from his saddle, intrigued by her slender, almost delicate frame and her long pale hair. Even her clothes were of unusually good quality, though they were torn and stained by her sojourn in the hills. She was not like the usual children of the tribes. 'How did you escape then, child,' he questioned, 'if the rest of your people were lost to the river?'

She'd gazed up at him, her wide green eyes dark with anguish. 'I don't know. But I knew it would happen,' she said brokenly. 'I knew the water would come, because I saw it in a dream. I tried to tell them, but they wouldn't listen to me. They wouldn't listen . . . Then the water came and swept me away, and threw me against the rocks.' Her voice became a racking sob that shook her small body, and Luad saw then that there was a deep cut on her forehead, presumably from where the flood had cast her ashore. He had said sharply, 'You say you saw what would happen, in your dreams?'

'Yes,' the girl had whispered. 'I often see the future as I sleep. But no one will listen to me.'

'I will listen to you,' Luad had said, his eyes alight with excitement. 'Who were they, your people?'

She drew a deep, shuddering breath to steady herself and said in quiet despair, 'I don't know. I can't remember. I can't remember anything.' It was true. Her mind had been emptied by the trauma of the flood. All she could tell him was her name, Catrina, and all she had

14

with her, apart from the clothes she wore, was the strange silver amulet on a chain round her neck. Luad looked at the amulet with silent concentration. It was beautifully crafted, and was engraved on one side with the image of a woman's head, her thick coils of hair radiating from her face like the rays of the sun. A goddess, he realised. The sign of a goddess, to avert the evil eye . . .

It was then that the young, ambitious Luad decided to take the striking silver-blonde child into his protection. She recovered well from her ordeal, though she would always bear a small, white arrow-shaped scar on her forehead, and soon she became his constant companion on his travels through the northern hills while he carefully trained her to develop her unusual skills.

Luad was not without skill himself. He had valuable medicines for the marsh fever and the eye-sickness, and he could heal the worst of festering wounds with his precious salves. Riding at his side on her little pony, Catrina had seen and learned much. From the shelter of a low turf hide, they'd watched the fierce cavalry patrols ride out as the Romans guarded the northern wall, and they'd followed the line of hostile forts from sea to sea. Luad had taught her to speak the Roman tongue, and once they'd even ridden within sight of the great stone city of Eboracum, with its vast legionary fortress. Catrina had been stunned by the sight of the roads filled with soldiers and ox-carts, by the bustling alleys and shops, the great mansions where the wealthy lived and the reed-thatched hovels of the poor. She'd caught her breath in delight at the barges and galleys that sailed up the river, unloading their precious cargoes at the bustling warehouses that lined the bank. It was another world. At first, she couldn't believe that ordinary men could live in such a vast, crowded place, but Luad had sensed her superstitious fear and said softly, 'They are mortal men, Catrina, the soldiers of the Eagle. They bleed from the bite of the sword, just as we do. Soon, if the gods are willing, they will all die.'

Lately, she'd heard the warriors talking around the fire at night, and she heard them murmur that the chief Roman commander, governor of all Britain, had gone away across the seas to fight. He had taken many of his soldiers with him, leaving the legionaries pitifully few in number. She knew that the northern tribes were gathering, waiting their chance to swoop down and kill all who were forced to remain behind in the beleaguered northern garrisons, and she knew where her loyalties should lie. These fierce, blue-painted warriors and their womenfolk were her people, after all, who had taken in the wandering priest and his handmaiden for season after season and given them food and shelter.

And yet, as Catrina sank back on to the mossy turf beside the little stream, her green eyes were dark with anguish as she thought about her Roman, the man she had dreamed about. Her whole body pulsed with newly awakened emotions that she didn't understand; she imagined him gazing at her with his splintering blue eyes and taking her into his arms, crushing her aching breasts against the cold breastplate of his armour and pressing his firm mouth against her lips. He was beautiful, her Roman, with his powerful, perfectly sculpted body and his bronzed, dangerous face.

Luad – priest, healer and her protector – was a figure of fear to her now, because he wanted the death of all Romans. She'd suspected for some time that his magical powers were not all he made them out to be, and that he was relying more and more on her, Catrina, to maintain his hold on the people of the tribe. Tonight, she had realised that he needed her in another way, and he wanted her all for himself.

She gazed into the darkness of the forest, her amulet warm and heavy against her breast, and felt her body surge with a mixture of despair and growing rebellion.

* * *

Away to the south, the soldiers rode steadily into the night, and the centurion at their head cursed softly as his big black horse stumbled slightly on the rough, muddy track. They'd left the proper road long ago, with its good, stone-flagged surface laid by his own legion, the men of the Sixth Victrix, during months of hard toil; and now they were heading relentlessly up into the dark hills, into the uncharted territory haunted by the barbarian tribes of Brigantia.

Alexius the centurion narrowed his clear blue eyes in thought while he murmured words of encouragement to his nervous steed. The bearded Briton at his side, in his greasy red leather cap and homespun cloak – Brant, he called himself – had ridden his foam-flecked pony to the gates of Eboracum just over an hour ago, and had babbled out some tale about a convoy of Romanised British people under attack from a tribe of wild hillsmen. Alexius had no alternative but to answer the call for help, because Brant said that the convoy contained women and children. But even so, Alexius cursed the timing of the attack because his men were out of their element up here in the hostile hills, and they knew it. He heard one troublemaker grumble a little too loudly into the darkness, and turned swiftly to lash him with his tongue.

The legionary instantly dropped his head, cowed. He should have known better. The centurion Alexius had risen through the ranks to become *primus pilus*, first among spears, the chief centurion of the whole sixth legion, and was therefore effectively military commander of the Eboracum garrison in the elderly legate's absence. Even the rawest *tiro* knew that Alexius was not a man to be trifled with.

They were rising up a steep incline into a narrow wooded valley. Somewhere a bird called out in alarm, its cry harsh and raucous in the silence of the night; Alexius, his skin prickling, felt the shoulders of the hills close around him and glanced sharply at the barbarian on his shaggy pony.

'You're sure it's this way, Briton?'

The man fawned, touching his forehead in grovelling humility. 'Yes, lord! I take you the swiftest way – I swear it, by all the gods!'

Alexius saw the shifting light in the Briton's eyes as the man glanced nervously into the shadows on either side. Suddenly, with a heart-stopping clarity, he knew. The signs weren't much – just the sound of a crackling twig in the darkness, an alien smell, the rasp of the Briton's sharp breathing, nothing more. But it was enough.

Alexius wrenched at his horse's reins so hard that the big animal lurched back on to its haunches. 'Mithras!' he swore. 'Sound the alarm. Close up. To arms!'

Even as he called out he knew it was too late. He could hear the terrifyingly familiar hum of noise filling the air as the Britons made their droning battle chant across their shield rims. And then the enemy were upon them, with their wild bearded faces and naked torsos glistening with paint, running down the hillside with their heron-tufted war spears singing through the air. The night was filled with the sound of their war horns braying, and their fearsome battle-cry swelled to an almighty roar as they swooped on the grim-faced cavalry.

The Briton had vanished into the darkness. Alexius, silently cursing himself for every kind of fool, held his sword high and rode forward to meet the enemy. In this narrow cleft, there wasn't even room for his men to make a proper battle formation, and they were hopelessly outnumbered. His only hope now was for a speedy death.

In the middle of the night, Catrina woke shaking from her dream with the perspiration dampening her brow and the terror constricting her heart. It had been an evil dream, and for a moment she couldn't breathe. All around her the other women slept heavily on their narrow straw pallets, crowded into the low thatched hut. Then she realised with a jolt that Luad was there, leaning over her in the darkness, with his eyes alight with triumph.

Pushing her hair back from her face, desperately fighting back the muzziness of sleep, she whispered, 'Luad. You startled me. What is it?'

He put his finger to his lips. 'Come and see.'

A tremor of nameless fear ran through her as she pulled herself up from her pallet. Wrapping her cloak around herself against the unexpected coolness of the night air, her throat tight with nameless apprehension, she hurried after him, desperately trying to keep up with the dark-haired priest's long strides as he made his way to the oak grove.

The ashes of last night's fires still smouldered, and there was an acrid smell in the air, of charred wood and pungent herbs. Several of the tribesmen were gathered there, waiting; one of them stepped forward quickly, murmuring low greetings to Luad.

'He's still alive?' queried the priest sharply.

The man nodded. 'Aye, he's wounded but conscious. He refuses to speak, but I reckon that with your permission, lord priest, we'll soon change his mind.' Meaningfully he jerked his thumb towards a place where the shadows gathered at the edge of the clearing, and Catrina felt her stomach lurch sickly.

A man was bound to the trunk of a sturdy oak, a soldier. They'd stripped him of his armour already; his linen tunic was dusty and blood-smeared, and a filthy bandage was wrapped tightly round his head so that it covered his eyes. Beneath the blood-stained horror of the bandage, Catrina knew that his eyes would be blue, deep blue.

Luad surveyed the bound captive for a moment, then said sharply to the other man, 'Is he blind?'

19

'So it would seem, lord Luad. He took a sword blow, just above the sockets. It might heal, or it might not.' The man let a slow, unpleasant grin twist his features. 'A pity, though, if he doesn't get his sight back, because then he won't see what's going to happen to him.'

Luad nodded appreciatively, while Catrina clenched her fists and gazed in horrified pity at the man who was so helplessly bound. They had tied him so tightly to the tree that the sinews of his upper arms and shoulders were strained and knotted beneath his tunic, and she could see all too clearly how he braced himself against his pain. The Roman was blind, as she had foreseen. Did he know their language? Did he understand what his captors were saying?

She swallowed hard and said, as steadily as she could, 'What will happen to him, Luad?'

A slow, triumphant smile flickered in the priest's eyes; his finely chiselled features were cold and dangerous. He drew her quietly to one side so the others couldn't hear and whispered quickly, 'This is my chance, Catrina. Now I can show the people of the tribe that the power of the old ones still lives on in me, their chosen one. The prisoner is mine.'

Even as Catrina drew away from him in instinctive fear, he turned to gaze at the helpless Roman and said softly, 'In answer to your question, why, he'll die, of course – on the night of the full moon. After the women have finished with him.'

Chapter Two

Julia lay face down on the soft towel that was draped over the smooth marble bench, her eyes closed in ecstasy. The skilled hands continued to rub and stroke at her oiled skin, bringing every inch of pampered flesh to a state of delicious, quivering anticipation. She turned her head slightly and her long, ringleted hair, as dark and glossy as the purple grapes that lay on the table beside her, slid luxuriously across her shoulders.

'A little lower, Nerissa,' she murmured.

The slave-girl's hands wandered obediently down the hollow of her back, drawing gently on Julia's beautiful, taut buttocks. Julia sighed with pleasure, feeling the warmth of the caress tingling through her, then decided reluctantly that she'd had enough for the time being and drew herself up to reach for her goblet of sweet Falernian wine that stood beside the grapes on the low wicker table. She felt no urge to dress, because the room was beautifully warm from the channels of heat that ran beneath the floor; and as if that wasn't enough, a wrought-iron brazier filled with glowing charcoal had been placed near to her. Even though it was midsummer, Julia knew the British climate well enough by now to take no chances. In the corner a palm-oil lamp cast its smooth yellow glow around the luxurious room, lighting up its intricately tiled walls and low, cushioned couches, and looking round it all, Julia couldn't help but breathe a little sigh of satisfaction.

When Flavius, her rich, elderly lover, had been appointed governor of the city of Eboracum and had asked her to accompany him to this cold, barbarian-infested northern province, she'd been filled with trepidation. But now, she found the place quite bearable. Especially now that Flavius was far away, dragged back to Gaul for this interminable civil war that people never stopped talking about, and that she found unbearably tedious.

'You can go now, Nerissa,' said Julia. 'No – wait a moment. Is there any news of Alexius?'

Nerissa was carefully putting the stopper back in the precious glass phial of perfumed oil. She hesitated a moment, her gentle eyes clouded with uncertainty, and said, 'There is no news yet of the centurion Alexius, my lady. But they are whispering in the town that the tribesman who brought the message was a spy. They say that he lied about the convoy of women and children, in order to draw Alexius and his men into a trap.'

'Dear me,' smiled the naked Julia, sipping appreciatively at her wine and admiring the gold serpent bracelets on her wrists. 'What a shame.' Putting down her wine, she began to stroke her skin, which was soft and scented from the oils. Her breasts were heavy and ripe, the nipples coral-tipped; she caressed them lovingly, teasing them into delicious stiffness. Thinking of Alexius, she felt the familiar lick of desire tonguing deep within her belly and frowned. Parting her slender legs, her jewelled fingers strayed absently to the soft, secret folds of flesh at the apex of her thighs, stroking the smooth, hairless skin where Nerissa had depilated her as usual after her bath. Her hard, sweet little bud of pleasure leaped at the brush of her fingertips; she dragged her hand away with an effort and fought down

22

her voracious need. Time enough for that kind of satisfaction. After all, she had the whole evening ahead of her.

And, to complete her pleasure, there was this news that Alexius was missing. The centurion Alexius, the handsomest legionary in the fortress, and the one she hated most, because he had dared to reject her, Julia, when she offered herself to him.

Nerissa was still waiting nervously by the door. Remembering her, Julia drew herself abruptly from her trance and hissed sharply, 'Before you go, bring me my gown, you lazy slut. The pale-green silk one, and the sandals that go with it.'

As Nerissa scurried to do her duty, Julia suddenly became aware of the constant murmur of the familiar noises of the fortress outside the high, small window; the jangle of harness, the hammer of the armourer's anvil, and the sound of the guards patrolling the long stone walls of the governor's house, the house she now occupied by herself. She could hear the soldiers' steady, measured paces, the muttered exchange of words, the sharp rap of the watchword on the hour. She liked listening to them, because it reminded her of home, the sunlit villa in Italy that Flavius had given her. Sometimes she called the soldiers in here, into her private apartments; and Flavius, besotted old fool that he was, had turned a blind eye to her private parties. When he'd sailed for Gaul three months ago, she'd asked him if she could stay here in Eboracum, and to her surprise he agreed. 'It will be safer for you here,' he'd said solemnly.

She laughed at the memory. The only danger she faced, had the old fool but known it, was the danger of complete, wanton overindulgence. She'd not realised then how the devastating centurion Alexius, whom she'd lusted after for so long and of whom she'd had such high hopes when he was left in charge of the garrison, would contrive to spoil her fun.

Sometimes Julia wished she could have married Flav-

23

ius. But she'd clawed her way up in society by entering the theatrical profession, and men of senatorial rank were forbidden to marry actresses. She'd have had more power as Flavius' wife. But, she consoled herself, she wouldn't have had as much fun.

Nerissa was patiently holding out her gown. Julia slipped it on quickly, not troubling with an undertunic, enjoying the feel of the soft, fine silk caressing her sensitised skin. She fastened the jewelled silver girdle round her waist, pulling it tight so that it emphasised her lovely high breasts and swelling hips; then she rapped out sharply, 'What are you waiting for? On your way, girl! And as you leave, tell the centurion on duty to report to me at once. I have some questions for him.'

Nerissa scurried out. Julia slipped on her delicate leather sandals, which were of a slightly darker green than her dress and fastened with criss-crossed thongs round her ankles. She scrutinised her reflection in a silver mirror, and frowned as she saw the faint tracery of lines at the corners of her eyes. Juno, she must get more of that precious salve from her little Egyptian shopkeeper, the beauty lotion of fennel, dried rose petals and myrrh that he'd promised her would make her skin like a girl's again. Then she moved across the warm, tessellated floor to recline becomingly on a curved, padded couch, and the frown faded altogether from her face as a tall, strapping young blond legionary from Gaul tapped at the door and came hesitantly inside.

Julia ran a hand artfully through her long raven ringlets and gazed up at him assessingly from beneath her long, silky lashes that had been carefully stained with antimony.

'My lady,' he said gruffly into the heavy silence, pressing his clenched fist to his leather-clad chest in the traditional salute.

'Well, soldier,' Julia murmured, her eyes drinking in his tall, muscular physique as he stood there, awkward amongst this unaccustomed luxury. 'I called you in

24

because I wanted to know if there's any more news yet of your commander, Alexius.'

'No, my lady Julia. We've heard nothing since he set out last night.' He hesitated, uncertain of how much more to say. He and the other soldiers in Eboracum were both fascinated and frightened by this beautiful woman. As mistress of the elderly legate Flavius, the lady Julia wielded informal but unprecedented power, even in her protector's absence. The old fool Flavius was away, curse him, having dragged most of the auxiliaries off to the civil war in Gaul and thus leaving the north pitifully short of troops. The Sixth Victrix legion was virtually isolated here at the great fort of Eboracum, and if the barbarians decided to flood southwards across the undefended northern wall built by the great Emperor Hadrian, then Jupiter help the men of the Sixth. But it was no good grumbling too much, because Flavius might return at any time; and all the legionaries knew that the exquisitely beautiful lady Julia, who had her spies everywhere, would be only to quick to report back in her elderly lover's ear as she warmed his bed.

Only Alexius had the guts to stand up to her. The young Gallic legionary fervently admired the *primus pilus* Alexius, who had risen the hard way, through the ranks, to become military commander of the entire legion.

And now Alexius was missing.

The young centurion nervously cleared his throat and said, 'There is talk amongst the men, my lady, that we should send out a patrol to follow Alexius' trail before it goes cold.'

Julia snapped, 'Are you mad? Isn't the city weak enough already? Would you really deprive us of yet more men, and leave Eboracum quite open to the barbarians?'

He winced visibly at her lashing tongue. Julia went on more gently, 'Presumably the chief centurion Alexius left commands for his deputies. What were they?'

He frowned, remembering. 'To – to maintain the guard as usual, my lady. To wait, either for his return or for his message.'

'Well, then. There you are.' She drew herself softly to her feet, and the big blond guard felt the colour rushing to his face. Jupiter, but she's lovely, he thought. As she swayed softly towards him across the tiled floor, with her luscious lips slightly parted, he realised that she smelled as divinely sweet as the summer roses he remembered seeing once during a posting in southern Gaul. She was within an arm's length of him now, gazing up at him with an expression of gentle amusement on her face as she ran one finger slowly down the tough leather of his tunic. She was so sweet, so unexpectedly fragile with her skin like pale gold and her wide, dark almond-shaped eyes. He wanted to crush her to his chest and run his fingers through her black curling ringlets and kiss the breath from her . . .

He stood ramrod straight, staring at the wall over the top of her head, trying desperately to ignore the surge of fierce hardness at his loins.

'I trust, soldier, that you know your duty,' she was saying softly.

'Of course, my lady,' he stammered.

She let her hand fall, and slid her fingers up along the hair-roughened, iron muscle of his thighs, invading his brief linen loincloth to let her cool palm graze the heavy pouch of his testicles. 'One of your duties,' she was whispering, 'is to keep the governor Flavius' lady happy. In whichever way she desires.' And her fingertips trailed wickedly along the hot, silken length of his rampant penis.

He groaned and clutched her to him, covering her face and lips with avid, greedy kisses. Julia submitted for a moment to keep him happy, but she found kisses boring. Really, there was only one thing she wanted, and judging by what she had felt beneath his tunic, this young centurion could evidently supply it. Gently removing

26

his big, calloused hands from her shoulders, she led him back to the low couch and arranged herself on it so that her back was settled against a pile of silken cushions. Slowly, smiling up at him with dark eyes that were liquid with desire, she unfastened the gold brooches that held her gown together at the shoulders and clasped her hands behind her head, so that the soft silk slithered to her waist and revealed the full glory of her high, jutting breasts. Then she raised her legs, bending them at the knee, and parted them gently. Her smooth, hairless folds of flesh, pink and succulent, glistened with moisture. The young legionary gave a strangled cry and lurched towards her.

'Ravish me, soldier,' she muttered hungrily, tangling her fingers in his thick blond hair as he kneeled between her spread thighs and took her pouting nipples in his greedy mouth. 'Take me, fill me like the barbarian you are.'

His lips pulled at her breasts as his tongue and teeth teased at their stiffened crests. She could feel how his heavy, massive phallus was nudging already at her honeyed entrance, and, moaning with excitement, she dragged her fingers across his shoulders, revelling in the harsh, sensual feel of the leather. He was thrusting blindly at her, engulfed by his own urgent lust, and she arched her hips to meet him, her abdomen tightening in sweet, hard pleasure as his hungry tongue tugged and licked at her engorged breasts. The fat, velvety red plum of his lengthy penis was prodding like a ravenous animal between her glistening sex lips. With a soft cry of rapture she felt him slip inside her and she engulfed his hardened flesh voraciously, drawing it up into her own tight silken cavity.

He stopped suddenly at her sharp cry, as if frightened he'd hurt her. Her dark eyes narrowed in impatient lust; she clutched at his tight, lean buttocks, feeling all the clenched power there, and hissed, 'Ride me! Ride me, soldier – fill me with your delicious weapon. Ah, yes . . .'

He gritted his teeth and pounded into her relentlessly, sliding out only to drive the whole of that wonderful thick length back inside her quivering flesh, until for Julia there was nothing but his massive, virile penis, pounding into her very core, filling her with such waves of delight that she clasped him hard against her so she could grind her throbbing flesh bud against him. She held her breath in an exquisite moment of tension as the shimmering sensations of orgasm started to engulf her, and then she cried out and soared high into a violent explosion of ecstasy that racked her whole body.

The young soldier grunted and thrust to his own climax moments later as the sweat poured down his face. She stroked him tenderly, holding him deep within her silken core until his last, racking spasms died away. This was how Julia liked them. Young, nameless and worshipping, with their exquisite, battle-hardened bodies.

In a few moments, of course, she'd order him out, and tell him never to bother her again. But for now she felt curiously tender towards him as she stroked his lovely thick blond hair and felt the sweet trickle of his spent seed starting to spill down her thighs.

Another handsome young centurion to add to her conquests. She would go and mark him off soon on the great scroll of parchment that was fixed to the wall in Flavius' neat, empty office.

Flavius – old fool that he was, with never a day's real fighting in his life – had been so proud to be made commander-in-chief of the Sixth Victrix. He'd told his careful old Greek scribe, with his scratching pen and ink, to list all the cohorts, with the names of all the centurions written in precise order of seniority on the big piece of parchment. Flavius used to like sitting in his office and gazing proudly at that list of officers under his command; he took great pleasure in drawing appropriate little devices next to the names of those who gained awards for valour, such as a tiny silver spear for those who were awarded the *hasta pura* for bravery, or a small device of an oak leaf for the centurion who was given the oak coronet for saving another soldier's life.

What Flavius hadn't noticed was that next to perhaps a score of the centurions' names was a tiny, curved letter 'J'. Julia really enjoyed inscribing her initial very carefully and discreetly just next to the appropriate name, whenever she was pleasured by yet another of her elderly lover's willing, virile young officers.

She had plenty more names to go, and so far she'd had no refusals, except one. The only person who'd ever turned Julia down was the officer whose name was at the very top of the list, the *primus pilus*, chief centurion Alexius himself; and for that, she would never, ever, forgive him.

Perhaps he was dead already, slaughtered by the savage barbarians up in the hills. A pity, that, because then she, Julia, would never get the chance to inscribe her mark next to his name.

Chapter Three

*I*t was evening, and the sun was starting to sink behind the high hills to the west, leaving the sky streaked with orange and crimson. Long fingers of shadow were already creeping across the heather-clad moorland, and the thin breeze stirred the wiry cotton grass that grew beside dark peat pools in the secret hollows of the mountainside.

As the light faded, Catrina was kneeling at Alexius' side. He lay very still on a hide-covered straw pallet in a tiny turf hut on the outer ring of the tribe's village, with his legs and wrists tethered, on Luad's orders, to stout wooden pegs that had been driven into the beaten earth floor. The Roman couldn't have escaped anyway, thought Catrina desperately, because he was unconscious with the fever. The smoky tallow dip that she had placed near his head flared and sputtered uncertainly, throwing long, sinister shadows around the bare hovel; Catrina clasped her small hands round her amulet and bowed her head, very close to despair. 'Great goddess,' she whispered, 'whoever you are, let the light be with this man. Let his eyes be opened. Let him see.'

She'd pleaded vehemently with Luad – too vehemently, perhaps – to be allowed to treat this Roman herself. The priest had listened to her request with narrow, suspicious eyes, and Catrina had fought to keep her voice steady as she pressed on. 'You do want him to get well, don't you, Luad? For the night of the full moon?'

He'd nodded then, and murmured, 'I certainly want him to be in full possession of his faculties.' The way the priest smiled had made Catrina feel sick.

The Roman had spent the last two days in a fever, drifting between spells of unconsciousness and deep, dark sleep. Catrina had plied him with draughts of Luad's precious poppy juice to soothe his pain, and had gently eased off his blood-stained clothing so that she could tend to his bodily needs. Then she'd tenderly washed the dust and the blood from him with bowls of warm, herb-scented water and precious soap.

As the priest's handmaiden, Catrina had ministered often to the menfolk of the tribe when they were wounded or sick. But this man was different, and the breath lodged in her throat as she drew her moistened washcloth down the ridged muscle of his body, feeling the softness of the silky black mat of hair that dusted his chest, and seeing how his beautiful bronzed skin was laced and seamed with old battle scars. Although he was probably only a few years older than she was, she surmised that he had been a warrior for many years, as she drank in the power of his wide shoulders and the ridged planes of his hard, flat stomach. He was so strong, yet so helpless. From his belly, a well-defined line of the same silky dark hair arrowed down to his loins, and as she followed it, her heart fluttered strangely at the sight of his heavy phallus lying so perfect, so innocently beautiful, against his powerful, tethered thighs. She reached out with trembling fingers to touch it; her palm grazed against the full, tender pouch of his testicles, and he stirred, muttering something in his sleep as the sweat beaded afresh on his wide forehead, just below the line of his thick, closely cropped dark hair.

31

Catrina pulled her hand away from his loins as if she'd been burned, and changed the bandage on his eyes, carefully applying fresh salve of bardane to the closed lids. Even in his sickness, his face was beautiful, she thought longingly. Hard, dangerous, perfectly sculpted, with a shadow of dark stubble outlining the strong contours of his jaw. She longed for his eyes to open, so she could gaze into their perfect, fathomless blue.

'He'll be better, Catrina?' enquired Luad abruptly that night. 'For the time of the full moon?'

It was a mild moonlit evening, the warmest so far of summer, and the people of the tribe were feasting out in the open on freshly roasted venison. Catrina hesitated, then she saw Eda's burning eyes on her and said slowly, 'If he should be better in time, what will happen to him, Luad?'

The priest had just started to tear at a meaty pork rib with his teeth, and the savoury juices were running down his chin. Eda leaned forward instead and said contemptuously to Catrina, 'Luad has promised that the Roman will be given to us women for our pleasure, of course. What did you expect, Catrina the cold one? The warriors of the Eagle took our best young men from us, and sent them overseas into slavery. They have much to make up for. We'll use the Roman's body for our satisfaction, before he is finally given up to the mother goddess.'

The goddess without a name. The queen of nightmares . . .

Eda's eyes glittered greedily; and Catrina, fighting down her sick, sharp fear, snapped out sharply, 'I can't say I'd noticed you going short of men lately, Eda. Is there something wrong with you, that it takes so many to satisfy you?'

With a yelp, the red-haired woman sprang towards her, her fists raised; but Luad, throwing aside his bone to the snapping dogs that sprawled hungrily before the fire, roared out his anger and Eda subsided sulkily. She reached out for some more meat, and as she did so she hissed in Catrina's ear, 'You are not a true priestess. You are not one of our people. And some day, we will cast you out.'

Eda disappeared shortly afterwards, and Catrina prepared to make her last visit of the night to the Roman. Slowly, her heart heavy, she gathered up her little leather pouch of medicines and salves, and filled a wineskin with clear water from the stream. Then she hurried away quietly towards the little turf bothie where the Roman lay tethered like a beast, knowing that if she had any true regard for the helpless prisoner, she would give him enough of Luad's powerful poppy draught to ensure that he slept for ever, before the night of the full moon.

The summer evening was dark and velvety, with the moon a silvery crescent above the trees, and she breathed in the peace of the forest, trying to drive Eda's menacing words from her mind. Then, with a spasm of fear, she saw that a soft light flickered already from the doorway of the Roman's hut. Had the warriors taken him already? Her heart tight with dread, she pulled back the oiled hide curtain and plunged inside; then a cry froze on her lips, because she saw that the man was writhing helplessly on the ground in his bonds, his clothing all cast aside, while the naked Eda straddled his hips with her powerful naked thighs, throwing back her red-maned head in a contortion of lust as she rubbed herself greedily against his erect phallus. Catrina, horrified, saw the beads of perspiration on the Roman's forehead above his bandaged eyes; burning with anger, she cried out, 'Eda! Stop, you stupid fool! He's sick – he's in a fever!'

Eda turned on her in scorn, her hips still gyrating frantically against the man's engorged penis, and snarled out, 'He's mine, all mine! I lost my man three years ago to the red crests, so I'll have this one instead. He's strong enough for anything – just look at his mighty weapon!' She licked her lips in a frenzy of desire and moaned

33

aloud as she pleasured herself, not taking him inside her hot flesh but just rubbing her juicy, parted sex-lips against the solid shaft so that the thick stem of it caressed her tingling bud of pleasure. Catrina saw how the woman's pendulous breasts swayed as she moved, then Eda dipped her shoulders to trail the stiffened dark crests across the Roman's pinioned torso, and as her nipples brushed his chest she caught her full lower lip between her teeth and groaned in aching delight.

Catrina said in a low voice that burned with anger, 'Leave the Roman alone, you slut. If you don't stop, I shall tell Luad that the goddess's offering has been violated.'

Eda, her face flushed, spat out, 'You want him for yourself, do you, little priestess? Why don't you say so? Ah ... ' And even as she spoke her body went into tremulous convulsions as she rubbed her honeyed folds dementedly along that helpless rod of flesh, shuddering and groaning as her fierce orgasm racked her hungry body. The prisoner's limbs, constrained by the leather cords, strained and pulled as she collapsed on top of him, her whole body shaking with her exertions. Then, laughing softly to herself, she drew herself slowly back up to feast her eyes on the Roman's helplessly aroused penis, seeing how the engorged rod of flesh was sticky with her free-flowing juices. With a cold smile, she drew her sharp fingernails slowly along the massively straining shaft, and a low groan burst from the man's lips.

Catrina thought that she had never felt such icy, burning anger. 'Enough, Eda,' she hissed flatly from behind her.

'Go find yourself another man to pleasure yourself with, oh sacred one! Go and make your priest happy! This one's mine!'

Catrina's green eyes blazed. 'Enough, I said!' And Eda swung round in sudden shock at the feel of sharp, cold metal. Catrina had pulled out the sharp little knife that

34

she always carried in her medicine pouch, and she was pressing the point very steadily at the base of Eda's neck.

'You – you wouldn't dare,' said Eda uncertainly, trying to jeer.

'Try me,' said Catrina, her green eyes blazing in the whiteness of her fragile face.

With a shrug, Eda rolled off the Roman and pulled on her tunic. Her eyes sparked with hate. 'So I was right. You do want him for yourself. Well, well, so our little priestess *is* made of real flesh and blood after all!'

Catrina, tossing back her long mane of silvery-blonde hair, raised the knife dangerously in both hands. 'Get out of here.'

Eda hesitated, then she spat in the corner, on to the beaten earth floor, and stalked out. Catrina stood there until her footsteps had died away, and then she flung herself on to her knees at the man's side. He had gone so still – *dear gods, is he unconscious again? If he should die . . .*

Eda had stripped him completely of his clothes, and his starkly muscled body was wet with perspiration. Her eyes skittered helplessly over his still erect, mighty phallus as it rose throbbing into the air; she caught her breath at the size of it, feeling her own loins churning with helpless arousal. The thought of that dark red, angry tip sliding against her own aching flesh, as it had rubbed against Eda, made her feel weak with a kind of sweet, helpless pain; her secret womanly parts quivered and trickled with moisture, and her small breasts were strangely hot and heavy in a way she didn't understand. With a great effort she dragged her eyes away from his helpless penis and laid her hand on his forehead, checking that the bandage across his eyes was still secure. Was he still breathing? He couldn't be dead, or . . . or . . .

His voice made her jump. '*Mithras,*' he groaned softly, 'whatever next?'

He spoke her own language, though his words were so quiet that she could scarcely make them out. Catrina reached quickly for one of the fur pelts to cover him

35

with, and said urgently, 'You must sleep, Roman. I shall put more salve of bardane on your eyes, and give you some cowslip medicine to soothe you.'

She was pulling the pelt quickly across his hips, averting her eyes from his blatant manhood, when he said, more clearly this time, 'You expect me to sleep? With – *that*?'

Catrina saw with a sense of shock that his mouth had twisted in grim amusement as his penis, with a life of its own, thrust yearningly against the covering. Unable to help herself, she pulled the fur aside and touched it, very softly. The man let out his breath in a long exhalation; the heat of his phallus burned her, and she couldn't drag her hands away from its beautiful, silken hardness. The man sighed aloud. 'That's better,' he said.

It was an offering to the goddess. That was what Catrina told herself afterwards. Gently, as if in a trance, she enfolded the mighty shaft of flesh in her hand and rubbed tentatively at the beautiful, velvety skin. The blood rushed to her cheeks as she felt the heat of the hard, powerful rod, and she felt a surge of immense, tender power as she saw how his body tensed within his bonds, how his lean hips clenched helplessly and the heavy bag of his testicles tightened and thickened against his body. He was all hers, and because she'd seen it so often at the tribe's secret ceremonies, she knew exactly what she had to do, though no one had told her how the feel of his hot, powerful flesh in her hands would send such fire through her blood. Catching her breath, she rubbed again, harder this time, feeling the tender skin sliding up and down the bone-hard core as the clear drops of juice started to ooze from the swollen, enpurpled glans. She shuddered gently to herself, her abdomen constricted with strange, painful longing as he gasped in extremity and his seed began to spurt across his tense belly in great, milky gouts. Catrina stroked him gently, lovingly until the last of his semen was spent, and then she held him until he grew soft again and drew the covers across his body. He said with a sigh, 'You Britons have strange ways with your prisoners.'

'It's all part of the healing,' she told him, smiling because she felt suddenly happy, and she heard his husky laugh in reply. She touched his cheek and bent to kiss him very lightly, feeling the dry, hard warmth of his beautifully curved mouth and the rasp of dark stubble against her soft cheek. Then she unbound his bandages and bathed his sightless eyes, and salved them with the special ointment she'd prepared and rebandaged them, before giving him the poppy juice to make him sleep.

Then she remembered that he was going to die.

After that, Catrina still visited him regularly but she was careful never to touch him again, and he never referred to her unusual ministration on the night that she'd driven Eda away. He grew stronger as the fever passed, and if she untied his wrists he could sit up and feed himself, though he needed her guidance because he still couldn't see. He told her that his name was Alexius, a name she had some difficulty in pronouncing; he smiled at her efforts, and teased her gently. He didn't ask her what her name was.

She treated him with a careful, distant coolness, as befitted her role as a priest's handmaiden, and she almost felt that she was completely in control of herself until one night, the night before the moon was at its fullest, he put down his bowl of thin beef broth and asked her quietly, 'What will happen to me?'

For a moment, Catrina couldn't speak. What could she tell him? That Eda and the other women would bind him and humiliate him, mocking him with their bodies and tempting him into arousal so that they could assault him and gloat over his shame? That next would come death, the death ordained by the powerful priest Luad in order to re-establish his own waning influence among the northern tribes?

The Roman broke the silence at last by saying quietly, 'I'm going to die, aren't I?'

Catrina felt a great lump in her throat. But she said, as steadily as she could, 'Isn't death at the hands of one's enemies the only true fate for the warrior? For your people as well as mine?'

'True.' She saw him grimace slightly. 'But I would rather have died fighting.' He picked up the bowl of broth and continued to eat, quite calmly. She'd left the bandage off his eyes, and the jagged gash across the bridge of his nose was healing well, but he still couldn't see. As she watched him, Catrina felt her eyes burning with pity and a hot tear rolled down her cheek and landed on his forearm. He turned to look at it, but of course he was blind, and then he heard her great, choking sob and put down his bowl and put his arm quickly around her.

'Don't weep, little wild one,' he said.

Catrina rubbed hopelessly at her eyes, but the tears still came. 'I – I'll set you free!' she blurted out fiercely. 'I'll leave your bonds untied this very night, so you can creep out of the village under cover of darkness!'

'Don't be foolish.' She remembered then that he was older than her, only by a few years, but he had seen so much more of the world than she had, and had his own kind of calm wisdom. 'They would know it was you who'd helped me escape, and your priest would kill you for it.'

She shivered, and he cradled her against his chest so that she could feel his heart beating steadily. This time tomorrow, he would be dead – if the goddess had mercy. He stroked her hair, and she said, shakily, 'I knew they would capture you, Al – Alexius.' She still found his Roman name difficult. 'I tried to warn you, as you rode out of your city.'

He seemed to go suddenly still. 'You mean – you could see me, even though I was many miles away? You have the sight?'

She looked into his blind, dark-lashed blue eyes and said quietly, 'Sometimes, I can see things very clearly. I knew, before they brought you here, that your eyes were blue like the sea.'

'You can see your own destiny, then?'

'No, not that.' She hesitated. 'And if I could, it would be of no use to me. It is the fate of our people to be helpless to evade our own end, even if we know it.'

He was silent for a moment, absorbing it, and then his hands reached up to flutter lightly over her face, pausing fractionally over the raised arrow-shaped scar on her temple before letting his sensitive fingers run through her long silky hair. 'I wish I could see you properly,' he said softly. 'I think you must be very beautiful. What colour is your hair?'

She smiled. 'My enemies say that it has no colour at all. Those who wish to please me say that it is like the moonlight.'

'Ah.' He let her hair slip through his fingers, breathing in its sweet scent. 'Your enemies – I wonder, do they include the voracious warrior woman who visited me the other night?' His hand rested on the silver chain of her amulet, lightly, just for a moment.

Catrina laughed ruefully. 'Yes. Her name is Eda, and she hates me.'

'Are you really a priestess, as she said?'

She said carefully, 'I am Luad's handmaiden. While he is training me, I live a life apart from the other women.'

'So no man has claimed you?'

'No,' she whispered, bowing her head.

He was silent for a moment, absorbing her words. Then he said suddenly, with an edge of scorn to his voice that took her unawares, 'He's a charlatan, your priest. All the true Druids died out long ago, and he knows it. He just uses his so-called magic to get an easy living from the British tribes. I'll wager he enjoys taking his share of everything without having to fight for it as the other men do.'

'No! That isn't true!' Catrina cried out. 'Luad has many gifts, he knows much of healing and wisdom! He *is* a priest. He is!'

The Roman's lip curled. 'And he pleasures you well, does he, this holy priest of yours?'

Catrina hissed out her anger, drawing back her hand to strike him. 'You lie, Roman! By the gods, you lie!'

Swiftly he knocked her raised arm aside, and then she heard herself gasp aloud in shock as he gripped her shoulders and his hands slipped deliberately down inside the loose folds of her woollen tunic. She held her breath, transfixed with sudden, unbelievable delight as she felt his warm, smooth palms grazing her small up-thrust breasts; then as he cupped them, kneading them slowly, she felt an incredible rush of longing, a warm, liquid melting right down at the pit of her stomach. A shuddering tremor ran through her as he bent his head to join his mouth to hers; she moaned softly as she felt the warm, masculine strength of his tongue exploring and caressing the velvety inner softness of her lips.

'Alexius,' she whispered, breaking away from him at last. 'Oh, Alexius, I don't want you to die.'

'Then untie me, *mea mellita*,' he said. His voice grated in his throat, almost harsh. With trembling fingers she did as he commanded, untying his bonds.

And then, suddenly, he was free, and she was in his arms, whimpering out her need as his body enfolded her, big and dark and powerful in the confines of the tiny hut. His lips brushed the top of her head, and she ran her fingers slowly across his wide shoulders, gasping at the warm strength of him. He whispered in her ear, 'Patence, little wild one. We have time enough . . .'

Then with cool, deliberate hands, he ripped her tunic at the neck, and bent to lick at her exposed breasts with long, rasping strokes of his tongue, drawing out the tender, rosy nipples and biting at them softly with his strong white teeth until the hard pain of desire tugged at her loins and Catrina squirmed with helpless longing in his arms. He lifted his head, his teeth gleaming whitely in the darkness as he said, 'This is what you want?'

'Oh, yes,' she whispered, gazing into those shadowy, beautiful blue eyes that couldn't see. 'Nothing more . . .'

He laid her gently on the ground, reaching for the fur pelts to slide them beneath her shivering body; then he bent to kiss her again. Spasm after spasm of liquid desire wrenched her limbs. She felt a shiver of fear, too, because she knew that his penis would be hot and hard and hungry; and she half-longed, half-dreaded to feel its strength within her. But the moment was not yet. Suddenly he was kneeling between her legs, gently parting her tender thighs, and before she could even guess what he intended, he was drawing his long, stiffened tongue lightly along the sweet, sensitive petals of her sex-lips, bathing them in heat and delight and rubbing his pointed tongue-tip very gently against her tiny bud of pleasure. She writhed beneath him as the exquisite, undreamed-of sensations flooded her body; then she tried to clamp her legs round his shoulders, forcing him to bury his hard face even deeper into her yearning flesh. Nudging at her gently with his long, high-bridged nose, he continued to lap steadily at her honeyed vulva until she thought she must surely die of pleasure, and her straining abdomen was so tight that she wanted to explode with the dark, voracious hunger that ravaged her womb.

Then he slowly reached down and drew out his penis. She could see it protruding darkly from his fist, a massive, hungry god of pleasure, rearing towards her with the tell-tale bead of moisture already gathering at its swollen purple tip. She whimpered with need and he bent forward to rub the moist glans with heart-stopping thoroughness round each of her rosy nipples, making her cry out hoarsely as the velvety hardness kissed her

41

tingling nubs; then he eased his hips between her thighs and took her aching teats one by one into his mouth, swirling and licking with his tongue until she felt she could stand no more of his exquisite torture. At last, she felt the full head of his thick penis thrusting, slipping steadily between her honeyed lips, sliding into her with such delicious, controlled strength that she thought she would swoon with pleasure.

He held himself very still, his body arched high above her. His face was chiselled, hard, dangerous; she gazed up at the strong lines of his unshaven jaw, at the wide, cruel line of his mouth, and a spasm of fear ran through her as she remembered that this man was her enemy, a soldier of the Eagles.

Then she stopped thinking altogether as he began to drive himself very slowly into her, and her mind was emptied of everything except pleasure. He was so deep within her, filling her, stretching her to the utmost; instinctively she felt her inner muscles contracting tightly around the long, thick shaft, and her womb began to pulse with rapture. Then he withdrew, slowly, leaving her empty, and she shuddered with loss, crying out softly to him in her own language; he smiled, and murmured, 'It's all right, *mea mellita*. It's not over yet,' and then she gasped with almost unbearable pleasure as he slid his hardened phallus deep inside her again, caressing her tender, soft flesh with slow, endless strokes that made her writhe in willing abandon. His warm hand slid across her belly, assessing its aroused tightness; then, without warning, his fingers plunged downwards, curling into the blonde silken down that was soaking wet with her juices; and his big, calloused thumb started to caress her leaping little pleasure bud even while he drove his massive shaft steadily into her.

Catrina gasped and threw her head back against the furs, hearing her own feet drumming ecstatically against the floor as his virile penis impaled her again and again. Her hips were arching upwards to meet her Roman lover; she felt herself gathering into an almost unbearable tightness as she rubbed her breasts against his face and began to soar into ecstasy, the great, sensual waves of pleasure roaring through her, engulfing her. Deliberately he bent to lick at her hard, straining nipples while his thumb still caressed her quivering clitoris; she heard her own sweet, sharp, animal-like cries as she writhed in incredible delight against his wonderful rod of flesh, dimly aware that he was driving to his own fierce extremity deep within her, his breathing harsh and fierce.

Then she lay still at last, her hands still caressing his heaving shoulders, her sated sex pulsing sweetly around him as her ragged breathing returned to normal.

After that, everything happened very quickly. The Roman drew several deep, rasping breaths to steady himself; and then, before Catrina could even begin to realise what was happening, he was reaching out in the darkness to find the discarded leather thongs and was tying her down with them, just as he himself had been tied. Catrina, stunned, felt the cold leather tighten against her wrists and ankles; her throat suddenly dry, she said, 'Alexius. What are you doing?'

He bent quickly to pull the fur pelts over her shivering body, to keep her warm, and then he was fumbling sightlessly for his tunic and boots, which were on the floor beside her.

'I'm escaping,' he said quietly.

The shock of it tore through her, so that she felt as if all the breath had been knocked from her body. He'd planned it all, every part of it. *Even her seduction* . . .

He said quickly, 'You wanted me to escape, didn't you?'

'Yes. But not like this. There was no need.' Her voice broke off, choked by her own agonised bewilderment.

'I told you,' he said almost gently as he towered above her in the darkness. 'I told you before that it was no good you just setting me free. Your people would have blamed you, punished you. This way is best, because you can tell them that I tied you up and forced you.'

The hurt gathered and welled in her chest, like a real pain. 'You did force me!' she gasped out at him. 'You did!'

There was a heavy silence, then Alexius said steadily, 'If you really believe that, little one, then you're deluding yourself. You surely don't think that uncultured barbarian women are to my taste?' She gasped aloud as he went on, 'But in spite of that, I gave you exactly what you wanted. And the encounter was nothing new to you; after all, you're the priest's whore, aren't you? Spare me your protests; you certainly seemed to enjoy what we've just done.'

She wrenched at her bonds, hissing, 'Bastard! Roman bastard!'

He was fastening his boots, saying calmly, 'Always remember that sexual indulgence is a fatal weakness, *mea mellita*. You should be grateful to me for tying you up like this. At least this way you'll be able to tell your people a convincing story about my escape.'

As his words lashed her, Catrina felt the hurt tearing through her, making her feel physically sick. He'd called her Luad's whore. Of course. He'd heard Eda's taunting words – *Go and make your priest happy* – and he'd remembered, and plotted. All the time she'd been tending him and healing him, he'd been laughing at her, and planning his escape.

'You won't get far with your useless eyes, Roman!' she spat up at him. 'You'll blunder all night round the forest, and if our warriors don't get you, then the wild beasts will!'

'My eyes are getting better,' he said quietly. 'I can't see your face, but I can make out outlines, make sense of light and dark. I'll circle your village until I find the track that leads downhill, to the road of the legions. Then I'll follow the paved road to Eboracum.'

'I'll scream! I'll let them know you've escaped!' cried Catrina, aching with hurt.

'No, you won't. But thank you for warning me of your intentions.' Swiftly he bent to find a coarse blanket and tore a strip of cloth from it, which he used to gag her, as gently as he could. She tried to lash out at him, but the knots that bound her were secure, biting into her flesh. At last, he stood up and looked down at her with his beautiful, sightless eyes; and she noticed, fleetingly, that he seemed to be holding something in his closed fist, something that gleamed coldly between his fingers. Then he said, 'I'm sorry that it had to be like this. But if you really have the power of seeing, as you claim, then you should have known that I was dangerous.'

His footsteps faded into the darkness outside the hut, and Catrina lay there, helplessly bound, his coldly scornful words knifing through her – *After all, you're the priest's whore, aren't you?*

Then she realised what the Roman had been holding in his hand. He had stolen her amulet.

Chapter Four

*T*he flickering oil lamps gleamed enticingly around the spacious living chamber, casting soft shadows on the warm reds and blues of the decorative friezes that adorned the lime-washed walls. At one end of the room, a fire of apple logs burned in the hearth, filling the air with their sweetly aromatic scent; while at the other end, a wide doorway opened out on to the courtyard colonnade, giving the lady Julia's guests a tantalising glimpse of the velvety, star-spangled summer night sky beyond the marble pillars. A solitary flute-player sat cross-legged in a shadowy corner and filled the room with his haunting, melodic cadences, while two Syrian slave-girls danced sinuously, utterly absorbed in his music. Their sleek brown breasts were bare, the nipples scarlet with rouge, and their dark eyes were heavy with kohl. Around their necks they wore heavy pendants of ivory shaped like serpents' heads that swayed pendulously between their breasts as they danced.

Towards the middle of the room, a big bronze lantern in an iron lamp-stand cast a golden pool of light over the guests, who reclined on a semicircle of couches around a low table laden with sweetmeats and wine. The main courses, of succulent wild boar and venison in a rich, piquant sauce, had long been cleared away at Julia's command; though her house slaves were still busy, as they moved silently amongst her guests in order to replenish their glasses with the sweet Cyprian wine.

They'd almost run out of gossip, and Julia felt restless and bored. For some reason her thoughts kept slipping to Alexius. It was a full moon tonight, and she wondered if he was still out there, somewhere in the bleak northern hills that were so desolate even in midsummer. She wondered if perhaps he was dead. She reached out thoughtfully for some of the luscious purple grapes that she so loved, and, as she did so, Drusus the tribune, who was reclining on the couch next to hers, touched her shoulder in a possessive, irritating way. Julia glanced at him with narrowed eyes.

'A fine feast, my lady Julia,' he said softly. 'One could almost imagine one was in Rome.'

'Hardly,' she snapped back. 'With this intolerable climate, and those savage barbarians ready to sweep down on us from the hills, Eboracum has certain noticeable drawbacks. Is there any news of the centurion Alexius yet?'

'Sadly, no.' Drusus poured himself some more wine, and smiled at the dancers as if the fate of the *primus pilus* was of no concern whatsoever to him.

Julia nibbled at her grapes, feeling the sweet juice spurt between her perfect white teeth. In theory, she knew that tribunes were higher in rank than centurions, and that tribune Drusus fancied himself in charge of the city now that Alexius was gone. Drusus' father was a rich, powerful senator in Rome, from one of the most ancient families; and for his son to be posted out to the imperial province of Britain was a well-proven career move. Though Drusus, thought Julia scornfully, wouldn't get much further up the ladder. In spite of his noble blood, he was conceited, senseless and shallow, and if it wasn't for the anticipated pleasure of scoring

47

her initial next to his name on the big scroll in Flavius' office, she wouldn't bother with him at all.

His hand was stroking her shoulder again, insinuating itself beneath the fine cream wool of her tunic. Irritably, she pushed it away.

'Something is wrong, my lady?'

'I just happen to be rather bored.'

His eyes lit up lasciviously. 'Should we retire, Julia? Perhaps to your private room?'

'So I can be even more bored?' she retorted, and rather regretted her impulsive words as his cold eyes narrowed nastily. She really ought to be more careful, because people like Drusus had important friends back in Rome. She ran her fingers quickly along his smoothly muscled forearm, rather liking the feel of the soft dark hairs there, and noticed that his skin had been scented with an extremely expensive unguent of spikenard and myrrh. Reminded yet again that Drusus was rather wealthy, she summoned up a seductive smile. 'I was hoping for something a little more novel before we retired. An appetiser, if you like, before the main feast.'

Drusus relaxed and smiled. 'So you want some entertainment. How fortuitous. I have a new slave, lady Julia; I bought him from my *optio*, who spotted him in one of the galleys down by the wharf. You and your illustrious guests might find him diverting for an hour or so.'

'He does tricks?' she drawled.

'Not exactly, but he's very, very beautiful.' Drusus paused. 'And he used to be a gladiator.'

Julia's dark, almond-shaped eyes lit up instantly. Juno, but she missed the Roman amphitheatre. Occasionally they had shows here in Eboracum, in the big arena just outside the city walls, but they were nothing compared to the magnificent shows in Rome.

'Gladiators are very expensive,' she commented, eyeing him speculatively. 'That's why Flavius wouldn't hold many shows here – he said it was too wasteful when they got killed. How could you afford to purchase this one?'

'This one was cheap,' smiled Drusus, seeing that he'd caught her interest at last. 'You see, he refuses to fight.'

Julia wrinkled her perfect nose. 'How extremely boring! However, I suppose you'd better fetch him, if only so we can laugh at him.'

Drusus obediently left the room, and she turned to talk lightly with her other guests. But when Drusus came back ten minutes later with his new slave in tow, silence fell around the room, and Julia felt her pulse quicken in sudden interest.

She'd expected somebody old and broken by the harsh life of the gladiator, but he was young, this slave: younger than Drusus, and several years younger than herself. He bowed his head in correct deference to his superiors, but even so there was a kind of quiet defiance in his stance. Julia saw that his sun-streaked blond hair was swept back thickly from his strong-boned face, curling delightfully down the nape of his neck; he had a sinewy, lithe young body with incredibly powerful shoulders that tapered down in perfect symmetry to his lean waist and hips. He was naked, except for his loincloth; his legs were long and heavily muscled, and his smooth, golden-skinned body gleamed as if he had just been caressed with body oil.

Julia sat up, her fingers tapping slowly on the scrolled end of her gilded couch. 'Well,' she said slowly. 'What is his name, then, Drusus, this proud gladiator who refuses to fight?'

'His name,' smirked Drusus, 'is Falco.'

'He must be about as much use as a lion who refuses to roar,' said Julia, and her guests laughed obediently at her joke. Feeling a small flutter of telltale excitement at the pit of her stomach, Julia got to her feet and glided towards her new guest. She knew she was looking good, because she was wearing her best gown, a beautiful long cream tunic that was girded with a jewelled gold belt;

her long, ringleted hair, lightly confined by a delicate circlet of gold, cascaded to her shoulders in dark, glossy curls. She heard the low murmurs of her guests die away as they waited in hushed expectation to see what she would do.

She walked right up to the slave called Falco and trailed her fingers lightly across the hard, ridged wall of his chest, then she let her palm glide in slow circles down his tense, flat belly. She could just glimpse the beginnings of a line of silky blond hair that disappeared tantalisingly below the edge of his loincloth; she caressed him there thoughtfully, twisting her fingers in the delicate strands of hair, and heard the slave's sharp intake of breath. Juno, but she guessed he was more than well-equipped down there. His body had flinched very slightly at her sensuous caress; looking up into his set face, she saw that his beautifully curved mouth had tightened, and a muscle flickered in his smooth-shaven jaw. Otherwise, his wide-set grey eyes were clear and steady above his slanting cheekbones as he quietly met her gaze.

'So,' she jeered up at him, intrigued. 'Here we have young Falco, the gladiator who refuses to fight. Are you going to tell me why, slave, or do you refuse to speak as well?'

Her guests sniggered at her witticism, but Falco continued to regard her steadily. 'Fighting is against my beliefs, my lady.'

Julia laughed mockingly. 'Is that so? Against your beliefs, you say? I'll tell you what, Falco. I don't think you were a gladiator at all. In fact, I think you're just a coward.'

Drusus, at her side, broke in quickly. 'He survived nigh on twenty battles in the Roman arena, my lady. Apparently he was a *retiarius*, highly skilled with the trident and the net.'

Julia's dark eyes glittered. Twenty battles, twenty deadly duels, which he had survived. That meant he must have killed at least twenty men in the arena, fought them to the death in the midst of all the heat and dust, with the sweat blinding his clear grey eyes and the voracious roar of thousands of spectators urging him on. As a net man, he would have fought without armour, with only the three-pronged trident and weighted net to defend himself against his heavily armoured adversary, the swordsman. He would have had to rely utterly on his own speed and skill and courage, and apparently they had not let him down.

Julia felt the warmth rising to her face as her secret excitement mounted. At the private box at the Games that Flavius had provided for her in Rome, she had often been aroused to orgasm; she'd got into the habit of taking a well-oiled ebony phallus with her, concealed in its soft leather purse, and once seated she would slide it carefully between her thighs beneath her gown before the games started, feeling it working slickly into her oiled flesh. As companion and guard she used to take a favourite slave, a big silent eunuch, who would obediently twist and caress her nipples as the heat and excitement built up in her aroused body, and she would squeeze dementedly on the fat ebony phallus, grinding herself against it, her soft groans of pleasure quite drowned out by the ecstatic roar of the crowds.

The grand finale of the show was usually the wild beasts, or the gladiators; but sometimes, to whet the crowd's appetite for variety, the circus masters would provide the spectacle of erotic couplings in the arena: exotic dwarves and giantesses, and once, memorably, a display of incredibly endowed, virile men from one of the remote eastern provinces. The show master had lined up a group of beautiful, willing female slaves to wait for them, and Julia would never, ever forget the delicious sight of six massive, well-oiled penises thrusting eagerly away into the excited women, who had arched their supple bodies back like bows to receive them. With the aid of her ebony phallus, Julia had orgasmed several times during that one, and still wasn't satisfied, so a little later she sent for the grim-faced Spaniard who'd won the chariot race and paid him to pleasure her. She still remembered how excitingly he smelled of sweat and victory and the dust of the arena as he ravished her roughly on the floor of her box, with the big eunuch keeping impassive guard.

Now this young, beautiful slave, Falco, brought all the memories flooding back. Julia's nipples tingled and chafed against the fine wool of her cream tunic, and she squeezed her thighs together hungrily, feeling how her sweet, naked flesh was pouting in anticipation of pleasure. 'The trident and the net,' she breathed huskily. 'Falco, I would like to see you in action. It will soon be the summer festival of the god-emperor Augustus, and there are going to be contests and games in the city's arena. I would like you to fight, one last time, against an armed warrior of my choosing, and, if you win, you will be set free and given a purse of gold as your winnings.'

Drusus gasped in alarm. 'Lady Julia,' he muttered under his breath, 'that is a great deal of money! And if the slave should lose in this contest, he will be killed, and my purchase price will have been entirely lost!'

Considering how wealthy he was, Drusus was extremely mean. 'I'm happy to pay the gold,' said Julia curtly, scarcely glancing at the tribune. 'And this man won't lose, not if he's survived the Roman arena. Well, slave, what do you say? Isn't your freedom worth one last, glorious fight?'

Falco turned his heart-stoppingly beautiful smile on her and said regretfully, 'I cannot do it, my lady. It is against my beliefs.'

Julia frowned angrily. 'These beliefs of yours intrude again. What nonsense is this?'

'He is a member of some obscure Judean sect,' explained Drusus hastily. 'This sect has a certain hold among the women and slaves of Rome, I am told, though you'll not get much out of him about it. They keep their rites a secret.'

Julia said impatiently, 'Rome has many gods, as befits the most powerful nation on earth. What does this god of yours say, Falco, that forbids you to do your duty in the arena to the glory of the deity Augustus?'

Falco was silent. Julia, her face darkening, said slowly, 'I take it that you do acknowledge the sacred deity of the emperors of Rome?'

He looked grave, but held his head high as he said, 'I accept them as emperors, but I do not acknowledge them as gods, my lady.'

Drusus hissed in dismay, and a shocked silence fell over the onlookers. Rome tolerated many religions within its vast boundaries, but always on the understanding that the supreme gods of Rome were fully acknowledged as well. Julia breathed, 'You *do* realise that it is a grave offence against the state to refuse to bow at the shrine of the Roman deities?'

He bowed his head in mute understanding, and Julia, her blood on fire at his beauty and his quiet, stubborn defiance, slapped him hard across the face.

'I'll make you!' she hissed. 'Juno, I'll make you fall on your knees in homage, slave, and cry out for mercy!'

The lamplight flickered uncertainly as a sudden current of air from the pillared courtyard stirred around the warm room. The flute player had fallen silent long ago, and the two dancing girls huddled in a corner, their kohled eyes wide; all the guests had stopped drinking and talking. They had all been infected by the whisper of dark excitements to come, by the air of erotic tension that coiled around the room.

Julia beckoned to the big Numidian house slave who stood impassively by the doorway with his arms folded across his naked chest. 'Fetch me the shackles, Phidias,' she ordered curtly.

He nodded. 'My lady.'

In a shadowed recess at the far end of the luxurious

chamber, a tiny taper of light burned constantly beneath the painted bronze images of the household gods. The beautiful blond gladiator said nothing at all as Julia's slaves forced him to his knees before the shrine. Drusus himself supervised the chaining of his arms behind his back, forcing the gladiator to his knees and hoisting his wrists high up his back so that his sinews were strained and knotted.

Julia watched it all, feeling the heavy silence settle like a cloak round the room. Then she moistened her lips and said, 'Make your obeisance, gladiator, to the goddess Roma, deity of our great empire.'

Falco said steadily, 'I cannot, my lady. I am sorry.'

Julia's hands bunched into fists. 'You will be sorry, I promise you!' she hissed. 'If you won't entertain us in the arena, then you will entertain us here, tonight!'

With that she snapped her fingers to summon the Syrian girls, and whispered curt orders to them. Then, her eyes still blazing with anger, she settled back on the couch among her silent guests with Drusus at her side, drinking more wine until it sang in her head and feeling her blood thickening with sexual need. Her guests, too, were inflamed with heated lust; she could see it in their eyes. This promised to be almost as good as the Roman arena.

She leaned forward, resting her arms on the curve of her couch, and offered no objection as Drusus reached out lazily to cup and stroke at her full breasts, sliding his hand beneath the folds of her gown. Her stiffened nipples pouted hungrily at his touch, and Drusus twisted them between his fingers, causing an aching shaft of sweet pleasure-pain to tug at her melting loins. Julia smiled drowsily. This evening was turning out better than she'd thought.

Her slaves were well-trained, needing little instruction in their task. By now, the big Numidian had ripped off Falco's loincloth, and as the blond slave kneeled help-lessly in his chains, the onlookers could assess the

54

incredible beauty of his lithe, muscular body, with his smooth golden skin and the tight twin globes of his buttocks. The Numidian dragged the gladiator's shackled legs apart suddenly, and Julia hissed aloud as she saw the bounty of his manhood, with the dark, heavy pouch of his testicles and the smooth length of his penis as it hung between his thighs, mouth-wateringly proportioned even in its detumescence.

As she'd guessed, he was splendidly endowed. She wondered what he would be like when aroused; and at that delicious thought, she felt her own sweet moisture gathering between her labia and trickling down her thighs. When Drusus slipped his hand up the skirt of her gown, to slide it up her silky skin and rub his knuckles gently against her bare, glistening flesh folds, she ground herself sweetly against him and coated his fingers with her juices. Meanwhile the two Syrian dancing girls, their heavy ivory pendants bobbing on golden chains between their scarlet-tipped breasts, were eagerly rubbing some musk-scented oil into the powerful muscles of Falco's back and shoulders. Between his legs, his phallus was thickening inexorably; one of the girls reached out to caress it, licking her lips longingly. Julia called out sharply, 'No – leave him!'

They turned to look at her, surprised. Normally in these games their mistress let them do whatever they liked. But this time, Julia's eyes warned them off, as she said in a low, meaningful voice, 'Let us see if you can bring this foolish slave to his extremity without touching him. Let us see how powerful this god of his really is.'

The man's head was bowed, either in despair or resignation; Julia couldn't tell. But oh, she wanted him in his suffering, wanted to feel that beautiful phallus driving into the aching void of her hungry sex . . .

The girls continued to knead and stroke him, running their soft hands rapturously over his tight bottom cheeks and strong thighs, while carefully ignoring his now strainingly erect phallus. Julia caught her breath at the sight of its magnificent, quivering length as it reared up helplessly from his groin; the girls too could scarcely keep their eyes from that thick, silken stem of flesh, and one of them sank to her knees just in front of him, parting her flimsy skirt so that her moist feminine parts beneath the little triangle of dark curling hair were fully revealed to him. Brazenly she parted her thighs only inches from his face, and as she murmured crooning endearments to the young gladiator in her own language, she began to stroke at her plumply glistening flesh folds, rubbing hungrily at her clitoris and lifting her fingers to suck and lick at her own juices. Then she pulled the long serpent's head pendant from around her neck and began to slide it slowly into her luscious flesh, gasping with delight as the cool shaft filled her pouting sex-lips. She began to drive it in herself harder, quicker, and her dusky, red-tipped breasts bounced with passion only inches from the captive slave's face as she ground into frantic orgasm, pumping her hips greedily against the thrust of the thick ivory.

Julia saw that the prisoner held himself very still, but the sinews stood out in his bronzed shoulders, and his massive penis trembled with need, its swollen purple glans oozing the clear droplets of desire. Then she saw that he had closed his eyes against the sight of the Syrian girl shuddering in the throes of ecstasy just in front of him. Enraged, she called out, 'If he refuses to look, then you must punish him! Punish him, I say!'

Beneath her gown, Drusus' fingers were thrusting enchantingly into her aching love channel, sliding between her flesh lips with firm insistence. She clamped her hot vulva desperately around them, while all the time gazing hungrily at the blond slave's beautiful, rampant phallus. It was so long, so thick; how she longed to take it in her hands, to feel its throbbing weight! Its lovely veined length beat in helpless desire against his taut belly as one of the Syrian maids ran to fetch a small switch made of birch twigs and then, standing just behind his chained, crouching body, began to beat with tantalising little strokes at the clenched globes of his buttocks. Julia gazed raptly at the dark, secret cleft between his reddened bottom cheeks, and imagined running her hands across the sweet tightness of that puckered rear entrance which she knew would be pulsing with shameful desire.

Her guests watched the erotic scene with scarcely restrained lust. At a word from Julia, the Numidian house slave moved silently around the room extinguishing nearly all the palm-oil lamps, so that the only illumination fell on the glorious golden figure of the naked gladiator. Taking advantage of the near darkness, the rapt audience shifted restlessly on their couches; somewhere a woman moaned aloud as a friend caressed her swiftly to a much-needed orgasm, and over in a dark corner a man on a couch rubbed himself slowly and tortuously beneath his long tunic, his hand working tightly up and down his excited penis until he spurted in silent ecstasy, his eyes still fastened on the young slave's desperate humiliation.

Julia felt the dark need gather and tremble in her own belly as she watched the gladiator's proud body tremble at the bitter-sweet caress of the birch twigs on his reddened buttocks. He was fighting in vain to subjugate the hunger of his own rampant penis. How Julia longed to kneel in front of him, to display to him her own luscious, flaring buttocks and feel him driving that hot shaft of flesh deep, deep within her aching void . . .

'Fálco!' she called out to him suddenly. 'Promise me that you will fight for me in the arena on Augustus' day, and you can have your fill of my handmaidens for the whole night!'

The girls waited eagerly for his reply, barely able to restrain their lust for the beautiful, young blond slave. But he turned to look at Julia, very steadily, and said, 'Your women do not tempt me, my lady.'

Julia could feel Drusus' loins hard against her own

buttocks as he lay beside her on the couch, the thick, swelling flesh of his penis pressing hungrily through the thin cloth of his tunic. Suddenly she was out of all patience with Falco as the voracious need for sex consumed her body. Her mouth curving thinly, she said, 'Really? You should have told me earlier, Falco, that you preferred men!' She nodded curtly to the silent Numidian. 'Take him, Phidias. He's yours.'

The whole room fell into silence. Even the Syrian handmaidens sank back, stunned, into the shadows as the big, dark-skinned Numidian stepped forward and slipped off his loincloth. Someone gasped aloud, then the silence reigned again. Phidias was already hugely erect; smiling slowly to himself, he reached for a phial of scented oil which he spilled into the palm of his hand. Carefully, yet with the utmost eroticism, he rubbed along the full length of his pulsing rod until the whole of its dusky stem glistened with the precious, sweet-smelling liquid. Then he knelt behind the chained gladiator, who had gone very still, and began to knead the blond slave's bottom cheeks. Picking up the glass phial again, he slowly trickled the cold liquid down the dark cleft, rubbing gently with his fingers, questing tenderly for the tightly-puckered hole; and for the first time Falco groaned helplessly, his proud shaft quivering and straining as it ached for release from this sweet burden of torment.

Slowly, so slowly that Julia could scarcely breathe for excitement, Phidias pulled Falco's buttocks gently apart. His swollen phallus was prodding already at the gladiator's secret orifice, nudging hungrily into its target; with a gasp Julia saw the slick, dark length slide through the collared hole, while the big Numidian gazed down at his crouching victim with a look of rapt intensity on his face.

He thrust once, hard; and then he was in, almost up to the hilt. The young gladiator's face was an agony, an ecstasy, as the hot, shameful pleasure of penetration flooded his loins; his corded muscles strained against his chains at the fierce onslaught of forbidden rapture, and he threw his head back, his eyes closed, his nostrils flared. Carefully the house slave started to move within him, clasping lovingly at his tight bottom cheeks and murmuring husky endearments. After a few gentle thrusts he drew his lengthy penis out, very slowly, so that his breathless audience could see almost the whole of that massive, dusky rod gleaming in the soft golden lamplight. Then he plunged it back in harshly, muttering lewd endearments, and reached down to stroke the gladiator's bulging testicles.

The young blond slave started to break. With sweat pouring down his forehead and his eyes squeezed tightly shut, he began to quiver and buck helplessly as the big Numidian impaled his shackled body. His penis leaped and throbbed in its extremity, searching blindly for release; then, as his tormentor pounded lovingly into him from behind, he convulsed and groaned aloud, his loins spasming in fierce, shameful ecstasy as his semen began to spurt forth. One of the lithe Syrian slave-girls threw herself beneath his arched body and seized on his climaxing penis with her tender little mouth, sucking and swallowing avidly as he jerked helplessly to his release. Meanwhile, Phidias threw back his head and let out a fierce cry as his own seed started to pump hotly from his loins.

Julia, unable to bear her own arousal any more, aware of the guests around her already coupling urgently on their shadowy couches, hissed fiercely to Drusus, 'Now! Take me now, damn you!'

Tribune Drusus needed no encouragement. With a swift intake of breath he flung Julia's gown up around her waist, lifting up her ripe, flaring buttocks as she crouched willingly before him; then he slid his ravening penis quickly between her clenched thighs and found her soaking vulva. With a guttural sigh he drove deeply into her hot, tight flesh; he felt her grasping at his shaft with fierce hunger, and he thrust quickly, with speedy but forceful strokes that almost instantly had her reeling in the blissful throes of climax.

Afterwards, Drusus wanted to hold Julia, and kiss her, and stroke her wonderful breasts. But she pushed him away impatiently, because she wanted to feast her eyes on the final act of the erotic drama being played out before their eyes. Her splendid slave Phidias, his seed all spent at last, was slowly withdrawing his softening but still lengthy penis in one final, tender caress from between the gladiator's trembling buttocks. Falco, meanwhile, had all but collapsed with the extremity of his ejaculation. The slave-girl who'd taken him in her mouth crouched beside him, stroking his shoulders gently; but he was oblivious to it all as he knelt with his cheek on the tiled floor before the painted shrine to the Roman gods, his powerful golden body shaking with deep, rasping breaths.

Julia, smiling softly to herself, drew herself up from her couch and smoothed down her long cream tunic. Then she sauntered up to him.

'Well, gladiator?' she drawled, indicating the bronze figurines before which he crouched. 'I take it you enjoyed making your obeisance to our Roman gods?'

He lifted his tousled blond head to look at her, and she felt a sudden, harsh shock jolting through her; because, in spite of his desperate humiliation, his grey eyes were still clear and steady, and they were filled almost with pity, not for himself, but for her, Julia.

'Your gods are not my gods,' Falco said quietly.

Then the deadly silence that followed his words was broken abruptly by the noisy clatter of nailed boots on the marble hallway outside, and the gruff exchange of curt, authoritative words as the watchword was repeated. Before Julia could even begin to collect herself, the main doors burst open, letting a flood of garish torchlight in on the decadently erotic tableau. Flanked by four *optios* bearing torches, a tall, dark-haired centurion walked slowly into the room, his face curiously expressionless; and at the sight of him, Julia stifled a low cry.

Alexius was back.

Chapter Five

*I*t was market day in Eboracum, and the thriving civilian settlement that had grown up in the shadow of the huge fortress was filled with more people than the bewildered, fair-haired girl in the threadbare grey cloak had ever seen in her life.

Catrina had been swept into the town on a human tide of people: merchants, tribesmen from the hills, and sharp-faced traders driving great lumbering ox-carts laden with produce. She was dazed by it all; by the crowded timber buildings pressing in on her, by the noise of the street sellers crying their wares, by the pungent, heated smells of frightened livestock and excited people.

It was seven nights and seven days since the Roman Alexius had betrayed her and stolen her amulet.

'Hey, you! Get out of my way! Damned little barbarian!' A trader driving a cart yelled and cursed at her as she hesitated, bewildered, in the middle of the street. Her cheeks burning, Catrina took refuge in the doorway of a wineshop and pulled her cloak more tightly around herself. She wasn't a barbarian – she wasn't! The tribes of the forests and hills had their own ancient customs, their own deep wisdom, stronger by far than the glittering, superficial display of military Rome!

She watched from her refuge, still trembling with indignation at the insult as people speaking all the languages of the empire pushed past her in a never-ending stream: pedlars and medicine men, jugglers and tricksters, even a bear-baiter with his shaggy, awkward beast in tow. The bear was blind. Catrina watched it with aching pity as it lumbered along in the midday heat, and she felt a sudden sharp stab of homesickness for the windswept, barren hills that were her true home.

Suddenly the street seemed to empty. There was the clatter of horses' hooves on the paved, dusty road, and Catrina pressed herself even further into the shelter of the doorway as a small troop of Roman cavalry rode past, their armour glinting ominously in the sun. The crowd seemed to melt away from their path in sudden, silent fear; and from her vantage point, Catrina forced herself to look up into their grim, helmeted faces, half-hoping, half-fearing that one of them might be the one she was looking for.

He wasn't there. But she knew that he was here, somewhere in this alien city. Instinctively, as the horses went by, she turned her head and looked across the river to where the pale limestone fortress, home to the Sixth Victrix, glinted in the sun, a stark reminder of Roman power. Somehow she, Catrina, had to get in there, into the very heart of the enemy's stronghold.

Luad the priest had been wildly angry when he learned of the Roman's escape, and his anger was tainted with fear. He was terrified, Catrina knew, that with the loss of her magical amulet, he would lose the veneration of the tribe; and he had agreed with her wholeheartedly that she must follow the Roman to Eboracum with all possible speed. The night before she left to travel south with a party of pedlars and native traders, he'd handed her a slender, dangerous-looking little knife with strange inscriptions on its hilt.

'It is engraved with the Roman's name,' he'd told her, answering the unspoken question in her troubled eyes.

'You know your task, Catrina. You are to bring the Roman Alexius back here with you, for the tribe's ceremonial revenge. But if all else fails ...' He stroked the knife's deadly blade meaningfully before handing it over to her. Catrina had nodded silently, and slipped the knife into the little leather pouch of salves that she always wore on her belt.

It was as well, she reflected silently, that the priest had not guessed exactly what had happened between her and the Roman on the night of Alexius' escape from the tribe's village. Catrina had hugged the knowledge of his betrayal despairingly to herself, realising that it was all her fault for being so stupid, so naive. The Roman's words still lacerated her: *You surely don't think that barbarians are to my taste? After all, you're only the priest's whore ...*

She would do anything, anything at all, to make the Roman pay for his insults.

Dragging herself back with an effort to the busy market scene, she watched in envious wonder as two beautifully dressed Roman women walked by, followed at a respectful distance by their silent servants. The hateful man Alexius would not dare to scorn them as he had scorned her!

One of the women saw Catrina looking at her and stared back contemptuously, her eyes quickly assessing the British girl's rough homespun clothes and long, unbraided blonde hair.

'Really,' she said loudly to her companion, 'the city grows more and more full of these savage tribespeople every day – you can smell them in the air. They are nothing but beggars and thieves. Something really should be done about it.'

They moved on, chattering and laughing before finally disappearing from view inside a goldsmith's shop. Catrina watched them, burning with rebellion. How dare they speak of her people so contemptuously? Every morning, Catrina used to bathe herself in the little stream that ran through the forest, keeping herself fresh and clean, as did all the women of the tribe. Even her clothes, ragged and threadbare though they were, were freshly laundered. It was they, the painted Roman women, who were heavily, falsely perfumed, with exotic scents and cosmetics that assaulted Catrina's finely honed senses! They were so different to her; a great gulf separated them. Yet – *they* were the kind of women that Alexius would be used to . . .

She drew a deep breath as realisation came to her. *That* was what she would have to be like. Beautiful in the Roman way; sleek, groomed, scented. No longer a little savage from the hills, but the kind of woman to make any man kneel at her feet in desire. Even Alexius, her enemy. Her eyes smouldered at the thought. How she longed to humiliate him, just as he'd humiliated her . . .

Just then, a heavy ox-cart laden with barrels of smoked beef lumbered slowly along the crowded street, scattering the pedestrians in its path. And Catrina, abstractedly watching its progress, was suddenly wrenched by such a fierce premonition of danger that her heart seemed to stop beating. In that same instant she saw that immediately behind the cart, trailing along in its wake, was a small boy who had wandered briefly from his mother's side. Catrina, almost blinded by fear, threw herself towards him and pushed him aside just as the cart lurched heavily and scattered half its load. The barrels bounced and split, most of them landing just where the little boy had been only moments before.

Suddenly Catrina was surrounded by an excited cluster of people. 'How did you know of the danger, lass?' they clamoured. 'What was it that warned you?'

The cart's owner, his face ashen as he examined his lopsided vehicle, muttered, 'The wheel's broken. Must have happened all of a sudden. How could she see it?'

As they crowded around her, Catrina, all too aware of the enormity of what she'd done, tried desperately to draw away. This was the last, the very last, thing she wanted, to draw attention to her gift in this way. But it was too late to regret it, because the excited crowds were pressing around her until she found it difficult to even breathe.

'She has the sight!' they were muttering openly now, and some of the voices were sounding hostile. 'The barbarian girl has the sight – she's been sent here to spy on us, to cast a curse on us! Seize her, or she'll destroy us all!'

Catrina, white-faced, tried to run; but it was too late. Several burly men had grabbed her; she clawed and spat and kicked with all her strength, her fair hair flying around her face in a tangled mane, but they were too powerful for her.

'Let go of me!' she hissed.

'A little wild-haired savage from the hills, who speaks our language!' they jeered. 'Just look at her worn rags. We'll have some fun with this one, eh? Before we hand her over to the magistrates!'

'Let me go!' hissed Catriona despairingly, still fighting, though her efforts were growing weaker. *Alexius.* The Roman's name invaded her mind like a poisoned barb. Oh, Alexius. How he would laugh if he knew how quickly, how pathetically, her lone errand of retribution had ended.

Julia was also in the town that day. She'd been purchasing some goods at an expensive Greek jeweller's shop on the south-west bank of the river; and now, her purchases completed, she'd returned to her sedan and had just ordered her escort to take her back to the fortress when she heard the all too recognisable noise of the mob in full cry.

'Stop!' she rapped out sharply to her bearers, and stepped outside to get a better view.

So the scum of the *vicus* had found themselves some new entertainment. Julia, pushing her way determinedly through the onlookers with her burly servants at her side, caught her breath when she saw their victim.

The girl, a native Briton to judge by her crude clothing, was stunningly beautiful, with her long, silky blonde hair and her small delicate face. And she had spirit, too; she fought dementedly against her captors, hurling her native insults at them with a passionate fury that made Julia lift her eyebrows in amused admiration. She stepped back a little and watched.

Julia was still stinging with resentment from the tongue-lashing she'd received from centurion Alexius when he'd arrived back at the fort so unexpectedly a few nights ago and broken up her delightful party. He'd rebuked her severely, in that deliciously stern way of his, telling her that she brought the name of Rome into disrepute. Julia, burning with annoyance and feeling at the same time a fierce upsurge of crude desire for the tall, scornful centurion, had riposted icily, 'So you're sorry you missed it all, are you, my dear Alexius? A pity you escaped from those barbarians just a little to late to join in. Just say the word, and I'll arrange a repeat performance for you!'

He'd looked her up and down coldly. She noticed then that there was a freshly healed sword-scar across the bridge of his nose, which merely seemed to add to his allure; his blue gaze was as hard and bright as ever, and Julia flushed even now as she remembered how scornfully he'd assessed her rumpled gown and disordered hair. Then he'd said, 'Don't trouble yourself. I don't think I'll ever be that desperate. From now on, as commander of the fort, I forbid you to hold such entertainments. I won't have the reputation of the Sixth Victrix besmirched in such a way.'

To Julia's annoyance, Drusus had stayed silent, even though he was technically Alexius's superior. Probably, thought Julia contemptuously, because he was embarrassed and angry at being caught in such a compromising situation. Alexius had just looked at him, in that

67

chilling way of his, and then he'd turned and marched out with his escort, leaving Julia helplessly hissing out her venomous rage. She'd get her own back on him somehow!

In the meantime, she'd purchased the beautiful young gladiator Falco from Drusus, and was busy planning all sorts of delightful torments for him. And now, the sight of this beautiful, struggling barbarian girl suddenly opened up all sorts of new possibilities.

She stepped into the crowd purposefully. 'Make way. Let me see her,' she commanded, and the girl's assailants, recognising her as the mistress of the absent legate Flavius, fell apart, bowing their heads swiftly in homage.

'She's a sorceress, my lady!' one of them muttered quickly. 'Planning harm to the city, no doubt!'

Julia ignored him, gazing instead at the panting, blonde-haired British girl whose smouldering green eyes still spat defiance. An exceptionally beautiful barbarian.

She reached out suddenly to touch the girl's hand. 'I think you'd better come with me,' she said softly. 'I live across the river.'

The girl's head jerked up at that, and her green eyes locked with Julia's dark ones, her bearing still proud and defiant in spite of her predicament. Julia shivered suddenly. There was something special about this girl, a kind of wild, innocent beauty. And ... didn't they say she had the sight?

The girl said quickly, in her broken, husky Latin, 'You live in the fortress?'

'Indeed I do.' Julia's exquisite eyebrows arched a fraction. 'And I rather think that you and I can help one another. If you choose to come with me, that is.'

The girl drew a deep, shaky breath, the mob's eyes still hot and avid on her slender form, and said in a low voice, 'You mean it? You will take me with you?'

'Indeed, I mean it.' And quickly, before anyone could argue, Julia took the girl's arm and drew her away from the suspicious crowd, murmuring quietly in her ear.

'You will have to learn to use your gifts with more caution, I think. Tell me – what brings you to our city?'

The girl gazed at Julia silently, as if memorising every detail of her face. Again, Julia felt that shiver of unease, as if the girl was looking into her mind. Then the girl said in a low, vehement voice, 'I want to learn to be beautiful, like you.'

Julia couldn't help but smile at this innocent-looking girl's fervour. 'I would have thought, my dear, that with your face and figure that shouldn't be too much of a problem.' Then a sudden thought struck her. 'You surely didn't come here to become a courtesan?' The girl looked at her blankly, not understanding. Julia said impatiently, 'A lady of pleasure, a lady who sells herself to men!'

The girl's amazing green eyes burned into her. 'I have no intention of selling myself,' she said scornfully. 'But I want to learn every art I can. I want to be able to make men bow at my feet. I am tired of being called a barbarian.'

'And you want me to teach you these arts you speak of?'

'If you think it is possible.' The girl's beautiful voice was steady, but Julia saw that her small, high breasts were still trembling slightly beneath her thin, threadbare cloak, as if she were some beautiful, untamed wild animal exhausted after the chase.

Julia smiled slowly. 'Indeed, I think it is possible. And I assure you that you've come to the right person.'

'I know,' said the fair-haired girl calmly. 'I knew the moment I saw you.'

Again, Julia felt a shiver of unease. She nodded coolly in acknowledgement, but inside, her heart was racing. An innocent, courageous barbarian girl, endowed with quite extraordinary beauty, and, it seemed, some very special gifts. A find indeed.

Suddenly, life didn't seem quite so dull after all.

* * *

Catrina lay back on the silk-covered couch feeling strangely excited, and conscious at the same time of being more luxuriously pampered than she'd ever been in her life before as she reflected on her strange, enchanted first day in the lady Julia's house.

At first, she'd had to fight down her fear when she'd crossed the river at Julia's side and entered the great Praetorian gates that marked the entrance to the fortress. The sight of the stern guards, the clamorous noise of armourers and blacksmiths at work and the shouted commands of a cohort of legionaries exercising on the nearby parade ground had made her senses swim.

But Julia had smiled at her, and taken her arm reassuringly as they'd passed along the straight, narrow streets lined with the legion's barracks and stores, until they'd passed without challenge into the cool, airy seclusion of the lady Julia's beautiful house, where the only sounds were the trickle of the fountain in the courtyard and, somewhere in the distance, the haunting notes of a melancholy flute. Catrina took a deep breath as she drank it all in – the cool, delicate beauty of the furnishings, the subtle luxury. Was this what Rome itself was like? If so, she wanted more of it – much more!

And now it was early evening, and outside the summer sky was as pearly and soft as a dove's wing. Bathed and refreshed, and dressed in a cool, filmy gown of the softest pale-blue silk, Catrina reclined on a low couch with a glass of wine and a bowl of fruit at her side. There was no one else in the room; she had been left in complete solitude. She felt the unfamiliar liquor singing through her veins, and again felt the throb of excitement, of something about to happen.

She was on her way. Her goddess was with her still, even though she had lost her amulet; she was on her way to learning how to defeat the Roman Alexius at his own game. He was here, somewhere, in the fortress. Her powers hadn't entirely deserted her, and she knew he was almost within her reach. She shivered at the thought of her enemy, as if a whisper of cold air had suddenly kissed her skin.

Julia had spoken to Catrina briefly, as she was being bathed and massaged with soothing, scented oils by the maid, Nerissa. Julia had glided in on a cloud of delicious perfume and sat beside her, asking solicitously if she had everything she required. Catrina thought that the lady Julia was the most beautiful woman she had ever seen; her skin was like palest gold, artfully enhanced by subtle cosmetics, while her lips were red and full and her eyes were unexpectedly dark and jewel-bright. Her hair was a mane of tightly curled, glossy raven ringlets that danced as she leaned towards the reclining Catrina to stroke her hand absently. Catrina had felt strange, sensuous little shivers running up and down her arm at that touch, and was not unaware that Julia's eyes were lazily roaming over her own naked, slender body, resting disturbingly for a few moments on her tender, pink-tipped breasts. Nerissa had gone out for more towels; Julia leaned forward, and Catrina blushed as she realised that her nipples were tingling and swelling under the older woman's gaze. Julia smiled and flicked them lightly, like a caress; then she said, in her low, throbbing voice,

'You meant what you said, Catrina? About wanting to learn everything there is to learn?'

Catrina caught her breath and met Julia's dark eyes with her own shadowy, haunted green gaze. 'Oh, yes. I meant it. It's what I want more than anything in the world.'

'You will do anything?'

Catrina responded steadily, 'Yes. Anything.'

Anything to get my vengeance on Alexius. Before he dies. Whatever it takes . . .

Julia gave a contented little sigh. 'My dear, by the time we have finished with your tuition, there will not be a man in the fortress able to resist you. Your lessons will begin as soon as possible. But for now, rest, and refresh

71

yourself. I assure you, you could not be in better hands. Your lessons will begin very soon.'

She turned to go, and Catrina gazed after her. At Julia's words, she'd felt a pulse of excitement surging through her whole body; and she knew that it wasn't just the wine.

And now, evening had fallen, and she was all alone in this spacious warm chamber to which the maid Nerissa had shown her some time ago. It was all so strange to her, so luxurious after the thatched huts of her tribe; and yet somehow it felt familiar, as if she had been here before, in a dream, as if she belonged. Her skin still tingled, moist and deliciously scented, from the ministrations of Julia's maid; the gown of pale-blue silk that lightly clad her body was cool and sensuous where it touched her flesh. This was a place of wonderful mysteries, from the patterned floor tiles that were warm beneath her feet, to the clear, cool water that miraculously spouted from the serpent's head fountain in the centre of the paved, sunlit courtyard. And she had so much yet to learn . . .

Gradually, the light from the setting sun faded away, until she was in a soft, sultry darkness, with only the tinkling music of the fountain in the courtyard outside for company. More than a little hazed by the sweet, strong wine she'd drunk, she stretched her limbs luxuriously on the curved, gilded couch, wondering lazily what to do next. Should she call for someone, or just wait here? The thought of talking to the lady Julia again excited her strangely. She wondered whether she should confide in her, and ask her if she knew anything of a tall, dark-haired soldier called Alexius amongst the thousands of legionaries who inhabited the fortress.

The memory of Alexius, her enemy, disturbed her, as it always did. Pushing him with an effort from her mind, she lay back against her cushions and closed her eyes, feeling the wine singing softly through her veins. And then, she heard a slight, unfamiliar noise from nearby, and tensed.

At the other end of the room was a low, shuttered window, which Catrina had assumed opened out on to the central courtyard. But as she watched, she saw that the shutters were being opened very slowly from the other side, by some unseen hand; and they revealed not the courtyard, but another chamber, similar to the one she was in. This other room was softly lit, whereas she was in the seclusion of darkness; and within the golden glow of the luxuriously furnished adjoining chamber, two girls were dancing slowly, utterly absorbed in the haunting music of the flute that echoed softly in the still air.

Catrina gasped, shifting her position so that she could gaze at them. They seemed completely unaware of her presence, and as she watched, spellbound, they swayed in time to the music with a graceful, sensuous charm that took Catrina's breath away. In the soft lamplight that bathed them, she could see that the two dancers were darkly skinned, and quite naked except for the short, flimsy skirts that were wrapped around their waists, and the golden bangles that encircled their slender arms. Their long, silky black hair hung in glossy swathes down as far as their breasts, and their beautiful, dusky faces were quite dominated by their huge dark eyes. Each one wore a heavy ivory pendant on a golden chain that bobbed between their pert, high breasts as they moved; and Catrina suddenly realised, with a stirring of strange excitement, that their nipples were painted red. They smiled at one another in secret pleasure as they moved, their hands sinuously outstretched, their fingertips curling gracefully. They looked, thought Catrina longingly, as if they were taking great pleasure in one another's beauty.

Then her breath caught raggedly in her throat as she saw what was happening next.

One girl had reached out lightly to stroke the other's

73

firm brown breast, her body still swaying in time to the rippling cadences of the music; and as Catrina watched, hypnotised, she cupped her partner's delicious globe of flesh and pulled gently at the tender red nipple until it stiffened and stood out proudly from the swelling flesh around it. The other dancing girl reciprocated, smiling, mirroring the other's actions; then, with both sets of nipples deliciously erect, they glided closer to one another until they were able to rub their breasts lightly together, so that their reddened teats seemed to kiss sweetly with a will of their own.

Catrina watched spellbound, feeling a sudden lick of violent desire deep in her abdomen. At the same time, she felt her own sensitive nipples tingle and harden, poking against the flimy fabric of her gown. Oh, what would it be like to feel another woman's warm, firm breasts rubbing so tantalisingly against her own hardened crests? At that delicious thought, she was suddenly aware that the delicate folds of flesh that enclosed her own most secret place, the place the Roman had violated, were pulsing with the sweet ache of arousal. Her gaze was wrenched back to the tableau in the adjoining room, because the two beautiful, dusky-skinnned dancing girls had wrapped their arms tenderly round one another, so that the shimmering golden bangles on their arms tinkled like music. And then, they began to kiss, very gently. Catrina, transfixed, could see how their small pink tongues protruded and entwined as their lips met, could see how their darkly painted eyelids closed in rapture, how their stiff-peaked, bouncing breasts rubbed together with even more urgency . . .

Catrina realised that her own breathing had become shallow, almost painful. She was used to the ways of men and women pleasuring one another in the open, lusty ceremonies of her tribe; but this strange, exotic decadence all but overwhelmed her, making her blood race thickly in her veins. If this was an example of the corrupting ways of Rome that Luad had warned her about, then she wanted to know more, much more! As the girls continued to kiss languorously, Catrina realised suddenly that her loose, flimsy silk gown had started to fall apart; her trembling fingers moved distractedly towards her own urgently aroused nipples, stroking and pulling as the sweet shafts of arousal arrowed towards her taut abdomen. At the juncture of her thighs, she could feel that her secret flesh was unexpectedly swollen and moist; instinctively she rubbed her legs together in an effort to assuage her need, desperately conscious all the time of the slick, betraying wetness that gathered in her womanly parts.

Then suddenly, as Catrina watched breathlessly, one of the dancing girls drew back from the kiss and dropped gracefully on to a small couch in the corner of the lamp-lit room. Her partner, smiling happily, knelt swiftly between her companion's legs, gently drawing them apart; and then she started to fondle her there with her slim fingers.

The dancing girl on the couch was quite naked beneath her flimsy skirt. Catrina's cheeks flamed with excitement as she glimpsed the intimate folds of her dark, plump sex-lips, glistening with arousal as they peeped from beneath her downy pubic mound. Swallowing hard to ease the sudden dryness in her throat, Catrina saw how the other dancing girl dropped her head and began to dance her pointed pink tongue skilfully up and down her partner's honeyed cleft, so that the reclining girl groaned with sudden, acute pleasure and grasped her own naked breasts, pulling and twisting at the red-painted teats as her excitement mounted.

Catrina, breathing shallowly now, felt her own trembling body racked with urgent need. She thought suddenly, despairingly, of the hateful Alexius, and of that night in the forest when he had bewitched her; she remembered his dark, fiercely rampant phallus as it had nudged at her velvety entrance, ready to dip past her honeyed lips and plunge deep, deep inside her. She shivered, hardly able to bear the hungry, throbbing ache at the pit of her belly. Reaching her hand urgently downwards to find her own slick flesh-folds, the shock of discovery juddered through her as her sensitive fingertips encountered the intricate, swollen petals of her most intimate, most feminine place. Slowly she began to explore.

Luad the priest had warned her that she must never, ever touch herself there, or she would lose her powers. But in that, as in perhaps so many other things, thought Catrina rebelliously, Luad may well have deceived her! Why had he tried to deny her such delicious, forbidden pleasure for so long? She gasped aloud with delight as her fingertip just brushed her hot, plump little bud of pleasure; she felt the fierce excitement leap through her body, and cupped her swollen vulva with her trembling hand, trying in vain to soothe the sweetly agonised ache of longing that engulfed her whole body.

Alexius. Oh, Alexius. My Roman – my enemy.

Then her gaze was drawn once more to the beautiful, erotic spectacle of the two girls pleasuring one another, and she gasped aloud. 'No,' she whispered, half-shocked, half-laughing aloud. 'Dear goddess, no. I must be dreaming!'

For the two dancing girls had shifted again, adjusting their position on the curved couch so that they lay snugly entwined top to toe, curled in an exquisitely erotic tangle of dusky limbs and gleaming dark hair as they gently licked and sucked at one another's lushly exposed femininity. Even as Catrina watched, hardly able to breathe in case the beautiful women stopped, one of them drew her serpent's head pendant from around her neck and used it to probe, very gently, at her partner's secret, tongue-moistened pink flesh.

Catrina thought she would die of need as she gazed at them. Her whole body throbbed with longing; her blood pounded with heavy languor through all her limbs as she watched how skilfully the beautiful dancers pleasured one another by sliding the long, thick serpent heads deep within each other's pouting flesh-lips. They pleasured one another slowly at first, then they started to plunge them in more quickly, with probing, powerful thrusts that ravished every inch of their lush inner flesh as they both started to tremble and writhe in the very throes of delicious orgasm.

Suddenly the shutters slammed across the aperture, leaving Catrina in a state of shocked, trembling arousal in the blackness of her room.

She couldn't believe it. Even the silence was absolute, except for the uneven hammering of her own heart. Her body, clad so sinuously in the pale-blue silk, was finely honed to a state of exquisite arousal, and she needed release, any kind of release, so much!

Then the door opened slowly, and she whirled round to see that there, in the open doorway, stood a man. The dim light from the passageway behind him outlined his massive figure all too plainly; he wore nothing except a scanty linen loincloth, and a glittering, somehow sinister, mask of gold that covered the top part of his face. His black hair was cropped close to his scalp; his smoothly oiled skin gleamed like ebony in the dark shadows.

Catrina shuddered with a helpless spasm of fear as she gazed at his heavily muscled body. And the fear was tinged with a dark, secret excitement as he stepped closer, his bulging arms folded across his broad chest, and she saw that a slight smile curved his full mouth. Who was he? What was he doing here, all on his own, so silent, so strangely menacing in his mysterious golden mask? Helplessly, her eyes were drawn down his powerful, naked torso to his scantily clad loins; she saw the taut bulge of his genitals, and recognised the gleam of pure sexual excitement in those dark eyes that glittered from behind the mask.

Had *he* been watching the beautiful dancers, too? Or – and she felt a hot stab of shame at the thought – had he been watching her, Catrina, as she furtively stroked her own heated body? Perhaps, she surmised wildly, he was some dark, primeval god, who had come in answer to her own surging, sensual need! She suddenly realised that anything, anything at all, was possible in this strange, exotically decadent household.

The man smiled, and said, in a deep, rich voice, 'You wanted something, my lady Catrina?' He reached behind him for the lamp from the passageway and carefully placed it on a small bronze table within the room. Then he shut the door, enclosing them both in the soft pool of light.

'Yes. Oh, yes,' breathed Catrina. Her words emerged in a whisper, because her throat was quite dry with excitement, and her whole body was tingling with wild anticipation.

The man smiled, and pulled casually at the knot of his loincloth, letting the linen garment slide to the floor.

'You perhaps wanted this?' he murmured, in his beautiful slow voice.

Catrina gasped. He had to be some kind of strange, beautiful demon, of the kind that the tribespeople described in their stories of olden times. A demon, or a god!

His massive penis was already erect, and rising like a ramrod from the heavy bag of his testicles. Catrina, transfixed, saw that it was beautifully long and thick, its dusky shaft ridged with veins; the swollen, rounded end seemed to rear hopefully towards her, adorned already with a clear, pearl-like drop of exuded moisture. Slowly, carefully, she saw him cup the pearl drop in his palm and rub all along the hot, quivering length of his phallus, licking his lips as he did so. Then he let his penis go, and it swayed heavily, ripe with virile power.

Catrina felt a heavy, pulsing ache deep within her as she gazed silently up at him, her green eyes dark and sultry. She felt ripe, wanton, ready for the taking. All she could think of, all she wanted, was to feel that delicious, hardened rod of flesh slide up into her tormented vulva, soothing her, filling her, stretching her with its exquisite masculine power . . .

She sank back breathlessly on to the silk cushions of the couch as if in a dream, her lips parted tremulously, her filmy blue gown slipping back from her shoulders to reveal her tender, luscious breasts in all their pink-tipped arousal. 'Yes, oh yes,' she whispered, holding out her slender arms. 'I want you. Now.'

Slowly the naked and masked god-man moved towards her in the pale golden light of the lamp, his rampant penis swaying heavily as he moved. Catrina reached out to brush it longingly with her fingertips as he knelt beside her, then she put her hand round it, shivering at its throbbing thickness; it was hot and silky, and quivered with a life of its own at her intimate caress. Uttering a little moan of need, she lay back on the couch, instinctively letting her thighs fall apart to reveal the very core of her femininity to her dark, unknown visitor.

'You are sure you are ready for me, my lady?'

Either he was some mysterious god from the world of the spirits, or she was dreaming. Catrina didn't really care which. 'More than ready,' she murmured, smiling dazedly up at his chillingly masked face.

His eyes glittered behind the mask as she spoke. Kneeling beside her, he bent his head to lick her tingling breasts adoringly with long, smooth strokes of his powerful tongue. Languorously he drew the stiffened nubs into the hot moistness of his mouth while circling and nipping with his tongue and teeth until she flung her arms round his massive shoulders, stroking his silken skin and feeling the powerful muscles ripple and tauten beneath her fingers. Uttering low, soothing words in some strange language that she didn't understand, the man gently pulled her churning hips almost to the edge of the couch, parting her legs wide so he could gaze at the dark pink folds of her lush femininity peeping from between the silky tendrils of blonde hair, all the while caressing the sensitive skin of her inner thighs with his big, strong hands. Then swiftly he dipped his head to rasp at her soaking flesh with his long, stiffened tongue, running it up and down her swollen nether lips until they were parted and ready. He let his tongue flicker along the base of her yearning clitoris, and she groaned aloud at the silvery touch and thrust desperately towards him, rubbing her vulva against his face, longing for fulfilment.

Her god-man smiled and lifted his masked head, so she could see that his mouth was smeared with her nectar. Purposefully gripping his rampant member in his fist, he positioned himself on his knees between her thighs so that he could rub the smooth, rounded glans against her glistening sex-lips; then, finally, he slid his penis deep, deep within her, carefully watching her face all the time as Catrina gasped aloud with joy.

Chapter Six

*J*ulia, meanwhile, was watching the progress of Catrina and her Numidian house slave with some interest through a cunningly concealed spyhole that linked the two rooms. Julia had listened with careful attention to the barbarian girl's little sighs and gasps as she avidly watched the two Syrian dancers so expertly pleasuring one another. And Julia, well-experienced in such matters, had sensed the exact moment in which to send in the willing Phidias. She'd already told him to put on the gold mask, which was one of the many treasures she'd brought with her from her days in the Roman theatre, and he looked just the part.

'I'm ready, mistress,' he had said, grinning.

Julia eyed him dryly. He certainly was. He too had been watching the Syrian girls avidly, and she could see how his magnificent phallus pushed and swelled already against the restraint of his loincloth. Julia felt her own inevitable surge of scarcely controlled desire. She was almost ready to abandon her plans and let the slave take her now, so she could experience the delight of feeling his dusky, rigid penis slide into her own luscious flesh.

But no. Control was part of the game. The beautiful barbarian girl would soon learn that for herself.

As for Falco, poor, suffering Falco, she felt almost sorry for him, except that it was his own fault. He was with her now, half-naked and in chains, of course, in case he should try to run. Since that first night, when he'd tried to defy her, she'd made him follow her everywhere, because she was determined somehow to make him give way. Getting him to bow down before her household gods was only part of it. She wanted to break him, to make him plead for mercy, to see his beautiful, strong young body totally abased. She wanted him all for herself, with a dark, hungry desire, almost as badly as she wanted Alexius. The thought of the two most desirable men in the fortress, with each other, with her, made her feel quite faint with need. It was one of her favourite fantasies.

Falco was behind her, kneeling and chained, his fair head bowed as the Numidian went into the room where Catrina was. 'Watch,' Julia hissed at him angrily. 'Watch them, gladiator, or I'll make you sorry!'

She could barely restrain her own excitement as she gazed through the secret spyhole and watched it all. Slowly and quietly, just as she'd instructed him, the big masked houseslave stepped towards the stunned Catrina with his lovely throbbing shaft in erotic display and Julia, with a pang of delight, saw how the British girl reached with trembling hands to touch it. She was perfect, this girl; wild, wanton, beautiful, with her silky golden hair and her supple, slender body and high, firm breasts. How eagerly and yet how innocently she responded to the big slave; how exquisitely her lovely body arched with pleasure as the skilful, powerful Numidian began to caress her, his penis throbbing and angry as it reared from his thighs.

Julia was desperate herself. Her nipples were thrusting achingly against the fine wool of her tunic, and her naked labia were swollen, melting with honeyed moisture. Glancing speculatively at Falco's beautiful, despairing profile, at his taut suntanned skin and thick fair hair, she let her eyes rove hungrily over the oiled golden muscles of his naked chest and biceps, taut and straining because of the way he was pinioned. He, too, could see the erotic tableau being enacted in the next room. She knew, because she could see the bulge in the fabric of his loincloth where his phallus strained in helpless arousal.

She wouldn't take him yet. She wanted his lovely body very much; but she wanted him to beg for her first.

She called for her Syrian girls by pulling on a corded bellrope. Julia was very fond of her two dancing girls; they were twins, and she'd bought them four years ago from the household of a bankrupt senator in Rome. Julia had renamed them Lark and Nightingale, because they reminded her of two delicate, graceful songbirds. Training them in the ways of her household had been a pleasure.

When the Syrian girls came in, their red-tipped breasts bobbing enticingly, she told them exactly what she wanted. Lark and Nightingale nodded eagerly and swiftly knelt on either side of her as she leaned back against her cushions. Julia sighed and closed her eyes as one of them obediently began to caress and tease her breasts with her hot little mouth, while the other, very gently but with wicked skill, reached to part Julia's soft thighs with her hands and bent her head to lick her there, to savour the warm, hairless, crinkled flesh and breathe in all the musky scent of her sex.

The touch of that hot, velvety little tongue nibbling at her swollen labia and flicking past her clitoris was so sweet that Julia shuddered and arched in delight. Quickly, sensing her mistress's nearness, Lark unlooped the heavy ivory serpent from around her neck and slid it slowly, tantalisingly, into Julia's throbbing vulva, twisting and pulling rhythmically at the delicious instrument of pleasure, tugging it out, slick with Julia's juices, and sliding it back in with blissful slowness while Nightingale continued to suck and lick and pull at the reclining woman's breasts.

Julia moaned in ecstasy and clenched her loins as the hot shafts of pleasure quivered and gathered in her straining abdomen. Her nipples were on fire, burning with exquisite need as the dusky Syrian girl bit and laved, swirling her dancing tongue round each turgid crest in turn. Between her splayed legs Julia could feel the satisfying fatness of the smooth ivory bulging between her vaginal walls, sending wave after wave of excitement through her. She writhed her hips, drawing the solid shaft deep inside herself, imagining that the cunningly carved serpent was alive, menacing, hungry as it plunged deep within her. Almost there, oh, almost there!

And then she heard Falco gasp, and she opened her eyes, to see that the sweat was beading on his wide, clear forehead, and his eyes were closed in the agony of his arousal. Julia let her eyes drop, and she saw how his strong phallus strained and bulged beneath his tunic.

Fighting down her own need, she wrenched herself away from her handmaidens' eager attentions, pulling herself off the ivory phallus, and sat up, her face flushed.

'Untie the gladiator,' she said curtly to Lark.

'But, *patrona* . . .'

'Do as I say!'

It was a risk, she knew. But it was one she was prepared to take, because no man would run from this. She settled herself again, back on her cushions, so that she could see the kneeling slave; she watched silently as the girls unchained him, their eyes lowered, and flicked back his tunic, so they could all see how his hot, angry rod leaped up and quivered against his taut belly. Julia caught her breath, and smiled. It was beautiful. Silken, strong, rippled with delicate veins, the swollen plum at the end already ripe to bursting. Some day soon, she would take him. When he had suffered enough . . .

She nodded to the girls to continue with her exactly

where they had left off, parting her legs in invitation. Then she glanced again through her spyhole into the neighbouring chamber.

She was glad Phidias had remembered to take a lamp with him. She could see everything clearly in the soft golden light; how the big Numidian was now tenderly ravishing the blonde girl with his massive dark shaft, gently and repeatedly sliding its great thick length juicily into her quivering loins and fondling her breasts with his big hands; she saw how the girl's delicate face was contorted with need, her wide green eyes smoky with desire as she arched herself to meet him and the skilful slave brought her slowly but surely towards certain ecstasy with each stroke of his deliciously lengthy penis.

Julia sighed and closed her eyes briefly with pleasure as the cool ivory serpent slipped welcomely inside her again; her vagina clenched lustfully around it, savouring its intimate caress, and her whole body surged anew with desire as Nightingale nipped and teased obediently at her nipples.

'Look at me, Falco,' Julia whispered huskily, turning her head towards the chained slave. 'Don't you want me? Wouldn't you like to stick your hot, huge penis right up inside me, and feel how ripe I am, how juicy? Wouldn't you like to ride me, to feel me grip and squirm against you, until you can't hold back any more? Wouldn't you like me to push my breasts in your face, gladiator, while you pump yourself deep inside me?'

It was too much for him. She knew it would be. His rampant penis jerked anew at her words, as if it had a life of its own, and its plummy tip was throbbing with desire. With a despairing groan he grasped it in his fist and rubbed and pulled feverishly at the thick shaft, sliding the skin up and down the bone-hard core, until his heavy balls tightened in warning. Then his entire body convulsed as his creamy seed suddenly jetted forth, spurting in great gouts across the tiled floor as he milked himself of every last, luscious drop. At the same moment, Julia, her eyes glazing over with lust as she watched him, began to thrust herself hard against the solid ivory serpent that her handmaiden wielded so cunningly, savouring every delicious inch of it and imagining that it was Falco's great weapon, spurting and thrusting inside her. Then she pushed her hot, aching breasts up into the other girl's face, to have them expertly caressed and licked, until, uttering fierce, high-pitched moans, she shuddered at last into a long, glorious orgasm that left her shaking and weak.

When she'd recovered, the young gladiator was kneeling in silence, his body still trembling with the force of his release as his semen cooled on the floor, his head bowed in an agony of shame. Julia said his name, softly, and his grey eyes, bleak and drained, were drawn towards her.

'That was rather decadent of you,' she said silkily, 'to debase yourself like that. I thought you had more self-control, Falco.' She turned to Lark and Nightingale. 'My little songbirds. Put his chains on again. I doubt he'll have the strength to resist you.'

The girls did as they were told, and Julia watched as the cold grey metal bit into the gladiator's smooth golden skin. His penis was somnolent now, a fat, dusky pink snake between his strong thighs; she longed to touch it, to see it surge into life once more. Then, suddenly, Lark was at her shoulder, whispering, 'Patrona. In the other room. Quickly . . .'

And as Julia swiftly leaned forward and gazed through her spyhole, she realised that the barbarian girl, too, was close to her extremity.

Catrina was pressing herself hungrily against the heavy, dusky body of the Numidian, her face flushed and joyous at the pleasure he was bestowing on her. Each time he slid himself into her lush, wanton flesh, she clutched instinctively with her vagina at his gloriously lengthy penis; and each time he withdrew, she gave a tiny sigh of disappointment, and dug her small fingers deeply into his broad, powerfully muscled shoulders. Her need gathered, sweet and hard, within her tight belly until she felt ready to split, like some luscious fruit; each time he lightly caressed the nubs of her nipples, or gently stroked her plump, throbbing clitoris, she felt herself gather on the brink in a longing for pleasure that was almost a pain, so acute was her arousal.

Then, at last, when she was a shivering, tremulous mass of need, the masked man smiled and planted his big hands firmly on the couch on either side of her panting body. His sleek, powerful body arched above her like a bow as he withdrew his glistening penis to the very brink of her swollen, pulsing vagina. Then, gazing down tenderly into her rapturous, flushed face, he began to thrust purposefully, almost grimly, with a steady driving force that emptied her mind of everything except pleasure; until she was aware of nothing except the delicious, bone-hard length of male flesh that filled her, stretched her and drove her into sweet, incredible realms of rapture. Gathering all her remaining strength, Catrina arched her trembling hips to meet him and ground her pubic bone against the hardness of his mighty shaft so that her desperately yearning clitoris was pressed and rubbed into ecstasy; and then she exploded into a long, mind-shattering orgasm, so that the lamp-lit room was filled with her whimpering, high-pitched cries of delight as her lover continued to drive his magnificent penis steadily into her spasming vulva.

The big Numidian came to his own climax very quickly after that, groaning aloud in the extremity of his release. Catrina, her own sated flesh still pulsing in sweet afterglow around his gently throbbing shaft, lay back dazed as her mysterious god-man let his velvety mouth drift across her pleasure-engorged breasts. If this was the way the Romans lived, then this was for her!

Then the door opened, letting in a draught of chill air, and Julia glided in.

'Well done, my dear,' she said. 'Full marks, I think, for your first lesson. Don't you agree, Phidias?'

Catrina sprang to her feet, pulling her gown across her flushed breasts in instinctive defence, while the man beside her rose with a satisfied smile on his face.

'She did extremely well, *patrona*,' said the man, carefully pulling the gold mask from his face and bowing his head in deference to Julia.

Catrina gazed from one to the other, speechless. So – the man with the mask was not some god, or spirit, but was a house slave, under Julia's orders to pleasure her!

'Lesson?' she blurted out, her cheeks burning while her skin was suddenly cold beneath her flimsy gown. 'I don't think I quite understand. You mean you were watching? All of it?'

Julia said, 'My dear, of course I was watching! After all, I arranged it all for you – with the help of my beautiful dancers, Lark and Nightingale, and, of course, Phidias himself! You realised that, surely?' She paused, scanning Catrina's small, anguished face, then went on anxiously, 'You *did* enjoy yourself, didn't you?'

She looked so worried that Catrina found herself almost laughing. *Enjoy* was not quite an adequate word to describe the utterly sensuous bliss that she'd just experienced! But even so, the thought of them all watching her was more than unnerving; it made her blood race with shame. She caught her breath at the enormity of it. Had Julia laughed at her naivety, just as the hateful Alexius must have laughed to himself when he walked off into the forest that night, leaving her stunned and desolate? His cutting words still lacerated her, even now: *You surely don't think that barbarians are to my taste?*

Struggling to appear calm and collected, she brushed her tousled blonde hair back from her face and said, 'Of course I enjoyed myself. But – forgive me – I didn't realise that I was here to provide entertainment for you all.'

Julia smiled approvingly. The British girl was incredibly beautiful, with her long, silken fair hair and her wide green eyes that were still smoky with sexual fulfilment. And it seemed that she was not without spirit either. Stepping forward to reassuringly touch her hand, Julia said quickly,

'Dear Catrina, please don't be offended! Of course I was watching. I had to observe it all, because you have placed yourself in my care, and it's my duty to assess your needs, your progress!'

She saw that the girl still hesitated, and pressed on, 'Just think for a while, Catrina. You can, of course, leave my house any time that you want to. But perhaps you should cast your mind back a little. What precisely was your situation when I came across you in the streets this afternoon?'

She saw the shadow of fear fall across the girl's small, exquisite face. Good. Catrina had remembered the mob, the hateful, peasant rabble out there in the township, who had been about to tear her to pieces as a sorceress. Julia went on quickly. 'Exactly. Those vile, rough people won't have forgotten you, you know. Stay here with me, I beg you – you'll be quite safe, because no one dares to offend me! And if you really, truly wish to learn our Roman ways, then you have come to the right place, believe me! We shall have such pleasure together!'

The girl's head jerked up at that, and her eyes fastened steadily on Julia's. 'I would like to stay,' she said. 'I would like to learn as much from you as I can about the ways of Rome.' Then she took a deep breath, as if making some kind of decision, and said in a low, yearning voice, 'I want to find a man.'

Julia, misunderstanding, put her hands affectionately on her shoulders. 'So you want to find yourself a wealthy, powerful protector! But, of course, what could be more natural? You are so ravishingly beautiful that you could have any man in the fort at your feet! Oh, we can teach you a little more about adornment, and the art of dressing like a fine lady. Lark and Nightingale will help. And between us, we can instruct you further in the many ways that Roman men like to take their pleasure . . .'

She'd seized Catrina's hand, and was drawing her out into the dimly lit passageway. Catrina, uneasily aware that perhaps Julia had not quite understood her, tried to pull back as she struggled to find the right words. 'No! I – I don't want just *any* man . . .'

'No, of course not!' broke in Julia abstractedly as they left the room. 'You want someone very special, very rich. Oh, you won't regret your decision to stay with me, I promise you!' Then she broke off, and said, in quite a different tone of voice, 'Falco. What are *you* doing here?'

A young blond slave was standing silently in the shadowy passageway with his hands chained behind his back. Catrina, her own maelstrom of thoughts quite driven from her head by his appearance, stared at him in wonder. He looked so beautiful, and so sad. Why was he chained up? She felt a shiver of unease. What else was going on in this strange, decadent household? Julia, seeing her staring, said, 'So you like my disobedient young gladiator, Catrina?'

Catrina felt the slave's grey eyes burning into her. She asked, 'Why is he chained up?'

'Because Falco has been very wicked. He thinks he's better than everyone else. But you aren't at all, are you, Falco? You're just the same as the rest of us!' She licked her fingertip and drew it down the slave's smooth, lean cheek; Catrina saw how he shuddered and closed his eyes, and felt her heart twist in pity for him.

Then Julia, with a little sigh, turned back to Catrina. 'Some day, you will meet Falco properly. But now, you must be tired. I'll show you to your room, and tomorrow we will make plans. And how very diverting that will be.'

Catrina felt a warning shiver of excitement as Julia summoned her maid, Nerissa, to show her to her room.

* * *

Julia was tired. Pleasantly so, but her body told her that she needed to rest after this evening's exertions. She decided that it was safest for Falco to be locked for the night in the slaves' quarters of the big house, but, just as she was about to summon Phidias to take him away, Falco said to her, in his quiet, steady voice, 'You should let the girl go. She is beautiful and innocent. She is not a plaything.'

Julia whirled round to face him, wildly angry at his presumption. 'How dare you tell me what to do! Have a care, gladiator. Remember that I can punish you even more!'

He said softly, 'You can do what you like. It doesn't matter to me.'

'But you *do* care, don't you, if I hunt out the other members of your precious sect! There are plenty of them skulking here in Eboracum, aren't there? Women and slaves and other lowly nobodies who claim to be followers of the *Christos*, as you are! Would you like me to punish them, as Nero once punished them, in the Roman arena?'

Falco's face paled; Julia said shakily, 'Ah, I see that you know what I'm talking about. So behave yourself, gladiator, and remember your place!'

He was silent then, and Julia, feeling in charge again, smiled suddenly. 'I think it's time I made more use of you, Falco, while you're in such an amenable mood. You speak Greek as well as Latin, don't you? Can you write both languages as well?'

Quietly he replied, 'Yes, my lady.'

'In that case,' said Julia, her eyes glinting with mischief, 'I have a most interesting occupation for you.'

When Nerissa had left her, Catrina lay awake in the darkness of her spacious bedchamber, listening to the distant, unfamiliar sounds of the fortress. Her wide wooden bed, with its soft, wool-filled mattress and heavy blankets, seemed strange and oppressive after the hide-covered bracken she was used to sleeping on. Her mind spun round and round, almost overwhelmed by the sensations she'd experienced on her first day in this strange, fascinating city.

Her body still tingled from the caresses of the powerful masked man, and she blushed as she remembered how she'd thought him to be some supernatural creature. Julia's house slave had pleasured her deliciously, and satisfyingly released her from the pressure of erotic tension that had been building up so relentlessly inside her. But he hadn't been Alexius.

As her memories enveloped her, the anguish of Alexius' cold betrayal shook her anew, like a physical pain, only worse. Pressing her hands to her forehead to calm herself, she tried to empty her mind of everything except the stillness that surrounded her. Outside, in the little courtyard that was at the centre of Julia's beautiful house, she could hear the fountain trickling musically in the warm night air; and somewhere a nightingale sang, its liquid enchanted notes echoing hauntingly in the stillness and reminding her of the distant forest, her home.

Silently Catrina reached beneath her pillow to touch her little leather pouch, feeling in the darkness for the slender, deadly blade that had the name of Alexius, her enemy, engraved upon its hilt.

The steam rose thickly from the heated water of the caldarium, and the high, frescoed ceiling echoed with the noise of splashing and laughter as Eboracum's military and civilian elite made its customary use of the luxurious bathhouse, built to recreate the comfort and civilisation of Rome here at the very frontier of the empire.

It was early evening, and there were many people here whom Alexius knew. If he happened to be free from his duties at this hour, he always made his way to the bathhouse, to relax in the warmth of the water, to drink a little wine with friends and avail himself of a massage, and to catch up with the latest news. Many people came here to exercise, taking advantage of the opportunities for weight-training, throwing and wrestling. But for Alexius, personal fitness was not a problem, because the many hours of military exercises and hard training kept his body honed and hard.

Feeling pleasantly relaxed, he drew himself slowly out of the hot water and, wrapping a towel loosely round his narrow hips, he made his way slowly to the small, private tepidarium where he prepared himself to be oiled and strigiled by his own attendant. It was good, after the harsh physical labours of the day and the constant pressure of command, to feel clean and relaxed, to have the sweat and weariness of the day stroked and scraped away by skilful masculine hands.

Because the chamber was dimly lit, he thought he was alone as he lowered his body on to the marble bench, but then he realised that the room already had an occupant. Someone stirred and grunted his name from a shadowy alcove, and Alexius, turning, recognised the civilian magistrate Elenius, who shared responsibility for the running of the township with two other elected officials.

'Well, friend Alexius, how goes it?' grunted the over-weight, perspiring official, his pallid flesh wobbling under the ministrations of his male attendant. 'I haven't seen you since you escaped from those painted barbarians up in the hills. Have you been back to raze their village to the ground yet? By Jupiter, that's what I would do, were I in your place!'

Alexius smiled politely as he arranged his long, powerful body face down on the soft towel that his attendant had silently placed on the marble bench. He said, 'They're elusive, these tribespeople. They could pin down half the legion and we'd still lose them in their mountains and forests.'

Elenius snorted. 'But you're commander of the Sixth –

surely you're not going to let them get away with it? You should ride out there and massacre them, my young friend. I certainly would, by the gods, I would!'

Alexius nodded politely. Elenius was fat and bald and well into middle age; the idea of him riding into battle and wielding a sword was unlikely. Alexius settled his head on his arm as the attendant began to attend to his heavily muscled body, skilfully oiling and scraping with the delicate silver strigil. He listened with only half an ear as Elenius chattered on about what he would do to the Brigantian tribespeople, and surrendered himself to a sheer sense of physical well-being. It had been a long day, with quantities of vital supplies arriving by river, so that there were inventories to be checked, crews to be paid off, and unloading parties requisitioned, as well as all the usual daily duties required of an isolated garrison. In addition, his men were throwing up an earthwork round the township; the fortress itself was well enough defended, but if the tribes came down from the north, as Alexius was convinced they would do soon if they took heed of the spreading rumours of central Rome's weakness, then the civilians would be the first to be slaughtered. It had happened before. People like Elenius, snug and sleek in their comfortable posts, thought that Rome, and any garrison of Rome's, was invincible. Alexius, who had served in Gaul against the wild German tribes who continually threatened the empire's northern borders, knew better.

'Should massacre them,' Elenius was still muttering comfortably. 'Take a cohort up into the hills, burn 'em out . . .'

Alexius rolled over at his attendant's gentle instruction and gave a sigh of pleasure as the man started work on his heavily muscled thighs, feeling how the soft hair on his damp skin was still whorled and clinging from the warm bath. Perhaps Elenius was right. Perhaps he should hunt them out. He closed his eyes. It was only natural, to seek some sort of vicious revenge on the natives for the treacherous night ambush, for the deaths of his men, for his own injuries. He'd heard others muttering the same as Elenius. But every time Alexius thought of those untamed barbarians up in their lair in the hills, he thought of the girl who'd healed him. And that was the trouble.

Mithras, he swore to himself, he didn't even know her name, or what she looked like! But he'd never forget the touch of her delicate, gentle hands as she stroked those near-magical salves into his wound, or the soft, rippling cadences of her quiet voice as she struggled to pronounce his unfamiliar name. She was beautiful, he knew it instinctively. Her body had been welcoming and tender as he prepared himself to take her. As he caressed her sweetly parted flesh, she'd opened to him and pressed herself against him like a tender spring flower yearning for the sun, shy yet deeply passionate; when he'd sheathed his hardness deep in the silky-soft depths of her flesh, her body had rippled with the first, dawning spasms of delight, and her sweet explosions of joy had taken his breath away.

Alexius had known many women in his lifetime. In the strict hierarchy of Roman society, the most beautiful of them, married or not, were always available to the powerful, handsome *primus pilus* of the Sixth Victrix. He had a certain reputation as a lover, which his fellow centurions, half-admiring, half-envious, had helped to spread; his evident determination never to link himself with one particular woman made him, he supposed, a challenge. Since joining the legion, he had maintained a simple rule of conduct where women were concerned; he gave them pleasure, he took his own pleasure, and nothing more was to be expected on either side.

But the barbarian girl in the turf hut on the dark mountainside, who'd come to him like a dream in the midst of his blindness, had stirred him strangely. Her soft little cries of wonder and love as he caressed her small, beautiful breasts inspired him with a fierce tenderness he'd not experienced before; the abandoned wildness of her climax as he pleasured her had taken him unawares, and left him shaken. Perhaps she really was a virgin, as she claimed; a virgin filled with a wanton, unleashed eroticism that he had been the first, the very first, to savour . . .

He'd been cruel to her. He'd told her that she'd asked for everything she'd got, and that anyway barbarian women were not to his taste, none of which was true. He had felt her hurt winging through the sultry air of the hut as he brusquely told her he was leaving. But to have implicated the girl in any way in his escape would have been in effect a death sentence on her; he knew the ways of her tribe, and he knew that they would kill her if they suspected her of connivance at his escape. So he'd left her there bound, left her hating him, no doubt, from the bottom of her heart; and ever since then he had been haunted by the memory of her. He felt his phallus beginning to thicken and swell inexorably as he remembered the sweet yet voluptuous innocence of her caresses. His attendant, who had finished now and was wiping the oil from his hands on a spare towel, tactfully ignored his arousal. Alexius sighed and tried to push the girl from his mind.

He wished he knew what she looked like. He wished he could meet her again. But of course, she would hate him.

And then, he was drawn swiftly back to reality by some unmistakable sounds from the other side of the dimly lit room. His own servant had departed, leaving a jug of cool wine and a bowl of figs on the low table at his side, but Elenius was still sprawled on his back on his own towel-strewn marble bench, and while Alexius had half-slept, his mind miles away, Elenius had summoned his own special attendant, a woman dressed in a scanty short tunic, who bent over to him to attend to his further needs.

Elenius' penis was still somnolent, noted Alexius

dryly. Evidently the middle-aged, corpulent magistrate, a pink and flaccid mound of naked flesh, was taking some time to appreciate what the woman was doing. She was certainly trying hard enough; Alexius found himself watching with some interest himself as the dark-haired woman loosened her tunic and let her large, plump breasts dangle over the fur-matted mound of Elenius' chest. She was licking sinuously at the top of his legs, lifting the magistrate's small, pale phallus in her hands to toy with it, then placing it in her mouth and sucking with evident relish, but to little avail. Alexius, stretched out with his head pillowed on one hand, reached out surreptitiously to pull a towel casually across his own loins, because he'd seen the woman glance at him and her eyes light up at his own rather more promising endowment. Ruefully he tried to fight down the stirring and hardening at his loins.

Elenius caught the gesture with the towel out of the corner of his eye and pulled himself up, puffing at the exertion, on one elbow. 'You want a girl, too, my friend Alexius?' he called out eagerly. 'Just say the word. I have plenty to spare!'

Alexius smiled and quickly raised his hand in dismissal. 'No, but thank you for your kind offer. Some day I might take you up on it, but I'm afraid I really must be on my way.'

'I know. Military duties – ah!' His voice turned into an exasperated wail. 'I've told you before, girl; put your hands round there – yes, your finger – just up there, you know the place – ah, yes! Yes, that's it . . .'

Alexius had already swung his legs from the bench, ready to get dressed in the fresh tunic the attendant had left for him. He paused in spite of himself to watch in wry fascination as the girl pulled Elenius' bottom cheeks apart and ran her well-oiled hands up his dark bottom-cleft, fighting her way through the soft whorls of dark, intimate body hair to find his anal entrance. Catching her full lip between her teeth and winking at Alexius, she slid her finger up deep into the tightly puckered hole. Elenius gave a squeal of pleasure, and at last his helpless penis began to stir into life.

'Now, girl!' he gasped. 'Take me in your mouth, wiggle your finger about a bit more – quickly – ah, yes, that's it!'

And the girl dipped her head to lick voraciously with her tongue, swirling her lips up and down the hot, angry little stem of flesh, her eyes closing with feigned pleasure, while her fingers continued to explore Elenius' secret hole. She paused for breath, and when Elenius gasped out his protest, she murmured silkily, 'Let me recover, please, my lord Elenius! With such a mighty weapon as yours, I have to catch my breath. It's almost too much for one woman!'

'Aye, it's a fine great staff, isn't it?' grated out Elenius, grabbing at the woman's rosy teats and rubbing their ripeness across his sweating face. 'Quickly, girl, faster!'

Alexius had to smother a smile. He turned away to fasten on his boots, but he could still hear his plump friend gasping and panting as the woman's head bobbed dutifully up and down. At last Elenius exploded, his hips lifting frantically off the bench in his excitement as his seed squirted hotly into the woman's luscious mouth. Alexius, fully dressed now and sternly willing away his own obvious arousal, turned to go.

But Elenius shot up, his face still pink with pleasure, and gasped out, 'Alexius, my friend! Don't go yet. The girl will see to you as well!'

The woman, kneeling at Elenius' side, gazed up at Alexius from under heavily kohled eyes. 'For you, commander, it's free,' she mouthed up at him, and licked her ripe lips wickedly.

Alexius smiled at her and said, 'No, Elenius, old friend. Thank you, but I must go.'

'You're not still on duty, surely?'

'Not officially, but tonight there's an anniversary celebration of the legion's arrival in Britain, and I should be there.'

Elenius looked knowledgeable. 'Ah, a party!'

Alexius smiled to himself. 'Of sorts.'

'Of course, I understand. But, Alexius, before you go – have you heard about the wild barbarian girl there's been such a fuss about?'

Alexius felt his heart unaccountably miss a beat as he said levelly enough, 'What barbarian girl?'

'Why, the one there was nearly a riot over in the township this afternoon. They say she has the sight. And by all accounts she's exceptionally beautiful – long blonde hair, delicate skin, a ravishing figure – in fact, not like a barbarian at all!'

Alexius had paused with his hand on the door. He said, 'What makes them say she has the sight?'

'Because she saved a child from certain death! There was some accident with a overladen cart. You know what it's like on market day, with all the scum from the neighbourhood, all the native beggars and traders and riff-raff crowding in, and apparently she foresaw that the cart's axle was about to break, and pulled the boy away just in time. A moment later and he would have been crushed to death. The whole town's still talking about it.'

Alexius stirred, pulling his thoughts back into order. 'And where is this girl now?'

'At the lady Julia's.' Elenius chuckled lasciviously, his hands absently wandering to stroke the heavy breasts of the woman at his side. 'Poor Julia. She was probably looking forward to introducing the barbarian girl to all sorts of delights in that decadent household of hers. How disappointed she'll be when we take the girl in!'

'Take her in?' echoed Alexius.

'Why, yes. We'll have to arrest her, of course. The girl's a sorceress, most likely sent here as a spy. If she's as beautiful as they say, then we'll have some fun with her before we turn her over to the mob.'

Alexius said carefully, 'And when are you planning to arrest her?'

'Early this evening, before Julia realises our plans. Ah, my dear, that's too, too delicious. You're very wicked, you know – Jupiter, don't stop, girl! Alexius, Alexius, you're not going already, surely?'

But Alexius had gone, and was already swiftly striding down the wide steps that led from the bathhouse, his scarred brow furrowed in concentration.

Chapter Seven

Next day, Julia was busy. In the morning, she checked that her intriguing new visitor was still sleeping soundly, and then she went shopping with her servants in attendance, choosing the freshest of imported food delicacies and ordering several amphorae of newly arrived Falernian wine from a warehouse by the river. She also called into the shop of a Greek merchant she knew, down a dark alleyway; he was expecting her, and she left half an hour later with a heavy object carefully wrapped in thickly quilted silk.

She spent the afternoon visiting certain friends in the luxurious south-east corner of the township. This was the quarter where the wealthiest of the non-military population of the city lived: the civic officials, the retired army officers and wealthy merchants – all of them *honestiores*, of noble and refined status. Here, well away from the smells and noise of the commercial quarter of the town, they dwelt in big, spacious stone houses, with large leafy gardens that commanded pleasant views across the river and the distant woodland that encircled the town.

Julia enjoyed visiting her friends. Some people looked down on her, even though she was the legate's mistress, because they knew she had once been an actress and therefore Flavius could never marry her. But Julia didn't give a fig for those who snubbed her; they tended to be the dullest people in the town anyway, boring matrons who had accompanied their husbands on official postings to the province and were counting the months till they returned to Rome. Julia enjoyed living in Britain. It presented one with such endless possibilities.

One by one, she called on her special friends during the course of the day and explained her plan for the night, and she smiled at the way their eyes lit up.

It was early evening by the time she had finished. On the way back, just before they came to the bridge across to the fortress, her sedan-bearers had to stop and wait while a company of mounted soldiers went by. Julia tapped her fingers impatiently, her mind still full of delicious plans. She jumped with shock when a familiar masculine voice said at her window, 'Well, lady Julia. I wonder what mischief you've been plotting today?'

She looked out with a start, and saw Alexius regarding her quizzically from the superior height of his beautiful black horse. She coloured faintly, and said, 'I've just been paying some visits, centurion, on a few old friends. Or am I forbidden that particular pleasure as well?'

'Oh, I wouldn't wish to deny you any *pleasure*, my lady Julia,' said Alexius, his deep blue eyes regarding her thoughtfully. 'As long as you don't intend implicating any more of my men in your sordid games.'

Julia crackled with anger. 'Feel free to join your men any time, centurion!' she hissed up at him. 'You never know, you might even enjoy yourself. It must be very frustrating, leading such a blameless life!'

Alexius laughed, and steadied his restless horse. Julia's gaze fastened helplessly on his long, strongly muscled thighs outlined beneath his tunic, seeing how effortlessly he gripped and controlled the big beast. She imagined those same beautiful, hair-roughened thighs gentling her own slender limbs into submission, exactly

102

as he was coaxing the horse, and she felt suddenly quite faint with wanting him.

'I don't lead a blameless life,' he corrected her steadily, 'but merely a discreet one. You should try it some time. And now is the perfect time to start, lady Julia; this evening, as you've no doubt remembered, is the sacred festival of Bona Dea. I take it you're fully aware that here, as in Rome, you and all the women of Eboracum are forbidden male company for the night?'

Julia laughed scornfully. 'Never fear, centurion. I shall endeavour to spend the evening in pious contemplation, just like a devout Roman matron!'

Alexius said mildly, 'I'm glad to hear it, though I must say I find it difficult to believe.' He stroked his horse's silky neck, then added, 'I hear you have a new guest.'

'Is that a crime too?' retorted Julia. 'Do I have to inform you of everything?'

'If it concerns the well-being of the fortress, then yes, you do. What do you intend doing with the girl?'

'She wants to learn the ways of Rome,' said Julia haughtily.

Alexius's eyebrows lifted in polite disbelief. 'The ways of Rome? I'm intrigued. Could you be a little more specific?'

Julia snapped, 'She wants to find herself a man, commander! A rich, powerful protector! Have you any objections?'

'No objections whatsoever,' replied Alexius calmly. 'But have a care as to what you teach her.'

'Why such interest?' Julia mocked. 'Do you have a fancy to try her yourself, centurion?'

There was a pause, and Julia was quite effectively silenced when Alexius said, 'Perhaps I do. Who knows?'

Then, with a mocking half-salute, he urged on his horse and headed back towards the fortress, the setting sun glinting on his sleek black hair.

Julia watched him go, her nostrils pinched with anger, her ring-adorned knuckles quite white as she clutched at the seat of her sedan. Damn the man for his arrogance. If only she didn't want him, as badly as ever.

She sank back against her cushions and closed her eyes and imagined his hard, sensual mouth covering hers, imagined the delicious iron hardness of his phallus pressing urgently, forcefully against her quivering thighs . . .

She rapped sharply on the side to signal to her sedan-bearers to take her home.

Tonight, as he'd reminded her, was the feast of the Good Goddess, when all women were supposed to stay at home and shun masculine company, filling their minds instead with pious thoughts of wifely duties and the glory of Rome. What Alexius didn't know was that she'd already laid her plans to enjoy herself in quite an unusual way, and the girl was going to be a part of it.

Catrina had woken late, some time after Julia had embarked on her expedition. She pulled herself up with a start as the morning sun streamed through the shutters of her small chamber, feeling heavy-eyed and confused in this strange place. She was late; she'd overslept! Anxiously pushing her long tousled hair back from her sleep-softened face, she washed herself hastily in the ewer of water that had been left on the coffer by the door, and wished with all her heart that it was the water of a cool mountain stream near her home.

Someone, kind Nerissa perhaps, must have been in that morning and left her clean clothes and food; there was a platter of small, freshly baked wheaten cakes with honey, and a beaker of ewe's milk. She dressed herself hastily in the long cream tunic that lay at the foot of her bed, and combed her hair thoroughly until it was silky-soft again, with a silver comb that had been left beside the clothes. Then she nibbled at the little wheat cakes, though she wasn't really hungry.

The house basked in the morning light, silent and deserted. Sunbeams danced on the white, lime-washed walls of her bedroom, which was curiously bare except for the bed and wooden chest. She suddenly shivered, very much aware that she was all alone, here in the very heart of the enemy fortress. With a surge of panic, feeling like a prisoner, she hurried towards the door, but it wasn't locked, and she was free to go. Shutting the door quietly behind her, she glided out into the corridor.

Doors seemed to lead off everywhere. The house was so big, so empty of life, so intimidating. Taking a deep breath, Catrina began to explore, passing room after room. She paused when she recognised the chamber where last night's erotic initiation had taken place, and she shivered anew as she recalled Phidias, remembering all too vividly how she'd thought him to be some demon lover, ravishing her in a dream. Her body tingled suddenly, freshly aroused at the mere thought of her wanton mating with the big, powerful house slave.

Slowly, stunned by the opulence of the building, Catrina wandered through the silent rooms, all of them spacious and exquisitely furnished, but with no sign of life at all. Then, from behind a closed door, she thought she heard someone cough, and impulsively she pushed open the door.

She found herself inside a big room lined with shelves, that were all filled with scroll upon scroll of Roman writing – a library. She recognised it immediately, from Luad's tales of the way the Romans lived. Luad had tried to explain writing to her when she was younger.

'Is it some kind of magical inscription?' she'd asked him, puzzled.

'No,' the priest had said. 'Not magic, but a cunning way of trapping words on parchment.'

Catrina had frowned in bewilderment. In the tribe, they relied on memory alone. The priests had some skill with inscriptions, but it was the way of things that tales of long ago were passed down reverently by word of mouth from generation to generation. To trap words with black lines on parchment sounded very like magic to Catrina.

She stepped further into the strange room, and only then realised that someone else was there. Sitting at a desk by the window to catch the light, with the morning sun glittering on his thick fair hair, was a young man, who wrote carefully with a quill pen and black ink, while his wide brow furrowed in concentration.

He looked up quickly as he heard her tentative foot-steps and smiled at her, a warm, heart-stopping smile. Catrina felt an unexpected surge of pleasure as she recognised him as the silent man who'd accompanied Julia last night. Then she went cold as she remembered that last night he'd been in chains.

But he wasn't in chains now. Appearing quite at ease, he leaned back in his chair, and Catrina saw that he was wearing a loose, pale tunic of fine quality which was slit at the throat to expose a golden triangle of smooth, gleaming chest. She also saw that he was quite, quite beautiful. Catrina gazed at him silently, drinking in the regular, clean-shaven features of his strong-boned face, noticing how his sun-streaked blond hair curled thickly down the nape of his neck. His shoulders beneath the fine wool tunic were wide and powerful; his forearms were strongly muscled, the golden skin dusted with fine blond hairs. And his eyes were wide-set and grey, and kind, as he said gently, interrupting her reverie, 'Greet-ings, lady. You were looking for someone?'

Catrina pulled herself together. 'Not really.' She smiled uncertainly back. 'Though I suppose I should be, because I'm not quite sure what I'm meant to be doing this morning. I'm here as a guest, you see, of the lady Julia.'

Was it her imagination, or did a shadow seem to cross his features, like the darkness of a cloud across the moors? He said slowly, 'Julia is out, I believe.' Then he put down his pen. 'How long are you staying here?'

She walked across the room towards him, gazing at

the manuscripts spread out on the table. 'I'm not really sure yet. What are you doing?' She reached out to touch one of the yellowed documents, noticing that it seemed to have some small illustrations engraved in one corner.

Quickly, the young blond man moved to cover it all up with a blank parchment. The colour seemed to creep into his smooth face as he said quickly, 'Nothing important.'

Catrina, feeling rebuked, said defensively, 'I suppose that it's Roman writing. You must be very clever to understand it all. I wish I could.'

The man seemed to let out a soft sigh, almost of relief. 'You mean you can't read?'

'No.' She gazed defiantly up at him, assuming he was laughing at her. 'No doubt you think me very foolish, but amongst my people, there is no need to capture words on paper. We keep all our knowledge in our heads and hearts.'

He said, 'I don't think you foolish at all. Of course, I remember now. They said you were British, but I'd forgotten, because to me you look Roman.' Then he recited, almost dreamily,

'Though brought up among the sky-blue Britons,
She has the spirit of the Latin race . . .'

Seeing her confusion, he went on swiftly, 'That's from a poem, by a great Latin writer called Martial. Sit down and talk for a while, if you're not going anywhere. What is your name?'

Catrina seated herself at the other side of the desk, looking warily at him. He was so beautiful that he made her feel a little warm and breathless. He wasn't dangerous and threatening, like the hateful Alexius, but friendly, and somehow touchable; his skin was like golden silk, and his mouth curved so beautifully when he smiled that she suddenly imagined herself kissing him, and felt herself blushing at the thought. She lowered her eyes quickly, aghast at her own wantonness.

There was a jug of water on the table; he poured her

some, and she was glad to moisten her suddenly dry throat. 'My name is Catrina,' she said.

He watched her for a moment with those steady grey eyes, then said at last, 'Strange. That is a Roman name. What brings you here, Catrina? This is no place for someone like you.'

She was taken aback. What did he mean? Perhaps he intended to remind her that she was an uncouth, uncultured barbarian! She gazed back at him heatedly and said, 'Why shouldn't I be here?'

'I meant no insult, lady,' he said quietly. 'Far from it.'

Something in the way he was looking at her unsettled her strangely. She knotted her hands together in her lap and said quickly, 'But why are *you* here, Falco?' Disturbingly, she remembered the chains, the look of desperate humiliation in his eyes last night. 'You know poetry – you know how to read and write. Why are you a slave?'

'I was well-educated, it's true. But so are many slaves. You see, my father, who was a wealthy Greek merchant, became bankrupted when some of his ships were lost, and he had to sell me to avoid prison for the entire family.'

'*Sell* you?' Catrina was horrified. 'As a slave?'

He shook his head. 'No – he sold me to the gladiator school in Rome.' His mouth seemed to tighten at the memory. 'I learned well, and was successful. But then – well, then something happened to me. And I didn't want to fight any more. Not for amusement, not for other people's sadistic pleasure.'

Catrina leaned forward impulsively. 'But that's awful, for your own family to sell you!'

'It happens often, in Rome. All sorts of things happen in Rome.' His quiet voice was tinged with sadness rather than bitterness. 'And what about *your* family, Catrina? Do they know you're here?'

'I have no family. I was taken in by the people of the tribe, and cared for by them.' Her eye was caught suddenly by the quill pen and the ink, and she said impulsively, 'Falco. Do you think I could learn to read, and to write? Or would I have to be very clever, like you?'

He laughed. 'In Rome, some of the most stupid people read and write, and call themselves poets. Of course you can learn, Catrina. If you like, I'll show you how to form your letters.' As he spoke, he lifted the pen quickly, and placed it in her hands to dip it in the bronze inkstand. She felt absorbed and happy as he began to show her the patterns, tracing out the curves and lines that made the mysterious marks called writing; she felt somehow that he was uncovering to her something she already knew, rather than teaching her something quite new, and the time flew by.

'You're good,' he said seriously. 'You're learning quickly.'

And then the door opened, and Lark and Nightingale came in.

'Here you are, lady Catrina!' said Lark happily. 'We have been commanded by our mistress to attend to you while she is out. But first, we have some business with the gladiator.'

And Catrina saw suddenly that at the sight of the two half-naked handmaidens, Falco had gone pale. The gladiator whispered to Catrina, urgently, 'Go now. Please, go.'

But Nightingale, gliding forward, her red-tipped, pert breasts swaying enticingly as she moved, said, 'Oh, but you must stay, lady Catrina. After all, our mistress told us to take advantage of every possible opportunity to educate you.' And swiftly, sinuously, she draped herself across Falco's knee and, curling her fingers through his thick, sun-streaked hair, reached up to kiss him languorously. Lark, meanwhile, was idly leafing through the parchments on the desk, the very ones that Falco had hastily covered up when Catrina came in. 'How far have you got with your task, Falco dearest?' Lark queried silkily. 'Have you been showing some of these poems to your visitor?'

Falco, fighting free of Nightingale's embrace, grated out, 'The girl cannot read.'

Lark laughed, a cold, tinkling sound. 'What a shame. But she can enjoy the illustrations, can't she? Look, Catrina dear. Look at what our handsome gladiator is working on! He's translating poems, for the lady Julia, from Greek to Latin. Isn't he clever? And such poems!'

'No,' groaned Falco, lunging forward to cover them again. 'No . . .'

Casually, Nightingale leaned forward from her perch on his knee and flicked a page towards Catrina; and Catrina, confused and bewildered by Falco's evident distress, looked down at it and felt the colour flood her cheeks.

It was a lewd drawing, in ink, of a naked woman on all fours, licking eagerly at a man's grotesquely enlarged appendage. Behind the crouching woman, another man, grinning broadly, held his erect penis in his hands and prepared to enter her from the rear. The pictures were simple, but skilfully done; utterly confused, Catrina felt a shameful stab of forbidden desire wrenching her body.

'The words are even better,' said Lark helpfully, with her light, melodious laugh. 'That is why we have to check regularly on Falco, to make sure that he is working hard, and not taking his pleasure illicitly. It requires willpower, you see, for a healthy, virile young man like him to concentrate on such wicked writings without becoming distracted.' And, grinning naughtily, she slid her delicate hands up under Falco's tunic, pushing it back to his hips. Catrina gasped aloud, and gripped the edge of the table.

For now she could see that Falco's exposed penis was a thick, fleshy rod of desire, already jerking hungrily upright as Lark's fingers trailed lovingly along its veined, silken length. Catrina gazed helplessly at it, feeling the wanton moisture flooding her own secret places. Aching with her own dark, hungry need, she heard Falco's voice say in quiet despair, 'Please, no. Not like this.'

Nightingale grinned, her teeth white and perfect against the dusky brownness of her skin. 'Every two hours, my lady said. To check you're not cheating on us, dear Falco; to ensure that you're doing your work thoroughly.'

'And to make sure that you're not being sly, and cheating us, by pleasuring yourself in secret!' giggled Lark. 'Oh, look, dearest Nightingale; read this, do!

'*My lady, I would part your silken thighs*
'*To find out where your glistening treasure lies* – oh! Did you enjoy translating that part, Falco? Did you?'

She gripped suddenly at the thick, quivering stem of his yearning penis, rubbing it cruelly, pulling the skin relentlessly up and down the bone-hard core. Catrina, gazing horrified at the young man's torment, saw how he gritted his teeth and closed his eyes against the punishing caress. Then Lark dipped her head, and, sticking out her hot, plump little tongue, began to lick at the swollen red glans, teasing and sucking until his whole body shook and trembled with illicit desire.

'Ah, gladiator,' whispered Nightingale, kissing his cheek and rubbing her naked breasts lewdly against his tunic-covered chest, 'what a fine erection you've got there! What a mighty shaft! I'll bet you were a favourite in the Roman arena! Did the noble Roman ladies summon you to pleasure them secretly afterwards? Did they pay you lots of lovely gold for the privilege of feeling your hot, throbbing rod sliding up into the juicy flesh between their legs?'

Lark's head dipped and dived, her eager little tongue teasing and stroking until Falco's penis glistened with her saliva. He was too big for her to take all of his massive shaft into her mouth, but nevertheless she slid her velvety mouth and lips over as much as she could, and then she gripped the base of his member with her

111

hand, toying also with the full, velvety sac of his balls; meanwhile, Nightingale kissed his lips languorously, and then positioned herself so that she could rub her breasts against his face, her bright scarlet nipples jutting proudly. Catrina, horrified by his degradation yet unable to move, conscious of her own churning desire gripping her loins and breasts, saw how Falco's strong thighs were clenched rigid in the extremity of his arousal. Lark's head dipped furiously over his throbbing member, faster and faster; until at last, judging her moment with fine precision, she pulled her head away and took his full, heavy testicles in her soft mouth, swirling her tongue across their hair-roughened skin as the gladiator's phallus began to helplessly spasm. Falco's head jerked back, blind, despairing as his seed began to spurt forth; the girls caught his copious sperm on their breasts, rubbing it into each other's skin avidly, murmuring, 'Oh, that's good, gladiator, that's good! You have so much sweet juice for us to milk!' At last, when his convulsions were finally over, they licked him clean with their eager, cat-like tongues.

Catrina watched helplessly, her blood racing, her body awash with the fierce ache of desire as the beautiful blond slave was so deliberately humiliated. She squeezed her eyes shut as his seed spurted, feeling her own nipples poking hot and hard against the soft fabric of her tunic. Her clitoris was a plump, aching kernel of desire, and she had to fight not to reach and touch it, not to send herself spinning into exquisite, shameful release.

Why did Falco endure it all? Why didn't he strike them away? He was strong and courageous, she could tell, and he hated what they were doing to him, even in the midst of such lewd pleasure. She hated it too, the way they made such sport of him; and yet another part of her longed to join in with Lark and Nightingale, longed to lick his lovely long, hard penis with her own worshipping tongue, longed to feel his rampant member sink deep within her own vulnerable flesh so that she could feel his strong body pound and jerk into her in helpless submission as his seed pumped hotly from his body...

She opened her eyes, shaken, unable to move. Falco had sagged forward, his elbows on the table, his head buried in his hands. His fair hair was darkly streaked with perspiration, and his wide shoulders trembled. Lark and Nightingale were giggling to one another in their own language, licking their lips as they smoothed the last of his creamy sperm into one another's naked breasts. Then they remembered she was there, and turned to her.

'You enjoyed that, lady Catrina?' lilted Nightingale. 'You will be pleased to hear that it is your turn next.'

Catrina leaped from her chair, her hands gripping the table.

'For your bath, we mean!' giggled Lark. 'Lady Julia informed us that we must spend the rest of the day tending to your needs and making you beautiful!'

They escorted her tenderly from the room. Just as she was about to pass through the door, Catrina turned round one last time and saw Falco gazing after her with a look of bleak despair on his beautiful, haggard face. But then Lark took her hand and pulled her away, saying tenderly, 'He enjoys it, so much. Believe me, he has never known such sweet pleasure.' And she gently shut the door on the silent gladiator.

The rest of the afternoon passed swiftly in a haze of new pleasures for Catrina. *We must spend the rest of the day in tending to your needs and making you beautiful*, they'd explained to her, with a hint of wicked promise in their dark eyes, and they certainly kept to their word. After a deliciously light repast of fruit and sweet honey cakes washed down with a delicate white wine, Catrina submitted with scarcely repressed excitement to the ministrations of the beautiful Syrian twins. She was still in a state of simmering arousal from the scene she'd wit-

113

nessed in the library, and as Lark and Nightingale bathed her and oiled her, their hands light and erotic on her naked, sensitised skin, Catrina tried her very hardest to push away the burning memory of the gladiator's fierce erection, and the way the two girls had pleasured him so relentlessly with their hot little tongues.

She had little success. It was difficult to be cool and calm when their full, red-tipped breasts, adorned so blatantly by the phallic ivory pendants, danced over her face and body all the time as the girls moved busily around her reclining figure. She felt quite dizzy with her own sexual need as they stroked and kneaded her flesh; their fingers were so light, so delicate as they caressed her body that she brimmed with shameful excitement, and felt the hot, dark need gather in her abdomen.

She recalled that Falco, too, had been ashamed; ashamed of his arousal and his fierce orgasm. Why was he working on those books? He'd tried to hide them from her, so he was not proud of his work. Why did he submit to it all? He was a slave, but even slaves could be driven too far.

She wondered, suddenly, what Falco's breaking point would be. And she wondered just how much she, Catrina, would be able to take of this decadent, erotic lifestyle. Yet so far, she had to admit, she'd found it all wonderfully pleasurable. How willingly she'd embraced the big, masked Numidian; how eagerly she'd welcomed his beautiful, strong penis deep inside her. And even the spectacle of Falco's humiliation had filled her with a sweet, dark longing to feel the gladiator's manhood pleasuring her own melting flesh.

Then, suddenly, with a jolt of anguish, she remembered the Roman Alexius' dismissive words to her on the fateful night of his escape. 'If you really believe I forced you into the act of love, then you are deluding yourself. I gave you exactly what you've been asking for.'

She closed her eyes and shivered, hating him fiercely

for what he'd done to her. She had to get her amulet back, to regain her lost power. And when she found the Roman, she would humiliate him as he'd humiliated her. She wanted him on his knees, abasing himself before her, pleading with her for mercy.

Then, and only then, would she tell him who she was, and see the fear in his face . . .

The thought of her beautiful, dangerous Roman had made her excited again. She shifted her bare thighs uncomfortably, feeling the familiar trickle of moisture in her palpitating vulva, and was aware of the tiny, insistent throb of desire as her heated clitoris began to stir anew. The Syrian girls giggled and chattered to one another in their own language as they put away their precious, oil-filled glass phials, then they indicated to her that she must lie flat on her back on the towel-strewn couch, and as they made her comfortable, one of them let her dusky breasts brush deliberately across Catrina's bare nipples. At the tantalisingly intimate touch, Catrina felt her own breasts tingle and peak uncomfortably; she shifted restlessly, embarrassed by the physical evidence of her own arousal, and the girls, laughing, indicated that she must just lie back and stay very, very still.

Then she realised why.

One of the girls had lifted up a tiny pottery jar with a slender goatshair brush dipped in it. The brush, when she drew it out, glistened with bright red paint. Suddenly, Catrina realised their intention. They were going to paint her nipples shameful scarlet, like theirs, blatant, arousing. She gasped and lifted herself on one elbow, half-laughing, half-confused. 'Oh, no! If you think you're doing *that* . . .'

Nightingale was poised above her with the tiny brush. 'But – it is our mistress's command, my lady!' Then she lowered her voice and whispered conspiratorially, 'She told us that it was your greatest wish to make men desire you. Is that not true?'

Catrina's thoughts whirled. Oh, yes. It was true. She

wanted, more than anything, to make men desire her, especially her enemy Alexius, when she finally tracked him down.

There was a long silence. Then . . . 'Proceed,' she breathed.

The paintbrush tickled her nipples, bringing the crinkled erectile tissue sharply into hard prominence. Only too conscious of her utter nudity, of her secret feminine flesh pulsing warningly between her thighs, Catrina found her eyes fastening helplessly on the pendants bobbing between the girls' high breasts. The serpents' heads were sleek and long and creamy smooth, with slanting, indented eyes that seemed to gaze at her slyly. The girls smiled at her fondly as they worked; Nightingale painted carefully while Lark caressed her belly lightly, knowingly. As the liquid rouge kissed her nipples, Catrina felt a fierce, aching spasm of desire wrench her vulnerable body; and then, the painting finished, Nightingale bent to kiss her on her mouth.

The girl's lips were sweet, silky, wickedly moist. Catrina, trembling, felt the intruding tongue bobbing tantalisingly inside her mouth, and as she gasped and tensed at the erotic caress she suddenly became aware of another plump, juicy tongue-tip licking its way up her inner thigh, darting and stroking, insinuously parting her honeyed sex-lips and bathing her swollen little bud of pleasure with delicious moisture.

A spasm of wicked delight shuddered through Catrina's prone body, and she instinctively parted her legs, spreading open her glistening pink sex. 'You are sweet, so sweet,' murmured Nightingale in her ear, running her tongue along her delicate fleshy lobe. 'So beautiful. And I want to make you happy . . .'

It was then that Catrina felt something cool and thick and solid prodding at her hot, exposed vulva, stroking her silky flesh with an insistent, urgent caress. With a jolt of alarm she realised that it was a serpent's head pendant, sliding and thrusting its way between her juicy, parted sex-lips. She cried out in surprise at the unfamiliar touch, but Nightingale, kneeling by her shoulders, moved swiftly to kiss her again, at the same time running her fingers over her lewdly painted nipples. Catrina shuddered with delight, her whole body a mass of rippling need, her breasts and belly tight to the point of bursting. Instinctively she splayed her legs still further, writhing and bearing down on the fat ivory phallus that impaled her so deliciously. Like a penis, it filled her with blissful thoroughness as the girl between her thighs smiled darkly and slid it in and out of her juicy sex lips with such tantalising skill that the entire ivory was covered in her slick juices. Catrina thought she would die of the sharp, sweet hunger that wrenched her body; she groaned aloud with disappointment as Lark withdrew the ivory serpent's head almost to its tip. She lifted her hips, silently begging for more.

Lark smiled darkly. Then she reached for the tiny paintbrush, and began to circle Catrina's clitoris with it, stroking and tickling the hot little protuberance with the silky soft goatshair until Catrina's whole body was a mass of churning desire to feel the fat ivory penis taking her, filling her, ravishing her hungry sex. The brush tickled again, with a caress that was almost a pain; the ivory was pushed in, deep and hard and thick, and Catrina clenched her vaginal walls desperately around the lewd shaft and bucked up and down, crying out in ecstasy as the sweet, cataclysmic orgasm started to roar through her. Her whole body arched and twisted to meet the cold kiss of the ivory deep inside her throbbing vulva.

At last she fell back, bathed in perspiration, melting with exquisite pleasure as her womb continued to throb lovingly around the thick phallus. As her orgasm slowly subsided, the Syrian twins kissed her and stroked her. 'You are beautiful. So beautiful, Catrina.' Catrina smiled dazedly back at them.

They offered her a loose silk robe to wrap herself in,

and more cool wine to drink, and sweet dates to nibble at; she pulled herself up lazily against the soft cushions they surrounded her with and let them pamper her, her eyes dark and smoky with satisfaction. She felt beautiful. She felt wonderfully powerful with the realisation of what her body could enjoy, what her body could achieve. A few days longer, and the Roman, when she tracked him down, would never, ever guess her to be the crude, naive barbarian he had tricked and seduced so easily. When she next saw Julia, she must remember to ask her if she knew anything of a tall, dark-haired soldier called Alexius – but there was no hurry.

She would take her time in finding her enemy, she decided, sipping languorously at the delicious wine and feeling it trickling down her parched throat. She would take her time, and enjoy her adventures along the way. For one brief moment she remembered Falco's bleak, despairing face, but she pushed it quickly to the back of her mind.

After that, Nightingale and Lark spent some time brushing and combing her long blonde hair, then plaiting it into braids and coiling it at the back of her head, like an elegant lady of Rome. They applied subtle make-up; a tinge of kohl and powdered green lapis lazuli to her eyes, a hint of lip-salve to emphasize the delicate fullness of her pleasure-swollen mouth; then some rice powder to enhance the translucence of her perfect, delicate skin. Then they took her through to Julia's dressing room, where several robes had already been laid out for her delectation; there, they held up various gowns in soft, radiant dyes that Catrina had never seen, accustomed as she was only to the bright reds and ochres of her own people's making. She chose a tunic of pale, delicate green wool; and the Syrian girls, nodding in approval, set to work.

First, they dressed her in a sleeveless silken undertunic that was almost transparent, its weightless fabric clinging like a whisper to her scented skin. Then, as Catrina gazed in wonder, they found a long, broad band of creamy linen and bound it round her ribcage and the underside of her bosom, so that her small breasts were lifted into a delicious, swelling prominence, and her scarlet nipples were thrust out brazenly against the flimsy fabric of the undertunic. Catrina gasped at the heady sensation of having her body so tantalisingly on display.

After that, they slipped the full-length tunic of pale green wool over her head, and as the filmy fabric settled in soft folds around her body, Lark and Nightingale bound her slender waist with a plaited silken cord that was exquisitely studded with pearls. Finally they fastened a pair of delicately made sandals of darker green leather on her feet, carefully wrapping and tying the supple leather thongs halfway up her calves.

Catrina was only too aware, as she moved, of the silk undertunic caressing her naked flesh. Her small but full breasts felt deliciously caressed by the cunningly tied linen band that thrust them into such prominence. Her bathed, scented skin felt wonderfully sensitive, and her intimate feminine parts still throbbed in dreamy satisfaction after the blissful attentions of the two girls and their ivory serpent. As they showed her her reflection in a long silver mirror, she gazed at her sex-darkened green eyes and tremulous red lips and felt freshly aroused by her own image, and ready for any adventure that this strange new world cared to throw her way. The girls brought her more honey cakes and wine, then left her alone; she drank another goblet of the sweet, heady liquid, feeling dizzy and excited, and nibbled greedily at the delicate treats they had prepared for her. Daylight was slowly fading; a silent house slave came to light the lamp, and the pale crocus-flame glowed enticingly on the richly painted frescoes that surrounded her. Catrina settled herself luxuriously on her soft cushions, and wondered, with a shiver of delicious anticipation, what delights the evening would bring.

Then, suddenly, as the shadows outside grew longer, she heard the ominous, measured tramp of booted feet coming along the silent street.

It's only the soldiers, she told herself quickly as her heart began to thud in alarm. They'll be changing the watch, or marching out of the fortress to some new duty . . .

Then the footsteps stopped, just outside Julia's house. Someone thumped heavily on the door; and in the threatening silence, Catrina's heart pounded with an agonising premonition of danger.

Chapter Eight

Julia, agitated by her meeting with Alexius, had summoned the slave Phidias on her return to the house and ordered him to pleasure her in order to wipe the Roman from her mind. Phidias had done so with a cool, reliable thoroughness, lifting her supple thighs high and wide as she reclined on the couch and penetrating her naked, pulsing mound with slow, delicious skill. Julia quickly exploded with delight, meeting him thrust for thrust until her very last spasm of erotic pleasure had died away.

And now she lay beside her obedient slave on the silk cushions in the darkening room, toying languorously with the big Numidian's somnolent but still lengthy penis, and making plans.

The girl, Catrina. Lark and Nightingale had looked after her today. Soon, Julia would go to visit her, and find out how she had fared in the Syrian girls' company. What other magic powers did she have? Could she make potions, love philtres, perhaps? Could she help her, Julia, to humiliate Alexius? She had certainly been exceptionally responsive and sensuous in her session with Phidias.

'You liked the British girl, didn't you, Phidias?' she said thoughtfully, her hand caressing his dark, tightly muscled thighs. 'You would like her again? In different ways?'

He licked his lips. 'Oh, yes, my lady. She was most rewarding.'

'Not better than me, though?' said Julia, frowning.

'Oh, no,' Phidias said quickly. 'No one could be better than you, my sweet *patrona*.'

She smiled, contented.

And then suddenly they, too, heard the commotion in the quiet street outside: the tramp of booted feet, the harsh exchange of curt masculine voices, then an ominous, heavy knocking at the door. Julia frowned. 'Whoever can it be, at this hour? Phidias, go and see.'

But before he even had time to get to the door, Nerissa flew into the room, panting and agitated.

'Oh, my lady, it's the commander's *optio*! Apparently the commander has heard of the disturbance in the town this afternoon, concerning the young British girl Catrina. It seems that the rumour has spread that the girl has certain magical powers, and the commander wishes to see her immediately!'

Julia sprang to her feet, her body tense with anger. 'Damn him,' she muttered. 'Will he persist in interfering with everything I do?' And, swiftly crossing the room, she flung open the shutters to gaze out into the street.

From outside came the familiar jangle of armour, and the muttered, impatient conversation of the waiting soldiers, their cuirasses gleaming in the light of the torches they carried. She turned quickly to Nerissa.

'If they've come for the girl, then they'll just have to wait. Go back and tell them that she isn't ready. I'm afraid that the commander's fine *optio* will just have to bide his time.'

Nerissa bit her lip anxiously. 'He won't be pleased, my lady. He's very anxious to carry out his duties as quickly as possible. I think he's new to the fortress.'

Julia's eyes glittered. 'Is he indeed?' She looked outside again, picking out the *optio* by his crested helmet, and she remembered suddenly that what Nerissa said was true; her informants had in fact told her the other day that Alexius had a new young assistant, recently posted up from Londinium. She suddenly smiled to herself.

'Wait a moment,' she said to Nerissa. 'I think I'll speak to the *optio* myself.'

Catrina tried hard to stay calm when kind Nerissa came to tell her the news that the commander of the fortress wanted to see her, but inside, she was shaking. Nerissa didn't tell her anything about the commander; she didn't even mention his name, but Catrina could picture only too well the stern, frightening old man with white hair who must command the legion, and the fear consumed her.

'What if I refuse to go?' she said shakily to Nerissa.

Nerissa frowned. 'You really have no choice in the matter. The lady Julia is angry about it, too, but she has to give way to the commander's orders. Everyone in the fortress does. She says that first you are to rest, and finish your meal, but after that, you must go with the soldiers to the commander's house.'

'May I speak to Julia myself?' Catrina said rather desperately.

'She is – somewhat occupied at the moment,' said Nerissa hesitantly.

'Then *you* must tell me, Nerissa! Please – this commander – what is he like? Why do you think he wants me?'

Nerissa, sensing her unspoken fear, said quickly, 'He is a stern man, but fair. Julia is always saying that he is virtually celibate, though I think she exaggerates. I really don't think you will have anything to be afraid of, Catrina. But – he does not like to be kept waiting.'

Catrina, realising that there was no escape, bowed her head in resignation. Why, oh why did the commander want to see her? To question *her*? To punish her? And now she'd lost her chance to question the lady Julia about her enemy, the soldier Alexius . . .

She longed for her amulet, to give her courage.

Julia, meanwhile, had called the *optio* in, and was occupied indeed.

'Yes . . . yes, that's it,' she breathed happily to the stalwart young *optio*, Felix. She was bent over a low marble table cushioned with rugs; Felix had rucked up her skirts round her waist and was ramming into her from behind and grunting with pleasure.

Felix had been worried at first when the beautiful lady Julia had told him that Catrina was not yet ready, and had ordered him to come inside with her. Julia was certainly amazingly beautiful, with her glossy black ringlets and beautiful smooth skin, but his commander had warned him that he was on no account to trust the legate's mistress.

'I should stay outside with my men, my lady,' he said apologetically when Julia invited him into her house.

She'd watched him then, her head on one side. Her high, rounded breasts pushed gently against the smooth fabric of her fine gown, and he thought he could see the hardness of her ripe nipples tantalisingly outlined; his mouth went dry and he stared helplessly into her dark, fascinating eyes.

'You're new to Eboracum, aren't you?' she commented thoughtfully.

He swallowed quickly. 'My lady, I was posted up from Londinium only ten days ago.'

'Then you must come inside. There are certain things about Eboracum that you should know, things that only I can tell you.'

He cast one last, despairing glance at his escort of stony-faced legionaries, who were carefully looking anywhere but at him, and went inside.

After the legionary barracks, the house was sumptuous, and the air seemed scented with exotic Arabian fragrances. Felix felt as if he were in Rome again. He was aware that his loins were stirring with excitement; and when the beautiful lady Julia led him into a cool, spacious chamber and turned to face him, he felt like a young, helpless boy, not a hardened legionary. She drew her finger down the lean, sun-burned skin of his cheek and whispered softly, 'Now. I want you to fuck me, soldier.'

He swallowed hard in disbelief. Those were, he decided, the most exciting, erotic words he'd ever heard in his life. His penis reared into hardness; desperately he gripped her shoulders and tried to kiss her. For a moment she responded, those luscious lips like honey beneath his mouth, but then she disengaged herself and dropped swiftly to bend face down over the table, looking back up at him over her shoulder with a wicked grin as she raised her bottom to him. 'Like this. Now.'

Swiftly he dropped to his knees and pulled up her gown to her waist with trembling hands. Then he pulled apart her ripely flaring buttocks and slid the tip of his throbbing phallus between her velvety-soft labia, feeling with a rush of excitement how she was already slick with her own moisture. She wriggled and moaned at his touch, pushing herself eagerly back towards him, and with a gasp of delight he thrust himself deep, deep into her quivering vulva.

Felix was too excited to last long. Breathing heavily, he gripped her bottom-cheeks and buried himself repeatedly in her juicy softness, pounding away as the fierce heat engorged his loins, half-hearing her tiny, yelping cries of pleasure as she squirmed against him. He was dimly aware that she'd reached down to rub frantically at her own heated clitoris as he ravished her, and she gasped aloud as her own climax drew near. 'Go on, soldier,' she moaned, 'fill me, ride me – oh, your mighty penis is so fat, so strong – '

Then she exploded, writhing around his pounding

shaft, letting out a long, high-pitched whimper of delight.

Felix juddered to his own climax within seconds, his loins twitching and jerking with the power of his release. Drenched with sweat, he drew himself slowly out of her. 'When can I see you again?' he whispered ecstatically as she turned to face him with her cheeks still flushed, her eyes glittering with sated lust. 'I'm off-duty later. I should be able to get away quite easily.'

But at his question, her dark, lustrous eyes seemed to harden suddenly, like stones. 'Oh, Felix. I'm afraid you don't quite understand.' She drew herself to her feet and smoothed back her hair, then walked towards the window. 'What makes you think that I particularly want to see you again?'

He stepped back as if she'd struck him, his young, handsome face suddenly dark with bewilderment and the beginnings of anger. 'But my lady – '

She moved back to face him, and lifted her finger to his lips, to silence him. She smelled of her own musky, potent juices and he shut his eyes despairingly, because already he wanted her again. She was the most beautiful, the most glorious creature he'd ever seen in his life.

'Be careful, soldier,' she said softly. 'What would your fine commander say, if he knew what you'd been up to, when you should have been standing guard with your men?'

He drew his hand across his forehead despairingly. 'Will – will you tell him, my lady?'

'Not unless you give me cause to.' She smiled at him. 'What is your name?'

'Felix. *Optio* to the *primus pilus*, Sixth Victrix legion,' he responded automatically. His voice was low, ashamed; Julia nodded approvingly.

'Very well,' she said. 'You may go. And, Felix, I might just need you again . . .'

His eyes leaped, and he started towards her, but she

turned her back on him. 'The girl should be ready for you now.'

After he'd gone, Julia went into Flavius's deserted office. Carefully she inscribed the soldier's name on Flavius's chart, and then she wrote a small 'J' next to it with a satisfied flourish. In fact, she felt extremely satisfied. It was against her own rules to take any of the soldiers more than once, but this time, she just might make an exception, especially as he was Alexius's man.

The *primus pilus* was becoming a nuisance. He had to be punished. And somehow, angry though she was that he'd purloined her new plaything Catrina, it was just possible that she, Julia, might be able to use the beautiful barbarian girl as a weapon against the commander Alexius.

Catrina stepped blindly out into the night, her coiled hair gleaming like a pale golden coin in the flaming torches borne aloft by the soldiers, her small head held high so that the escort who eyed her so curiously wouldn't be able to detect her fear.

Nerissa had lent her a beautiful cream mantle to wear, and Catrina was grateful now for its warmth against the chilly summer night. The soldiers' nail-studded boots tramped the dark streets of the fortress with grim precision; Catrina shivered and drew her cloak tightly around herself, hurrying to keep up with them as they strode past the great buildings of the citadel, the granaries, the barracks, the workshops that were the lifeblood of the legion. Their stone walls gleamed coldly in the light of the soldiers' torches, and Catrina realised with a tremor of fear that this was a man's world, a soldier's world, where someone like her had no place. She was in the very heart of enemy territory, and she felt small and weak and vulnerable. Oh, if only she had her precious amulet to protect her!

They'd stopped at last before a big, single-storey stone building, its doorway brightly lit by torches flaming in iron brackets on the wall. Two guards stood on either side of the door, standing stiffly to attention as the small foot party approached; the young *optio* who led the escort took Catrina's arm brusquely and stepped forward, saluting.

'The British girl to see the commander, as requested!' The guards saluted back briskly, then looked with bored indifference at the new arrival. Catrina let her mantle drop from her head and stared back defiantly, glad to see that their eyes opened wider and their jaws dropped as they got a closer look at her. Doubtless they'd been expecting a savage, wild-haired barbarian dressed in rags, not a perfectly groomed woman with coiled blonde hair who looked every bit as Roman as any of their womenfolk! Taking a deep breath, she lifted her chin and said scathingly, in her huskily accented Latin, 'Well, gentlemen? Are you going to let me in, or is it your intention to keep me waiting out here indefinitely?'

At her words, they hurried to open the door, fumbling in their haste. One of them beckoned to her to follow and she stepped inside the principia after him, her heart thudding beneath her calm exterior.

Immediately, she realised that this was very different to Julia's house. The rooms were similarly elegant and spacious, but there the resemblance ended; this was so much a man's place, sparely yet elegantly furnished. As they hurried along the lamp-lit corridors, the only colours in evidence were stark black and white, with the occasional gleam of ornamental bronze. Even the air smelled different, masculine; a spicy, fragrant scent that was somehow hauntingly familiar ...

It was then that Catrina's blood began to pound warningly in her veins. She started to feel a strange, icy dread clutching at the very pit of her stomach, in spite of the heated warmth of the building. The thudding of her heart made her feel sick, and it was all she could do to follow the guard through the maze of rooms. Danger threatened, growing closer with every step she took, and there was absolutely nothing she could do to avoid it.

At last, the soldier stopped by an open door, and beckoned to her to go inside without him. Catrina, dazed by the sudden bright light, found herself in a spacious lime-washed chamber with bronze lamps set in high wall-holders, and a charcoal fire burning low in a brazier at the far end. There was a heavy carved table in the centre of the room, covered with scrolls and parchments and a bronze inkstand; a man sat there with his back to her, with his head bent over his papers, a wide-shouldered man with close-cropped dark hair, and a pen in his hand. He was busy writing something, and for a moment he ignored her, though he must have heard her footsteps. Then, after what seemed to be an interminable pause, he stood up slowly, deliberately pushing back his chair and turning to face her.

And Catrina's heart pounded so painfully against her chest that she almost cried out aloud.

Alexius. Her Roman. As devastating as ever – no, more so, she corrected herself desperately, because now his fathomless blue eyes were alive with hard, bright intelligence as they raked her from top to toe. So Alexius, her enemy, was the commander of the fortress, in control of the entire sixth legion. Oh, goddess . . .

Somehow Catrina managed to meet his gaze defiantly, but her heart hammered so violently that she was sure he must hear it. He doesn't know who you are, she kept telling herself. He can't possibly recognise you, because he was blind in the forest, he could see nothing, he doesn't even know that you speak his language!

But she felt very much afraid as he started to walk slowly across the room towards her. He was tall, forbidding, frighteningly powerful somehow in his officer's leather tunic, with his dark-green cloak slung carelessly across his wide shoulders. On his bare arms were several cunningly wrought bronze bracelets, and the sinuously coiled metal contrasted breathtakingly with the man's smooth brown skin; her eyes fastened helplessly on the silky dark hair that dusted his forearms. She found that her mouth had suddenly gone dry. Dear goddess, whatever had made her think that she could take on this man, commander of the entire legion?

He spoke curtly to the soldier who hovered at the doorway. 'I'll let you have the duty lists shortly. For now, you may go.'

'Sir.' The man saluted respectfully and backed away, closing the door behind him; Catrina drew a deep, dizzying breath and gazed up at her enemy, painfully recognising each well-remembered feature in the symmetry of his hard, perfectly-sculpted Roman face; the jutting cheekbones, the high-bridged nose with the jagged line of the fresh scar just above it, relic of the wound that she herself had tended; the thin, almost cruel mouth that had kissed her so devastatingly. And those splintering dark blue eyes, regarding her now with such cool, contemptuous disdain . . .

'Well,' he said. 'You took your time in obeying my summons.'

Drawing herself up to her full height, which was not great compared to his, Catrina retorted, 'Why *should* I obey your summons? I would like to know by what right you ordered me here. I have done nothing wrong.'

His dark brows lifted in ironic surprise at her defiance. 'You sound disconcerted. Have I by any chance interrupted some kind of entertainment at the lady Julia's house?'

'That's none of your business!'

'Oh, but I rather think it is. You see, I just happen to be the commander of this fort, and all its occupants.' He was watching her carefully. 'Julia is somewhat obsessed with sex, as you've no doubt discovered. I can't prevent her adventures, but I can try to limit the scope of her activities. Are you her new accomplice?'

Catrina drew a deep breath. 'I only met her yesterday!'

'Time enough,' he replied coolly, his eyes assessing

her braided hair, her kohled eyes, her elegant clothes, with such scorn that she wondered, with a throb of fear, if he knew. About the dancing girls, and the magnificent masked slave ... He went on steadily, his lips curling round the words, 'They say you saved a child from certain death in the township yesterday afternoon. They say that you have the sight, and can make magic potions and philtres. Is that why Julia took you in? So that you could help her with her games?'

Catrina tried her very best to face up to him, but inside she was trembling. Oh, if only she'd been prepared; if only she had her amulet, to protect her! She said, in a low but defiant voice, 'The lady Julia rescued me yesterday, because the mob had surrounded me. Yes, I rescued a child, a child about to be crushed under the wheels of a cart. The mob was going to tear me apart for it. Tell me, is that your Roman idea of gratitude, commander?'

His cold blue eyes raked her, and Catrina felt the colour rising to her cheeks. At last he said, 'Oh, I imagine the lady Julia had her own kind of reward for you, didn't she? What was it? The Syrian dancing girls? The Numidian house slave? One of my legionaries, perhaps? I know she has a weakness herself for them.'

How did he *know*? Aware that her guilt must be written all over her face, she took refuge in attack, and hissed back at him, 'You certainly seem to be rather well-acquainted with the lady Julia's household! Which of her accomplices do you prefer, commander? Girls or men?'

A spasm of cold anger suddenly shadowed his face, and inwardly she trembled with fear. But then, to her amazement, he seemed to relax, and his thin-lipped, sensual mouth twisted into a smile. 'Well, well. The lady Julia seems to have met her match in you,' he said. 'What is your name?'

'Catrina!'

He nodded slowly. 'Strange that you have a Roman name.' Then he wandered back to his table, and casually

131

poured himself a glass of thick red wine. Catrina stayed where she was, helplessly transfixed by the lean, powerful grace of this soldier's body. He drank, taking his time; then he turned round suddenly to face her again. 'You do realise, Catrina,' he said softly, 'that sorcery is a criminal offence under Roman law?'

She gasped. 'Why should that concern me, Roman, when I am no sorceress?'

'Then how did you know that the wheel was about to break on that cart? They're saying in the township that it was you who actually caused the accident, with your magical powers. Is that true?'

Catrina glared up at him scornfully. 'Your spies are imaginative, but not accurate!'

'Answer my question. Are you a sorceress?'

Through Catrina's mind flashed all the wonderful knowledge, all the beautiful age-old wisdom of her people. How could she even begin to explain to this man? She drew a deep, shuddering breath. 'There is no point in trying to answer your question, commander, because you've already decided on the answer. Why don't you just throw me in prison? That's why I'm here, isn't it?'

He folded his arms across his chest and said, almost patiently, 'I don't know, Catrina. Why *are* you here? That's what I'm trying to find out.'

She swallowed hard, her heart thumping. If he ever found out why she was really here, then death would be too good for her. 'Why should I tell *you*?' she breathed.

He drank some more of his wine. 'No particular reason, except that I was intrigued by something Julia said about you. She told me, you see, that you came to Eboracum to learn our Roman ways.'

What else had Julia told him? Her mouth dry, Catrina said, trembling, 'And is that a crime, commander?'

He was walking slowly towards her, and she fought down the instinctive urge to shrink away from him. 'I take it,' he said softly, 'that you're hoping to find some rich, elderly Roman to make a fool of. The town is littered with native women like yourself, openly selling their wares. Though I must say you're rather more enticing than most of them, and you've certainly found yourself a worthy mentor in the lady Julia. How much have you learned so far, I wonder?'

And before she could even cry out, he'd reached out to pull at her tightly coiled braids, so that her silvery-blonde hair cascaded to her shoulders. Then, with one casual hand he roughly fondled her breast through the thin fabric of her gown, so that the nipple peaked and stiffened painfully with desire, until Catrina almost buckled at the knees with the wild waves of forbidden excitement that coursed through her blood. With his other hand he cupped her face and bent to kiss her almost savagely, his tongue possessing her soft mouth with a cold sensuality that speared her very core. Then he stood back, and she struggled to hold herself steady as the tears stung her eyelids.

'It seems to me,' he said softly, 'that you still have a lot to learn, little barbarian.'

'And you're going to teach me? What do you know about such things?' she hissed up at him, desperately pushing her disarrayed hair back from her face and smoothing down her crumpled clothing while her breasts ached treacherously for his cool, exquisite palms. 'You, the stern, pompous commander of the legion? I thought you regarded such lowly indulgence as a fatal weakness. Why, according to Julia, you're almost celibate!'

'In comparison with the lady Julia, almost everyone is virtually celibate,' he murmured, his blue eyes glinting with dark amusement. 'But perhaps your idea isn't as foolish as it sounds. Perhaps I *will* teach you. And we'll start right now. Put your cloak on again. I have to go out, and you're coming with me.'

Utterly bewildered, she stammered, 'Going out?'

'Why not? You want to learn more about Eboracum,

don't you?' His lip curled. 'I'll make it my mission to show you the city and its sights. Or are you afraid it will be too much for your tender sensibilities?'

She bridled at the scorn in his voice, and said breathlessly, 'Oh, I'm ready, commander! Where are we going?'

He put the documents on his desk into some sort of order and blew out the candle. 'There's a legionaries' celebration in the town tonight. I'm already late, because I had to wait for you to arrive. My men will be waiting for me, and as there's no time to make any alternative arrangements for you, you'll have to come too.' He was drawing his own cloak across his shoulders, and fastening it with a bronze fibula; then he held the door open for her, and beckoned her through.

'By the way,' he said conversationally as she walked past him, 'what made you assume that I regard sexual indulgence as a fatal weakness?'

Caught off guard, remembering too late that it was what he'd said to her in the forest, Catrina went pale. 'I – I heard the lady Julia say it.'

His mouth thinned. 'Really? You must have had some interesting conversations with her.' He didn't pursue the topic, but whether he was convinced, Catrina couldn't say, as she followed him, dazed and uncertain, through the silent corridors of the *principia*. He'd said, *Perhaps I will teach you*. His words thudded through her like dark, potent magic, as powerful as any of the magic of her tribe.

This man was her hated enemy. She had vowed to pursue him remorselessly, to get back her amulet that he'd so treacherously stolen from her, and then to expose him to the revenge of her tribe.

But her blood raced inexplicably as she hurried after him out into the dark night. What, exactly, did he intend to teach her?

Chapter Nine

*J*ulia was at a friend's house that evening, and the company was all female, which would, she reflected wryly, have pleased Alexius. At the thought of Alexius, a small frown puckered her forehead, which she quickly erased, because frowns caused wrinkles. Instead she sighed, and reached for her fluted goblet of wine.

'I was going to bring the British girl tonight,' she said regretfully to her friends, 'to show her to you all. But Alexius, as usual, has contrived to interfere, and has taken her in for questioning. You would have loved her. She's so untamed, yet so innocent, with her wide, dark eyes and her long fair hair – not like a barbarian at all. And her figure is entrancing. I tell you, my slave Phidias found her absolutely irresistible.' Julia's voice trailed away, and her voice grew smoky with lust. She leaned back on her couch and carefully smoothed down her gown, which was of heavy ivory silk and embroidered with gold thread and pearls.

'You mean – you *watched* them?' breathed her friend Melina. They were at Melina's villa, Julia and three other carefully chosen guests, all reclining in a circle of silk-clad couches in the atrium after a delicious meal of succulent roasted fowl and salads followed by sweetmeats coated in honey. Melina was the plump, spoiled wife of a rich merchant who'd made his fortune importing red Samian ware into the northern province; her fine house, on the southern outskirts of the town, was richly opulent, filled with elaborately inlaid furniture and draped with the finest of silks and linens brought in from the distant corners of the Empire on her husband's galleys. Melina was more than a little drunk on the sweet Falernian wine that filled their goblets to brimming, as were all her guests.

'Oh, yes, I watched them,' sighed Julia contentedly, reaching for more wine.

The other women stirred uncomfortably, enviously. They all knew the extraordinarily well-endowed Phidias. Unknown to their pompous husbands, they had all enjoyed the big house slave at one time or another during Julia's various entertainments.

'Tell us about it,' whispered one, wriggling a little closer.

Julia smiled and patted her dark curls, which were adorned with delicate ropes of tiny pearls. As she did so, her golden serpent bracelets jangled softly on her slender arms. 'It was really quite a straightforward encounter. The girl, you see, was more than ready for him.' She reached for another honey-coated date, knowing that her friends were hanging on her every word, and said archly, 'How you would have enjoyed seeing it all!'

'Seeing what?' someone breathed.

'Why, seeing him ravishing the barbarian girl with his mighty shaft, of course!'

There was a delighted gasp of horror from her audience, and they all shifted closer as Julia carried on. 'It really was magnificent. Every time Phidias withdrew his long penis, I could see how slick he was with her love juices. Then, my dears, he would slide in again, gripping her buttocks to steady himself, and the girl would wriggle about ecstatically, completely impaled upon that mighty weapon! The barbarian girl is naturally, exquisitely wanton, though I don't actually think she realises her talents yet. Oh, we would have had such fun with her tonight!'

'But now Alexius has taken her,' sighed Melina.

'Lucky her,' muttered another woman, drinking down her wine.

Julia stiffened, feeling a sudden sharp spasm of jealousy. Surely Alexius wouldn't be interested in the British girl in *that* way! 'He's only taken her in to question her,' said Julia scornfully. 'You don't seriously think he'll try to seduce her, do you? Our pure, upright Alexius?'

'Not so pure,' said the plump Melina quickly, crossing her ankles as she lay back against her quilted silk cushions. 'My husband says that when he was in Rome there was quite a scandal over some senator's beautiful wife. And there have been others . . .'

'I would give half my jewellery to have Alexius in my bed for one night. They say he's a wonderful lover,' sighed another woman longingly.

The lamps seemed to flicker in a sudden cool draught. Julia snapped sharply, 'Then he certainly keeps his talents hidden, doesn't he? I must say that I find him quite unattractive, and overbearingly arrogant! The only pleasure he seems to get is in spoiling other people's fun!'

Her friends glanced quickly at one another from beneath lowered lashes, wary of Julia's anger. One of them coughed, and said quickly, 'And how is your sweet, handsome young gladiator, Julia?'

Julia's face lightened as she thought of Falco, but then she felt a curious, nagging discomfiture as she remembered his quiet defiance. She wanted him to submit to her, and yet his resistance stirred her in a way she couldn't understand. 'Stubborn. Very stubborn. But I think I have found a way to tame him.'

'How? Do tell us!'

Swiftly, her dark eyes sparkling, she told them how she'd ordered Falco, who was surprisingly skilled in languages, to translate her prized collection of erotic literature. She'd brought the scrolls of poetry with her from Rome, she explained to her friends, because when poor old Flavius was flagging, a quick glance at a few of the choicest of the poems, together with their explicit illustrations, used to do wonders for his performance in bed.

'Inevitably, my dears,' she expounded, 'my gladiator Falco becomes helplessly aroused as he studies the delicious accounts of strange and unusual adventures. So at regular intervals I send in Lark and Nightingale to service him. They enjoy their task greatly, as you can imagine, and the gladiator is becoming quite dependent on them. He's not so defiant now, I can tell you.'

There was a breathless silence. Then someone said longingly, 'Oh, Julia! All this talk of delightful men makes me feel quite faint with longing!'

'But you know that we're not allowed to indulge in pleasure of that kind tonight!' said a slightly older matron with a sigh. 'Tonight is the festival of Bona Dea, and we must desist from such delights!'

Julia and Melina exchanged wry glances. Then Julia got up swiftly and walked across the rich mosaic floor to the niche in the wall where the small bronze household deities rested. Lighting a taper from an oil lamp, she lit the wax candles that surrounded them, and poured out a tiny offering of wine as a libation.

'There,' she said calmly. 'That's our duty to the goddess over and done with. Now we can begin to entertain ourselves properly.'

'But how?' her friends chorused desperately. 'When we have no men?'

Julia, still standing, smiled down at them, her face glowing in the flickering candlelight. Then she went over to a small table in the corner and lifted up a heavy, silk-wrapped package. 'I have something to show you. Something I got from my Greek merchant earlier today. He kept it specially for me.'

'What is it? Show us, do!' Her friends leaned forward excitedly; Julia's surprises were always worth waiting for.

Slowly, catching her full lower lip between her small white teeth in the pleasure of anticipation, Julia unwrapped the heavy object and placed it carefully on the low ebony table around which her friends reclined. The gasps and exclamations of her audience were suitably satisfying.

Her purchase turned out to be a small bronze statue of a kneeling winged figure, perhaps a foot high. He was naked, except for a belt fashioned like a snake that was wrapped round his waist. Rising mockingly from between his thighs, almost as high as the top of his head, was a thick bronze phallus, curved and strong, cunningly carved to the likeness of a generously life-sized penis, complete with a smooth, swelling glans at its rounded tip. On the statue's face was engraved a lewd, mocking grin, as if the manikin was amused at the grotesque size of his own appendage. Julia ran her fingers lovingly over the smooth bronze phallus, fondling it meaningfully, while her friends gasped and crowded forward.

'Let me see it, oh, let me see it!' clamoured one, reaching out eagerly to touch the posturing little statue. 'It's beautiful. Wherever is it from?'

Julia purred with secret satisfaction at her friends' delight. 'My Greek merchant whispered to me that it was once used in secret rituals in Persia,' she explained with slow relish, her fingers ringing and sliding over the cold, thick and more than life-size bronze phallus. 'It represents the Mithraic devil, Ahriman the mighty; and each of you may have a turn with it.'

'Me first ... oh, me!' they all clamoured, stirring restlessly on their silken couches.

'On one condition,' grinned Julia. 'You each have to recount your favourite dream. And if it entertains us all sufficiently, then the little statue is your reward.'

There was a heavy silence. Then someone said, 'I think Julia should begin.'

'So do I,' said Melina decisively. 'Julia, will you start us off?'

'With pleasure,' breathed the Julia. 'But first, Melina, you must call for more wine; plenty of wine ... ' She drained her goblet deeply, her cheeks already flushed as the sweet liquor raced through her veins. She was aware of them all waiting with bated breath as she got softly to her feet and went to blow out the candles, leaving only one dim lamp burning at the far corner of the atrium. The heated excitement that filled the room was almost tangible. 'So much for you, Alexius,' she whispered under her breath. 'No one tells *me* not to enjoy myself!'

She glided back to her place and lay back voluptuously against the silk cushions. 'So. You want to hear my dream?'

'Yes – oh, yes!' they breathed, their eyes sparkling in the flickering lamplight. Julia sipped at her replenished glass, and closed her eyes happily.

'Well,' she began softly, 'it starts like this. The other night, I dreamed that I was watching two beautiful men wrestling in a warm, moonlit courtyard. They were naked, and their bodies gleamed with the soft sheen of oil; I could see how their powerful muscles rippled beneath their taut, smooth skin. One was beautiful, blond and golden-skinned. The other was a few years older, somehow more dangerous, with cropped dark hair and a sun-burned, magnificent body that was laced with old battle-scars. As I gazed at him, I saw that he had the most wonderful deep blue eyes.'

'Falco and Alexius!' breathed Melina raptly.

'Yes, yes ... ' Julia had reached across to the table, and was cradling the statue with both hands, resting its weight in her lap. 'In my dream, they didn't know I was there. They were wrestling not for some prize, but for the sheer pleasure of the physical contest. I could see from their faces how they relished the animal strength, the sheer vitality of one another's bodies. They were aroused, I could see, by each other's beauty; each of them was exquisitely endowed, and I stood in the shadows of the colonnade, seeing how their long, thick members hung heavily against their thighs as they moved to and fro across the courtyard, their sinewed arms locked in the embrace of battle.'

Someone gave a little sigh of longing. Julia paused, and went on. 'Both men were exceptionally strong, but Alexius was the more skilful combatant, the more cunning. He moved suddenly, quickly; and Falco, taken by surprise, thudded heavily to the floor, the breath knocked from his body. Alexius dropped gracefully to his knees beside him, to check that he was not injured, and as I watched, breathless in the shadows, I saw how his blue eyes fastened suddenly on Falco's soft penis as it nestled so sweetly in its cradle of thick blond hair. Silently he reached to touch it, to caress it, running his fingers lightly over the heavy, dark pouch of the gladiator's testicles. As he did so Falco's eyes opened wide, and he looked up at the dark, powerful, naked centurion with eyes that burned with need. And then they kissed, their mouths caressing one another with lewd, obsessive passion.'

The silence was so intense that they could hear the flutter of a moth as it beat its wings against the shutters outside. Someone swallowed, and breathed, 'Did they see you?'

Julia looked at her, and went on in her low, husky voice. 'Yes, because it was then that I stepped forward. In my dream I too was naked, except for my serpent bracelets and a pair of flimsy leather sandals that were thonged halfway up my calves. My hair was loose, and gleamed like a raven's wing around my shoulders and naked breasts, while my nipples and my hairless mound were tinted subtly with rouge. I was already aroused by what I had witnessed, and I knew that my dark-pink

141

flesh folds were peeping out, wet and slick between my thighs. And I carried a whip . . .

'The men stopped in my dream, stopped kissing; and they turned from where they crouched on the ground to look up at me. I said sternly, "You are both very wicked to take such lewd pleasure in one another's bodies. I am going to punish you accordingly. See how your rampant members have risen at one another's caresses; see how vilely you have imagined ravishing one another!" And all the while, as I spoke, I rubbed myself slowly with the stiff leather handle of my whip, parting my swollen sex-lips and caressing my tender flesh until the whip was soaking with my body's sweet nectar.

'"Punish us," the two men groaned aloud. "Oh, beautiful lady Julia, punish us – we are your abject slaves!"

'So I whipped them. I made them bend over on all fours, there in that moonlit courtyard that was scented with roses and gum-cistus, and I stood astride them and drew the lash of my whip down hard across their tight buttocks, seeing how their phalluses leaped up, strong and proud and urgent. They'd wanted one another, but now they were desperate for me, and they were going to have me – both of them!'

Her friends gasped aloud, and Julia, the little bronze statue resting heavily in her lap, had almost forgotten them. Her eyes were half-closed with pleasure and her hands had moved to her nipples, to pull them and stroke them in secret bliss through the soft silk of her ivory gown.

'Go on,' breathed Melina.

Julia stirred, the wine coursing sweetly through her veins. 'By now, Falco's grey eyes were wide with anguish, with wanting me. The centurion Alexius, still on his knees, was more guarded, but I could see, from the pulsing of his mighty penis and from the way his blue eyes blazed beneath his heavy lids, that he was desperate for release. I whipped them both with loving care until their bottom cheeks were red, while beneath

142

their bowed bodies their stiffened pricks wept tiny tears of moisture. Then I said, "Falco. Lie on your back. On the floor."

'He did so, grovelling obediently. Meanwhile I beckoned to the soldier to stand, and he did so impassively, as if he already suspected his fate. As Falco lay on his back on the stone flags of the courtyard, his prick rose quivering into the empty air, hot and huge and angry. I stood over him, fondling my proud breasts, parting my thighs slightly so he could see how the love nectar trickled from my smooth, silken folds of flesh. Slowly I straddled him, gazing down at his helpless, beautiful face all the while.

'"Tell me what you want, Falco," I breathed.

'He groaned. "I want you, sweet lady."

'"That's not enough. Tell me more."

'The sweat beaded his wide forehead. He whispered, "I want to drive my hungry cock into your luscious body. I want to take your ripe breasts into my mouth, and wrap my tongue around your glorious nipples. I want to hear you cry out in need as you writhe on my stiffened rod of flesh . . ."

'I glanced round. Alexius was standing there in silent agony, his face pale, his penis dark and lengthy as it jutted rampantly from his loins. I repeated coldly, "Now tell me what *you* want, Alexius."

'He said, in his grating, anguished voice, "Lady Julia, I cannot. It is too shameful."

'I smiled thinly and moved myself a little more on the gladiator's helpless shaft, squeezing and caressing with my inner muscles until poor Falco closed his eyes in despair, and his chest rose and fell rapidly with the sheer effort of self-control. I said, "Then, Alexius, I shall tell you what you are going to do. You are going to kneel behind me, and you are going to sink your wicked shaft deep into my tight bottom-hole. You are going to drive it slowly in and out; you are going to ravish me until I am filled to the brim, with you and with Falco pounding

143

into me, until my beautiful body explodes with pleasure."

'I lifted my flaring bottom cheeks mockingly towards his anguished face, and saw him shudder with need. "Isn't that what you want, soldier? Isn't it?"

'He bowed his head in despair. "Nothing more, my lady."

'"Then go ahead," I challenged him softly. "Do it."

'His face still dark with the shame of his desire, he nodded silently. Falco, beneath me, had gone despairingly still, though his penis still throbbed hungrily inside me. Then, as I watched, Alexius picked up a glass phial of body oil, and, pouring a few drops into his palm, began to rub it slowly up and down his lengthy prick until it gleamed. As the moon gleamed down on the warm, open courtyard, I could see the veins standing out on the shaft, could see how the dark, plummy tip was all ripe and juicy for me, and I gasped at the thought of that great, quivering beast taking my tiny, puckered hole in such a wicked way.

'I writhed on Falco's solid stem until my juices flowed desperately. Then I grinned challengingly up at Alexius. "Come on, then, soldier. Show me you're a man!" and with a violent exclamation, he knelt naked behind me, and gripped my pouting bottom cheeks with his big, strong hands.

'I gasped aloud as I felt his mighty phallus nudging and prodding at my dark, forbidden hole. Already, I was almost at the brink, with Falco's hard penis filling me so exquisitely. And then, as the soldier probed and pulled at my bottom cheeks with his skilful fingers, I felt his great, oiled prick sliding deliciously into my tightly puckered entrance, and I gasped aloud with the sudden dark pleasure of it . . .'

Julia broke off suddenly, her face flushed, her breathing agitated. She glared at Melina. 'Don't just sit there. Touch me, damn you.' And her friends, quiet and intent as they crouched around her in the near-darkness, silently began to pull back her robe and to caress her urgently throbbing breasts.

Julia swallowed and went on in a low voice. 'The two of them were deep within me, both mad for me. My whole body was heavy and ripe and aching for release. I could hear their animal grunts, their harsh breathing as they pounded away, one from below, one from behind; could feel every caress of their magnificent shafts as they slid in and out of me, both so hot, so rigid, so delicious – oh, give me the phallus, I beg you, Melina!'

Quickly her friend pushed the devil-statue towards her clenching hands; Julia grabbed it and kneeled urgently on the couch, her eyes half-closed, her face flushed with excitement. Then, rucking up her long silken tunic and splaying her thighs so that her dark pink sex-lips were exposed to her friends' view, she positioned the little god between her legs so that she was able to slide his gigantic, lewdly curving penis deep between her pouting labia.

She gave a sigh of exquisite relief and held it there for a moment, very still, her hunger temporarily assuaged as her vulva fastened around the cold bronze shaft. The friends closest to her leaned silently forward as if in homage, to lick and mouth her throbbing breasts.

'Oh, gods,' she breathed, her eyes glazed with lust, 'I dreamed I had both of them, both of them longing for me, both surging into me, ready to explode. Alexius drove himself into my bottom, and Falco, his penis still deep within my vagina, reached up to take my nipples in his hot mouth, and I writhed with rapture, feeling both their massive shafts impaling me so exquisitely, and I came, I came.'

Frantically, her eyes shut now, she started to slide the bronze phallus rapidly in and out of her soaking vulva even as she spoke, leaning back against the padded cushions and panting aloud with need as her friends' tongues circled her pouting nipples. She couldn't hold back any longer. The cold, solid bronze penis stretched her, filled her; she clenched her vaginal muscles tightly around the lewd object, feeling as if she were about to burst asunder with pleasure. Then she bore down on the grotesque phallus, pressing down hard so that it caressed her soaking clitoris, and she screamed aloud with pleasure as the heavy, thudding waves of long-awaited orgasm convulsed her straining body.

It was some time before she opened her eyes. The phallus lay smooth and thick inside her contentedly pulsing vagina. With a little sigh of pleasure, she slowly pulled it out, and the bronze manikin's head grinned up at her as if in triumph, his curved phallus shiny with her body's inner nectar.

Her friends' eyes followed it, hot and envious.

'And Alexius forbade me to enjoy myself tonight,' Julia grinned triumphantly. 'Wouldn't he have enjoyed *that*?'

Melina said, awed, 'Did you really dream all that?'

'No, of course I didn't.' Julia smiled sweetly, and reached with a sigh for her wine. 'Now, whose turn is it next?'

Chapter Ten

*I*f Catrina had thought the town busy by day, then the sight of it by night took her breath away. Hurrying to keep up with Alexius' long stride, she felt the crowded timber buildings that lined the streets closing in on her, shadowy and oppressive; while the brightly lit winebooths and gambling dens of the *vicus* overflowed and spilled men noisily out into the streets, men of all races, all ages and all languages, already drunk on cheap, potent liquor. Where the market stalls had been set up earlier, there was now a noisy cock-fight in progress, and Catrina found herself shrinking against Alexius for safety in the light of the smoking cressets as he carved his way with silent authority through the drunken, brawling throng. *Safety?* With this hateful man? She mocked herself despairingly for the thought. A large rat scuttled by her feet; she caught her breath in revulsion and longed suddenly, desperately, for the peace of the forest at night.

Alexius wore a plain, drab cloak instead of the distinctive green one of a centurion, but even so, as the light from the street stalls flickered garishly on his tall, wide-shouldered figure, the men from the fortress recognised him and instinctively saluted, with muttered greetings of 'Commander'. There were women, too; shabbily dressed women with luridly painted faces, who lurked in the doorways of hovels with their friends or walked arm in arm along the narrow street with an off-duty soldier or native trader. They eyed Alexius with open interest, and threw scornful glances at the silent, slender girl who hurried along in his shadow. Catrina glared back at them as she stumbled breathlessly after her tormentor.

Abruptly, Alexius swung away from the main thoroughfare into a narrow, badly lit alleyway which smelled of the tanning works nearby. A mangy dog scuffled in the shadows and Catrina jumped, her nerves jangling. Then she saw that Alexius had pulled up beneath a faded, creaking sign that carried a crude painting of a boar's head that had once, perhaps, been painted with gold. The emblem was scarcely discernible now, even by the light of the little lantern that had been hopefully strung up beside it. But, nevertheless, they seemed to have come to the right place, because Alexius pushed open the narrow door below the sign and beckoned her to follow him.

Instantly, Catrina's senses were assailed by the noise and reek of tightly pressed humanity, and by the ripe fumes of a variety of strong liquors as as he led her into the dimly lit and crowded wineshop. At first, she had to shut her eyes to adjust them to the feeble light from the smoking lamps set high in brackets on the walls. Then, drawing a deep breath, she saw that the room was packed with men, sitting or standing around the stained wooden tables, drinking, laughing, throwing dice or eating from big wooden platters of stew. The noise and the near-darkness stunned her; she saw Alexius watching her with his cold, mocking eyes.

'Welcome to the Golden Boar,' he said. 'Favourite off-duty haunt of the men of the Sixth Victrix.'

She gazed up at him, her green eyes wide with apprehension. 'Why have you brought me here?'

He shrugged. 'You wanted to learn about the ways of Rome,' he said softly. 'But tell me – is this too much for you?'

'Of course not! You . . . you think I haven't been in this kind of place before?'

His eyebrows lifted, mocking her. Without saying any more, he guided her over to a small table set against the wall, from which the wine-booth's owner had hurriedly cleared away a group of drunken skin-traders. Then Alexius ordered a jug of wine. 'Here's your chance to increase your knowledge, then,' he said. 'Tonight is a special night for the legionaries; it's the anniversary of their arrival in Britain. You'll be able to see how my men celebrate.'

Catrina glared at him and sat back on her bench with her arms folded defensively across her chest, her heart hammering as she surreptitiously surveyed the smoky, dimly-lit room and its crowded occupants. At first, she thought that there were no other women beside herself but just men, most of them off-duty soldiers; she could tell them by their hard, clean-shaven Roman faces and closely cropped hair. But then she saw that there were in fact several women, serving the wine. Their lips were painted red, and their eyes were gaudy with eye-colour; they wore shabby, revealing tunics, and the men reached out carelessly to fondle them as they moved past, and whispered in their ears. At the table next to theirs, a girl was sitting on a soldier's knee, and Catrina could see that she was stroking his thigh provocatively in the shadows, her fingers sliding up beneath his tunic. Catrina's face flamed at the intimacy, and she turned away quickly. Alexius seemed calmly indifferent to the spectacle. Why had he brought her here? To mock her? To punish her? Or – did the arrogant Roman really think she belonged in a place like this, with these women?

A serving girl with saffron-dyed hair brought an overflowing jug of red wine to their table, and smiled enticingly at Alexius as she set it on the table together

149

with two earthenware beakers. Then she glanced at the tense, silent Catrina with undisguised contempt. 'Let me know if you want some real company, commander, won't you?' she laughed to Alexius, and moved off, her hips swaying voluptuously beneath her tattered gown.

Catrina sprang to her feet, her hands gripping the edge of the wine-scarred wooden table. 'I'm going!' she said decisively. 'I can see what sort of place this is! You've had your amusement at my expense. Now, take me back to Julia's!'

Alexius, still sitting, fastened his hand round her wrist like an iron band. 'You're not going anywhere,' he said, his eyes glinting dangerously. 'Least of all to Julia's. Believe me, she'll have entertainments of her own organised for tonight.' His grip relaxed, just a little. 'I thought you wanted to learn, Catrina. Sit down, and wait.'

'I won't!' But her pathetic defiance was drowned out suddenly by the shrill, mocking blare of a trumpet, the *bucina*, which Catrina had already heard several times in the fortress, calling out the changes of the watch. Its unexpected sound, here in this dark, smoky drinking den, was met by gasps, then by laughter and roars of spontaneous applause as three young women came marching into the room, in an impudent imitation of the tramp of the legionaries' martial stride. Alexius pulled so hard at Catrina's arm that she sat down with a jerk.

The three females wore gleaming, red-crested helmets and sturdy thonged leather sandals which somehow emphasized the slender curves of their long, smooth legs. Their bodies were scarcely covered by flimsy leather tunics, a lewd parody of the legionaries' uniforms; the skirts were made of short hide strips, fastened at the waist, while the bodices consisted of a series of buckled vertical straps, loosely connected at shoulders and waistband, through which their full, high breasts could be glimpsed trembling provocatively as they marched into the area that had miraculously cleared for them at the corner of the room.

'Signa inferte!' their leader called out in her clear, feminine voice. *'Legio – expedita!'* The many soldiers in the crowded tavern roared with laughter at the familiar battle commands; Catrina glanced, aghast, at Alexius, commander of the legion, to see how he reacted to this mockery, but he seemed to be enjoying the spectacle as much as anyone. His profile was hard and knowing; his mouth twisted in amusement as he glanced down at Catrina's stunned, questioning face. 'They're the legion's mascots,' he said dryly. 'Stop looking so horrified, and watch. You said you wanted to learn.'

Catrina glared back at him. But she did watch, and she felt hot all over as the lights went down everywhere except for the lamp that flickered high on the wall in the corner where the soldier-girls paraded. With the darkness silence fell, but it was a hot, hungry silence that made her skin tingle.

It all started innocently enough, with two of the girls prancing across the floor and doing tumbling tricks. There were gasps of appreciation as their tunics fell back to reveal their shapely thighs. Their modesty was preserved by soft undergarments of fine leather that were attached to the waistband of their tunics and were cunningly shaped to pass tightly between their legs, covering their secret places. But their breasts bounced enticingly as they whirled and spun, and the third girl, who had closely cropped black hair that gleamed like jet in the lamplight, ran laughingly round the room with her helmet inverted to collect the coins that were flung enthusiastically towards her.

Then the trumpet sounded again, and silence fell, with a kind of hushed expectancy that made Catrina squirm uncomfortably on her hard wooden bench. The girl who was collecting the money carefully put down the now heavy helmet and pulled a small, gleaming dagger from the waistband of her tunic. Slowly, in an atmosphere of breathless expectancy, she kneeled on the floor, pushed aside the slit apron of her tunic and carefully peeled back the soft leather undergarment that concealed her pudenda.

A gasp went up from the crowd, and Catrina felt the blood burning in her cheeks. The girl slowly splayed her thighs, so that the black, silky down of her pubic mound was revealed; then, catching her lip between her teeth in concentration, gazing defiantly at her stunned audience, she inverted the dagger and began to caress herself, slowly, subtly, with its rounded bronze pommel.

The silence was absolute as the girl rubbed the weapon very slowly up and down her secret folds of flesh, as if relishing every touch of the cold, hard metal against her femininity. Then, licking her lips, she held the dagger's pommel carefully poised, pulling her sex-lips apart with her other hand, and started to slide it carefully up inside her vulva.

The room exploded. There were cheers, and whistles; men thumped their heavy wine goblets on the tables, as the girl, smiling meaningfully at her audience, her eyes dark with pleasure, began to rhythmically slide the thick, solid shaft up between her thighs.

Catrina burned all over with the shame of what she was witnessing, yet she was filled at the same time with a fierce, incredible excitement. In a dark corner of the room, not far away, Catrina could see a man openly fondling himself beneath his tunic, his glazed eyes fastened on the performing girl; she felt her own face flaming as her gaze was drawn helplessly back to the beautiful, crop-headed soldier-girl who was pleasuring herself so obscenely with the cold metal. Catrina could see that the girl was close to orgasm now; her breasts, thrusting out shamelessly from between the tight leather straps of her bodice, were flushed and pouting hungrily, and as she drove the fat pommel faster and faster between her legs, Catrina could see how the dark-pink flesh of her labia was swollen and distended, while the dagger's hilt gleamed with her love juices. She spread her kneeling thighs wider, to savour the dagger's lewd caress; then swiftly her two companions knelt at either side to finger her breasts through the slits of her leather uniform, pulling her stiffened nipples out yet further and caressing them with tender fingers and velvety mouths so everyone could see how they were darkly distended with need. Suddenly the girl threw her head back and began to moan and shudder, driving her loins in quivering frenzy on to the hard, smooth hilt; faster and faster she thrust, while her companions fastened their lascivious lips around her breasts until at last she began to convulse in a shuddering, ecstatic climax.

Catrina, unable to tear her eyes away, felt quite weak with need. She was aware of her own private parts melting and swelling moistly, as her juices of arousal trickled shamefully between her thighs; she could feel her own blatantly painted nipples poking urgently against the soft, clinging fabric of her gown and yearned to touch them, to soothe their painfully stiffened crests. She glanced at Alexius beside her, who was gazing at the exploding soldier-girl and drinking his wine, imperturbable as ever. She shivered with a sudden dark need as she drank in his harsh Roman profile, seeing the fresh scar above the bridge of his nose that she herself had tended so lovingly. Her gaze fastened helplessly on his strong brown hand resting on the battered table, and she longed to take it in her own hand, and press his cool palm against her throbbing, swollen breasts. She wanted him to do what he'd done to her that night in the forest, wanted him to ravish her with his exquisite, masterful penis until she writhed and moaned to her own sweet climax in his arms. Her eyes skidded helplessly down to the firm strength of his thighs beneath his tunic, longing to run her hands along the iron-hard muscle, to slip her fingers secretly up the hair-roughened flesh until she could stroke the silky, exciting bulge of his genitals . . .

Surely he too must be desperately aroused by what he had just witnessed? If so, she thought bitterly, glancing up at his calm, indifferent face as he watched the erotic floor-show, he hid it, only too well.

Sexual indulgence is a fatal weakness, mea mellita . . .

He turned to look at her suddenly, catching her off-guard. His blue eyes were glacial in the hard, controlled perfection of his face, and she shuddered at the coldness in them. *He knew.* He knew how much she wanted him, and yet he felt nothing at all for her. He was exposing her to this lewd display to humiliate her, to punish her, to show her that she, as one of Julia's minions, meant nothing to him at all. He was hateful! She whipped her gaze away from him and turned back defiantly to the dimly lit tableau that was changing once more.

The girl who'd pleasured herself so erotically with the dagger had swiftly recovered her composure, and was now swaggering around the crowded tables nearest to her with a thickly corded vine stick, the centurion's symbol of office, clenched in her hand. She tapped it authoritatively on a crowded table, making the brimming wine-beakers jump and spill. 'Any new recruits this week, lads?' she called out in her pure, clear voice. 'Any valiant new soldiers for the Sixth Victrix?'

There was much raucous laughter and jostling, and in the end, a tall, brown-haired youth was pushed forward by his comrades. He blushed and grinned in delighted embarrassment. The girl strode arrogantly up to him.

'Name?' she snapped, slapping the heavy vine-stick in the palm of her hand.

'G–Galba,' stammered the young man.

'Last posting?'

'Trier, Gaul. With the training cohort.'

'Commander!' hissed the girl. 'You must address me as commander!'

The crowd roared with laughter as the youth blurted out, 'Yes, of course – commander!' and Catrina, glancing quickly sideways, saw that a thin smile of amusement was curving Alexius' sensual mouth. So at least he had a sense of humour.

The soldier-girl was still tapping her big stick in her hand, gazing up at the tall young legionary with challenging, bright brown eyes. 'And which is the best legion in the Roman army, soldier?'

'The Sixth Victrix – commander!' Galba responded promptly, grinning with delight; and the room exploded with roars of approval and the sound of wine-beakers being thumped on tables. But the girl silenced them instantly by holding up her corded stick. Then she planted her other hand on her slender, leather-clad hip and called out, 'Well, Galba. Any misdemeanours yet?'

The soldier hesitated, but his comrades started to roar with laughter. 'By Mithras, he keeps us awake with his snoring! Isn't that worthy of punishment?' Another called out, 'Ask young Galba if he's paid for his share of the wine yet! He's certainly quaffed enough!'

The girl gazed up at Galba sternly. 'Well? Have you paid?'

He hung his head sheepishly. 'No. I mean, no, commander. Not yet.'

'And do you snore?'

'So they say.'

The girl lifted her eyebrows to the crowd. 'Punishment?'

'Beat him!' they yelled back. 'Use the vine-stick on him!'

The other two soldier-girls pounced easily on Galba, who was dazed with wine and excitement. Pushing the burly young soldier to his knees, they stripped him of his off-duty linen tunic so he was left wearing only his loincloth, and the powerful muscles of his back and shoulders gleamed naked in the flickering light of the smoky lamp. The crop-haired girl who held the vine-stick stood behind him, and lifted the club high, as if she was about to bring it down heavily on his back in the harsh, traditional punishment of the legions. There was a breathless hush.

Then, with a wicked smile to her rapt audience, the

girl flicked her stick deftly, unexpectedly, to tug at the crouching man's brief white loincloth. It fell away instantly, revealing the nakedness of his taut, muscular buttocks. Licking her lips, the soldier-girl drew the rounded end of the thick stick down the dark cleft between his bottom-cheeks, and prodded meaningfully at the secret entrance there. The crowd, swiftly recovering from the shock, openly roared its delight, while the soldier Galba moaned in despair as the other two soldier-girls knelt quickly beside him and started to stroke his phallus. They played with it mischievously, making sure that he had a good view of their own enticing, half-naked bodies; and in no time at all his penis was throbbing, dark and angry, against his belly.

'Punishment?' their leader asked the crowd again, her vine-stick hovering and stroking meaningfully at the helpless soldier's buttocks.

'Use the stick on him!' they yelled again, wild with excitement.

Catrina, with a tremor of horror, saw how Galba's head hung with shame, how his shoulders heaved with great, shuddering breaths that racked his body as his virile penis quivered and surged with a life of its own beneath its tormentors' avid ministrations. She felt a desperate, overwhelming ache at the pit of her own belly, and squirmed silently against the hard wooden bench, realising with despair that her musky feminine juices were starting to dampen her skirt. With a sudden surge of dark desire, she imagined what it would be like to feel that rampant, solid penis sliding deep inside her own yearning vulva.

She shut her eyes, and instantly felt Alexius' strong, calloused hand gripping her shoulder. 'You're here to watch, Catrina. Do so.'

Catrina glared defiantly up at him. 'Do I have to watch every detail? I find your legion's idea of entertainment somewhat childish!'

He raised his dark brows, mocking her. 'Really?' His

eyes rested for a moment on where her stiffened nipples poked betrayingly against the soft fabric of her gown, and Catrina burned with helpless rage as he went on, in his soft, masterful voice. 'I got the idea you were rather enjoying it.'

She opened her mouth to furiously deny it, but just then a deafening roar from the crowded room prevented any further exchange. Seething with resentment, Catrina turned back towards the lamp-lit tableau, and gasped. The girl with cropped hair, turning her back on her avid audience, had dropped gracefully on to all fours, flicking up the dangling strips of her leather tunic so that her ripe, luscious bottom-cheeks were fully revealed, while her breasts dangled ripely between the straps and buckles of her bodice. Her two companions did likewise, swiftly lifting their tunics so that they too presented naked bottoms that were pouting temptingly at the audience. Galba, still kneeling helplessly, stared at them in disbelief.

'Come, Galba,' whispered the leader of the soldier-girls enticingly. 'Your punishment. Take us, all three of us – if you're man enough, that is!'

The young soldier obviously thought he was dreaming. With a hoarse cry of lust, his penis quivering and his eyes hot with greed, he leaped at the first girl and kneeled upright behind her, gripping her flared bottom cheeks and gritting his teeth as his mighty shaft found its target and slipped with delicious ease into that hot, juicy passage. He bucked and thrust eagerly for a while, his eyes tight shut with ecstasy while the crowd roared out its approval. Then the next girl nudged him hard and whispered enticingly, 'What about me, my fine Galba? Don't I get a taste of that magnificent prick?'

'And me!' cried out the next girl. 'Save some for me, I beg you! I want to feel your fine, sturdy weapon deep inside me, soldier!'

With a gasp of disbelieving joy, the naked, rampant Galba worked his way along the line, grunting out his acute bliss each time he impaled one of the waiting girl-soldiers, sliding his hot red penis between their plump buttocks until it was glistening with their love juices. The quantity of wine he'd drunk had numbed him and served to sustain his valiant erection for some time, but suddenly it was all too much for him. Clutching fiercely at the lifted bottom-cheeks of the girl he was currently pleasuring, he started to drive himself faster and faster into her luscious ripeness, his face gleaming with sweat, while the crowd roared out its approval. Catrina caught her breath as she saw the glistening length of his angry great shaft appearing and disappearing rhythmically as he pumped himself avidly into her loins; she saw how the girl's face was alight with pleasure as she writhed ravenously on his stalwart member while pulling hungrily at her own pouting nipples and gasping, 'Oh, yes, soldier, oh, yes! Drive it into me, all the way ...'

And the other girls, acknowledging their loss, sighed and turned eagerly to watch, kneeling with splayed thighs and rubbing their swollen labia hungrily with their fingers as they muttered under their breath, '*Celeriter*, soldier. Faster, faster!'

Catrina felt weak and warm with her own desperate need. All around her, in the flickering shadows of the tavern's dark, secret corners, she could hear the harsh breathing of the onlookers, the grunts and sighs of arousal as the erotic tableau ran its course. She gazed despairingly up at Alexius, who was watching it all with cool, cynical detachment. Roman brute, she muttered to herself. As far as he was concerned, she might as well not be there! Suddenly, she could bear no more. Watching the young soldier Galba as he pumped so furiously into the girl's loins, she imagined it was her, Catrina, kneeling there before him in that erotic leather tunic, her beautiful, sexually aroused body on full display before all these hungry, virile men, all avid to touch her, to pleasure her, to ravish her with their hungry shafts.

Desperately she slid her palm across her thighs

beneath the table and ground it surreptitiously against her pubic mound, feeling through the folds of her gown how her flesh was hot and slippery and already responding joyously to her touch. Her labia parted eagerly, moistening the thin fabric of her gown as her fingers slid against them; with a little jolt of agonised bliss, she found her tiny, throbbing bud of desire, the secret heart of all her delight, and through her flimsy gown she caressed it swiftly, feeling how the pleasure, hard and sweet, surged swiftly through her loins. Her whole body tightened in a dark rush of rapture. She felt her breasts throb and the colour rush to her face as she rubbed hard with one eager finger, and she swiftly exploded in hot, silent release, trying desperately to control the instinctive spasming of her hips, clamping her throbbing lips tightly shut against her deep, ragged breathing.

When she opened her eyes at last, dizzy with the force of her secret explosion, the dazed but happy Galba had staggered back to join his friends. The soldier-girls were coolly rearranging their disordered clothing, laughing and saluting with mock military precision as the men got to their feet and stamped and cheered. Then they marched off, arms swinging at their sides, breasts poking out jauntily through the leather straps of their bodices. Slowly the room returned to its normal noisy bustle as the lamps were relit and more wine was served. Catrina leaned back against the wall behind her and drew a deep, shuddering breath.

And then, suddenly, she felt Alexius' hand touching her shoulder, his firm grip slowly but surely turning her round to face him. She quailed inwardly because his eyes were dark and mocking. Had he realised what she'd been doing just now? The colour burned anew in her cheeks.

'You enjoyed the entertainment?' he drawled out.

Catrina swept back her loose silver-blonde hair from her face with her hand, and scornfully met his gaze. 'You call that entertainment, Roman? I feel sorry for you all, if that's the best you can do!'

Before she could realise what he intended, his hand slid down from her shoulder to her breast. Cupping it lightly in his palm, he caressed it with slow deliberation and pulled lightly at her peaked nipple through the thin fabric of her gown, sending fresh waves of anguished desire flooding through her body. Then, abruptly, before she could even gather the strength to pull herself away from him, he let her go.

'Perhaps you'd better go back to your hills and forests, barbarian girl,' he said softly. 'You're out of your depth here. You say you want to learn Roman ways, but I don't believe you. What are you really doing here in Eboracum, Catrina?'

She drew a ragged breath. 'It looks as if I'm being given a good demonstration of the depths to which you're all prepared to descend!'

'How very self-righteous of you. Can't you match us, then, little wild one?' His lip curled into a cold smile as he spoke, and Catrina, still shaking from his unnerving assault, was just summoning the strength to reply when she realised that someone was pushing through the crowds towards them and heading for their table. It was one of the soldier-girls, the one with the beautiful face and the cropped, jet-black hair that was somehow so amazingly feminine. She'd pulled a cloak on over her tunic to conceal her half-exposed body, but her face was still flushed with arousal as she directed herself at Alexius. '*Salutatio*, commander,' she breathed softly, her dark brown eyes shining. 'It's been quite a while since we last met. I certainly didn't realise you would be here tonight. Did you enjoy our little entertainment?'

She perched herself on the edge of the table as she was speaking, and Catrina saw how her cloak had slipped back to display her long, well-shaped legs with their high-thonged sandals. And the soldier-girl's eyes were fastened familiarly, almost hungrily, on Alexius, as if she knew him well . . .

Alexius smiled, and said, 'Very much, Claudia. I shall have to take you on to my official staff, I think.'

The girl grinned back, and hesitated before saying, 'We've finished for the night now, the girls and I. Are you free later, Alexius?'

'Sadly, no.'

Claudia pouted. 'You've not forgotten that night at the fort in Calleva? With the three of us?'

'How could I?' he replied graciously. 'But duty calls, I'm afraid.'

The girl looked suddenly at Catrina, and her eyes grew hard. 'Duty,' she said. 'Is that what you call it? I can't believe that your tastes have changed so very much, commander.' She slid from the table and walked off with a defiant swagger until she was lost in the crowd. Catrina stared after her blindly, seething at the contempt in her voice. So *that* was the kind of woman Alexius preferred, was it? But before she could recover herself she suddenly realised that someone else was pushing their way urgently through the noisy throng towards their table; not a girl this time, but a man in soldier's uniform, who saluted quickly then leaned and whispered in Alexius' ear. 'Sorry to disturb you, commander. But there's a brawl outside, and some of the soldiers are involved. We could do with you there, sir, to cool things down.' Instantly Alexius was on his feet, his face intent and purposeful. 'Stay here,' he said curtly to Catrina. 'I'll be right back.'

Catrina retorted, 'Don't worry. I'm not going anywhere. How could I?' But in spite of her defiance, she felt desperately alone without him, here in this alien crowd.

The entertainment, it seemed, was over. The men in the tavern had turned back to their wine and their gambling. And Alexius seemed to be a long time. She tried not to be anxious, but her agitation grew. Perhaps he wasn't coming back. Perhaps he'd grown bored, and had just decided to leave her here, as a kind of punishment for her defiance!

She tried to fight her fears down, but the panic rose like a hot tide in her chest, and she felt more and more isolated in the smoky, crowded wine-booth. Just as she was wondering whether to get up and fight her way to the door, two burly legionaries suddenly appeared from nowhere, and sat on either side of her bench, trapping her. One of them stroked her hair and murmured drunkenly, 'All alone, sweetheart?'

Catrina knocked his hand away. 'Leave me alone!'

The soldier's rough face darkened. 'Ah. Playing that sort of game, are we?' His hand slid down to her breast, and he fondled it roughly. 'Don't give me that. You're here for pleasure, just like the rest of us, aren't you? I've got some of my pay with me; how much do you want? You look a bit new to this sort of thing, but you're a pretty enough wench . . . Tell you what, I'll give you ten *sesterces* if you'll go outside with us, both of us at the same time, eh?'

The other soldier leaned forward, nodding eagerly; his breath stank of sour wine. Catrina, pale with fear, tried to get up, but they gripped her wrists, pinning her down.

'Let me go!' she cried hoarsely.

'You're joking, sweetheart,' responded the first man. 'Let go of a fine, juicy little morsel like you? Or is this all part of the games you like to play?'

Each man was formidably strong, and together they were far too much for her. Standing up, they hauled her to her feet and started towards the door with her, her struggles going completely unnoticed in the noisy, constantly shifting throng of the crowded tavern.

But before they reached the door, it opened suddenly, letting in a draught of chilling air, and Alexius came in. Immediately he assessed what was happening and barred their way.

'Let her go,' he said, in his quiet, icy voice, and the first man fell back.

'Sorry, commander,' he stammered. 'Didn't realise . . .'

But the second, brazen with wine, said, 'Why is the girl here, damn her, if she's not prepared for a bit of fun? We were going to pay her well – '

But he got no further, because Alexius, drawing back his clenched fist, punched him so hard on the jaw that he slumped to the tavern floor like a felled log.

The room had gone silent. Swiftly, Alexius caught Catrina's arm and dragged her outside. She tried to hold herself steady, but she was trembling with fear.

Alexius gripped her shoulders and twisted her round to face him. 'I think it's time I sent you back to the fortress before you get into any more trouble.'

Catrina, still shivering from the shock she'd had, looked up at him with wide, defiant eyes and retaliated. 'Why bother with me at all, Roman? Why don't you just let me go, seeing as I'm such a nuisance to you?'

His mouth thinned as he assessed her forlorn, defiant figure. Then he said, 'Firstly, because you've yet to tell me exactly what you're doing in Eboracum. You're no courtesan; your reaction to tonight's display told me that clearly enough. You're an innocent, Catrina.' He paused, letting his words sink in. 'Secondly, I'm keeping you with me because the civilian magistrates who are in charge of the township will need some convincing that you're not a danger to them. They were going to arrest you at Julia's house this evening, but fortunately I got word of it and managed to forestall them by claiming military jurisdiction over you.'

'Fortunate for whom?' spat back Catrina. 'What fate do *you* have in store for me, Al–Alexius?' She stumbled in the agonisingly familiar way over his name, and there was a heavy silence. Then his blue eyes gleamed suddenly.

'I'm not sure yet,' he said, and his hands, gripping her shoulders, seemed suddenly lighter, almost caressing.

Catrina felt the helpless, treacherous ache of wanting him so badly, and struggled to break free.

'If your taste runs to brazen, half-clad girls who don't mind exposing themselves to half the legion,' she shrugged up at him, 'then I'm afraid you'll be disappointed!'

He smiled calmly down at her. 'I'm not so sure I *will* be disappointed, my little wild one,' he said, and his blue eyes seared her in a way that made her feel quite weak.

It was no good. Without her amulet, she was quite powerless against him. She gazed after her enemy helplessly as he went off into the night, concerned now only with his duties as commander of the legion.

Alexius' *optio*, Felix, escorted her back across the river to the fortress with silent deference. After exchanging words with the duty guard at the door of the *principia*, Felix left her there all alone, behind the locked doors of Alexius' forbidding residence.

The brawl having been settled, Alexius moved swiftly, purposefully about his last duties of the night, accompanied by a grizzled older centurion as he inspected the guards posted at the watchtowers. Up here, high on the bastions of the fortress, the township appeared smaller, less significant, a cluster of flimsy wooden buildings gathered under the shelter of the fortress's grim walls with the silvery gleam of the river throwing back the moon's pale light. Around, all was blackness, the blackness of the wooded plains, and, unseen to the west and north, the high, bleak hills where the native British took their shelter and waited, he knew, for the slightest weakness in Rome's defences.

He rubbed his forehead, because tonight the scar that slashed his forehead seemed to throb anew, bringing back memories of that darkness in the forest, when the girl with soft hands and a beautiful low voice had tended to his bodily needs in every way possible. And there was something, something that disturbed him badly about the husky, accented voice of the girl Catrina; about the way she couldn't quite pronounce his name . . .

He shook his head, calling himself a fool, and moved on to the next watchtower, making the usual curt enquiries and answering the clenched salutes of his men. He was overreacting. The girl Catrina was from a British tribe; that was why her voice seemed so familiar. Catrina – strange, it was a Roman name. She was beautiful, by Mithras she was beautiful, with her long, silky hair that was like moonshine, and her wide green eyes that sparked with rebellion, or darkened with her secret pain whenever he spoke sharply to her, which he seemed to do so often.

My enemies say it has no colour, except, perhaps, the colour of moonlight.

The words spun round his head, and he stopped, gripping the parapet. That voice. Dear Mithras, that voice . . .

'Sir. Are you all right, sir?' The grizzled centurion, who was well aware that his young master had not recovered from the wound as completely as he liked to make out, moved towards him anxiously, but Alexius brushed him away.

'Yes. I'm fine, centurion. You have the duty rota for the next watch? Then let me see it.'

They moved on, and in the darkness Alexius reached to touch the silver amulet that he wore around his neck, concealed beneath his tunic. His mind was playing tricks on him. The girl Catrina, who claimed she had the sight and had come to Eboracum to learn the ways of Rome, couldn't possibly be the girl who had tended him in the forest – the girl he had seduced and tricked in order to save her from certain death at the hands of her tribe. She couldn't be.

But somehow, he had to make quite, quite sure.

Chapter Eleven

To Catrina, the house where Alexius lived seemed huge and silent and forbidding. Did Alexius have servants? she wondered, as she wandered around the sparsely furnished rooms, with their stark lime-washed walls. He must have some domestic staff, a man in a position of such power, but perhaps they came only by day; certainly there was no one around at this late hour. Except, of course, for the guard at the outer door, reminding her that she was a prisoner just as surely as if she was in chains.

There was a central room, a little less bleak than the others, with rich tapestries breaking up the harshness of the walls and a wrought-iron brazier filled with glowing charcoal. Settling herself cross-legged on a thick wolfskin rug that had been spread before the fire, she hugged her knees to her chin and gazed into the flames, trying desperately to make sense of everything.

Seeing Alexius again was like the pain of a sharp knife twisting in her heart, making it difficult for her to think straight. He was her enemy, and her one purpose in coming to the city of the Eagles was to get her revenge on this man who had humiliated her so badly. But it was going to be so difficult when his every look, his mere presence even, disturbed her so treacherously. Oh, if only she had her precious silver amulet to help her protect herself from him!

She gasped, and sprang to her feet. Of course – her amulet! Why didn't she think of it before? Here she was, all alone in Alexius' house. If her amulet was anywhere, it was here, and she was wasting infinitely precious time, sitting here like a fool bemoaning her fate instead of getting on and looking for it! While Alexius was away, she would search the building from end to end. Her heart hammering with excitement, she picked up a bronze lamp from the table, and began to explore.

Holding the lamp high so that it cast a small circle of golden light, she moved swiftly from room to room, looking for some place where her amulet may be concealed. There were chests and coffers in the big room that seemed to be his office; but when she opened one of them, it was filled with nothing but dry, dusty documents. Catrina put down her lamp and ran her hands agitatedly through her loose fair hair. Soon the Roman would be back, and she had got no further in her quest.

Without any real hope, she tried one last door that led from a dark corner of the central atrium. It was unlocked. Holding out her lamp into the darkness, she saw that it revealed a shallow flight of stone steps leading down into the murky blackness. Some kind of cellar, or store-room? Perhaps *this* could be the hiding place for her precious amulet! Swiftly she made her way down the steps and found herself in a wide, vaulted chamber that had been built underneath the main body of the house. Holding her lamp high, she gazed with wondering eyes as the faint golden light struggled to penetrate the pillared alcoves; then, in the shadows, she saw something gleaming coldly. Her footsteps sounded unexpectedly loud in the heavy silence as she walked slowly across the tiled floor towards it; as the light of her lamp fell on the mysterious object, she gasped with surprise.

167

There in the shadows of the candlelit alcove, gleaming with unexpected brightness as she raised her lamp high, was a magnificent bronze effigy of an eagle, set high on an ornately carved pole that was adorned with badges and scarves. The eagle's fierce talons gripped the cross-bars to which it was secured, and its sightless eyes seemed to gleam down at her, proud and cruel and strong; like a god, a cruel eagle god ... She felt a shiver of fear tingle down her spine, and at the same moment she heard the sound of a door thudding open in the distance.

Too late, much too late, she became aware of the heavy footsteps crashing down the stone steps behind her. She whirled round, and was instantly dazzled by the blaze of torchlight. Blindly covering her eyes with her hands, she heard a gruff voice shouting, 'That's her, com-mander! I've been following her as she crept round the house, just like you ordered! And look at her! Just as I guessed, she's after the legion's treasure. We should turn her over to the magistrates straight away, and have her locked up!'

There were more soldiers behind him, their armour clanking, their swords raised as they plunged down the steps towards her. And behind them, his face cold and grim, was Alexius.

Catrina tried to run, but it was hopeless. Two of the soldiers caught her arms, and she knew her struggles were in vain. Gasping for breath, she tossed back her hair from her face and tried her best to meet Alexius' gaze with proud defiance, but his blue eyes, quietly contemptuous, chilled her to the bone.

'I wasn't after your treasure!' she hissed. 'I didn't even know it was here!'

'Then what were you looking for?' he said quietly.

She gazed at him in helpless silence. That was the one question she could never answer.

'Take her to the magistrates, sir,' suggested one of the

soldiers. 'She's obviously a barbarian spy. They'll have ways to make her talk.'

Alexius said, 'So do I. Secure her to the wall; it's best if I question her down here, where we are private. She's obviously cunning, and we don't want any chance of her escaping.'

Again, Catrina struggled and fought, but her efforts were in vain as the two soldiers dragged her swiftly across to the nearest pillars and bound her wrists tightly with leather thongs, so that her arms were spread high and wide. She pulled and jerked helplessly, but she knew that there was no escape. 'Oh, goddess,' she murmured silently, 'help me. Please . . .'

Then she realised that Alexius had dismissed his men, and was walking slowly towards her. They were quite alone, in this strange, secluded shrine of the eagle god. Fighting back her fear, she tugged at her bonds and hissed up at him, 'Let me go, Roman! You've no right to keep me here!'

'Haven't I?' His gaze raked her lazily. 'I don't think you quite realise yet, Catrina, that within the walls of this fortress, I can do whatever I like. I'll ask you one last time; what are you doing here?'

Catrina swallowed hard, her small face remained taut with defiance.

He shrugged at her silence. 'Perhaps I'd better leave you down here until you decide to answer me.' And he turned, and started walking towards the steps, taking the lamp with him.

Catrina felt dazed with fear. He was going to leave her, all alone in this strange underground chamber, with only the cruel eagle god for company! In the dark. 'You – you're not going to leave me down here?' she stammered out at last.

He stopped and turned back. 'You'd rather go to the magistrates?'

'Perhaps!' she retaliated wildly. 'They at least might offer me some sort of justice!'

169

He folded his arms and surveyed her coldly. 'If you believe that, then you're even more of a fool than I thought. If the town magistrates get hold of you, then they'll turn you over to the mob. You know what that means, don't you?'

She had a good idea. The blood drained from her face at the prospect, but somehow she managed to meet his gaze as she said with apparent indifference, 'Why don't you give me to the magistrates, then?'

'Because,' he replied, 'I want to know what you're doing here in Eboracum. That's why I left you alone here, under the watchful eye of my soldiers, in the hope that you might give something away. You're after something, Catrina, aren't you? But what?'

She gasped. 'You've had people watching me? All the time?'

His lip curled. 'Did you really think that the legion's Eagle is ever unguarded?'

'Then – it really is a god?' she breathed, turning to gaze at the great bronze effigy.

'To a soldier, it's the most powerful god there is. If the Eagle is lost, the legion is finished. You've been watched very carefully, Catrina.' He took a step closer; she was suddenly aware of his height, his strength as he towered over her pinioned body. 'I'll ask you one more time; why did you come to Eboracum?'

She shrugged scornfully, as far as her bonds would allow. 'I've told you. I came here to enjoy myself. Is that against your Roman law?'

'It depends,' he said softly, 'on how you intend to take your pleasure. And with whom.' And with that, he reached out to grab at the neckline of her tunic, and pulled sharply at the pale fabric, ripping it from throat to waist. Catrina shuddered in despair and closed her eyes.

'Well,' said Alexius, his voice heavy with contempt. 'I see Julia's been busy with you already.'

Catrina felt quite sick with degradation. Her eyes were

170

still tightly shut, but she knew only too well what the Roman would be looking at. As he'd ripped her gown and her silk undertunic in that one powerful gesture, he had exposed her high, firm breasts, with their erotically painted red nipples, just as garish as anything on offer from the prostitutes she'd seen in the town tonight. Then she felt his hand there, smooth and warm and strong, and as his thumb caressed her already stiffening nipples one by one, she opened her eyes to gaze up at him, her face white with despair, because even as he stroked the tender scarlet crests into life, the arrows of sharp, savage desire were winging down to her loins.

He must have seen what was written in her face, because with a casual tug he pulled at her girdle so that her gown slipped completely to the floor in heavy folds. Then his cold blue gaze travelled steadily downwards, taking in her slender hand-span waist, her softly swelling hips, and the soft golden down that curled enticingly over the mound at the apex of her thighs. Catrina, with a stab of despair, felt the warning throb at the very core of her femininity. Already, she was warm and moist for him. If he knew how desperately she wanted him, then he would show her no mercy.

She tossed her head and said scornfully, 'You could have bought your pleasure on the streets tonight, centurion. Are you so mean with your money that you prefer to take a helpless captive?'

He smiled dangerously. 'Oh, I couldn't have bought anything like this.' And Catrina gasped aloud as she felt his hand hard between her legs, cupping her. The pleasure ran through her like a tongue of flame, as his blue eyes held her, hypnotised her. She trembled with need as his strong, lean brown fingers slowly parted her swollen sex- lips, assessing the juicy nectar that gathered there so shamefully. Wickedly his fingertip slid upwards between the delicate folds of tissue, only to stop as they brushed against her pulsating clitoris; she moaned aloud with the sweet pleasure of his caress, and bit on her soft

171

lower lip in an effort to suppress her urgent need. His touch was diabolical. With a despairing effort, she hissed at him, 'Leave me alone, damn you! Go and pay for your pleasures somewhere else!'

His hand stayed there, softly stroking her melting labia until the pleasure invaded every point of her pinioned body. She could feel her juices trickling down her silky inner thigh; his finger penetrated lightly, teasingly and she had to fight the urge to clamp her thighs round him, to press down against the hard caress of his insolent hand . . .

'Look at me.' His voice was quiet but insistent. 'Look at me, Catrina, and tell me what you want.'

She gazed helplessly up at him, feeling the bonds pulling all the time at her wrists, and knowing that this powerful, sexually experienced man would see all her yearning hunger in her smoky pupils, her tremulous lips. His hand continued to stroke insolently. Taking a deep breath, she hissed out defiantly, 'I want you to let me go!'

He smiled, and the slow, dangerous smile sent explosions of need racing through her blood. 'So you keep saying. Now tell me the truth, Catrina. What do you really want, more than anything?' And he began to circle her clitoris very slowly, with the tip of his forefinger, not actually touching its sensitised tip, but making it leap and throb with longing. In spite of her cool nakedness, she was burning, burning with exquisite need, and she could feel the hunger gathering dark and heavy within her. 'Not you, Roman,' she whispered despairingly, 'that's for sure!'

With his free hand, he started to rub her scarlet nipples. They leaped and thrust out proudly, longingly; then with agonising slowness he licked his finger and circled them until her whole body seemed to centre on the tingling, throbbing ache that pleaded so desperately to be assuaged.

'Are you quite sure about that?' he said. 'I saw you

172

earlier, you know. You were pleasuring yourself secretly, back there in the wineshop, weren't you? You're very wanton, Catrina the barbarian. Did you enjoy your solitary little climax? Or would you rather have a real one, with me?'

The shame flooded her cheeks. She was shaking her head silently, helplessly, because all the time his delicious fingers were pulling at her nipples, and sliding up and down her sticky labia.

'Tell me,' he went on, tugging with exquisite insistency at her yearning red nipples, 'tell me what I should do. More of this? Or this?'

She was grinding her vulva helplessly against his knuckles now, bearing down on him as far as her taut bonds would allow, desperately trying to rub her swollen, glistening flesh against his tantalising fingers, her whole body a quivering, helpless mass of desire. Desperately she lifted her breasts to him, longing for his mouth to take them, to soothe their burning crests. And then she almost stopped breathing, because suddenly his fingers were sliding deeply into the juicy cleft at the apex of her thighs, pausing tantalisingly at the hot, pulsing entrance to her vagina. She bore down desperately against his strong hand, grinding herself against him, smearing him with her love juices, beyond all control.

And then, he drew his hand away and stepped back from her, saying thoughtfully, 'Sexual indulgence is a fatal weakness, *mea mellita.*'

He was cruel. So cruel. She hung her head, so that her long, silky blonde hair curtained her burning face and veiled her despairing eyes; her slender body sagged helplessly in her bonds.

Suddenly, unbelievably, she felt his hand cupping her cheek in a tender caress. He tilted her face up to meet his, saying softly, 'And it is also, undoubtedly, the sweetest of pleasures.'

Then he kissed her.

His mouth was warm, and sensitive, and wonderful.

173

His tongue gently caressed her inner lips in deep, probing promise, while his hands soothed and cupped her tingling breasts, twisting her hardened teats in delicious pleasure-pain. She melted at his touch, trembling in exquisite delight at the unbelievable tenderness of him, at the hard maleness of his powerful lean body pressing against her sensitised naked flesh.

And then, while he was still kissing her, she felt his exposed phallus, hard and hot and proud, nudging greedily against her thighs. She uttered a soft moan of pleasure as she felt him lower his hips slightly to adjust to her lesser height; then she felt the full, throbbing glans of his manhood prodding insistently at her pouting, nectared labia, and she gasped with shock at the thick, hard power of his engorged penis as it slid slowly, irrevocably, up between her swollen folds of flesh.

He was inside her, filling her, stretching her exquisitely. Her eyes opened very wide at the unbelievable male solidity of him; and he smiled gently down at her. Then, with wonderful prowess, he supported the taut curve of her naked buttocks with his powerful grasp in order to pleasure her slowly, lovingly, with his lengthy shaft, while his dark head bent low to nuzzle at her hungry breasts.

He knew everything she wanted. All her deepest, darkest, most shameful desires were laid bare to him. Silently lifting his head from her swollen breasts, he reached with his hand to finger her soaking, exposed clitoris; and Catrina felt the delicious, burning heat gathering at the very core of her womb as he drove himself ever deeper into her tethered body, his thick rod of flesh pulsing steadily within her hungry love-channel, his dark blue gaze searing her with passion. Dazed with desire, she glanced down and caught her breath at the erotic sight of his slim yet powerful hips slowly driving his stiffened manhood up into the very heart of her femininity; then he withdrew, slowly, tantalisingly, and she felt dizzy with longing as she saw the thick, dark base of his proud shaft rearing forth from its nest of soft black hair, the silky veined stem of it glistening with her womanly juices.

She gazed up at him, helpless with need, almost forgetting that her arms were still bound. Her enemy smiled back at her, his smile darkly masculine, and full of wicked promise. She felt her whole body gather itself into an exquisite, shuddering knot of erotic tension, and then she heard herself utter a long, blissful moan as he pounded into her and drove her whole body into a wonderful, mind-searing explosion of rapture.

With devastating skill, he continued to pleasure her, drawing every last essence of delight from her trembling body, kissing her breasts and cupping her buttocks gently as the waves of languorous ecstasy swept through her, over and over again. Then, at the very end, he gave way to his own pounding release, and she felt his body throb and spasm inside her. Catrina experienced a heady sensation of sheer power when she saw that his eyes were tightly closed, and his face was racked with dark pleasure as his extremity wrenched his whole body.

For a moment he continued to hold her in perfect stillness, while his thick, still powerful penis pulsed deep within her. Then with the utmost tenderness, he withdrew himself and began to carefully untie her wrists. Catrina would have fallen as her bonds were released, but he caught her round her slender waist and held her easily upright with his strong arms. Carefully he reached for his cloak, and wrapped her shivering, tremulous body in its soft folds. For one unbelievable moment she felt safe and loved. Silently she gazed up at him, her green eyes dark with emotion, waiting for some word of tenderness.

But she should have known better. His blue eyes were like ice, and she felt the shock of it jar her body into alertness. *Her enemy . . .*

He was watching her, assessing her. He said at last, 'You show some promise, little wild one. And you remind me of someone I once knew. The sound of your voice, the feel of your hair . . .'

Catrina shrank away from him, her heart thudding against her ribs. He was playing games with her. Oh, goddess, if he knew who she was, then she was lost. Forcing herself somehow to sound calm, she shrugged and said, 'Indeed? There must be many women who look and sound like me.'

'No,' he said quietly, 'there's no one quite like you, *mea mellita.*'

The endearment he'd used in the forest made her blood run cold. Then, abruptly, he turned towards the steps, beckoning to her to follow. 'It's late,' he said curtly, 'and I have to rise early tomorrow. I'll show you to your room.'

She drew the cloak tightly around her shivering body and stared after him stubbornly. 'And what if I want to leave, Roman? Am I your prisoner?'

He regarded her thoughtfully from the foot of the steps. 'It's more a question of your safety, Catrina. The magistrates have issued an edict for your arrest, and I'm probably the only person with the power to keep you safe from them. I thought I explained that earlier.'

She said scornfully, 'So you're trying to tell me that you're keeping me as your prisoner in order to ensure my safety?'

'Partly.' He smiled coldly. 'But there is another consideration.'

'What?'

'There is the question of pleasure. Yours and mine, while we find ourselves thus – forced together.'

The colour warmed her cheeks. 'Pleasure?' she repeated in a low voice. 'I thought, Roman, that barbarian women were not to your taste!'

He regarded her thoughtfully, a gleam of laughter in his eyes. 'Now, who in the name of Mithras told you that? I have found that the women of the northern tribes have a certain primitive, if uncultured, charm.'

176

Catrina hissed, her green eyes sparking, and sprang towards him; Alexius grinned openly, holding up his arm to ward her off, and gestured towards the steps. 'Time for bed, my little wild one. And tonight, though I hate to disappoint you, you will sleep alone.'

'What makes you think that news disappoints me?'

For answer he merely laughed and turned to go.

Then, just at the bottom of the stairs, Catrina noticed that Alexius seemed to hesitate and stumble slightly as his foot caught against the bottom step. He paused uncertainly, and she knew, beyond a shadow of a doubt, what had caused him to almost fall.

His eyes. His beautiful blue eyes. The effects of his old wound still lingered, and for one terrible moment he hadn't been able to see at all.

Without pausing to think, she rushed forward impulsively, crying out, 'Alexius!'

He'd put his hand against the wall to steady himself. The whole episode only lasted a moment, but his sudden weakness devastated Catrina. He looked so much younger in his vulnerability, and she felt her heart twist painfully as he struggled for control. But before she could even form the words to offer help, he'd recovered and was drawing his hand across his scarred forehead as if to push the darkness aside. Seeing her there in front of him, he caught her frozen, anguished expression and grinned slowly. 'Sympathy for me, little barbarian?' he mocked. 'Surely not.' Then he was moving swiftly on up the stairs without a trace of hesitation.

Briefly he showed her to her tiny sleeping chamber, bare except for a small bed and a high, narrow window through which the high, pale moon gleamed. After he'd gone, Catrina, despite her tiredness, lay awake long into the night, hearing the lonely call of the trumpet sounding the changes of watch, and the distant footfall of the guards along the ramparts.

Alexius. His every word, his every gesture seemed to

haunt her, and her body was still warm from his love-making. Was this hate?

She closed her eyes, the weariness washing through her, and tried desperately to push the turmoil of her thoughts aside. She wished she had some of her medicines with her so that she could prepare a soothing infusion that would help her to sleep.

But she *had* brought some medicines! In the little pouch that was fastened to her girdle . . . Then, suddenly, she remembered, and her heart seemed to stop beating.

She'd left the clothes that she'd travelled in at the lady Julia's. With them was her little purse of salves; and concealed within that purse was the deadly little knife.

The knife with the name of Alexius engraved upon its hilt.

Chapter Twelve

*L*uad the priest had been gathering herbs. In order to impress the watching people of the tribe, he had made all the necessary incantations, murmuring the ancient words of wisdom in suitably hushed tones before he went out alone into the dark forest to find the holy plants of the Druids. Then, clad in his hooded white robe as his people would expect, he returned to the sacred clearing for the ceremony of consecration. This next part of the evening was entirely a figment of his own fertile imagination, though fortunately the gullible tribespeople did not realise it.

The moon glittered fitfully through the clouds, piercing the canopy of high, interlaced branches and gleaming coldly on the pale, rabbit-cropped turf below. In the little clearing, Luad's cloaked figure was imposing and coldly handsome, with his long dark hair emphasising the gaunt, compelling structure of his intent face. The most beautiful, wanton women of the tribe gathered round him in hungry silence with Eda at their forefront. They were waiting for the final consecration.

The summer breeze soughed gently through the full-leaved oaks, making the shadows twist and jump suddenly as if there were strange, secret creatures of the night weaving their purposeful way through the undergrowth. It was time. Luad carefully kindled the fire in the centre, and laid his bowls of freshly gathered herbs – wolfsbane, yarrow, comfrey, belladonna, and, the holiest of them all to the Druids, vervain – all around the yellow, leaping new flames that as yet cast no warmth.

They were ready for him, waiting for him. Eda, clad in a thin, pale robe, moved forward proudly to hand him the big bronze cup of metheglin, the fiery native liquor that stirred a man's senses and sent his blood leaping through his body. 'My lord, we are ready for you,' she said softly, her eyes an open invitation. Luad drank deeply, feeling the liquor warm his taut belly, and gazed into the tangle of trees that surrounded the firelit glade. And all he could think of was Catrina.

Away to the south, many miles away, its pale ramparts rising threateningly from the lowland plains, was the city of the Eagles, Eboracum, where Catrina had gone. He hoped, very much, that she was not going to betray him.

She had vowed to him before she left that she hated the Roman who had stolen her amulet, but Luad remembered how she'd tended the prisoner as he lay injured, and he guessed that she was playing a dangerous game. He needed her back, quickly. Without Catrina and her sacred amulet, he, Luad, was virtually without power, and it would not take long for the people of the tribe to realise it.

What if she never came back? How long would it be before the natural cravings of her body led her into the arms of another man?

He felt a wild rage engulf him. And then, at the thought of Catrina experiencing the sweet joys of the flesh, he felt the lust starting to rise in his body like the spring sap in a young forest tree. She was his, the girl with the incredible pale hair, and the wide, innocent green eyes, and the slender yet womanly figure, and no one else would have her.

As he drank deeply from the bronze bowl of methegelin, and gazed frowning into the flames, he remembered one particular day last summer, the day when he'd followed her and watched her bathing in her secret mountain spring when she'd thought she was all alone. Luad had crouched in the shadows, behind a thicket of dog roses and alders, fondling himself gently as he watched her undress. He'd felt the blood race in his veins as he saw how she let the cool, trickling spring water play over her high, womanly breasts and glimpsed how her ripe, rosy teats stiffened and peaked beneath the relentless spray. His pulse had quickened with desire as he saw how she fondled her own tender nipples, that, despite her maturity, were as yet untouched by a man . . .

Sliding his hand carefully beneath his robe as he crouched there, he'd rubbed slowly, luxuriantly, at his throbbing shaft till it was thick and bone-hard. He imagined stroking its velvety purple tip against her sweet nipples, and seeing the startled shock on her face change to flushed, melting pleasure as she learned to take womanly joy from the lewd touch of his mighty, virile shaft. Even as he rubbed, imagining it all so vividly, she rose naked from the pool, running her hands uninhibitedly through her long wet hair; Luad's refined face grew dark with arousal as he glimpsed the delicate mound at the top of her slender thighs, so delicately clad in softly curling golden hair. As she climbed gracefully up on to the mossy bank, he caught a tantalising glimpse of the darker pink folds of flesh that were the entrance to her delightful femininity.

Catching his breath, he had rubbed harder and harder, feeling his seed gather helplessly in his pulsing testicles. Then with a choked gasp he spurted hotly, feeling his whole body convulse with the shuddering ecstasy of release as the milky fluid shot in great jets from his body.

By the time he had recovered himself, Catrina, unknowing and innocent, had gone on her way. Somehow she remained magically untouched by the wanton rituals she observed; as well as the protection of her amulet, Luad wondered sometimes if she was guarded by her magic powers, as if the goddess had marked her out for something other than the base coupling of ordinary mortals. Yes, she was marked for something special – for him, Luad, priest of the northern tribes!

But now she had gone, and he very much feared that he had made a bad mistake in letting her go.

'My lord priest.' Eda was on her knees before him. Her head was demurely covered with her pale hood, but her eyes glittered hungrily as she looked up at him. 'We are ready for your ministrations.'

He was ready, too; more than ready. His penis was already stirring, thanks to his memories of Catrina bathing so innocently in that clear mountain pool; eagerly it thrust against the folds of his priestly robe, angrily demanding his attentions.

'Then it is time,' he announced grimly, holding out his hands towards the glittering fire, gazing into its glowing heart. There were five women kneeling in the circle, the most comely of the tribe, chosen specially by Luad himself. At his words they bowed their heads, their faces a mixture of fear and excitement as Luad began to murmur the ritual words of blessing over the newly gathered herbs.

Luad went through it all as quickly as he could, in a low droning voice, rushing through the spell that he had half-made up and half-remembered in a doggerel mixture of Latin and Celtic. He knew it was not the true magic of the old hooded ones, but the people of the tribe did not know that, and it served his purpose well enough – the purpose of his, Luad's, pleasure. He thought of the true priests finding out, the old ones of the ancient ways who still lingered up in the high, secret glens of the northern mountains, and he shivered. He knew, more than anyone, that he abused his power, and he accepted that this was why his gift had waned over the years into a tiny fragment of what it should have been. But for the time being, there was the pleasure, pleasure which he could not live without.

One by one he touched the bowls of freshly lifted vervain root and cowslip and belladonna, his voice droning constantly in murmured blessing. The moon, riding high between the clouds, shone brightly on the little secret clearing, and somewhere in the distance an owl hooted as it pursued its nightly prey. He felt the fear, the awe, gather in the watching women, felt his power over them as he intoned the final words of the ritual. He could not give this up.

'And now, goddess of ancient ways, be with us as we
Prepare to honour thee.'

He stopped, his hands spread wide, his long dark hair falling back from his finely chiselled features as he lifted his face to the cold moon. The silence was intense; he could hear the tiny rustlings of secret animals in the undergrowth, and the sighing of the leafy branches overhead as the breeze stirred once more. The smoke of the fire billowed suddenly, and one of the women, overawed by the tense atmosphere, gave a low cry of fear.

Luad fastened his pale eyes on her, and she blenched. 'Prepare yourselves,' he said sternly in his soft, hypnotic voice. 'Prepare yourselves, for the final ritual of consecration.'

The moon gleamed down on the pale globes of their breasts, as trance-like, they pulled back their robes for his delectation. The cool night breeze caressed their naked flesh, drawing out their nipples into stiffened peaks; as they gazed up at him, he saw the open hunger in their eyes. Earlier they had drunk sweet mead, into which Luad had secretly dropped pinches of the special yellow-green powder he'd prepared, containing tansy and other herbs. It was a magical infusion he had learned

183

from the old hooded ones on his travels, and it never failed. Tonight would seem to the women as a wild, trance-like dream. They were more than ready; they knew they were not allowed to speak, but their expressions spoke for them.

Luad, standing impassively before them, parted his long, priestly robes so that his throbbing, rampant penis reared out into the empty air, like a hungry beast ready for its prey. The women moaned and whimpered with desire at the sight of his perfect male body, and he gloried in this moment of triumph, knowing that his powers had not entirely deserted him, because each of them would be pulsing and wet between her thighs, and longing for his mighty member to bring pleasure and release, such release.

One of the women, a plump little brunette who had drunk more than her share of the mead, had let her robe fall back completely as she knelt before him, and was caressing herself dreamily between her spread thighs; he could see how her forefinger tenderly teased and pressed her hardened clitoris between her juicy labia. 'Take me, lord priest,' she muttered. Her eyes fastened on Luad's jutting penis as she wriggled surreptitiously closer, and her big, freckled breasts swayed heavily.

Eda struck her angrily aside. 'You have drunk so much mead, Silda, that you have forgotten you are enjoined to silence!' she hissed. 'The priest will dismiss you from the ceremony if you dare to utter another word!'

The dark-haired woman darted an angry, rebellious look at Eda and pressed her lips shut. Luad frowned. He was growing tired of Eda's possessiveness. She had always been fiercely jealous of Catrina, and had expected, with the blonde girl out of the way, to share the priest's bed every night. Luad decided that it was time now to teach Eda a lesson. Reaching out his hand, he beckoned to Silda; she smiled in answer, and with a mocking glance at Eda she rose and walked proudly naked towards him, tossing back her long mane of dark hair.

Luad watched her appreciatively. The firelight gleamed on her pale, freckle-dusted skin; her breasts were large and ripe, while her hips were sleekly voluptuous, and between her thighs her curling black hair glistened already with her feminine moisture of arousal. He could glimpse her full, dusky labia protruding stickily from the secret place between her thighs, and his penis quivered and leaped in fresh excitement. The woman saw it, and licked her lips meaningfully.

Luad said to her, 'You spoke to me earlier, Silda. You know that speech is forbidden, unless I myself give the word. I give that word now; you may speak, and tell me what you wish!'

She lifted her head proudly, and said in her delicious, husky voice, 'I wish to give the handsome lord Luad the greatest pleasure he has yet known. I wish to taste him with my tongue, and let him savour the moist, delicious warmth of my lips enfolding his exquisite manhood. I wish to take him within my waiting body, and ride him and ride him until he feels that the goddess is truly with him tonight.'

Luad smiled thinly. 'Then proceed.' Eda gasped and darted forward in protest, but he beckoned her sharply away, and she sank back into the firelit circle with the other disappointed women, her face flushed with anger.

Silda moved towards the priest, her tongue already darting and flickering between her full lips. Sinking to her knees before his tall, cloaked figure, she positioned herself before his erect penis and started to lick it slowly, drawing the moist tip of her tongue in featherlight strokes along the thickly veined shaft.

Luad groaned inwardly with delight, and braced himself against the onslaught of bliss. His penis was throbbing, burning; the wetness of her wicked tongue cooled it and yet excited it still further. With an effort, he opened his eyes, and saw the circle of bare-breasted

185

women all watching Silda's possession of his great manly weapon with hot, jealous eyes. Some of them were openly pleasuring themselves, unable to control their own fierce need; he saw how they were stroking and pulling hotly at their own breasts, and rubbing their secretive fingers surreptitiously down their glistening flesh folds as they hungrily watched his great, thick shaft sliding so deliciously into Silda's wanton mouth.

She was taking him all in now, or at least as much as she could of that pulsing length; he could feel the back of her throat caressing his exquisitely sensitised glans with its soft, velvety resistance. He groaned, wrapping his hands in her tangled hair and starting to slide rhythmically in and out of her deliciously moist lips, feeling how they rimmed and gently squeezed his tender, throbbing shaft. Then suddenly he felt her plump, mischievous hands caressing his testicles, her sharp little nails scraping his scrotum, and he shuddered. He had to have her. Soon.

Luad had more strength, more staying power, than any other man of the tribe; it was yet another reason why the women clamoured so hungrily for his attentions. It was a secret he had learned from a travelling wise man long ago, who, like Luad, had also absorbed much of the almost-forgotten magic of the old hooded ones. The man had given Luad the recipe for an unguent, which, when used to anoint a man's phallus, produced a pleasant sensation of numbness that delayed the moment of crisis and extended the pleasure further than could be believed possible. Luad had made up the unguent himself, using wolfsbane, which he already knew could quieten the pain of a bruise or an injured place. Then he added to it all the other secret ingredients which the man had whispered to him. It worked well, and had pleasantly extended many a sexual encounter. But even so, even he, Luad the priest, had his limits.

Carefully he gripped Silda's shoulders and slid himself out of the embracing suction of her skilful mouth; his

186

so red ... He muttered the words rhythmically to himself as the very last of his semen spurted forth; and then it was over. He was drained, magnificently spent. The women bent to lick his seed adoringly from Silda's still-quivering buttocks, and slowly Luad got to his feet and reached for his robe as the old obsession returned.

Catrina was still his. He would know, surely, if any other man dared to defile her. She was his, the orphan of the floods; for years now, he'd protected her from the hungry eyes of the men of the tribe, and guarded her from her own desires with his careful instructions as to what the goddess required from her. He'd saved her all this time for himself. He was not going to lose her now.

Luad's hard, clean-shaven face was sheened with perspiration after his exertions as he smoothed down his heavy robe. The potent metheglin he'd drunk lay heavy in his stomach. The fire was dying down, and the breeze sighed once more through the little clearing. Although it was summer he felt suddenly cold. The women gazed up at him, awaiting his bidding; curtly he told them to dress and go back to the turf huts of the village. Disappointed, they slowly did as they were told and melted away into the darkness.

Lingering by himself in the moonlight, Luad felt increasingly restless and uncertain. Catrina must return. Without her and the power of her amulet, he was in danger of losing his authority over the tribespeople; he was well aware that earlier tonight some of the warriors had watched him with dark expressions on their faces, muttering angrily as he chose the best of their women for this evening's ceremony. He had to act, now, before their jealousy of his gifts made them conspire against him.

Making his way to the edge of the clearing, he called for Brant, who he knew would have been spying hungrily from the shadows. Swiftly, Luad told the red-capped little tribesman exactly what he had to do that night; and Brant, nodding eagerly, hurried off to find his shaggy pony and ride south, towards the city of the Eagles. Then Luad went back to the dying fire, and threw a pinch of dried vervain powder on its dying embers.

'A curse on you, Roman,' he said softly, and the flames leaped menacingly up in the darkness of the night.

The same moon that haunted the forest clearing flickered and gleamed coldly on the great stone walls of the fortress of Eboracum, making its pale ramparts appear wraithlike and insubstantial against the enveloping darkness.

As the night wore on, Catrina, lying alone in her small lime-washed bedchamber in Alexius' house, slept fitfully at the very heart of the enemy citadel, and her sleep was riven by dreams. Towards dawn she dreamed once more of the great forest to the north, where amongst the mighty oaks she saw Luad in his pale hooded robe, with his long hands outspread towards the glowing fire in the heart of the secret clearing, and his gaunt, compelling face lifted to the high, cold moon. She could almost feel the heat of the flames, which leaped and crackled menacingly as Luad threw a scattering of his magic herbs on to them; with the heat came the sudden awareness of evil, and she imgined she could even smell the bitter, acrid smoke as the flames licked and spread with frightening ferocity around the tinder-dry clearing.

A forest fire! Although a figment of her dream, it seemed to scorch her lungs, suffocating her; with a stifled sob, she pulled herself up in her little wooden bed, suddenly wide, wide awake.

Nothing but silence in the cold, empty, hostile *principia*. Just the sound of her heart hammering stupidly against her ribs; just the moonlight piercing a chink in the high shutter, its cold, thin shafts spearing her narrow bed. She sat there very still, clutching at the woollen covers, frighteningly aware of the presence of evil, of danger. Was it really just a dream? She drew her hand across her forehead in desperate confusion.

Then she smelled the pungent reek again, more clearly this time, and her blood went cold, and she realised then that, dear goddess, this was no dream, because now she could see the blue-grey spirals twisting under the door into her room, stretching out long, choking tendrils, reaching for her . . .

She jumped from her bed and ran to fling open the door, her bare feet flying across the cold tiled floor, her skin rising in goose bumps beneath the thin white cotton of her shift. Then she gasped in horror, because further along the passageway, she could see a flickering, lurid glow, the light of the fierce fire god; the flames leaped high, lighting the darkness with their mocking red light, and already they were licking up against the door of Alexius' chamber.

Her heart thumping with fear, her eyes already stinging from the black, acrid smoke that swirled menacingly towards her, Catrina looked round wildly for help. Suddenly she spied the rich tapestries that adorned the *principia*'s otherwise bare walls. Hardly thinking what she was doing, she wrenched one down and threw its thick, smothering length across the edge of the swirling flames, then another, while she cried out through the choking smoke, 'Alexius – oh, Alexius! Please wake up!'

Then the big door that opened on to the street was wrenched suddenly open, and four big, uniformed soldiers burst in. They took in the fire-scorched scene with horrified eyes, and while two of them continued to stamp out the flames, the others seized Catrina and wrenched her arms painfully behind her back.

'Little sorceress!' one of them growled. 'Set fire to the commander's house, would you?'

Catrina coughed and choked as the black, dirty smoke from the extinguished fire rasped against her throat and lungs. 'Let me go, you brutes!' she gasped, struggling desperately. 'I didn't start the fire!'

One of the soldiers, who was stamping out the last glowing embers where a tapestry still smouldered, hissed out to his comrades, 'It's oil. Lamp-oil. Look how it's been splashed all over the floor, right up to the commander's door! Lucky we were here on time!'

Catrina looked wildly to where the man was pointing. Yes, there was a trail of oil – and the tell-tale wet gleam started just below a high-barred window, from where it trickled down the wall to the floor. Someone had poured it through the grating, and then tossed a brand in afterwards, to send the whole building up in flames! She went cold at the realisation; the men meanwhile were shaking her till her teeth chattered. 'Little witch. We stopped you getting away with our Eagle, and now this!'

'No!' she whispered. 'It's not true! You beasts, let me go!'

And she was still fighting desperately when Alexius, already clothed in his tunic and leather boots, opened the door of his bedchamber, saying, '*Mithras*, but you make enough noise between you to waken the dead. What's happening?'

Then he paused, his cold blue eyes suddenly alert, taking everything in: the desperate, wild-eyed Catrina in her thin cotton tunic with her loose fair hair tangling round her face and shoulders; the grim guards who pinioned her arms; the charred hangings and the filthy, clinging smoke.

He said, 'Let go of the girl. You're hurting her.'

'But sir! She started the fire – there was burning oil spilled right up to your door! She's a spy, a Druid witch, sent here to kill you!'

'No!' breathed Catrina, white-lipped. 'I didn't start it! It's not true!'

There was a heavy silence; then Alexius stepped towards the men's prisoner. 'How could the girl have started the fire,' he said softly, 'when she's been in my bed all night?' He took Catrina by the arm, and the guards shrank back, stunned. Alexius went on, 'So, you see, you may return to your duties outside.'

'But, sir -'

'You can send a work party to clear up the damage later. Now go.'

The four men saluted stiffly and retreated, shutting the door heavily behind them. But Catrina didn't see them go; she was gazing up at Alexius, her cheeks smeared with smoke, her eyes still stinging from the fumes.

'Why did you say that to them, Roman?' she said hotly. 'That I'd been with you all night?'

Already he was starting to buckle on his heavy sword belt. 'Isn't it obvious? If I hadn't, they would have hauled you off and lynched you as a sorceress. You certainly have an appetite for dangerous situations, Catrina. First you're caught with the legion's Eagle, and then you're discovered wandering around just as a conflagration threatens to engulf the commander's house.'

She gasped, the colour flaming in her cheeks. 'I – I wish I'd let it burn!'

He was watching her with narrowed eyes. 'How did you know there was a fire before anyone else did?'

She gazed up at him helplessly. 'Sometimes I have dreams. Sometimes I see things that turn out to be real.'

He was watching her with that steely, penetrating blue gaze that made her body feel weak and helpless as a child's. He said, 'If *you* didn't start the fire, then who did?'

She felt the tendrils of fear curl round her heart, because she thought she might have an answer. 'How should I know, Roman?' she declared at last. 'It must have been an accident!'

He indicated the trail of oil on the wall below the high barred window. 'No accident, and I think you know it. Fetch yourself a cloak, my little wild one – it's almost dawn, and time for the first roll-call. From now on, you'd better stay with me. That seems to be the only way to keep you out of trouble.'

'You're still keeping me a prisoner, then?' she said scornfully.

His eyes gleamed. 'Let's say that you're a hostage rather than a prisoner.'

Catrina trembled with fear and exhaustion and anger. She thrust back her tousled hair from her face and felt the hot tears of vexation sting her eyes. Why had she tried to save this man's life, when he was her enemy?

Yet she felt sick at the thought of the fire engulfing him; and at the realisation that someone else was trying to kill him.

Chapter Thirteen

Catrina felt dizzy with the heat as she stood by Alexius' side and gazed down into the vast, sanded arena that was the legion's parade ground. The sun's rays glinted fiercely on rank after rank of pennants and armour and upraised swords, almost dazzling her. Wings of cavalry had been drawn up at either end of the infantry lines, and the horses stamped restlessly, their nostrils flecked with foam as they chafed at their bridles. Again and again, the hoarse battle trumpets blared out in the ceremonial of display, and the barked commands of the grim-faced centurions reverberated through the ranks of immaculately arrayed legionaries.

A cohort of Gallic auxiliaries was preparing to leave for garrison duty in one of the bleak forts on the northern wall, and it was being sent off with all the pomp and ceremony of Rome. Alexius was watching it all from a vantage tower that adjoined the *principia*; a pillared stone balcony had been built many years ago on to the first floor of the tower in order to give the legion's commander a perfect view of the parade ground below.

And, alone with Alexius on the high balcony, was Catrina. His hostage. She had struggled so much at her confinement that Alexius had fastened a chain round her

195

wrist, which was looped to his sword belt. Amongst the watching legionaries, the sight of their commander, formidable in full armour and crested helmet, accompanied by his blonde barbarian prisoner, had caused no little stir. Catrina, feeling their curious eyes upon her, burned with shame and humiliation.

She and Alexius were quite isolated here on the balcony. To their rear was a closed door into the watchtower, while encircling them on the other three sides was a waist-high stone wall. Catrina gazed down at the parade ground, fascinated yet horrified by this evidence of the might of Rome, by the wheeling, marching ranks of legionaries all taking their turn to salute their Eagle and their commander, Alexius. No wonder her people had been conquered, thought Catrina faintly. The dust of the tramping feet and the prancing horses seared her throat; the sun glinting on their armour dazzled her. Seeking some shade, she sank to her knees behind the solid stone wall and leaned her cheek against its coolness, feeling the chain round her wrist tighten threateningly as she moved.

Alexius – hateful, arrogant Alexius. She'd tried to save his life – but why, when she'd come here to kill him? She gazed distractedly around the small balcony that was her prison, thoughts of escape from her impossible situation churning in her mind. Then she felt Alexius' hand tug warningly at the chain that encircled her right wrist, and he was saying gently, 'Careful, Catrina. Don't even think of making any mischief.'

Tossing back her loose fair hair, she glared up at him, only to see that his blue eyes were still fixed calmly on the parade ground, and his hand was outstretched over the sill of the balcony as he returned the salutes of rank after rank of legionaries. Suddenly, her blood boiled. How dare he! How dare he chain her up and parade her in public as his barbarian hostage!

Her green eyes gleamed with rebellion as she gazed up at his powerful, proud figure. Mischief, he'd said.

Perhaps there was more than one way to inconvenience the high and mighty commander Alexius!

And, very quickly, before he could even realise what she intended, she ran her hand up the bronze greaves that encased his lower legs and began to explore the long, hard, hair-roughened line of his thighs. Beneath the thick leather strips that formed the skirt of his tunic, he wore only a soft linen undertunic; she heard his hiss of indrawn breath as she pushed her hand higher and found what she was looking for: the long, thick flesh of his naked manhood, lying heavily against the silken skin of his inner thigh.

She sensed his whole body go rigid, and felt a sudden, sharp lick of desire at the base of her own belly at the exciting, forbidden caress.

'For pity's sake, Catrina!' he hissed through thinned lips, his arm still raised in salute as the legions gazed up at him. 'What in the name of Hades are you doing?'

Her hand began to stroke and fondle the detumescent phallus. Her eyes glittered. 'Just another of my barbarian ways, lord Alexius,' she said in her broken, husky Latin. 'After all, if I am to accompany you everywhere, then I have to find some way to amuse myself.'

'*Mithras . . .*'

She glanced up quickly, and saw that his face was dark with anger, but there was nothing, absolutely nothing, he could do, because although the kneeling Catrina was hidden from the view of the arena by the stone wall of the balcony, Alexius himself, the focus of this parade, was on full public display from the waist upwards. As if to emphasise his dilemma, the trumpet blared again, and another century marched by; again and again he had to acknowledge and return the salutes of his men.

'Catrina,' he said through clenched teeth, 'behave yourself, or -'

'Or what, Alexius?' She gazed up at him demurely, suddenly enjoying herself. 'Will you beat me with your

197

centurion's stick? You'd enjoy that, wouldn't you? So would your men down there. How they'd love it if they knew what was going on . . .'

Both her hands were running tantalisingly up his legs now; she felt him brace himself despairingly against her caresses, and recognised her own mounting excitement. She loved the texture of his hard, hair-covered bare thighs beneath her palms, loved the heady feeling that he was utterly helpless to do anything to stop her. Very gently, surprised at her own daring, she inserted her face beneath his linen tunic and began to press her warm, dry lips against his clenched leg muscles. She heard him moan under his breath. And then, she slipped her hand upwards to find his phallus again.

It was thickening inexorably. As she stroked it with her fingers, she could almost feel the blood rushing to its dark, heated length; she remembered how this beautiful weapon had pleasured her so sweetly last night, and she felt suddenly quite faint with wanting him.

Her own body tingled and throbbed with need. The legion in its dusty arena seemed a world away, the sound of tramping feet and the blare of trumpets just a mirage. Still holding his penis, she rubbed her small, high breasts lightly against the solid hardness of his thighs, feeling her nipples peak and harden inexorably through the flimsy linen of her plain tunic; the dark, heavy throb of arousal started to gather in her belly, and she was suddenly aware of a tiny, pulsing core of need at the apex of her thighs, where her labia swelled and moistened, betraying her own dark need.

Concentrate, Catrina, she told herself fiercely. Concentrate, on humiliating your enemy! Alexius' shaft had swelled into glorious, rampant erection beneath his tunic as her busy little fingers stroked and fondled. Running her hand along its magnificent length, feeling her own senses reel at the strength of it, she reached to cup and enfold the heavy purse of his throbbing testicles; at her intimate caress she heard him catch his breath in despair, and his body went rigid. Fighting down her own urgent arousal, trying to ignore the soft rasp of her tingling, stiffened nipples against her linen tunic, she took his beautiful, bone-hard penis in her hands and gently stroked it, feeling the veined ridges of its jutting shaft and the velvety smoothness of its swollen tip as it reared and jerked like some live animal in her hands. She closed her eyes, breathing in the musky maleness of him, mingling with the scent of harness and leather, and started to rub, harder.

Suddenly she felt his free hand entangle in her loose blonde hair. 'Catrina. For Jupiter's sake . . .'

She pulled herself away a little so that she could look up at him; but her fingers were still delicately stroking the rigid, lengthy shaft that prodded so urgently against her hands, desperate for release. Suddenly remembering the ways of the women of her tribe as they pleasured their men, she let her fingers travel past his testicles to find the dark, hairy cleft that ran between his taut bottom cheeks, and as she began to explore that mysterious place, she queried innocently, 'Yes, Alexius? You want me to stop?'

'Catrina, you witch. We're in full sight of the entire legion here!'

'*You* are, Alexius,' she responded sweetly, her fingers still tantalising his secret places. 'But they can't see me, or what I'm doing. I thought that as I'm just an uncultured, captive barbarian, you really wouldn't have any trouble at all resisting me!' Then she leaned forward again, placing her face between his thighs, and whispered, 'Sexual indulgence is a fatal weakness, remember?' Then, very carefully, she began to circle the swollen head of his thick, dark penis with her tongue.

Instantly it jerked and reared towards her, weeping with tears of salty moisture. She pulled her head away and gazed up at him demurely. 'Do you still wish me to stop, Roman?'

She saw his face go dark and tight. She could tell by

199

the sound of clattering hooves and jingling harness that a cavalry wing was sweeping past now; the trumpets shrilled, and again Alexius had to stretch out his clenched fist across the high wall of the little balcony in acknowledgement of their passage. 'Mithras, little wild one,' he grated out in despair through clenched teeth, 'if you stop now, I'll punish you indeed.'

Throbbing with excitement herself, the fevered blood sweeping through her veins, Catrina formed her mouth into a perfect circle in the manner of the women of her tribe when they were pleasuring their menfolk; and then, her heart beating very fast, she let her tongue dance round the fat, plummy rim of his penis, and slid her moistened lips slowly down his thickly engorged shaft.

He tasted warm, and male, and good. She felt his whole body go taut at her moist, intimate caress; and she felt her own despairing shudder of need as the rod of warm, solid flesh slid slowly, irrevocably, between her moist lips. Her breasts swelled and ached beneath her tunic, longing for his cool hands to take them and soothe them; at the apex of her thighs, she felt her moist labia puff out and tingle with need, and she wished it was her yearning vagina that was caressing and enfolding his beautiful, proud penis.

She sucked and pulled gently with her tongue, filled with wonder at the silken taste and feel of him, only too aware that she had the pulsing, virile core of this man at her mercy. Somehow the thought filled her with a strange, searing delight. Tenderly she slid her encircling lips up and down him, feeling how his penis swelled yet further to fill her mouth with its hardness; already the fat glans was stroking the back of her throat, and, realising with a gasp of wonder that there were still several inches of him that her mouth could not take, she instinctively gripped the base of his shaft with one hand, while with the other she began to gently squeeze the velvety twin globes of his testicles. She felt a fresh surge of power as she realised that he was responding help-

200

lessly to her caresses, thrusting his loins towards her face with urgent, rhythmic jerks; she could feel his heavy balls thicken and tighten beneath her fingers, and, withdrawing her mouth for just one tantalising moment, she wrapped her tongue hotly round the rim of his glans, flickering and darting with teasing little licks before plunging her mouth down and down, as far as she could, while squeezing and rubbing with her fingers at the base of his agonised shaft.

She felt him shudder, his free hand desperately gripping the parapet of their little balcony as he braced himself against the onslaught of passion; and then, in a moment of intense, primeval victory, she felt him start to helplessly spend himself into the velvet cavity of her mouth, his semen spurting again and again as the force of his release convulsed him. Catrina swallowed hungrily as the hot seed sprang from his loins. She felt the fierce tremor of answering need run like fire through her own body and rubbed her aching breasts desperately against his thighs, feeling her tight, thrusting nipples quiver in an echo of his violent passion, while her moist vagina churned hungrily for penetration. Avidly, almost despairingly, she licked and sucked at his spasming penis, taking every last drop of his warm, salty fluid into herself.

At last, he was spent. Dazed at the enormity of what she had done, Catrina shrank away from him, still on her knees, her own aroused body clamouring desperately for release as she waited for the inevitable retribution.

Then she felt his hand on her hair, touching it lightly, as if he was caressing it. Her gaze shot up to meet his, and she was utterly shaken to see that his beautiful blue eyes were still molten with passion.

'For that, my little wild one,' he said, 'I shall pay you back, never fear.' And he pulled gently on the chain, reminding her that she was his prisoner.

She swallowed hard, feeling her own excitement surge anew at the dark promise of his words.

All day Catrina was Alexius' silent shadow, linked to him inexorably by the hateful chain around her wrist. So much of his world was strange to her. She had not realised before just how much responsibility rested upon the commander of the Eagles; she had assumed that, unless the Romans were at war, his life would be an easy one, but there was the day-to-day living of five thousand men, plus their auxiliaries and servants and staff, to be ordered and controlled; and Alexius spent much of the day in meetings with his stern-faced officers, discussing supplies and troop movements while assiduous secretaries took down every detail with their scratching pens. Then, after midday, when they had taken a brief cold lunch, Alexius rode out to view some defences that were being built along the river bank to protect the township from flooding, and Catrina too was given a little pony to ride. Even though her chains had been removed, she stayed close by his side, awed by the great wharves that lined the water, and by the bustle and noise of the galleys that plied their way into Eboracum's harbour, bringing supplies of oil and wine and luxury goods from the south.

If anyone thought it strange that Alexius should be accompanied everywhere by a silent blonde girl from the British tribe, they did not venture to pass comment. Only one thin-faced officer with unpleasant eyes, who was accompanied by three big wolfhounds and soldiers bearing hunting weapons, rode up to Alexius as he inspected the flood walls and said, 'Well, centurion. Are you so besotted with your latest concubine that you have to trail her around at your side?'

Alexius, his eyes like splintered ice, said, 'The girl is a hostage, sir.'

'Scared of your safety, Alexius?' jeered the tribune. 'Scared to find a British knife through your ribs?'

'It is the girl's safety I am thinking of, not my own,' said Alexius quietly. 'Enjoy your hunting, tribune Drusus.'

Tribune Drusus snorted with contempt, and rode on his way, taking the paved road to the forest where good game could be found. Catrina had listened in bewilderment to the brief exchange. Why had Alexius said that it was *her* safety he was thinking of, not his own? Who presented any possible threat to her, other than her enemy, Alexius himself?

And she was puzzled, too, because the thin-faced tribune Drusus seemed in some strange way to be Alexius' superior, even though he appeared to have little to do with the army itself. The tribune's sneering expression somehow made her afraid; she found herself instinctively guiding her little pony closer to Alexius' steed, and she jumped when he looked down at her and said, 'You feel safer with me, my little wild one?'

Her eyes flashed. 'You must be jesting, Roman!' she retaliated, quickly jerking her pony's reins away from his side. But somehow the disturbing feeling persisted that Alexius was protecting her, though she didn't understand why.

At last, when the shadows of late afternoon were lengthening into dusk over the city of the Eagles, they rode back towards the *principia* through the high, guarded gates of the fortress. Catrina was tired and aching in every limb after her long, exhausting day trailing around after Alexius. She would have died rather than admit it, but he must have known how she felt because, as she slid from her pony, he caught her in his arms and gazed down at her, saying seriously, 'Little one, you are white with weariness. I think I know what you need.'

She struggled to get away from him, when really all she wanted to do was sink gratefully into his strong embrace. 'I need my freedom, Roman! You're going to let me go?'

He laughed softly. 'Oh, no. Not yet. You and I have some scores to settle, I think. But first, let me show you something of Rome that I think you will enjoy.'

Mystified, but too utterly weary to argue, she followed him through the *principia*'s colonnaded courtyard to a shallow flight of steps that led up to a wide, single-storied building of stone. Carefully Alexius opened the door and beckoned her through.

The light was different. That was the first thing she noticed. The evening sunlight poured in from high, recessed windows, but there was a dancing, ethereal quality to it, as if it was the light of will o' the wisps, in the moonlight. Then she realised why. In the centre of this high, vaulted room was a pool; a deep blue pool of pure, clean water, whose little waves sparkled and danced as if a breeze stirred them mischievously.

She glanced panic-stricken up at Alexius, mindful of the strange, dark tales of her own people. She had heard whispered legends of the old days, of the ritual drownings that were the accepted sacrifices to the ancient water gods, with the victim held underwater until the water spirit accepted his struggling body. She remembered, suddenly, the dark roaring of the flood, the terrible fear she had felt as a child when the tumultuous river had swept away her home and her family, and had obliterated the life she had once known but could no longer remember.

Alexius said quickly, 'What is it, Catrina? Something's disturbed you. What is it?'

She drew her hand dazedly across her eyes, feeling the old agony of loss sweeping over her, and said, distressed, 'Once there was a flood. It took away my home and my people.'

She felt his hands grow tense as they clasped her arms. 'Where was this? When?'

She shook her head, overwhelmed by the painful memory. 'It was so long ago. I was only a child. The flood swept me away, and cast me against the rocks;

they tell me that the blow to my forehead wiped out all my memories.' She fingered the tiny, arrow-shaped white scar on her temple, and Alexius, seeing it, went suddenly very still.

At last, he said, 'So you remember nothing of your old life, Catrina?'

'Nothing at all. But there are things that remind me.' She gestured blindly towards the dancing surface of the pool behind them. 'The water looks so deep, so frightening.'

He said quickly, 'It was built for bathing. At its deepest, it will come only to your shoulders, I promise you, Catrina.'

She tried to smile up at him. 'It is not the home of a water spirit, as our streams and pools in the mountains are.'

'No,' he assured her gently, 'but the water is clean and warm and very, very safe, I assure you.'

'Then . . . this is not my punishment?'

His lips twitched. 'Punishment? Why should I punish you, Catrina?'

She blushed, but lifted her green eyes defiantly to meet his. 'For what I did to you earlier.'

'Ah, yes. Perhaps the word is not punishment, but retribution.' For a moment his eyes seemed to dance, matching the rippling blue of the water; then he said, 'I must place my armour somewhere safe. Meanwhile, you can undress and climb in. No one will disturb you.' Then he was gone, leaving her quite alone. She felt very shaken, because he had spoken to her so tenderly. Remember he's your enemy, she reminded herself silently. And he always will be.

Drawing a deep breath, her heart strangely sad, she turned towards the pool.

The water looked deliciously tempting. For a moment, she hesitated, feeling shy even though she was all alone. Then, taking a deep breath, she pulled her tunic over her head and unfastened her shoes, stepping tentatively with bare feet across the cool marble tiles until she was at the water's edge. Before she could have time to feel afraid again, she quickly climbed down the wide, shallow steps that led so enticingly into the clear depths.

The warm pleasure of the water took her quite by surprise. It wasn't cold and bracing, like her favourite mountain pool, but gentle, and voluptuous, seeming to caress her whole body. There was a broad, submerged ledge along one side of the pool, on which she could sit and feel the water lapping up to her chin; she leaned back with a sigh, closing her eyes and letting her loose hair billow out around her head. Her legs swayed gently apart, their weight supported by the translucent water, and she gave a little gasp of shock as she felt the caressing touch of the liquid against her labia, penetrating her secret folds and places with gentle, insinuous caresses. Closing her eyes, she ran her fingers gently over her breasts, and sighed. The water had reminded her that she was still burning for Alexius' forbidden touch, longing for his hands, his mouth, his tongue to savour all the sensitised parts of her aching body. She remembered the powerful throb of his angry phallus between her lips this morning, when she had been so deliciously in charge, and her loins convulsed with sudden, hungry need. Her hand slid down to her silky mound and strayed down between the silken folds of her private places, stroking softly to ease the ache of longing. Alexius, her enemy . . .

Suddenly the silence was broken by a loud splash that sent agitated waves rippling towards her, bubbling up against her chin and mouth. With a gasp she hauled herself up spluttering on to her ledge and saw Alexius, his dark head glistening with drops of water, pulling himself with powerful strokes through the water towards her.

She tried instinctively to move away, but somehow she stumbled, unused to the pull of the deep water and the feel of the smooth tiles beneath her feet. As she went under, he caught her in his arms and said, with a husky laugh, 'And now, *mea mellita*, for my punishment, as you like to call it.'

He pulled her towards him and kissed her, and in the same moment Catrina realised two things.

Firstly, that he was naked. As his firm, warm mouth moved seductively over hers, she could feel the long, powerful length of him pressing insistently against her trembling body.

And the second thing she noticed was that he was wearing her silver amulet on a leather thong around his neck.

Her senses reeled under the double onslaught. But there was no time to say anything, or even to think, because already his warm lips had pierced her feeble resistance and his strong, mobile tongue was possessing her, ravishing her inner, velvety softness with rhythmic insistence. Then he pulled her closer, against his hard, lean body, so that her soft, already aroused breasts were crushed remorselessly against the hair-roughened wall of his chest; she gasped as she felt the cold metal of the amulet against her skin and rubbed helplessly against him, feeling her nipples harden deliciously at the meeting of their water-caressed bodies. By now his strong hands had travelled round to the small of her back and he was stroking her hips and moulding her body hard against his so that she could feel the solid line of his thighs against her loins, and very soon she could feel something else; dear goddess, she could feel the hot hardness of his aroused genitals pressing relentlessly against her belly ...

With a little gasp she tried to pull away. But, laughing softly deep in his throat, Alexius moved one wicked hand upwards to caress her wet breast, and a surge of such intense pleasure radiated from her tingling nipple that she heard a soft moan of longing escape from her throat. At the same time, she realised that her hands were somehow sliding helplessly up the wet, bronzed muscles of his shoulders, to clasp the back of his neck and pull his face downwards as the passion of their kiss intensified and their tongues mingled in delicious intimacy.

At last he withdrew very gently from her swollen, feverish lips. 'Patience, *mea mellita*,' he said huskily. 'We have time enough.'

Gently he gathered her naked body up in his arms and climbed out of the water, taking her to a small, lamp-lit room that adjoined the main chamber of the bathhouse.

Dimly she was aware that the walls and ceilings of this room seemed to be adorned with exotically painted tiles, and she saw that there was a glowing charcoal brazier in the corner which gave a welcome warmth to her water-chilled body. Against the wall lay a soft pile of freshly laundered linen sheets; gently Alexius spread one on the floor and laid her down on it, and then he used another of the sheets to start rubbing her body dry.

She gazed up at him helplessly as he worked, seeing how every inch of his strong, bronzed body, still glistening with water, was the magnificent epitome of masculinity. His dark, silken body hair clung slickly to every sinew and muscle, and the heart-touching silver tracings of old battle scars only served to enhance the perfection of his powerful frame. As he steadily chafed her with the soft linen, she saw with a stab of longing that his lengthy penis was still erect, standing proudly and without shame from the mysterious cradle of hair at his loins. Suddenly Catrina felt quite weak with wanting him.

Dragging her gaze away from his gloriously unashamed manhood, she looked upwards, and saw for the first time that the decorated walls she'd noticed earlier were painted with lewdly graphic scenes. Just above her, a colourful goat god was vigorously thrusting into a plumply fleshy Roman woman who was clad only in wisps of the thinnest material; Catrina felt the colour flood her face as she saw how the dark, thin phallus protruding from the man's hairy loins penetrated the voluptuous hips of the eager Roman matron. The artist had graphically detailed the wicked grin of the goat man as he did his work, as well as the woman's look of shocked delight as he gripped her thighs. And behind them, the artist had painted another almost naked female, whose eyes were alight with pleasure as she played with another goat god's erect penis, rubbing at it with both hands while she splayed her own luscious thighs temptingly, ready to receive his lusty homage.

Alexius' voice broke in gently. 'The paintings were commissioned by the previous commander of the fort, so I can't take responsibility for them.'

Catrina, her cheeks burning because he'd intercepted her gaze, cleared her throat and said, 'This place is for your own personal use, Alexius?' She still found his Roman name difficult.

He smiled. 'This is the commander's private bathhouse, Catrina. Rank carries certain privileges.'

He stood up at last and, drawing a linen sheet for himself, he began to rub lightly at his own body to remove the lingering moisture. Catrina sat up slowly, wrapping her bare arms around her knees, and gazed up at him, her heart full and troubled. Rank carried its own dangers, too.

'Alexius,' she said quietly, her eyes drawn once more by the silver amulet that gleamed on his chest, 'it was not I who started that fire this morning.'

He paused as he rubbed at his cropped dark hair. 'I'm glad to hear it, my little wild one. But perhaps we should discuss that later.' He glanced ruefully down at his heavily swaying erection. 'I think there are certain, rather more urgent matters we should attend to.'

She looked up at him wonderingly, and his voice softened. 'I desire you, my little silvery-haired barbarian, just as I think you desire me. Enough for the moment of lies and games and tricks.'

'Our two worlds meet,' she said softly.

He bowed his head. 'Our two worlds meet.'

And then he lowered himself on to the sheets beside her. She gazed up at him, serious and wide-eyed, and then she held out her arms to him, wanting him so much that it hurt.

First he kissed her breasts, lightly circling the nipples with his tongue and tugging lightly on the raspberry nubs with his teeth until Catrina whimpered out her delight, running her hands urgently through his cropped hair. Then she felt his hands moving down to stroke her hips, and she gasped aloud as she realised that his strong hands were gently parting her thighs. Lifting his head, he smiled darkly at her and eased himself down between her legs. Then she was utterly overwhelmed by the exquisite sensation of his warm, rasping tongue parting her swollen labia and licking steadily up and down, pausing at the extremity of each delicious tongue-stroke to lightly caress her heated, throbbing pleasure bud.

Her juices ran hotly. Desperately she clamped her legs around his body and thrust her glistening vulva hard against his mouth so that his strong tongue was sliding into her, pleasuring her innermost flesh. 'Oh, Alexius,' she breathed. 'Please. I want you, now.'

He lifted his head and used his darting tongue to caress her taut belly, licking at the tiny indentation of her navel with slow strokes that sent stabs of pleasure rippling through her. 'Patience, little wild one. The pleasure is all the greater for waiting.'

His hands were caressing her breasts again, and she shifted wildly under him, longing to feel the dark, magnificent rod of his phallus pounding within her. She threw back her head, gasping for breath; and all the while, as if aware of her sweet torment, Alexius was rubbing his fingers slowly, lazily up and down the swollen folds of her labia, carefully avoiding her hard, hot clitoris, which tingled and burned for his touch. She clenched her legs around him desperately, longing to feel the thick masculine hardness of him sink deep inside her; warm waves of hungry need rolled through her as she helplessly rubbed her breasts against his teasing hands. Oh, goddess, his touch was delicious, but she longed to take all of him, deep within her, to pleasure his flesh as he was pleasuring hers.

His blue eyes glittered down at her as he said, 'You like the ways of Rome, Catrina?'

She said, in a low, husky voice, 'Is it your way to torment me for ever, Roman?'

'Oh, no.' And with a smile he raised himself slightly and reached out his hand to pick up a small glass phial of scented body oil, which he unstoppered and slowly emptied into the palm of his hand. The perfume was deliciously exotic to Catrina, smelling of sweet, piercingly scented flowers whose blooms she could only guess at. Gently he rubbed the oil on her breasts, caressing and kneading at her slippery, sensitised flesh until she felt the burning heat gather and tighten in her nipples as if she was about to explode.

Then he eased himself between her parted legs, and her face burned with desire as she watched him anoint his own hotly pulsing rod until it gleamed with promise. She shivered with wanting him, longing to feel that great shaft of flesh sliding into her, pleasuring her, ravishing her . . .

Gently gripping his swaying, heavy penis, he poised it at her quivering entrance. He rubbed it carefully up and down between the swollen petals of flesh, driving her demented with the hot, silken feel of it, and then he was sliding into her, his phallus deliciously solid and thick, pleasuring her and ravishing all her tender places.

Catrina let out a great cry of joy at feeling her vagina so deliciously filled and stretched by his magnificent shaft. Instinctively she started to rise up against it, lifting her head so that she could see the strong, thick base of his glistening penis sliding repeatedly into her honeyed flesh. She wanted it to go on for ever, this beautiful, mutual pleasuring. How she adored the feel of his great silken rod caressing her soft, silken love passage as she gripped and stroked.

Then he lowered his face to her breasts, pulling and licking urgently with his tongue and teeth, and she felt his strong yet gentle finger slide against the bursting bud of her clitoris. Gasping aloud, she went very still as the languorous pleasure-pain tightened in her belly until she thought she would burst asunder, and then she writhed her hips urgently against him as the hot, soaring rapture began to take over her body. As his phallus pounded deeply and steadily withing her and his finger caressed her anguished pleasure bud, the near-pain was suddenly transmuted into gloriously sweet pleasure, and she clutched with her spasming inner muscles at his massive penis as if her life depended on it, while the harsh ecstasy of her release rolled over and over her trembling body.

She ground her fingers into his shoulders, raking his back and sobbing aloud as she felt him drive to his own convulsive climax deep within her, his breathing ragged as he thrust powerfully into her tender body. At last she nestled against him, her body still melting with the sweet after-sensations, breathing in the scent of him, feeling the warm, musky perspiration of his body as her soft femininity unfurled against his hard soldier's body. Alexius, her enemy. She felt the touch of her stolen amulet cold against her breasts.

He was stroking her cheek gently, drowsily. Then suddenly he said, 'Catrina. You spoke of the fire just now.'

She stiffened, her heart beating fast. He went on, in the same lazy voice, 'You're quite sure that you didn't start it, little one?'

Suddenly feeling cold, she whispered, 'No. How could you think it?'

He was coiling a tendril of her still-damp blonde hair idly round his finger, but she was no longer deceived by his pretended air of casualness. 'Because,' he said, 'I thought at first that you had come to Eboracum to kill me.' He smiled. 'Foolish of me, wasn't it?'

Catrina felt suddenly sick. Did he know? Had he known, all along, who she was?

'Is that why you chained me up?' she said in a low voice.

His finger was absently stroking the tiny arrow-shaped scar on her temple, and his eyes suddenly seemed distant as he said, 'Perhaps. Such games we play with one another, *mea mellita*. You know, I don't think I can bear to let you out of my sight.' Casually he stroked the silver amulet that hung at his throat. 'I've noticed you keep looking at this. You admire it?'

Catrina swallowed hard. 'I – I have seen something like it before, that is all.'

'That's hardly surprising,' he replied calmly, 'as it is an effigy of the goddess Minerva. Amulets like this are worn frequently as a charm by the better-off Roman families.'

Catrina watched him, stunned. 'No!' she breathed. 'It is the image of a sacred deity of my own tribe, the goddess Brigantia!'

'I'm afraid not,' said Alexius politely, still stroking the silver engraving of the sun-like face with its radiant halo of hair. 'But, seeing as you like it so much, Catrina, you must take it.' And lightly he lifted the leather thong from around his own neck, and lowered it over her head, so that the weight of the cold silver burned into her skin. 'It suits you, Catrina,' he went on, his blue eyes glinting. 'But you look startled by my gift. Don't you want it?'

Alexius' action had stunned her. He was playing games with her.

'Is – is it yours to give?' she stammered out at last.

He pulled himself to his feet and reached out for the fresh clothes he'd brought for himself. 'Spoils of war,' he said lightly. 'But keep it. It's yours.'

Suddenly Catrina felt very afraid, and sick with unknown fear, the old, piercing kind of fear that sometimes possessed her until she could think of nothing else, setting her nerves jangling and her blood racing warningly in her veins.

'No!' she said quickly, pulling it off and jumping up to thrust it back into his hands. 'No. I don't want it. You must keep it, Alexius!'

He looked at her in startled query, but already she was pulling her tunic on with her back to him. He let the silver amulet slide over his neck again, and waited until she was ready. Then, silently, she followed him outside.

It was almost dark, though cressets flared in defiance of the night from the iron holders set in the stone walls of the fortress. The canopy of the sky was dark blue, pierced with tiny bright stars; the light breeze seemed cold after the warmth of the bathhouse. A train of pannier-laden mules was being driven by towards one of the warehouses; the men who drove them were not soldiers, but muleteers from the vicus. Catrina and Alexius had to wait for them to pass by, and as Catrina stood there, the anxiety gathered and curdled in her stomach until she could have cried aloud with fear.

Then she saw the face of one of the mule-drivers beneath his greasy red cap, and he saw her.

'Alexius,' she screamed out, 'oh, Alexius – ' And she flung herself in front of him just as the red-capped man sprang towards them, his cruel knife ready to plunge into Alexius' heart; she felt the cold sting of the blade bite her arm, and then Alexius, his sword already drawn, thrust her aside and ran the man through with the lightning speed of the professional soldier. His attacker slumped at his feet, the lifeblood draining from his body. The knife that was meant for Alexius' heart lay in the gutter as the other mule-drivers, stunned by the speed of it all, began to shout out in alarm.

Alexius was gripping Catrina's arm, his face drawn and grim, not realising she had been injured. 'How did you know?' he said, shaking her slightly when at first she refused to answer. 'How did you know what he intended, before he even moved?'

She was trembling violently now with pain and shock. She could feel the warm blood starting to trickle along her sleeve and her teeth chattered helplessly as she struggled to say, 'That is how it happens sometimes. I just know that there is danger, as I did with the child and the cart!'

'I think,' he said softly, 'that you are not telling me the entire truth.'

She was stung almost to tears. Pulling herself away, heedless of her wounded arm, she hissed up at him, 'What would you rather, Roman? That I said nothing? That I had let the man knife you?'

'I would rather,' he said between gritted teeth, 'that you told me everything.'

She held his gaze defiantly, though her face was still pale with shock. 'Why should I tell you everything, when you are my enemy?' Then she seemed to stagger, and nearly fall. Alexius reached quickly to support her, thinking her merely to be badly shocked, and as he swung her up into his arms, she whispered, 'It was the amulet that saved you. My amulet.'

Already, the soldiers were pounding down the narrow street towards them as news of the attack on the commander spread like fire around the fort. Alexius, after some curt words of explanation to one of his senior centurions, carried Catrina swiftly back towards the *principia*.

As she lay dazed in his arms, she felt sick and totally drained. In those few, heart-stopping moments, she realised that now she had no alternative but to tell Alexius everything. If he had not already guessed.

She had already known, long before tonight, that she herself had not got the capacity to do him harm. But someone else had. The deliberate fire this morning, and the knife attack just now, left her in no doubt of that.

She would never be able to tell Alexius, but she *had*

recognised the man with the knife, the red-capped Briton whom Alexius had killed. He was Brant, one of the priest Luad's minions. And he would not have been alone. Who else was there in the fortress, secretly pursuing them? Who else had noticed that Catrina had actually tried to save the Roman by throwing herself in front of him, so that *she* took the knife's blade instead of him?

She gazed up at Alexius, painfully aware of his arms wrapped tightly round her as he moved swiftly towards the *principia*. She could feel the steady beat of his heart as he cradled her against his chest. If she had not been there, Alexius would have died.

She felt sick, and the shallow wound on her arm burned and stung. Suddenly, she remembered something else; something that made her blood run cold. It was the habit of the tribe's warriors to anoint their knives with poison before they attacked ... 'Alexius,' she faltered, her mouth dry as the blackness swept towards her again. 'Alexius ...'

But the shadows were closing in. She closed her eyes as the pain of the knife-wound whipped through her arm, and she fell back into merciful unconsciousness in his arms.

Alexius, still not realising that she'd been wounded, gazed down at her as her delicate, blue-veined eyelids drifted shut. He'd been right, of course. She was the girl from the forest. That tiny, arrow-shaped scar on her temple had been the final confirmation. But why was she here? His brow tightened in perplexity.

Then, suddenly, he saw the bright blood that freshly stained her sleeve, and he called out, urgently, for help.

216

Chapter Fourteen

*T*wo nights later, Julia had something very special
arranged. The evening, true to her hopes, was warm
and starlit, and her spacious paved courtyard, open to
the skies, was filled with the scent of summer flowers.
From somewhere beyond the marble colonnade came
the faint, rhythmically sensuous throb of lyre and cymbals, played by as yet unseen musicians. Meanwhile,
Lark and Nightingale were gracefully strewing the
paving stones with clusters of brightly hued roses from
the wicker baskets they carried, and Julia, reclining on a
padded velvet couch on the lamp-lit terrace, picked some
of the soft, stray petals and crushed them thoughtfully
between her ringed fingers.

Drusus, draped on a couch beside her, drank down
his wine as he watched the two bare-breasted Syrian
girls. His eyes were already narrow with lust. 'Those
two are good,' he said to Julia. 'Will you sell them to
me? I could make a fortune with them back in Rome.'

'Sell my little songbirds? They're not for sale,' said
Julia, smiling. 'They're my friends. Hush, now Drusus.
The entertainment is about to begin!'

Lark and Nightingale ran swiftly out of sight. There
was a bold clash of cymbals, and the moonlit courtyard

217

was suddenly filled by several lightly clad, silent females, who wandered around picking up the freshly strewn flowers as if in a trance.

'Who are they?' murmured Drusus to Julia, gazing at them from his vantage point on the terrace.

Julia whispered back, 'See the one who plays Persephone, the one in emerald silk? She's the wife of one of the magistrates. He doesn't know she's here, naturally. And her friend, the dark-haired one, is the wife of one of the decurions. All the women have drunk far too much wine, of course.'

Drusus laughed. 'Your experience on the Roman stage stands you in good stead, Julia.'

'That's why they asked me to direct them in this little ... entertainment.' She grinned back at Drusus. 'On the strict understanding, of course, that their privacy is guaranteed. You won't breathe a word to anyone about this evening?'

'Of course not.'

Julia nodded, and went on thoughtfully, 'As you know, Alexius has forbidden me to hold any further parties here. But, careless man, he never mentioned theatrical entertainments ...' The cymbal clashed again; she dropped her voice and whispered conspiratorially, 'Watch carefully. The god of the underworld should be making his entrance soon, to seize poor Persephone and drag her down to his dark domain. This is when the fun really begins.'

Drusus settled back on his couch to enjoy himself as the unseen musicians exploded into a menacing flurry of sound. Suddenly the women started to run about the courtyard in mimed distress, throwing their hands to their faces and dropping their flowers as dark, menacing shapes began to stir and shift in the shadows behind the marble pillars. The shadows were men, moving in on them threateningly in the moonlight, men with masks and loincloths and bare, silent feet. One of them wore a

218

magnificent lion skin, with the beast's head all but covering his face; Drusus gasped at the sight of it.

'He's wearing the Eagle-bearer's headdress! In the name of Jupiter, Julia, how did you contrive to get *that* from under Alexius' eye? Isn't it kept in the strongroom with the Eagle itself?'

Julia laughed shortly. 'I bribed young Felix, Alexius' new *optio*, to bring it here for me. I didn't think our virtuous Alexius would miss it for one evening. Or do you think he enjoys dressing up in it, in private?'

'It's probably the only pleasure he does allow himself,' sniggered Drusus. Then he corrected himself. 'No. I'm wrong. After all, he's kept the little barbarian all to himself.'

There was a moment's frozen silence. Then Julia breathed, 'What did you say?'

'Oh, didn't you know? It's true, I assure you. Our Alexius didn't waste much time. The two of them slept together the first night she arrived, according to the guards, and now she's well-ensconced in the *principia*. Apparently she received some kind of minor injury in a skirmish, and Alexius is taking care of her. They say he's quite besotted.'

In the uncertain light of the flickering lamp, Julia had gone pale. Alexius, and the barbarian girl. How *dare* he? How dare he reject her, Julia, then take that slut to his bed?

Her hand gripped the edge of her couch until her knuckles showed white. Trying to appear calm, she turned back to the theatrical spectacle unfolding in her sheltered, moonlit courtyard, and thrust all thoughts of Alexius temporarily from her mind. He wouldn't spoil her pleasure tonight.

The silent men were spinning and whirling around in primitive dance as the drums beat faster and faster, their bare feet pounding the flower-strewn paving stones. The women shrieked and squealed, pretending to escape, but in reality they were running into the men's arms. Julia smiled at their antics. *The Abduction of Persephone*, highly popular in Rome, had always been one of her own favourite plays. The big, silent men caught the women easily, and started on the real work of the evening; Julia sighed with pleasure as she watched the burly masked actors tear at the women's flimsy garments and fondle their breasts lewdly. Shifting restlessly on her couch, she felt the sudden flow of nectar between her thighs, and Drusus reached silently across to touch her pouting nipples, his face dark with lust. Soon, every woman had been caught. The men, still wearing their contorted animal masks, had torn off their own loincloths and were starting to make thrusting, erotic gestures as their victims whimpered eagerly in their arms.

Just in front of Julia was the man wearing the Eagle-bearer's costume. He had removed his loincloth, but the lion head and its tawny skin were still securely attached to his lithe, handsome body. Julia had paid him well in advance to place himself carefully where she could see him when the play really began to get going. He'd chosen his woman well, too, Melina the merchant's wife; she was breathless with wine and excitement, running her fingers up and down his big, muscled limbs as if she could scarcely believe her luck. This was her annual treat. Her husband, innocently trusting, thought that she was at a demure women's supper.

If he could see his wife now, grinned Julia to herself, the plump merchant would have the shock of his life. Melina was gasping and squealing in the throes of erotic excitement as the big, lion-masked man ripped her flimsy gown from her body and fondled her roughly, his already erect penis riding high between his sinewed thighs. Then he swung her from the ground, and eagerly she clasped her thighs around his waist, wriggling on to him as he thrust his massive weapon deep within her. She squirmed frenziedly at the luscious impalement, rubbing her plump breasts desperately against his chest and orgasming almost immediately in shameful excitement. Julia shuddered with need herself as she watched; Drusus, sensing her acute arousal, let his hand slip steadily up between her thighs and start to press against her swollen sex, but she wanted more, more, as she absorbed all the varieties of lewd pleasuring that were being enacted in her secret, moonlit courtyard.

She saw, with a spasm of delicious shock, that the prim tax-collector's wife had crouched to suck at the dark, magnificently rampant penis of the man playing Pluto, the god of the underworld. As the woman's head bobbed eagerly up and down, another man kneeled quickly behind her and gripped her bared bottom-cheeks, pulling them apart so that he could slide his own lusty shaft deep into her juicy vulva. He gave a shout of triumph as he homed in, and reached round her front to play with her dangling breasts; the woman wriggled with delight and slid her mouth up and down the penis she was savouring, reaching her own feverish climax just as Pluto pumped his hot seed greedily into her luscious mouth.

Julia swallowed hard as she watched, wishing she was that woman. Juno, but she was almost at the brink herself. The sweet, dark ache gathered and brimmed at the base of her belly, and she ground her nectared labia against Drusus' insistent hand, feeling her breasts tingle and swell tormentingly. By now, the music was wild and abandoned, spiced with the cadences of the Orient; the shadowy courtyard seemed to be full of writhing, copulating figures. She thought suddenly of Alexius. Alexius with Catrina, damn him . . .

Drusus had pulled his rigid penis out from beneath his tunic, and was lying behind her. She gasped as he slid its swollen end between the tops of her thighs and started to nudge and rub gently, drawing out the juices from her heated vulva. His hand was still rubbing insistently down her cleft, bringing her almost to the brink. Then he seemed to retreat slightly, and she moaned aloud as his hot shaft seemed to disappear, only to gasp in shock as she felt it prodding insistently at her tiny, puckered anal hole.

She went very still, and her dark eyes narrowed. How dare he? But then he rubbed again at her swollen flesh folds with his fingers, and she felt the hot, shameful pleasure take over as she fastened her eyes on the lion man, who was kneeling a few feet in front of her and sliding lasciviously in and out of a plump, giggling matron, his tight, neat buttocks working with sinuous energy as his dusky penis impaled her willing body. Feeling her body flush with need, Julia thrust her bottom cheeks hard against Drusus' loins. Suddenly she felt his slender cock slide into the tight collared rim of her forbidden entrance, and she felt the hot, shameful pleasure of it invade her abdomen. Drawing in her breath, she rubbed her heavy breasts against the velvet pile of the couch and surrendered to the degradation of having her bottom-cheeks plundered, feeling the delicious warmth rippling in seductive waves through her melting body.

'Good?' whispered Drusus, nibbling and biting at her neck as he thrust away.

'Good, oh good. Drusus, I want more, please – oh, fill me with your delicious cock . . .'

By now, in a torment of desire, she was playing avidly with her own breasts, tugging and pulling at her stiffened teats, moaning and gasping as he drove quickly and silently into her, while his hand still rubbed against her soaking vulva. Gazing at the lion man as he spurted to his climax over the breasts of the woman he had just pleasured, Julia bucked helplessly against the man behind her, writhing in abandoned delight as his hot, stiff penis impaled her so shamefully, hearing his ragged, hoarse breathing in her ear as he started to convulse into orgasm. With a gasp, she thrust hard back against him, feeling him filling her with his hard, solid flesh; then she started to cry out as the ecstasy rolled through her in sweet, solid waves, her muscles clutching and spasming around him as her whole body jerked into climax.

At last, when both of them were completely spent, Julia drew herself up from the couch and rearranged her scanty clothing. For the moment, the courtyard was still, with sated couples lying lazily around on cushions in the fragrant darkness. Then Pluto stepped forward to speak, still clutching a naked, pleasure-hazed Persephone at his side. Julia noticed dryly that Pluto's phallus, although he had so recently spent himself, looked almost ready for action once more; it hung long and thick between his sturdy thighs, and she licked her lips, imagining the taste of its fat softness in her mouth. Pluto cleared his throat and made his speech, concluding solemnly, *'Thus Pluto with vile strength abducts his bride,*

'And direst mourning cracks the heavens wide.'

'The play's nearly over,' Julia informed Drusus dryly, forgetting Catrina for the moment. 'Pluto's about to drag his Persephone down to the underworld. I doubt if we'll see much of them for the rest of the evening; sweet Persephone looks quite besotted. Wait here a moment, Drusus, while I go and see what entertainment my guests would like next.'

She swept from beneath the shelter of the terraced colonnade into the open courtyard, smiling, and an expectant hush fell on the exhausted company of women. All the men had disappeared, following Pluto and Persephone into the darkness. Julia clapped her hands and a bevy of silent servants appeared, relighting the soft lamps and bringing in trays of wine and sweet little honey cakes. The night air was fragrant and velvety in the sheltered courtyard; the moon glittered overhead, and a moth fluttered helplessly around a bronze lantern. The women reclined on low couches that were clustered on the sheltered terrace around wine-laden tables, and gazed at their hostess with vibrant expectancy.

'What next, lady Julia?' breathed the tax-collector's

wife, whose face was still flushed from her erotic exertions.

'What next indeed?' breathed Julia, her eyes glittering with speculation.

'Where is your gladiator?' someone asked, and the question was quickly taken up.

'Yes! The beautiful young gladiator!'

'Make him fight! Let's watch him fight!'

They began to chant Falco's name in the fashion of the Roman arena, and Julia thought, why not?

She went to find Phidias, and explained to him, and he nodded, smiling. Then she went quickly out into the courtyard again, and told her friends to be patient.

When the two men came in at last, there was a low sigh of pleasure from the women, and no wonder, thought Julia, who felt excited again just looking at them. Apart from their sturdy thonged sandals, both men wore nothing but little pouches made of leather to constrain the exciting bulge of their genitals, and their beautiful bodies formed a glorious contrast. Phidias was big and dusky, with his oiled muscles flexing and sliding beneath his smooth, shiny skin; while Falco was young, heartbreakingly beautiful, a golden demi-god. A slave who still dared to defy her . . .

Both men carried the sword and shield that she'd ordered them to be given. The swords were the wooden, blunted weapons that were used in the legionaries' training; Phidias bore his with a proud flourish, flamboyantly saluting Julia with it, a grin on his face. But Falco stood expressionless with his sword loose in his hand, his wide grey eyes dark and stormy.

Julia walked slowly across the courtyard to gaze into his set face, and felt a sudden surge of violent desire grip her body. Fighting it down, because, she, Julia, was always in control, she said coldly, 'You will fight for our amusement, slave.'

He said, 'My lady, I have told you before. I do not fight for the crowd's entertainment.'

Julia clenched her fists. 'I think you mistake me, Falco. It was not a request, but an order!'

His grey eyes surveyed her impassively, and she suddenly felt heated, lustful, tawdry, and she hated him for the way he made her feel. Then he said quietly, 'I am truly sorry that you cannot think of any better amusement, my lady.'

Julia's eyes sparked with rage. Damn him, but no one felt sorry for her! The blood hot in her cheeks, she swung round to the waiting Phidias.

'Phidias,' she said shortly, 'make him fight!'

Phidias moved forward threateningly, but Falco just stood there, proud in his defiance, yet gentle too. 'I will not fight,' he repeated, almost regretfully.

Julia hissed, 'In the arena, the masters of the games use sticks and whips to make cowardly gladiators fight. He's all yours, Phidias.'

The women started to call out and jeer from their couches, as if they were in the arena in Rome. Phidias, sensing their excitement, tossed his practice sword aside and swaggered up to Falco, his hands on his hips. 'You're a filthy coward, aren't you, gladiator?' he taunted. 'What's the matter? Are you scared of being shown up in front of all these women?' He drew one finger mockingly down Falco's smooth-shaven cheek and gripped suddenly at his thick mane of blond hair. 'Perhaps instead of fighting you'd prefer a repeat of the kind of entertainment we put on for them the other night. Is that what you want?' His big hands slipped down suddenly to grip Falco's taut buttocks and caress them meaningfully, tugging at the thin leather strap that split his bottom cheeks. Then he thrust his hips lewdly at the young gladiator, rubbing the big leather pouch that restrained his genitals hard against the other man's loins.

Falco's face was drained of colour, and his high, jutting cheekbones were taut against his smooth skin. Phidias laughed, pouting his lips in a mocking kiss, and reached to fondle the leather-clad bulge of Falco's private parts.

But he had gone too far. Suddenly, Falco's muscles rippled with frightening power and his clenched fist shot out to land on his tormentor's jaw. With a surprised grunt, Phidias swayed and tottered to the floor.

Falco seemed to shudder, and Julia saw how he closed his eyes, his face tight with some secret agony as the women stamped and cheered with delight, banging their wine-beakers on the tables. Julia felt the quickening of excitement surge through her. So he *was* human, after all. He was starting to break at last.

She stepped forward. 'Well, my sweet gladiator,' she said softly, 'that was rather disobedient of you. For that, I fear you really must be punished.' She turned back to her eager guests. 'I think it's time for another play, don't you, my friends? How about *Achilles and the Daughters of Lycomades*? We haven't done that one for a long time.'

The tax-collector's wife stepped eagerly forward. 'You mean the one where Achilles is kept from going to the Trojan wars by Lycomades' mischievous daughters? Oh, yes. And the gladiator can be Achilles!'

Phidias was pulling himself slowly from the floor, rubbing tenderly at his bruised jaw. 'My lady,' he said hotly, 'I am the one who usually plays the part of Achilles!'

Julia looked at him disdainfully. Phidias was getting too full of himself. He needed taking down a peg or two. 'Then we are in need of a change, aren't we?' she said coldly.

Bowing his head stiffly, he retreated into the shadows, shooting a furious look at the immobile gladiator as Julia went on. 'Tonight, Falco will play the part of the suffering Achilles.'

She saw Falco's head jerk up at that, and saw his grey eyes meet hers in mute resistance. He knew the story, she thought with a tingle of delight; he knew what was coming, but he did not dare to utter a word of protest, because he knew it was pointless. A sacrificial hero indeed, thought Julia, and she realised, looking at his taut, nearly naked body, with the delicious bulge in the leather pouch at his groin, that her blood was pulsing hotly with sexual need again.

But she gave the signal impassively, then stood back and watched with cold detachment as the excited, wine-heated women swarmed over him, swiftly overpowering him and dragging him to the floor. Then they began to oil him and finger him, stripping him at last of his leather loin-garment and bending over him to lick and savour every inch of his beautiful, struggling, perfectly formed athlete's body – every inch except for the most beautiful part of all, the magnificent phallus that already was starting to swell and thicken with shameful excitement as the young gladiator struggled to evade the women's lascivious attentions.

But his attempts were in vain. The women crowed and laughed as slowly, remorselessly, his virile rod jerked into life, thrusting up hungrily from his loins, pulsing with need into the thin air. Julia, watching, was over-come with lust. She licked her dry lips as she saw how they'd tethered Falco to the floor with their hands and bodies, so that he was lying on his back with his long golden limbs spread out helplessly as his hot, lengthy penis waved helplessly into the air, searching for some enveloping orifice to tightly caress it and give it release. His weapon was beautifully thick and sturdy, patterned with a light tracing of veins and ending in a fat, swollen plum that Julia knew would feel exquisitely firm yet tender against her own wanton secret parts; she trembled as she imagined that strong, bone-hard shaft of flesh sliding up deep into her own quivering womb, and she suddenly stirred into action, striding across the room swiftly and purposefully.

'Pin him down, daughters of Lycomades. Hold him so he can't move,' she ordered, her throat tight with lust, and then, flinging up her own flimsy gown, she stepped across his body and straddled him. Lowering herself gradually so that she was kneeling on the floor, her

227

thighs splayed wide across his hips, she pulled apart her sex-lips, so he could see the dark pink, glistening flesh ready to swallow him, and reached to steady his jerking, angry penis with her hand; then carefully, catching her lower lip between her teeth in concentration, she lowered herself on to his mighty rod.

She sighed and shut her eyes in ecstasy as his beautiful, rampant penis slid deep, deep within her, filling her, stretching her, sending dark waves of passion through her whole yearning body. She moved slightly, lifting and lowering herself in blissful impalement, feeling how his huge shaft surged and quivered within her as she coated him slickly with her honeyed nectar.

And then, suddenly, she felt a searing dark wave of tenderness that shook her to her very core. It struck her, in the very furnace of her lust, that Falco the gladiator was beautiful, and strong, and valiant, and not a coward at all.

She opened her eyes and was shaken again by unexpected emotion as she registered his wide-eyed expression of helpless, resigned despair while the other women continued to stroke his beautiful body, and lick his exposed flesh, and murmur lewdly in his ear. Julia frowned. This humiliation was what he deserved, wasn't it? He was nothing, a failed gladiator who belonged to some obscure religious sect, and yet he dared to defy her, to feel sorry for her! Gritting her teeth, she started to slide up and down on him, seeing him tremble as she hissed, 'This is what you've been longing for, isn't it, my fine gladiator? Don't you like the feel of me gliding about on your fat, sturdy prick? You think you're going to resist me; you think you're going to hold back, and show me how you scorn my beautiful body. But I'm going to ride you now, I'm going to pleasure myself with your great strong penis until you can't hold back. Soon you'll be begging me to release you from your exquisite torment!'

And, almost dementedly, tugging at her own clothing

so she could free her breasts to twist them and pull at them, she pounded fiercely on top of him, feeling his massive shaft quiver and jerk inside her. She writhed with heated pleasure as the warm flood of ecstasy washed through her body, forcing her to cry out her delight.

He'd lasted well, but her own abandoned climax proved too much for him. Despairingly he bucked and strained beneath her, his masculine, exquisite face taut with the approaching agony of defeat. Swiftly, sensing that he was about to explode, Julia pulled away from him, feeling his hot, slippery penis slide helplessly from between her swollen, sated vulva, and the women moved in eagerly with little sighs and whispers to stroke and caress his tormented body.

Julia herself reached to feel for his heavy, velvety testicles, handling them with delicious, tormenting fingers and seeing how his mighty red phallus quivered and strained in desperate need. Then, as she squeezed the hair-roughened pouch a little harder, his body arched convulsively and his seed began to spurt in great hot jets into the air. The women shrieked with pleasure at the sight and fought to catch the copious milky fluid on their breasts and faces. One of them leaned forward to hungrily rub her dark, pouting nipples against the tip of Falco's pulsing shaft, shouting with excitement at the lewd touch of his swollen, semen-smeared glans.

Julia leaned back, satisfied. Her feeling of tenderness had been an aberration, nothing more, caused by his youth and beauty. She, Julia, used men for convenience and pleasure. In Rome, it was the only way for women without birth or money to survive. Thoughtfully, still slightly shaken, she stroked the spent gladiator's heavily muscled thighs. His breathing was ragged and shallow; his flaccid penis lay helpless against his thighs, and his gaunt face was sheened with perspiration. His eyes were closed in despair.

Suddenly, Julia decided that she had had enough. She

beckoned the women away from him, and he rolled over silently on to his side, burying his face against his outstretched arm. He was almost broken, but somehow, his prostrate, exhausted figure didn't give him quite as much pleasure as she'd anticipated.

Phidias was glowering in a corner of the courtyard, still angry because the role of Achilles was usually his. Julia curtly beckoned to him to lead the gladiator away, and lock him up in the safety of the slave quarters.

Soon afterwards, the women left for their homes, chattering happily and reminiscing about their evening's glorious entertainment as they made their way out to their waiting sedans and servants. Drusus reappeared then, to share the last of the wine with Julia. He'd been watching the torment of the gladiator from his place in the shadows, and she could tell from the hot look on his narrow face that he'd enjoyed it all excessively. He'd probably pleasured himself at the same time, she speculated, picturing him rubbing away excitedly at his slender white penis as Falco reached his excruciatingly public climax. Not a bad evening's entertainment, for all of them.

And then, suddenly, she remembered about Alexius and Catrina. Damn Alexius, damn him! How dare he favour the little barbarian girl above herself? Drusus had refilled her goblet, and was handing it to her as they stood there in the courtyard. The night was still warm, but she felt suddenly cold as the balmy night breeze shifted and stirred the remnants of the flower petals that lay around. Shivering slightly, she sipped at her wine and said, as unconcernedly as she could, 'Is it really true, what you said earlier? That Alexius has kept the British girl for his own private pleasure, and is rutting with her in the *principia*?'

'That's what they say.' Drusus shrugged. 'What does it matter? He has to have his entertainment. The soldiers have their brothels, and all the officers have got one – or

230

several – slave-girls tucked away in their private quarters. Or boys,' he added thoughtfully.

Julia hissed, 'It's still not fitting! And anyway, the girl was mine!'

'No longer, my sweet. Apparently, he's hardly let her out of his sight. The little barbarian must be to his taste. He is only a common soldier raised from the ranks, after all.' He placed his hand meaningfully on her shoulder. 'It's growing cold. Why don't we move indoors, Julia, and find somewhere more comfortable?'

But Julia's heart was still twisted with rage and envy. She moved quickly away from Drusus' insinuating hand, and said, 'I'm tired, Drusus. It's been a long evening.'

'Very well. As you wish.' His lip curled in disappointment, but with controlled good manners he escorted her to the door of her bedchamber and then, looking round quickly to make sure there was no one about, he hurried off towards the slave quarters at the far end of Julia's house.

Phidias was very angry with Falco. Not only had the young gladiator knocked him almost senseless, but he'd also stolen the part of Achilles that should have been his. Phidias had got his revenge quickly as soon as they were away from the courtyard, by assaulting the naked gladiator with a vicious punch to the stomach that had him gasping on his knees. 'That was for your arrogance,' said Phidias grimly as he glared down at the retching man. 'Now let's get you to your sleeping cell, gladiator, before you can cause any more trouble.'

But Falco, utterly exhausted, seemed unable to get up. Hissing in anger, the big Numidian hauled him to his feet and wrapped his arm round his shoulder, dragging him along the endless, dimly lit tiled corridors. 'Too much for you, were they, those women?' he muttered as he went. 'Serves you right. Now I would have pleasured them all, and come back for more.'

Grunting, Phidias at last reached the door of Falco's

room and struggled to open it while still supporting the gladiator's weight. Finally he succeeded, and pushed Falco in so that he sprawled across the bed. Then he turned suddenly, because someone else had come in the room. Drusus.

The tribune stood there, fingering his belt, gazing down at the prone, naked man on the bed, and drawled slowly, 'Phidias. I liked what I saw a few nights ago.'

Phidias raised his eyebrows enquiringly. 'My lord. You mean – me and him? The first night you brought the gladiator to this house?'

'Exactly,' said Drusus. 'And I feel in the mood for a repeat performance. Do you think you can manage it? Six gold pieces for you, if you take the gladiator here and now. He doesn't look as if he'll offer much resistance.'

Phidias glanced down proudly at the promising bulge in the smooth leather pouch that clad his own loins. 'My lord, I am always ready. And the cowardly gladiator will enjoy it, too, I promise you.' He licked his lips. 'Six gold pieces, you say?'

'Six. With a little extra, perhaps, if your performance is particularly good.'

Grinning, Phidias pulled off the leather pouch that contained his genitals, so that his penis hung thick and unrestrained. With his eyes fastened meaningfully on Drusus, he began to fondle and pull at it, and inexorably the great, dusky shaft began to swell and rise. He saw how the tribune's eyes glazed over as he watched. Phidias knew his sort. There would be more money, no doubt, if he, Phidias, gave the arrogant Roman exactly what he wanted. But first, he would put on a good display, and thoroughly humiliate the gladiator who'd dared to hit him. His penis was fully engorged now, and rearing proudly from his loins; feeling the hot, dark need churning in his blood, Phidias turned to Falco, who lay face down on the bed, his tight bottom-cheeks tantalisingly exposed. He seemed asleep, or unconscious, and would offer little resistance. Standing beside him, the Numidian pulled his legs slightly apart, so that he could see the dark, plump sac of the young gladiator's balls; then he ran his finger experimentally up and down the dark, secret cleft, and felt his own rampant penis jerk with greed to plunder that tight little bottom hole. He heard the rustle of clothing behind him in the darkness, and knew that the lascivious tribune would be fondling his own tiny prick, rubbing at it hotly beneath his tunic.

Then suddenly the door opened, and there was a waft of fragrant, expensive Arabian perfume. Julia stood there, her face white with rage.

'What are you doing?' she hissed. 'Get out of here, Phidias! And you, too, Drusus! Who gave you permission to enter my slave quarters? Leave, at once!'

Drusus looked hot and embarrassed. 'Look, we were only continuing the evening's entertainment, Julia,' he drawled. 'Why all the fuss?'

'This is my house, and I arrange the entertainment, as you call it! Get out, Drusus!'

The tribune's face was dark with anger as he clamped his lips shut and quickly turned on his heel, striding off down the corridor. Julia watched him go, then turned to Phidias, whose erection was rapidly subsiding. 'And you, too. Go. I will speak to you about this in the morning.'

With a resentful bow, Phidias turned and left. Julia, feeling rather shaky, sat at the side of Falco's bed, and touched his shoulders gently. She didn't understand why she was feeling like this. Normally, she would have stayed to watch, to join in.

But suddenly, inexplicably, she didn't want the gladiator to be hurt any more.

His golden athlete's body was so beautiful, so perfect as he lay face down on the bed, with his broad, powerful shoulders tapering down to his slender waist and hips, and his small, rounded bottom cheeks with their imperceptible covering of downy golden hair. Gently, she bent to kiss him there, to run her tongue delicately up and down the shadowy cleft, pushing slightly at the secret entrance. He was asleep, exhausted, and she could take her pleasure in him just by looking at him, by softly caressing him so he wouldn't waken.

Then, slowly but deliberately, he turned over, and drew himself up. He hadn't been asleep at all. She saw that his grey eyes were wide awake, and smiling at her, and that his beautiful, silky penis was fully erect again, surging towards her. 'My lady,' he said softly, and drew her down so that she lost her balance and fell into his arms.

Julia lay back on the tiny hard bed, helplessly confused, her heart thudding. Why was he so tender to her after what she had made him endure? Then she stopped thinking about anything, because he had skilfully removed her tunic, and his golden head was dipping between her parted thighs, and he was licking and kissing her so sweetly there that she arched desperately towards him, suddenly churning with need. His long tongue caressed and savoured her plump, naked flesh-folds with such exquisite attention that she thought she would die of pleasure; desperately she gripped his hair, his shoulders, lifting herself and grinding her vulva hard against his beautiful face until his nose was pressing down on her quivering pleasure bud. Goddess, but she had never known such wild, sweet rapture.

Then slowly he lifted himself, arching like a taut bow over her helpless body, and she saw his beautiful, lengthy penis jutting purposefully towards her. With a soft cry of need, Julia raised her legs and locked them around his wide, heavily muscled shoulders. Falco smiled down at her and positioned himself carefully above her loins so that he could slide his manhood deliciously between her parted, swollen sex-lips, his bone-hard phallus so exquisitely thick and fulfilling that she drove herself hungrily against him, faster and faster, her clitoris grinding against the stalwart base of his solid shaft.

And then she began to orgasm in intense, wrenching spasms that matched each thrust of his beautiful penis, feeling her womb convulse with such a hard, sweet pleasure that she thought she would die of it. At the same time, she felt Falco's own pace quicken inexorably, and was aware of his powerful, jerking thrusts deep within her own trembling body as he reached his own harsh climax.

Afterwards she lay back stunned in the darkness of that tiny bare room as he held her in his strong arms and let his hand trace lazy, seductive patterns on her breasts that were still swollen with satisfaction. She moved slightly, just for the joy of feeling his powerful, muscle-hardened body rasp against her own soft, languorous flesh. Then she took a deep breath and said quietly into the silence, 'Falco, perhaps I have been harsh with you. If you wish, you can have your freedom.'

He lifted his head and gazed down at her, his grey eyes wide and steady. 'What makes you think I want my freedom?'

Julia felt the shock run through her. She tried to laugh, and said lightly, 'You cannot enjoy the life of a slave, with all the things I have made you endure.'

'It was all worth it,' he said quietly, 'to have *you*.'

She was speechless. No. He'd got it all wrong. He couldn't care for her, Julia. Nobody did. She chose her men only for pleasure, and they came to her for the same, and that was all! Pulling herself almost violently from the bed, she wrapped herself quickly in her discarded tunic and said harshly, 'You have made a mistake, gladiator. You would do well to put tonight's happenings from your mind.'

'Will *you*?' he asked her quietly.

With a hiss of indrawn breath, she hurried from the room and slammed the door shut on him, locking it securely. He was a slave, a beautiful, useful slave, nothing more. She couldn't afford for him to be anything more.

And besides, her next task was to get her revenge on Catrina and Alexius. Especially Catrina, the seemingly shy, innocent barbarian girl who had turned out to be as intrepid a schemer as Julia herself, worming her way into the commander's bed where Julia herself had failed!

Suddenly she remembered the little leather bag that Nerissa had found beneath Catrina's pillow. At first, Julia had thought it contained nothing of importance, just a few dried herbs and salves. Primitive barbarian medicines, nothing more.

But then, at the bottom, wrapped in soft deerskin, she'd found the sharp little knife, with Alexius' name engraved on it.

At the time, it had puzzled her greatly, but she'd decided to keep quiet about it, and bide her time. Now, it seemed that the moment had come. She would tell Alexius about it, and see what happened next.

Even better, she would let Alexius find the knife himself . . .

Chapter Fifteen

Catrina awoke from a long, heavy sleep of exhaustion to find herself alone in the little bedchamber in Alexius' house, lying between cool linen sheets. Someone had undressed her and clad her in a thin cotton shift, and there was a clean bandage round her arm.

At the sight of the bandage, she suddenly remembered everything. Drawing herself up, she ran her hands dazedly through her long, loose hair, her mind spinning. Three long nights and days had passed since Brant had launched his deadly attack on Alexius and injured her instead. The cut had not been deep, but as Catrina had feared, the knife's blade had been tipped with wolfsbane, and she had succumbed to a low fever as the poison contaminated her blood. The empty, sunlit days had passed almost in a dream as she lay in her small bed, her isolation broken only by visits from a silent elderly woman who bathed her hot forehead and gave her soothing infusions to drink. At night she slept heavily, dreamlessly. Of Alexius she saw nothing, although she heard his voice in the distance, speaking in low tones to the woman who tended her.

And now, she felt almost well again. Her arm, though still bandaged, seemed quite healed, although she felt light-headed and insubstantial after the fever. She judged that it was late morning by the way the sun poured in through her high little window; the shutters were wide open, and outside she could hear the rumble of a passing ox-cart on the paved road, and the distant clanging of an armourer's hammer as the inhabitants of the great fortress went about their business.

Catrina rubbed her palm across her forehead as her memories flooded back. She realised afresh what she had realised so sickeningly on the night of the attack: that Brant must have been sent to Eboracum by Luad the priest. Brant was dead now, killed by Alexius. But who else from the tribe was out there, lurking in the fortress, spying on her? It was doubtful that Brant had been on his own. Another of Luad's followers might well have seen Catrina save Alexius from Brant's deadly blade. By now, Luad the priest would know of Catrina's betrayal of the tribe.

Alexius was still in terrible danger, and so was she. Now she had no choice but to tell Alexius everything, before it was too late.

Then the door opened quietly, and Alexius himself came in. The hard, dangerous planes of his face were softened by something that was almost tenderness as he gazed down at her. She felt her heart lurch painfully.

He had stopped just inside the door; she saw that he was dressed for duty, in his centurion's armour, with his sword buckled to his belt and his helmet under his arm. He said quietly, 'You slept well, Catrina?'

'Yes, indeed. I feel as though I have slept for days. Alexius, have you a moment? I must speak with you!'

As if she hadn't spoken, he interrupted, 'How is your injured arm?'

'It was nothing but a scratch. I don't think I even need the bandage any more.' She drew her breath to try again. 'Alexius, there is something I must tell you.'

He gazed down at her, his dark blue eyes unreadable in the stark perfection of his face. 'It will keep safely enough for a few hours,' he said. 'I must go now, Catrina, and you must rest. You'll be well looked after while I'm gone. We'll talk later.'

It might be too late by then! Luad would have his men planted in and around the fortress, watching Alexius, waiting for their chance. And the Druid had more subtle weapons at his disposal than a knife-blade dipped in poison . . .

'Please!' she begged, struggling to pull herself upright. 'You must listen to me *now*, Alexius! You're in terrible danger!'

'You think I'm not used to that?' he said quietly.

She clutched at the bedsheet, feeling all the strength drain out of her. He wasn't going to listen to her. He wasn't going to believe her. 'When – when will you be back?'

'By dusk,' he replied. 'And then we will talk.' He turned, about to go. Then he seemed to change his mind, and said, 'Catrina, listen to me. You must not leave the *principia*. You must stay here, you understand? You will be well guarded.'

'I'm still a prisoner, then?' she flashed back in despair, her green eyes wide and dark in the whiteness of her face. 'I think I know that already, Alexius!'

'It's for your own safety,' he responded gravely. 'Believe me.'

She suddenly thought of Brant's shadowy, hooded face, full of hatred for her as he realised that she had recognised him, and she shivered. 'Alexius,' she called out desperately as he turned to go. 'You are wearing the silver amulet?'

He looked at her oddly. 'Why, yes,' he said. She sighed with relief, knowing that it would protect him; and then the door closed, and he was gone.

The silent but kind-faced old woman attended her some time later, with a platter of tiny wheat cakes and a beaker of ewe's milk which Catrina didn't really want. There was a bowl of medicine, too, some sweet, honey-flavoured liquid that the woman indicated would ease the throbbing in her head. Sipping it, Catrina worried again about what had happened to her little pouch of medicines that she'd left in her room at Julia's house. Her blood ran cold when she remembered that it contained the small, deadly knife that Luad had given her, the knife with Alexius' name inscribed on its hilt.

Slowly she drank the medicine and lapsed into a troubled, hazy sleep. She dreamed of Alexius; his arm was around her, and he was smiling into her eyes, and she felt safe, and loved. She awoke with a wrenching sense of loss, because she knew that her dream was impossible.

She realised that she must have slept for a long time, because the sun had moved across the sky and the shadows had lengthened across her room, warning her that it must be late afternoon. And suddenly, she thought she heard soft footsteps, not far away from her door. Her heart thumped with fear, and she scolded herself for her stupidity, telling herself that it was most likely only the old woman who had tended to her. But the footsteps sounded heavier, somehow more deliberate, more masculine. Alexius? But why would he be creeping about so silently in his own house?

She pulled herself out of her little bed, and shakily put on her gown and sandals. Then, girding her belt around her waist, she carefully opened her door and went out into the long passageway that ran the length of the building.

A man was hurrying away towards the main door. He glanced round, and she realised with a jerk of surprise that it was Alexius' *optio*, Felix, the man who'd escorted her here from Julia's house.

He looked startled to see her, and somehow not pleased. She expected him to speak, but he quickly moved on, and she heard the front door slam as he left.

She felt strangely shaken. Of course, it was quite natural that he should be here. After all, he was Alexius'

240

second-in-command, and Alexius had told her that the *principia* would be well guarded. But it was almost as if he didn't want to be seen by her.

Unable to settle again, she wandered restlessly round the house. It was growing dark now; a lamp had been lit in the atrium, and she wandered into the spacious central room, noticing that a chequered marble square adorned with beautifully carved animal and soldier figures had been left on a low table, as if some sort of game had been interrupted. She kneeled on the velvet couch beside it and examined the little figures with rapt attention. Outside, as darkness fell over the fortress, she was dimly aware of the blare of trumpets announcing the first watch of the night, and in the distance she heard the steady, tramping feet of a band of legionaries, marching to their centurion's gruff command.

Then she heard the front doors of the *principia* open suddenly, and she heard the sound of footsteps coming quickly towards the atrium. Felix again?

In her confusion, she dropped the figure she was holding and was reaching hurriedly to the floor to pick it up when a figure suddenly darkened the doorway.

She looked up, and saw Alexius.

Her first, foolish instinct was to run towards him, but something made her hesitate. He stood there, strangely still in the big doorway, formidably outlined in the pale glow of the lamp; he had already removed his armour, and she saw that his leather tunic and boots were streaked with dust, his face strained with the exertions of his long day.

'Alexius!' she exclaimed, swiftly getting to her feet. 'I thought you were never coming. I . . .'

Then she broke off, because she'd seen his expression: cold, cynical, almost indifferent. She almost stopped breathing and her lungs seemed painfully tight.

'Well,' he said, his voice like splintered ice. 'So, my little wild one. It's certainly a dangerous game that you're playing.'

Moistening her dry lips, Catrina said, 'I – I don't know what you're talking about.'

He walked slowly towards her. 'For a while,' he said softly, 'when you warned me of the fire, and even saved me from that knife, I was almost convinced that I'd misjudged you. But then, I realised the truth. You were protecting me so you could kill me yourself, weren't you?'

She shrank back, her eyes wide in the whiteness of her face. 'No! You're lying!'

'Am I?' His mouth thinned. 'Then what about this?' He held out his hand, and for the first time she noticed that he was holding her precious little leather pouch.

'My medicines!' she burst out.

'So you admit they're yours?'

'Of course! Those are my medicines, and salves – I'd lost them. Please, Alexius, let me have them back! They're very precious to me!'

'I'm sure they are.' He smiled coldly, and she began, too late, to realise her mistake. 'And so I can assume that this too is yours, Catrina?'

Pulling harshly at the leather cord that fastened the neck of her bag, he tipped it upside down so that little wrappings and sticks of powders and salves were scattered all over the tessellated floor. And clattering to the ground in the midst of them was the small, deadly knife with his name on it. He picked it up and fingered it thoughtfully, and Catrina felt quite sick, as if all the coldness in the world had gathered in her stomach.

'Well?' he pressed on softly. 'Can you explain this?'

She whispered, 'How did you find it? I left it at Julia's house.'

Alexius smiled thinly. 'Really? Your memory seems somewhat faulty, Catrina. My *optio*, whose duty it is to guard my life, found it here, this afternoon, secreted behind a loose tile in the kitchen.'

Felix – this afternoon. Her blood ran cold. 'No!' she cried out. 'That's not true! I never hid it there!'

'I thought you at least had some honesty,' he said softly. 'Do you deny that you came here to kill me, Catrina? Do you deny that you made a vow to your charlatan priest, back there in the forest, to follow me here and get your vengeance?'

Catrina gazed up at him as the shock jarred through her. 'Then – you know who I am?'

He was fingering the knife, slowly caressing its deadly blade with the ball of his thumb. 'Of course. I think I've always known.'

She shrank back; he went on coldly, 'You confused me, I must admit. I even made arrangements for your protection. I thought it was *you* that your priest was trying to kill, with the fire, and that knife attack the other night. I even thought you gave me your amulet to protect me, but it's more like a curse, isn't it? What were you going to do to me, *mea mellita*? Stab me in the darkness while I slept in your arms?'

'No,' she whispered helplessly, 'no . . .'

He looked scornful, angry, tired. He said, 'Really, Catrina. You begin to try my patience. Spare me your protestations. I think that you're a spy and a sorceress, and I should have handed you over to the magistrates on the very first night you arrived. Now tell me the truth – all of it.'

And slowly, menacingly, he started to walk towards her.

Catrina clenched her fists at her sides, burning with rage and despair. Oh, she hated him. She hated him!

Suddenly she realised that a tiny twist of feverfew powder from her scattered pouch was lying just by her feet. Moving in the same instant that she noticed it, she crouched to pick it up, unwrapping it as she rose. With a hiss of defiance, she flung the dried, aromatic contents straight into Alexius' face.

He gasped and put his hands to his eyes, temporarily blinded as the pungent powder assailed him. Without pausing to think, she plunged past him towards the open door as he struggled helplessly to recover from the unexpected onslaught.

'Catrina!' she heard him roar after her. 'Catrina, damn you, come back here! Don't you realise? You've nowhere to run!'

She did not even hesitate. Racing frantically along the echoing corridor, she rushed through the open door, and out into the dark, still streets.

By now, darkness had enveloped the fortress completely, and the smoky flare of the burning cressets set in iron brackets at each street corner served only to confuse rather than help her find her way. Her first instinct was to run, to get as far away from the *principia* and Alexius as she possibly could; but, finding her headlong flight stopped by a high wall at the end of a narrow alley, she drew up in despair, her breath coming in hoarse gasps.

She needed to get back across the river, to the relative freedom of the township that sheltered beneath the fortress's grim walls. But to do that, she had to get out through the heavily guarded gate, and she would never manage that, because as soon as Alexius had recovered, he would raise the alarm, and the whole garrison would be after her.

She stared round blindly. To her, every street was the same, every forbidding stone building, workshop, barracks or granary; all were laid out in neat right angles with chilling Roman precision. Her only hope, perhaps, was to find somewhere to hide, until the hunt for her had died down.

Taking a deep breath to steady her pounding heart, she gazed round, desperately hoping to get her bearings.

And then, her blood froze in her veins, because in the distance she could see a tall, familiar figure flanked by two others coming slowly towards her, clinging to the shadows that edged the buildings. A man in a dark, rough cloak; a man whose compelling hooded gaze fastened on her like that of a hunter on his prey as his

pace increased until he was walking swiftly, purposefully towards her hiding place.

Luad the priest. No time to wonder how he had
tracked her down, how he had penetrated the fortress's
defences, how he had known that she had failed in her
mission to destroy the Roman. No time for anything
except the harsh, searing agony of premonition telling
her that Luad's intention was to punish her, Catrina, for
betraying the sacred trust of the tribe.

Sobbing with distress, she ran desperately back down
the narrow alleyway she had just left, but all the time
she heard the footsteps of the swift, powerful men
coming closer and closer. Then Luad was standing in
front of her, barring her escape, and saying in his soft,
cold voice, 'Well, Catrina. If you won't bring the Roman
to us, then we shall have to force him to follow *you*,
away from the safety of his fortress.'

Catrina gasped, 'No! You're wasting your time! Don't
you understand? Alexius will never follow me, because
he hates me!'

She tried desperately to push past them all, but
something dark and swirling and heavy, like a cloak,
enveloped her head and shoulders, and she felt a blow
on the back of her neck. She called out Alexius' name in
despair as she felt the blackness close in.

The soldiers of the Sixth Victrix noted that their commander Alexius was unusually harsh and demanding in
his inspection that evening as he went about his final
duties before the night watch took over. No doubt it was
something to do with the fact that the blonde barbarian
girl whom he'd taken a fancy to had gone missing. The
fortress had been searched methodically, but there was
no sign of her, and now the search had been called off. It
was generally considered that the legionaries of this
isolated northern fortress had more serious enemies to
contend with than a single girl.

It was rumoured that the commander thought the girl

to be in some sort of danger; but from whom, and why, nobody was quite clear. There were, of course, the usual sorts of soldiers' gossip, claiming that the girl was a witch or priestess of the barbarian British tribe, and that she had cast some kind of spell on the commander; but no one dared to ask him directly about these rumours. Those who'd seen her close up said that she was breathtakingly beautiful, and that just to look into her bewitching green eyes was enough for a soldier to lose his soul. Making the sign to avert the Evil Eye, the soldiers muttered that the gods would surely punish any Roman who dared to bed her, as their commander had done. The girl was a sorceress, no doubt about it.

As the commander went silently about his evening rounds, his *optio* Felix followed quietly with the auxiliary escort, feeling guilty and ashamed. Felix admired the *primus pilus* excessively, and he hadn't particularly enjoyed the look on Alexius' face when he'd shown his commander the place where, on Julia's instructions, he'd hidden the girl's leather pouch with its deadly, incriminating little knife. Felix wished he'd had the strength to refuse to do it. But Julia had commanded him, and he was the lady Julia's slave.

Last night, in the privacy of her luxurious quarters, Julia had tied him up and encased his genitals in a kind of buckled leather harness, so that his penis and testicles were thrust out obscenely in all their pink, swelling nakedness. Then she'd got her two fiendish Syrian girls to anoint his manhood with sweet, sticky Egyptian wine, and they'd licked it all off again with their delicious little tongues while their scarlet-tipped breasts bobbed about in front of his face, until Felix was so excited that his phallus stood out hugely, and his youthful face glistened with sweat.

Julia watched him as she reclined on a couch in the corner of the room. She was wearing one of her beautiful sheer gowns, with a silk bandeau criss-crossed tightly around her breasts to emphasise their fullness; she had a cool smile on her face as the two Syrian girls giggled and licked his throbbing shaft and bulging testicles.

'Please,' he'd begged, 'please . . .'

'You'll have your fun in a moment,' said Julia calmly. 'When you've agreed to do exactly as I say, and to spy on your commander for me.'

'No!' Felix had gasped. 'That I will not do!'

Julia nodded coolly to Lark and Nightingale. 'My little songbirds. You know what to do next.'

They tightened the grotesque little harness round his hips, just a little, so that his purple genitals strained forth in exquisite, scarcely bearable tension. Felix felt the blood pound in his loins, and moistened his dry lips. 'Yes,' he breathed despairingly, 'anything. Anything at all . . .'

Julia leaned forward to stroke his perspiring forehead. 'Well done, my Felix. You're to take this little leather pouch, which belongs to the girl Catrina, and conceal it behind a loose brick in the *principia*'s kitchen. Make sure the girl doesn't see you. Then, some time later, you must tell Alexius that you saw the girl hiding it there herself. You think you can manage that?'

Felix hesitated, his brow furrowed in torment. Then one of the girls bent over him, her moist coral mouth hovering inches from his purple, engorged shaft. 'Yes,' he gasped out, 'anything!'

Julia nodded, and Lark's lips went down over his agonised penis in an exquisite, enfolding caress as she wrapped her pink little tongue deliciously around the throbbing stem. Shouting out hoarsely, he pumped his floods of semen into her luscious mouth while his whole body shuddered with relief.

Now, when it was too late, he wished he'd had the strength to withstand Julia's devilish ways. He'd known there was going to be trouble as soon as he showed the commander the hiding place with the little bag in it that contained the deadly knife; and trouble there was, with the barbarian girl running off into the darkness, and all

Hades let loose in the attempt to find her – without success.

And now, the commander had looked over the guard lists for the night, and had issued the watchword, and had almost finished his tour of the sentry posts. The night sky was quite black overhead, unrelieved by stars or moon; a warm, stifling wind blew up from the clustered hovels of the township, and from the docks beside the river came the tang of pitch and salt-caked canvas. Felix jerked back into alertness as the trumpets blared for the second watch, and decided that he would be glad to finish for the night. He felt hot and uncomfortable in full armour, and his crested helmet scratched his scalp.

At last, Alexius was formally dismissing his escort, and Felix gave a secret sigh of relief. He didn't seem to have so much stamina these days. Perhaps his adventures with the lady Julia were wearing him out.

Some of the more senior officers seemed to be talking about going down to the town, for some wine and entertainment. Felix was just debating whether or not he had the energy to join them, when he blinked suddenly with surprise. That the centurions should have a night on the town was nothing unusual. But it was certainly highly unusual for the commander, Alexius, to head towards the common fleshpots of the *vicus* with them.

Swiftly, Felix muttered his excuses and hurried off to report the interesting news to Julia.

Alexius went with his fellow-officers through the winding streets of the *vicus* to the dark little alley where the creaking, faded sign of the Golden Boar hung above the entrance to the wineshop of that name. Inside, it was already crowded, because it was rumoured that the soldier-girls would be appearing there that evening, and every table was full with off-duty legionaries drinking and dicing, or eating bowls of the thick stew that were on offer. Smoking lamps cast a dim glow about the room;

the air was already hot and thick with fumes from the charcoal braziers as the landlord, a tough, retired legionary who knew his duty, quickly cleared a space for the senior officers and ordered his prettiest serving girls to bring them jugs of his best Gallic wine, with just a little water to thin it down.

Alexius joined his comrades at the scarred wooden table that had been vacated for them, and drank a good deal of the strong red wine without showing it, and talked easily with his companions of distant campaigns they'd endured together. But all the time, he was obsessed by one thought – Catrina.

He'd underestimated her badly. *Mithras*, but she'd got under his guard, in just a few days! He'd realised, as soon as Felix had shown him the knife with his name on it, that she'd meant to kill him all the time. And he, fool that he was, had thought *she* was the one in danger, from that charlatan priest and his pagan followers.

One of the officers, who'd drunk a little too much to know when to hold his tongue, leaned conspiratorially towards Alexius and said, 'Hear you've lost your tasty little barbarian wench, the one you pinched from the lady Julia. Never mind – plenty more where she came from, eh?'

Alexius thought suddenly, No. No, there wasn't anyone else like Catrina, with her stunning, silky fair hair, and her wide, vulnerable green eyes, and the way she clung to him, crying out her joy, when he held her in his arms. But he smiled coldly and beckoned for more wine, and silently fingered the silver amulet that still hung on its leather thong beneath his tunic. 'Plenty more,' he said.

The soldier-girls turned up as promised, tantalising and delighting the packed room of soldiers with their performance until all three of them had to run round the tables to collect the proffered coins in their upturned helmets. Alexius, the memory of the girl still a hard, dark pain in his chest, scarcely noticed them until one of the soldier-girls stood directly in front of him, her hands on her hips.

'My lord Alexius?' she said, almost hesitantly. 'It's been a while since we spent some time together. You look as if you could do with some company tonight.'

Claudia. Her voice was hesitant, but her lively face, piquantly enhanced by her cropped, boyish dark hair and her dancing brown eyes, was full of challenge. He realised then that Claudia had a companion with her, likewise dressed in a slit leather parody of a soldier's tunic, with her high, luscious breasts pouting lasciviously through the bodice straps so that the pink buds of her nipples were enticingly exposed. This one's hair, though, was concealed by her helmet, and her face was all but covered by a soft, clinging leather mask through which her eyes glittered strangely. She, too, was watching him, waiting silently; he was aware of a sudden dark stab of arousal, and he felt the eyes of the other officers on him, watching him enviously.

He stood up, and put the coins for his wine down on the scarred table. His smile was cold. 'Perhaps you're right,' he said to Claudia. 'I could do with some company.'

The women smiled secretly at one another and silently escorted him from the packed, noisy room.

There was a narrow, twisted flight of stairs outside the Golden Boar, which led to a small private chamber just above the wineshop. It was quiet and clean, and was often rented out by the landlord to various visiting dignitaries who had to travel up to Eboracum on the empire's business. Softly illuminated by an ornate bronze lamp in the corner, the room provided certain discreet comforts, in that the big bed was freshly draped with clean linen, and there was a flask of good wine on the table, together with a ewer and basin of water for washing.

'Well, commander,' breathed Claudia, gazing at Alexius' tall, silent figure with hungry eyes, 'it's been a long time. Remember Calleva? We thought you'd forgotten us.'

'But we haven't forgotten you,' smiled the other one, the woman in the strange leather mask that seemed moulded to her features. Who was she? She'd taken off her helmet, tossing her head so that her dark, glossy hair cascaded to her shoulders; but the mask remained. Alexius, gazing at her, frowned and wished he hadn't drunk so much of the numbing wine. Her husky, musical voice was somehow familiar . . .

But then they set to work on him, and he stopped thinking, letting the wine and the touch of their fingers take over his mind.

Carefully, they unbuckled his armour and his leather tunic, and pulled the boots from his legs. Then, when he was completely naked, they gestured him down on to the bed, and caressed him carefully with the citrus-scented water, running their tantalising fingers lingeringly over the old wounds and scars that made silvery patterns on his bronzed skin. His phallus was already hardening relentlessly; they abstained carefully from touching it, but smiled at one another in a kind of mutual conspiracy. They worked nimbly, sometimes kneeling by his side, sometimes astride him, their breasts bobbing ripely between the tight leather straps of their soldiers' tunics, and Alexius, closing his eyes, let the sensation of hard, purely physical lust overwhelm him as his penis surged and thickened inexorably.

The masked woman, seeing his throbbing phallus, licked her lips. Her eyes were glittering brightly through the slits in her black leather mask as she nodded to Claudia, and squatted beside Alexius on the wide bed.

'Take me now, my beautiful commander,' she whispered huskily. 'I'm ready for you. See how I'm ready!' And, her tongue still protruding slightly through the mouth-slit of the mask in anticipation, she flicked aside the leather strips that formed the brief skirt of her tunic and splayed her folded thighs, then reached with tender care to unfurl her swollen, nectared labia.

And Alexius saw, with a dark jolt of desire that made his already engorged penis leap and strain, that between her thighs she was completely naked; her dark pink feminine flesh was totally denuded of hair. As she reached to pull her juicy petals wide apart, he could see how the crinkled folds glistened with moisture; he could see the tiny bud of her clitoris throbbing hotly at the brink of her honeyed cleft, and as her finger moved, very slowly, to rub it and caress it, he felt the hot surge of desire flood through his own body. Her hungry eyes were fastened all the time on his penis; with a hiss of indrawn breath he raised himself and lunged towards her, and she fell back beneath him, her supple legs twining instantly round his waist as she gasped, 'I'm ready, commander – oh, I'm ready!' Alexius, gritting his teeth as she writhed beneath him enticingly, positioned his heavy, throbbing shaft at her honeyed entrance, and plunged it deep, deep within her; she gasped and moaned, gripping him to her, pushing her half-naked, straining breasts up against his face. He took his weight on his elbows and started to ravish her slowly, thoroughly, as the masked woman rose to meet his plunging shaft and whimpered out her need.

From behind them in the shadows, Claudia watched enviously, her brown eyes rapt at the sight of the soldier's beautiful, lengthy shaft sliding steadily in and out as he pleasured the masked woman with slow, skilful strength. The masked woman had come to the soldier-girls earlier as they prepared for their show, offering them good money if they would allow her to join in with them for one evening; Claudia hadn't quite realised that the bargain would include *this*. She had known Alexius for a long time, and knew only too well the exquisite pleasure he could bestow. Now she was jealous, because she wanted him as well; she too wanted to feel that delicious, sturdy weapon impaling her own secret flesh, which was already moist and pulsing with need. She gazed raptly, hungrily, as the soldier's tightly muscled bottom-cheeks clenched and drove rhythmically into the squirming woman; saw how his heavy, delicious balls swung with each thrust, and caught a glimpse of the dark, enticing hole in the cleft between his taut buttocks, its puckered little entrance whorled with dark, silky hair.

Claudia, panting with sexual need, let her hand slide across her own tingling nipples, pulling and pinching at the swollen teats and enjoying the way the tight leather straps of her bodice constricted and squeezed her soft flesh. Then, rucking up her tunic impatiently, she let her other hand slide between her thighs to caress her exposed vulva. Already it was swollen and juicy, and she uttered a little moan of need as she slid her finger deliciously up and down the unfurling folds of flesh and lightly brushed her throbbing clitoris. The heavy, languorous waves of need that swept over her made her grit her teeth as she jealously watched the masked woman being so exquisitely serviced. Oh, she wanted him, too!

Suddenly, Claudia leaped up on to the bed to kneel behind Alexius. Then, before he'd even realised she was there, she gripped his tight buttocks and dipped her head, to begin to lick and nuzzle her way down the dark, hairy cleft between his taut bottom-cheeks. He smelled musky, masculine, delicious; with a little shudder of rapture she let her hot little tongue trail right down to the top of his thighs, and pressed through to lick with her eager tongue at his heavy, hair-roughened balls.

She heard him gasp, and felt his whole body go rigid at the wicked kiss of her tongue. She reached even further, to caress the very base of his strong shaft, licking down as far as she could until she could feel where his phallus became buried in the fiercely gripping flesh of the masked woman. Oh, but he was beautiful! She heard the masked woman whimper with need as she thrust her hips hungrily up against his magnificent shaft, trying desperately to regain control; Claudia, longing to feel the length of it herself, rubbed her stiffened teats yearningly against the man's tight, trembling buttocks, feeling the dark arrows of pleasure shivering through her hard nipples. Then, with sudden inspiration, she remembered the small, gleaming dagger she kept in the waistband of her tunic, the one she used in the floor-show. Swiftly she eased it from its sheath, inverted it, and thrust the rounded end of the narrow bronze pommel into the tightly puckered hole between Alexius' bottom-cheeks.

Alexius reared up and swore aloud at the lewd assault, and Claudia, tingling with excitement at the discovery of her unexpected power over him, renewed her assault with fresh vigour, sliding the dagger's hilt deep between his quivering bottom-cheeks with mischievous, wriggling strokes then retreating in a slow, languorous caress. At the same time the beautiful masked woman beneath him, who to judge by her passionate moans was almost at her own extremity, wrapped her sinuous calves more tightly than ever around the soldier's waist and pounded her hips convulsively upwards against the solid pillar of flesh that impaled her. Claudia heard Alexius draw a deep, searing breath; then he began to pound into her with his rampant, hungry penis, while Claudia, making sure that her little dagger handle followed his every thrust, caressed his tight anal crevice with rhythmic, loving strokes.

They were all on the brink of explosion. The masked woman gasped and shouted her delight as his shaft vigorously pleasured her, and she thumped the bed in ecstasy as her orgasm swept over her, crying out, 'Oh, yes. Fill me with your wonderful prick, soldier – ride me, ride me!' And as she fell back sated, Claudia felt Alexius pull himself swiftly out of her. His seed began to spurt ravenously across her flushed, trembling breasts, making the leather straps of her tunic sticky with the creamy liquid as he rubbed his spasming penis dementedly against her pouting nipples. Somehow Claudia kept her smooth dagger-hilt deep inside his delicious bottom-hole as he came, wriggling it hard, while with desperate fingers she rubbed her own soaking clitoris into a heated, ravenous climax, imagining that massive, spurting penis tightly clenched inside her own hungry, rippling vagina as she shuddered to her own noisy release.

They were all finished at last, completely sated, their perspiration-soaked bodies in a tangled, trembling heap on the bed. Claudia threw her dagger to the floor and lay with her head against Alexius' hard, hair-covered thighs, feeling the sweet, melting after-glow of pleasure wash through her. There was no one quite like Alexius . . .

Alexius himself lay utterly spent, the wine still throbbing through his head. Then he became aware that the masked woman was starting to ease herself with sinuous, cat-like movements from the bed. Still wearing her mask, she reached to kiss him lingeringly on the mouth, then she got to her feet and stretched contentedly. And suddenly, Alexius felt his skin start to prickle in warning.

'Magnificent, my dear Alexius,' she drawled as she gazed down at him. 'And I think you would find it rather hard to deny that you enjoyed yourself thoroughly too.'

Then she pulled off the close-fitting leather mask, and her dark, almond-shaped eyes glittered triumphantly in the exquisite oval of her face.

Alexius drew himself up, suddenly effortlessly sober. Julia. Julia had got the better of him at last.

Slowly he reached for a towel and started to rub himself down, drawling as he did so, 'I see you've found your role in life at last, Julia. How much should I pay you?'

Julia hissed, and her eyes suddenly became black, venomous pools. 'Be careful, Alexius,' she warned.

'Come now, Julia,' he said, starting to pull on his

clothes with casual ease. 'You, at least, should acknowledge that we both got what we deserved.' He gave her a blue, glacial smile; and Julia, swiftly pulling on her long cloak, ran from the room, slamming the door behind her so hard that the lamp faltered and nearly went out in the draught.

Claudia, not understanding what had spoiled their glorious encounter, gazed in bewilderment as Alexius, looking strangely distant and abstracted, gave her a brief kiss of farewell and slowly went down the stairs to rejoin his comrades.

Chapter Sixteen

*T*he sun was setting slowly behind the high western escarpment, sending long fingers of shadow across the tumbled rocks that crowded the steep summit of the remote northern valley. It was still warm, almost oppressively so; but all the same Catrina shivered and drew her shabby cloak around herself as she watched the sun's last rays glimmer and fade beyond the horizon. Another night was drawing in, and another day had gone. Another day without Alexius.

She sank on to a craggy boulder with her chin in her hands and gazed into the distance, south towards far-off Eboracum, her eyes shadowed with a despair she couldn't hide.

Four nights had passed since Luad and his men had captured her and dragged her up here to their rocky hideout in the barren hills. After the blow that had stunned her, they'd bundled her into the wooden cart that had got them into the fortress on the pretext of bringing in some overdue supplies of grain; then they'd covered her up with empty sacks as they returned across the river into the civilian township. After that they'd abandoned the cart and pushed north through the night on their shaggy ponies.

Catrina, feeling sick and dizzy, had been roped to her pony, which in turn was tethered to Luad's larger steed. Luad kept glancing back over his shoulder into the darkness as if he could hear something. Catrina said to him, defiantly, 'I assure you that Alexius won't follow me. I don't rank very high in his priorities.'

Luad had smiled unpleasantly. 'I think you might be mistaken. I think he'll come after you very soon. And when he does, we shall be ready for him, believe me.'

Catrina felt the cold fear constrict her heart. Another trap for Alexius, and this time she was the bait. 'I told you, Luad,' she said as calmly as she could. 'He hates me.'

His gaunt, finely chiselled features seemed cold and dangerous. 'Really? Then why did you allow him to ravish you, Catrina? Why didn't you kill him?'

As they jolted up the steep, stony track, she lifted her head to meet the priest's pale eyes, trying her best to hide her fear that he knew everything. 'Perhaps because I never had the chance!'

Luad's eyes narrowed. 'According to my informants, you had plenty of chance – in the Roman's bed, in his arms! You realise that you are no longer one of us? That you have forfeited your right to be counted as one of the tribe?'

To be cursed by the tribe was to be cast outside the circle of life. Catrina felt sick at his malediction, and shaken to her core that the priest knew everything. He must have had spies everywhere, watching her, following her.

'If I am no longer one of the tribe, then let me go, Luad!'

He laughed contemptuously. 'Where would you go to? You have nowhere left to hide, Catrina. You've lost your amulet; you've lost your sacred powers. The tribe will never have you back. You've only one use for us now; to lure back the Roman for our revenge.'

After a hard climb up the steep mountainside where

nothing grew but heather and bog-moss and the occasional twisted upland thorn, the little company had stopped at last, just as the bleak, grey dawn was starting to push away the darkness. Catrina had gazed around this solitary, remote hiding place amongst the high rocks, where Luad and his followers seemed to have made their camp, and she suddenly wondered, Why? Why were they hiding here, in this desolate spot, so far from the usual haunts of the tribe? Why were there so few of them? She recognised a few faces – Deta and Cernwi among the men, and Eda, glaring at her malevolently, from among the women – but they were no more than a dozen in all. Acting on sudden impulse, she took a deep breath and said coldly, 'You too have lost your place in the tribe, Luad, haven't you?'

Luad, pulling the saddle off his weary pony, looked at her with fury, and she realised she'd hit home.

'I decided to leave *them*! They wouldn't follow the ways of the old gods, they wouldn't listen to me! For that, I blame you, Catrina, for losing your sacred amulet which the tribe held in such esteem. But I still have my powers, and there are still many who honour me.' He laughed shortly. 'As for you, little priestess, you might still have some use for us; after you've drawn the Roman into our trap. You're still very beautiful, Catrina.'

Catrina felt a jolt of fear shoot through her at his ominous words, but somehow she fought it down. Looking scornfully at Eda, who was lapping up her old enemy's disgrace, she said clearly, 'I thought you had whores enough, Luad.'

Eda hissed and sprang for Catrina with her fingers stretched out like talons, but Luad put out his arm to restrain her, saying, 'Patience, Eda. You'll have time enough for your revenge.'

Eda slunk away, and Luad said to Catrina suddenly, 'You've got one last chance, Catrina. Go back to the city of the Eagles and somehow bring the Roman back here, so that we can kill him.'

Catrina caught her breath and said coldly, 'How could I? I told you, he despises me. He would never follow me anywhere, least of all into a trap of *your* making, Luad.'

'Then there's no escape for you,' said Luad softly, his pale eyes assessing her weary, defiant figure.

When he'd gone, Catrina pressed her clenched hands tightly to. her sides, feeling dizzy and sick. She would have run, but there was nowhere to run to, as Luad had pointed out. If she tried to scramble down this barren, rocky hillside, the nimble tribesmen would recapture her immediately.

Nowhere to run. Alexius had told her that as well; in fact they were his last words to her. Oh, Alexius. She fought the memory of him away, but it lingered like a deep, dark pain.

During the days and nights that followed, Catrina was very much afraid that Luad was losing his mind to the moon goddess. There seemed to be a cruel, almost feverish quality to his words and actions that chilled her blood. He was more avid than ever for sexual pleasure, as were the others of his little company; she'd already noticed that the men and the women he'd drawn with him were the most wanton and licentious of the tribe. Every night he and the others would pass round a bowl of fiery, potent metheglin and then they would carouse under the stars in the still, midsummer heat, thinking up new entertainments each evening. Catrina would turn her head away blindly from their excesses; from the voluptuousness of the eager women, led by Eda, and from the basic licentiousness of the men: the big warrior Cernwi, the silent, red-haired Deta and salacious, sharp-tongued little Tan, who whispered new ideas into Luad's ear each night.

Catrina had grown up with the joyous celebrations of the tribe, with the festivals of the seasons, and the sacred fertility rituals when the pleasure taken in one another's bodies was a joyous offering to the deities, to life. But this, this degrading exploitation of one another's bodies

260

night after night, was different. And she, Catrina, was being kept apart for some purpose, she knew.

The weather continued to be hot and airless, even through the short hours of darkness. After the group had made their evening meal of dried deermeat or freshly killed rabbit or hare, they would all swill down the strong barley brew and then Luad would play his licentious games with them. He would encourage the women to expose their luscious bodies to the handsome but simple Cernwi, who had a huge gnarled penis. Laughing at him, Eda and her friends would caress their own naked bodies lewdly in front of him and persuade him to show them his throbbing phallus, which curved enticingly when fully erect; and then they would run away from him, jeering scornfully when he lunged helplessly after them. Cernwi was obsessed in particular with Eda's voluptuous form; when he could stand no more of her tormenting ways, they'd offer him the woman Moren instead, whose plumply ripe body was always hungry for him. She would bounce up and down on his rampant weapon in gleeful joy, savouring every inch of his massive erection, while the others looked on and laughed. Luad would silently watch their antics, sprawling on the mossy turf with a beaker of barley spirit in his hand, while Eda or another of his favourites would be constantly at his side, fondling his penis as it rose hot and hard from his loins. Luad was always careful, though, to delay his own climax of pleasure while the others copulated at his command.

Catrina noticed that Luad no longer even pretended to dress or act like a priest, but wore a rough homespun tunic like the rest of them. He would rub himself sometimes in slow pleasure while Eda performed for him, then he would tell eager, salacious Tan to buck between her parted thighs like a rabbit, while Eda took someone else's penis in her mouth. But he was always careful to postpone his own extremity of pleasure until the very end.

261

As the final act, Luad would coldly take his pick of the beautiful, eager women. He liked his chosen partner to crouch naked before him on all fours, with her bottom-cheeks flared hungrily, then he would kneel behind her and drive his hot, hard penis slowly in and out of her vulva, relishing the clenching wet tightness that enveloped him as the woman beneath him squirmed and groaned her pleasure. And as he serviced her, the dark-haired priest would turn his head to make sure Catrina could see him, as if to say, 'This is what you will enjoy, very soon.'

She tried at first to hide herself away as the evenings approached, but he made his men guard her, so that she had to watch. She grew to dread the evenings, and as the night of the full moon grew nearer, the weather seemed to grow even hotter and more oppressive, so that the sparse mountain grass shrivelled and died and even the birds grew silent.

One afternoon, when she had asked permission to go a little way downhill to relieve herself and wash her hot, dusty body in a little mountain stream that flowed between the rocks, Cernwi suddenly appeared, smiling in gentle appeal. Catrina, diving in dismay for her clothes, realised that he must have been watching her for some time; his purple phallus was already throbbing as he exposed it to her, and he caught her easily as she tried to run and pinned her against him. His mouth was wet over her breasts, and she could feel his huge penis prodding hungrily against her naked belly. She struggled and tried to scream, but he pushed her gently to the ground, crooning endearments all the while, and pinned her hands to the ground; then, breathless with excitement, he crouched astride her and began to masturbate over her, tenderly rubbing the swollen plum of his great, purple shaft against her nipples. 'My little priestess,' he was murmuring. 'Don't be frightened. How I've longed for you . . .'

Catrina bit on his hand, still struggling, and screamed

aloud. Luad came striding down the hillside towards them and pulled Cernwi from her just as the big man's seed was starting to spurt, and he whimpered in disappointment, rubbing himself softly in his extremity as he knelt and rocked on the hard ground. Catrina, shaking, pulled herself up and grabbed for her tunic to shield her body. Luad said coldly, 'He means no harm. He doesn't understand your rejection. The other women find him attractive.'

Shaking her head, Catrina whispered, 'I want no part in your games, Luad.'

His lips thinned. 'You still think you're better than the rest of us? You're no longer a priestess, Catrina.'

'And you can no longer even pretend to be a priest! Let me go, Luad. Why are you keeping me here?'

'It's your fault that I've lost my hold on the people!' he grated out. 'It vanished the day you lost your silver amulet. But you still belong with me, Catrina. All will be well when the Roman comes for you.'

Catrina caught her breath. 'I've told you! He'll never follow me. Why should he, when he hates me?'

'So you keep saying.' Luad laughed. 'But I think he'll be here soon. And afterwards – why, afterwards, you'll learn to be happy with me, Catrina.'

'No!'

But Luad, no longer listening to her, was hauling the shivering Cernwi back up the hillside to punish him, and Catrina sank to her knees in despair.

She tried not to think of Alexius. But her fright, and Luad's harsh words, had broken down her defences, and she felt a great, tearing wave of longing. Had Alexius troubled to search for her? Did he even think of her?

She swallowed hard on the lump in her throat, knowing the answer. He despised her. He thought her a spy, a pathetic deceiver, who had failed in her attempt to kill him and had fled back to her tribe. *I thought you at least had some honesty*, Alexius had said, flaying her with his final words.

263

Sometimes, as they slept in the open under the shadow of the rocks, she dreamed that he came looking for her, and when she awoke from those dreams she felt again the searing pain of loss. She knew she ought to be glad that he hadn't tried to find her. If he came looking for her, he would die; Luad would make sure of that.

She waited in growing despair, feeling helpless and alone.

In the full heat of the afternoon, Julia roamed restlessly around the praetorium, impatiently wafting the still air against her cheeks with a tiny hand fan carved from ivory. Everything was going wrong. She was wearing her flimsiest silk gown, but even so, the hot, humid weather seemed to sap her energy. She'd tried bathing herself in cool water, but it brought her only temporary relief, and even the peace of her shaded courtyard failed to soothe her. It was as if the hot, fetid air from the squalid township below the fortress walls had risen up here to plague her, and even the scented lavender bushes she'd planted amongst the paving stones seemed to have lost their fragrance.

This morning, she'd received a sealed wax tablet, brought up from Londinium with the rest of the legion's business. It was inscribed with a message from Flavius. It said briefly that as he had now vowed his allegiance to the victorious new emperor Severus, he would be travelling north soon and hoped to be with his darling mistress again in a matter of days, if the gods were willing.

The news that Flavius was so close to returning had shaken Julia badly. It would mean the end of everything; her freedom, her independence, her pleasure. With all this churning around in her mind, she swept her dark curls tiredly back from her face and wandered listlessly through the empty chambers to Flavius' office. At the thought of the return of her elderly lover, even his precious chart seemed to have palled. At the very top, she'd put her mark next to the name of the man she'd wanted so desperately for so long – Alexius, first centurion of the legion. It should have been a moment of triumph, but instead his name seemed to mock her coldly.

It had been such a wonderful idea – one of her best ever – to pose as one of the soldier-girls, and Alexius, as a lover, had been everything and more that she expected. She shivered suddenly at the memory, her inner flesh palpitating at the recollection of the acute, astonishing pleasure she'd experienced as his delicious, strongly thrusting penis had taken her to the edge of rapture and beyond. Then suddenly she felt cold as she remembered the look of utter derision in his wonderful blue eyes when he realised who she was. Quickly, she dashed the burning tears of humiliation from her eyes. She hated him, hated him! And soon, Flavius would be back, and she didn't think she could bear her elderly protector to come near her. But what else was there for her? No one of standing would marry her, an actress, and she wasn't young any more. Only this morning, she'd noticed yet more tiny lines creeping hatefully around the corners of her eyes. The thought of dyeing her hair with soot, as some of her former companions of the stage had to do, and painting her face with more and more cosmetics to enhance her fading charms, was utterly repugnant to her. She would rather die.

The door had opened softly behind her, but in her rage and misery she heard nothing of the slow, measured footsteps until the warm masculine hands fastened gently around her silk-clad breasts. Gasping, she breathed in the delicious, heady scent of warm, clean male skin that was smooth with sandalwood oil, and she whirled round, her eyes wide with astonishment. 'Falco! How dare you follow me? Who gave you permission to leave the slave quarters?'

He smiled, gazing down at her with his beautiful grey eyes, and shrugged his wide shoulders. 'How can I stop myself from following you everywhere, when you're so beautiful, so exquisite?'

She tossed her head proudly so that her dark ringlets bobbed around her face, and hoped desperately that he couldn't see the traces of her stupid tears. 'Who do you think you are, to speak to me in such a fashion?' she demanded scornfully.

'I think,' he said softly, 'that I'm the man who can make you happy.' And before she could draw in her breath to react, he imprisoned her in his arms and kissed her.

Julia gasped in protest. She didn't like being kissed! But, with a little shiver, she realised that this was different. Falco's mouth was so firm, so warm, cherishing her full, tremulous lips as if they were infinitely precious; she felt his strong tongue gently caressing the inner silk of her mouth, felt him probing and thrusting with a patient masculine tenderness that made her senses ache with wanting all of his sweet young beauty. Slowly her hands crept up with a will of their own round the back of his neck, drinking in the powerful muscles beneath his tunic, reaching to tangle in his mane of thick blonde hair as she felt her swelling breasts crushed gently against his hard chest. Closing her eyes, Julia felt a sudden shock of happiness.

Her gladiator.

Falco broke reluctantly away from her at last, but he still held her very close in his strong arms, gazing down into her bewildered, suddenly vulnerable face with his familiar, steady grey eyes. 'We belong together, you and I,' he said calmly.

Julia shook her head, half-laughing, half-crying. 'You must be mad! I'm much older than you are. And – and I had a message today to say that the legate Flavius is returning any day now.'

'Do you want him back?'

'No! But what alternative have I?'

'We'll go away together,' he said steadily. 'We'll live

somewhere warm, by the sea, and I'll earn enough to keep us both.'

Julia laughed mockingly, but the colour had risen in her cheeks. 'You are my slave! Even if I were to make you free, we couldn't possibly marry!'

'Then we'll live together,' he said.

'You – you don't know what I'm like, Falco! I need people, entertainment, excitement, luxury . . .'

Slowly, letting her go, he reached up behind her to the wall and deliberately ripped down the parchment with the soldiers' names inscribed in rows. 'I think', he said calmly, 'that you have had enough of this kind of thing to last you for some time.' And, still watching her with that mischievous glint in his eyes, he began to tear the parchment into small shreds with his strong hands and let the pieces drift to the floor.

Julia sank rather faintly into Flavius' big leather chair and gazed up at him. 'You're mad, gladiator,' she said a little breathlessly. 'Quite, quite mad! Flavius will be furious!' But her eyes were dancing as she watched him, and she suddenly felt very, very happy.

He threw the last scraps of parchment into the air and came to kneel on the floor beside her, resting his hand on her silk-clad thigh so that she could feel the strong warmth of his fingers there, and gazing at her with steady, loving eyes. 'I've never been more serious in my life,' he said.

She blushed like a young girl. No one had ever looked at her like this before. Usually men's eyes were filled with lust, or calculating greed, whenever they looked at her. She said lightly, 'This crazy scheme of yours. When do you suggest that we leave?'

'As soon as possible,' he replied calmly, 'if Flavius is on his way back. We'll take a galley for Rutupiae, and then sail to my homeland, Greece. There are islands there, beautiful islands, like jewels in a wine-dark sea . . . But first, there is something you must do.'

Julia gazed at him, still bewildered. 'What is that?'

He said, 'The girl Catrina is in trouble. You must tell Alexius.'

The old bitterness welled anew in Julia's heart. She sprang to her feet and paced the room, saying, 'Alexius? Catrina? Why should I care about them? They are nothing to me!'

'I know that,' he said softly, standing in the corner with his arms folded across his chest. 'And the best way to show everyone that is to help them in their trouble. Catrina is in enemy hands, and desperately needs help.'

'How do you know this? Everyone says that she ran away because Alexius discovered her for what she was – a scheming little spy!'

Falco was shaking his head. 'The slaves have their own means of intelligence. Someone saw Catrina the other night, being abducted by some strangers to the city. The girl must have known her attackers, because she called out a name – *"Luad"*. Apparently Catrina struggled desperately, but they took her by force. Will you send to Alexius, and warn him?'

Send to Alexius? When she hated him?

But Falco was beside her, stroking her shoulder tenderly, and suddenly Alexius didn't seem to have the power to hurt her any more.

'I – I'll think about it,' she said at last.

Then Falco said quietly, 'You know something else, don't you? About the little knife with Alexius' name on it, the knife that the girl thought she had lost. It turned up again, didn't it, in Alexius' living quarters? And Alexius thought that Catrina had hidden it there.'

Julia hesitated, and her cheeks flooded with shameful colour. Falco kissed her forehead tenderly.

'I think,' he said, 'that we had better go and find Alexius. Don't you?'

Chapter Seventeen

*I*t was the night of the full moon, only there was no moon, because the sky was black and heavy with the storm-clouds that had been building up all day in banks of ominous purple behind the high mountains to the west. The craggy, barren landscape was airless and oppressive in the unnatural stillness; the only light on the hillside came from the glowing peat fire that flickered and sparked dully in the encampment of the tribesmen.

But Luad did not care that there was no moon. Feeling a little dizzy from too much metheglin, vaguely aware that his pale robe was torn and stained, he stood gloating in the turf-clad hollow among the rocks where the fire blazed, with his long dark hair flowing to his shoulders and his face lifted exultantly to the night sky. Yes, he was a true priest! He had the power! Tonight he could feel it surging through his body, and the others could sense it, too; he could see them all waiting, trance-like, for his every word . . .

He glanced across the clearing at the girl, the girl priestess that he himself had trained, and he moistened his lips. She'd been tied naked to a tall rock carved with ancient magical inscriptions. Her head was still held high and proud, but he could see the despair in her green eyes, and her long moon-silver hair hung in a wild tangle around her shoulders.

Earlier that evening, as the fierce sun was smothered by the lowering purple storm-clouds and even the birds grew silent at the threat of an approaching storm, Eda and the other women had stripped the little priestess and painted her with the blue paint of the tribespeople, tracing the lines of curling dye in rich whorls and circles around her breasts and thighs and loins. They'd had to hold her still as they did it, and their touch had not been gentle. But she had to be reminded where she belonged.

Soon, Catrina would forget Eboracum, and the Roman who had violated her. Soon she would realise that she belonged to him, to Luad. She would welcome the pleasure he and the others could offer her.

He gazed at her high, painted breasts and let his gaze drop thoughtfully to her tenderly curved belly, to the little triangle of soft golden hair that dusted her tender womanly parts. He felt himself grow hot and hard as he thought of exploring her there. Later tonight, that moment would come. But because she'd violated her own sanctity, because she'd given herself to the Roman, she would have to be punished, and tonight she would be anybody's. Big Cernwi was panting for her; he'd had to pull the great simpleton off her only the other day. And Luad had noticed Deta following her, too, his eyes dark and hungry.

Well, they would all enjoy her tonight. She would be a sacrifice to the cold goddess of the moon, because she'd lost the sacred protection of her amulet. He, Luad, would watch them all, while perhaps Eda and one or two others caressed him and stimulated him in the secret ways they knew he enjoyed. And then, in full sight of them all, he would take her, and show her that he was her lord.

Excited already, feeling his penis throbbing hot and hard beneath his robe, he raised his hand to Eda. She came quickly up to him. 'What is your will, lord?'

Luad smiled thinly. 'Make her ready,' he said. 'The ceremony is about to begin.'

Catrina saw Luad pointing towards her from across the clearing, and closed her eyes, shaking. They were closing in on her, and there was no escape. 'Oh, goddess,' she breathed, 'help me.'

The great towering rocks that looked as if they'd been piled up by some primeval giant loomed all around, and the black, threatening night sky seemed to press in on her. Her skin prickled with heat and tension; she could feel the perspiration beading the painted bands and spirals that the women had smeared all over her naked body. So still, so hot, so silent. Somewhere below the rocks, she thought she heard something stir; a pebble clattered, and then all was quiet again. Only some night animal, stealing through the undergrowth.

And then Luad was walking towards her, with the women crouching behind him like a hunter's dogs advancing on their prey.

'She's all yours,' said the priest softly to the women.

Suddenly they all seemed to be upon her, touching her, stroking her, caressing her mockingly. Eda was at the forefront, of course, her eyes gleaming with malevolence as she hissed in Catrina's ear, 'Not too good for us now, are you, little priestess? We'll make you forget your Roman, never fear!'

Catrina shuddered with revulsion, and summoned the last of her strength for a final, desperate appeal.

'Luad,' she called out, 'you must set me free! Remember, I am one of your people, marked out by special gifts. If you offend me, you offend our gods!'

Luad walked forward slowly, and her tormentors fell back.

'Oh, no, Catrina,' he said softly as the firelight flickered on his gauntly handsome features. 'You're not one of us. You never have been. You're one of the enemy. A Roman.'

271

'No,' she whispered, shaking her head. 'No, I don't understand.'

'Oh, yes. You see, soon after I found you all those years ago, I made some investigations. I discovered that it was a Roman settlement that had been flooded, Roman families who'd drowned. That's why you're so different – why you've always been different to us. You're of Roman blood, Catrina. And that's why no one will lift a finger in your defence no matter what happens to you.'

Catrina felt as if she had stopped breathing. The memories crowded in on her, making her dizzy: Eda, hissing, 'You're not one of us.' Falco, murmuring, 'Catrina. Strange, but that is a Roman name.' Alexius, telling her that her amulet was Roman, not British. 'Many families round here wear a similar trinket . . .'

And Luad, watching her with calm deliberation, was saying, 'So, my little Roman. Still rebellious?' He turned to the others. 'Let Cernwi have her.'

With a groan of pleasure Cernwi stumbled forward from the shadows, and the women turned on him quickly, laughingly divesting him of his ragged homespun tunic. As they stripped his big, handsome body completely naked, they saw that his lewdly curving penis was already swollen and purple; Eda giggled and stroked it lasciviously as it jerked hungrily towards her. 'There now, my fine, beautiful Cernwi!' she crooned, running her fingers tantalisingly up and down its lengthy stem. 'Let me have a taste of this first, and then you can have the Roman girl. I'll get you properly warmed up. Stick it up me, Cernwi – ravish me. Let's see what a man you are!'

Laughing, she squatted back on the turf and parted her sex-lips, tossing back her wild, coppery hair. Cernwi gazed in delight at her most secret parts and started to rub hungrily with his fist at his fiercely distended shaft, his dark eyes glittering with lust.

'Come on, Cernwi!' challenged Eda. 'Give me a taste

272

of that fine weapon! Is the Roman girl to have all the fun?'

Suddenly Cernwi lunged at her, still gripping his rampant phallus. Flinging himself between her legs, he shoved and prodded desperately until the rounded, velvety tip slid lustfully between Eda's parted labia. She guided him and caressed him all the way, crooning encouragement as the big man, gasping, drove his shaft deeply into her hungry vagina.

'Oh, yes, Cernwi!' gasped Eda, wrapping her legs tightly around him. 'What a beautiful fat prick, drive it into me! Let me feel all of it, filling me, fucking me!'

Grunting out his passion, Cernwi, red-faced, bucked and pounded at her command, while the others watched avidly, lapping up the sight of his angry great penis sliding so hungrily in and out of Eda's greedy love passage. Eda was climaxing already, her face flushed and sweating as she pushed her swollen breasts up against Cernwi's mouth, urging him to take and suck her distended scarlet teats. Cernwi thrust harder and harder, and was soon uttering his own hoarse cry of fulfilment as he convulsed to his own release deep within her.

Catrina felt the despair wash over her as the bonds chafed her wrists and ankles, knowing that she was a prisoner of these people. Yet her traitorous body trembled with instinctive arousal at the sight of the crude copulation; she could feel that her own nipples were tingling and stiff as they protruded from the whorls of blue paint that encircled her breasts, and her swollen labia pulsed with a strange, deep hunger. But she wasn't hungry for Cernwi, with his avid eyes and his hugely distended weapon, which he was even now pulling out from Eda's sated loins. Not him. Oh, she wanted Alexius . . .

She heard a low, menacing rumble of thunder in the distance, rolling across the high hills, and she closed her eyes. Oh, goddess, give me your aid . . .

Then, suddenly, she heard the jarring scrape of metal against rock, and there seemed to be tall, silent figures springing out from the shadows all around them. Someone – she thought it was Eda – let out a moan of fear as the half-naked tribespeople huddled together around their tiny fire, and Catrina's head jerked up in disbelief.

Soldiers. Soldiers of the Eagle crest, wearing sinuous chain-link armour that glittered in the firelight as they closed in on Luad and his followers. Their gleaming swords were raised high. And at their head, his harsh Roman profile starkly outlined against the towering black rocks, was Alexius.

Catrina held herself very still as her heart thudded against her ribs. This must be the end. He had followed her here to kill her.

In the same instant, she felt the sting of cold metal at her throat, and she realised that Luad was beside her. He was panting heavily; she could smell the potent metheglin on his breath, and his small, sharp knife was pressed against her neck.

'Come any closer, Roman,' Luad hissed out, 'and I'll kill her.'

'If you touch her, priest,' said Alexius softly, 'then rest assured that you and all your people will die.'

'Not me, Roman!' Luad was fiercely hacking at her bonds; in a moment she was free, and he was holding her tightly so that her back was pressed against his chest, her body a naked, blue-painted human shield for him, with his knife still pricking her throat. 'You'll not get me without killing the girl first!'

His other hand encircled her waist tightly. Grinning because he was still drunk, he slid his hand up to stroke and pull at her painted nipples, taunting, 'She's a little beauty, isn't she, Roman? You've had your turn of her. Was she good? Now she's mine!'

Alexius raised his hand, and his men surged forwards. There was a warning glitter of light as Luad raised his knife, and Catrina closed her eyes, her insides churning with sick despair. She almost felt sorry for Luad. He didn't realise that Alexius didn't *care* if she lived or died. She prayed desperately to her goddess.

In the heavy stillness of the hot night, there was a searing flash of light that brought day to the lonely mountainside, starkly illuminating the terrified faces of Luad's followers and the grim features of the soldiers who surrounded them. It was followed by a fierce rumble of thunder that gathered and rolled amongst the bleak, high rocks overhead, gathering strength until the ground itself seemed to shake.

Luad's followers cowered in terror, covering their eyes. 'Taranis is angry!' they whimpered helplessly. 'Taranis the thunder god is hurling down his wrath upon us for daring to violate the holy priestess!'

And in that moment, Alexius stepped towards them with his hand held high. Yet another blinding flash of lightning exploded across the mountainside, and they saw that he was gripping a small silver object that glinted and flashed in the lightning's glare.

Catrina's amulet.

Luad hissed aloud at the sight of it, and his hand that bore the knife fell unsteadily to his side.

Alexius, still speaking the tribesmen's language, said clearly, 'Yes, Taranis is angry with you, and with good reason. By the power of this sacred silver amulet, I command you to let the girl Catrina go unharmed. See how the gods rage at you for daring to harm their holy priestess!'

The thunder rumbled again, almost drowning out the last of his words. But it didn't matter, because he'd said enough. Luad, crying out in fear as the ground seemed to shake beneath his feet, flung himself to the ground with the rest of them, covering his face with his hands. And then, as the rain began to pour down from the overloaded sky in torrents, Alexius strode across the rocky clearing towards Catrina and said quietly, so that only she could hear him, 'I think you'd better come with me. Now. Before they realise that the thunder was just a lucky accident.'

She gazed up at him white-faced as the rain poured down on her helpless, naked figure. 'Alexius, you shouldn't have followed me here. It was just a trap to lure you up here and kill you! Go while you can, Alexius, please!'

He gazed down at her, his face slick with rain beneath his bronze helmet, while his blue eyes gleamed with something that was almost amusement.

'*Mithras*,' he breathed, 'you mean I've tracked you all this way for nothing? You don't want to come with me?'

'I do, oh, I do! But I've brought you nothing but trouble, and you must hate me for it – '

'Allow me,' he said, 'to be the judge of that.'

Another jagged sheet of lightning trapped them in its glare. Alexius gazed down at her slender, shivering body, with its garish blue paint marks already starting to trickle wetly down her skin under the onslaught of the rain.

'Perhaps from now on,' he went on quietly, 'I'll have to look after you better, my little wild one.' Then he put her silver amulet around her neck and wrapped her in his heavy soldier's cloak before carrying her over to his horse. Luad and his minions crouched and prayed desperately as Taranis the thunder god rumbled overhead and the rain sluiced relentlessly across the bleak mountainside.

A blackbird sang in a leafy birch overhead, and the morning sky was a pale, rain-washed blue. The grass, still beaded with bright drops of moisture after last night's storm, sparkled in the rays of the warm sun.

After leaving Luad's camp, the soldiers had ridden south through the darkness for many miles with Catrina in their midst. At last, just when she'd felt as if the relentless rain had penetrated to her very bones, they pulled up to shelter in a warm, dry cave in the lee of a hillside. Alexius had brought Catrina a fresh tunic and cloak to wrap herself in, and then, as she knelt shivering beside the fire they'd built, one of the other soldiers brought her food: smoked strips of savoury venison, and wheaten bread, and a beaker of warming red wine that brought life at last to her chilled limbs. After that, she'd slept in a recess of the dark cave, too weary to think.

And now that morning had come, she was bathing herself in a tree-shaded stream, as Alexius had told her to do after they'd broken their fast. 'They'll never let you in through the gates of the fortress if you turn up looking like a blue-painted barbarian,' he'd pointed out.

Catrina had been about to react fiercely to his autocratic tone, but she swallowed down her retort, because she didn't even like to guess in what role she was going back into the fortress of Eboracum. She was a prisoner, naturally. *His* prisoner. But what then?

She dipped herself in the clear water, trying very hard not to think about Alexius or her future because it was all too confusing and too painful. The fast-flowing stream had carved itself a deep, fern-fringed pool here beneath the shade of the birch grove, and she was able to submerge herself with ease. Slowly she rubbed at her skin, watching the blue dye float off and trickle away. The last trace of her past, because she wasn't British, but Roman. Luad had told her so, in his last, vicious verbal thrust. Her amulet felt strangely heavy between her breasts, almost alien; she rubbed sadly at the smooth silver, thinking how even her precious talisman had betrayed her, because that, too, was not what it seemed.

The blackbird had hopped nearer now, and was trilling joyfully on a branch overhead. She leaned back in the water to listen to him, feeling the sun kiss her face, and she wished, she wished . . .

'A water spirit,' said a familiar male voice thoughtfully from the bank behind her. 'Not a priestess, but a nymph. A naiad of the pool.'

Catrina gasped and whirled round, spluttering as the water caught her throat. Alexius!

She crossed her arms protectively across her naked breasts, but he just laughed. Unselfconsciously removing his leather boots and the knee-length linen tunic he wore beneath his armour, he slipped into the pool beside her, sending the blackbird chattering away in alarm. 'You need some help,' he said seriously. 'Here, let me.'

And with slow, warming strokes, he began to caress her shoulders and back, rubbing the blue paint from her skin. Catrina, feeling helpless tremors of desire tearing through her as he worked, said desperately, 'I'm not a naiad, or a priestess, or anything, Al-Alexius!' Her tongue stumbled familiarly on his name. 'I'm not even one of the tribe!'

'I know,' he said gently. His hands had travelled up to her breasts, and were gently caressing her taut raspberry nipples beneath the water.

'You knew?' she gasped, feeling the last of her brain-power rapidly departing as his fingers did their slow, relentless work. 'You knew I was Roman?'

'I'd long suspected it,' he said gravely. 'I took your amulet on an impulse, a wrong impulse, I admit. But, you see, I was curious. Even without seeing it, just the shape of it reminded me of something I'd seen before, and when I made enquiries, I discovered why. It turned out to be the emblem of a well-known patrician family, who were lost in the terrible floods that engulfed the plains around Eboracum many years ago.'

Catrina gazed up at him silently. 'No one else survived?' she whispered in a small voice.

His hands gentled her shoulders. 'I'm sorry, no. But you have a name now, Catrina, an identity. I made further enquiries, and also discovered that there is a substantial amount of money and property awaiting you in Rome. We will hire lawyers to prove your claim; the amulet will be invaluable evidence.'

She shook her head slowly, her green eyes dark and

haunted in her small face. Rome was the end of the earth. It meant nothing to her. She tried to imagine her future, and could see nothing.

'But I'm your prisoner,' she whispered. 'How could I get to Rome, even if I wanted to? What are you going to do with me, Alexius?'

The current was swirling around them; he held her more firmly, closer to his own powerful form. 'What, precisely, do you mean, *mea mellita*?'

Catrina gasped. Was it her imagination, or was there a glint of wicked humour in his eyes? And – dear goddess – she could feel his body pressing against her in the cool embrace of the water, could feel him warm and throbbing into hard life against her naked belly . . .

She licked her suddenly dry lips, conscious of her heart pounding painfully against her ribs. 'I mean . . . oh, Alexius, you thought I was going to kill you! You found that knife – you must have hated me!'

He looked suddenly serious. 'I never hated you. But finding the hidden knife disturbed me, because it didn't seem to make sense.'

She gazed up at him. 'That knife, with your name on it. It was mine, but I'd lost it, and I had no intention of looking for it. I – I *did* come to Eboracum to get my revenge, but then I found that somehow, I didn't want vengeance any more. And Luad had sent spies, who reported to him that I'd failed. That was why he sent his men after you, to start the fire and to attack you in the streets. But I just don't understand how the knife came to be hidden in your house!'

He touched her cheek gently. 'Julia could explain it all to you. If she was here. But she'll be on board ship by now, bound for warmer climes, with her gladiator Falco.'

'No!' breathed Catrina. 'But how – '

'Little one,' said Alexius, tenderly interrupting her, 'my men are preparing the horses. We have to set off again very shortly. And you still have much to learn of the ways of Rome. Before I make you my wife.'

279

She gasped in surprise, but he silenced her by kissing her, and she felt her blood surge as his warm, firm mouth moved gently over hers. With swift, powerful movements, he lifted her on to the mossy bank so that her legs still dangled in the clear water. Then he parted her thighs gently.

'You still need some attention – here,' he pointed out, showing her where the blue warrior-paint still streaked her loins and pudenda. She bent anxiously to look, her wet blonde hair trailing silkily along his bronzed, muscled forearms; and then he dipped his head carefully at the apex of her thighs and ran his rasping tongue gently up and down the crinkled folds and crevices of her labia.

The heat of his tongue after the cold water of the pool was such bliss that Catrina instinctively clutched at his dark cropped head with her hands and pulled him towards her. 'More,' she whispered softly, 'oh, more, Roman . . .'

He gave her more, thrusting and pleasuring with his strong, skilful tongue as she leaned her head back and felt the dappled heat of the sun caressing her tingling breasts.

Then he was heaving himself out of the water, shaking the moisture from his bronzed skin like a big hunting dog. She barely had time to gasp at the sight of his darkly erect phallus before he was on the turf beside her, crushing her in his arms as she nestled joyously against his damp, beautiful body. She ran her fingers lasciviously over the silky-soft mat of dark hair that adorned his chest.

'*Mea mellita,*' he whispered, 'you will make a wonderful Roman wife. You will forget your British ways very quickly, I promise you.'

A shadow seemed to cross Catrina's face, but Alexius didn't see it. Pushing and caressing with her small hands, she gently persuaded him to lie on his back. He did so with a contented sigh, and Catrina started to kiss and bite at the hard brown nubs of his nipples, while her hand strayed downwards to stroke the iron hardness of his hair-covered thighs, tantalising him with the nearness of her busy fingers, until at last they fastened round his hardened phallus, coaxing it to swell and thicken even more as it reared up from its dark cradle of hair.

Catrina ringed her forefinger and thumb and began to stroke up and down his bone-hard penis very slowly, watching his face all the time. 'If I have much to learn of Rome,' she whispered, defiantly tossing her long wet hair back from her face, 'then you, my Alexius, have much to learn of the ways of the tribe.'

And with that she flung her leg across him, straddling his hips with ease, and took his deliciously lengthy phallus deep into her hot vagina, moaning and writhing as she felt the pleasure engulf her.

He smiled lazily up at her, his hands pillowing his head, but his body was growing tense and his breathing was becoming faster as she rode him voluptuously. 'I've told you before, Catrina,' he said huskily, 'you're not one of the tribe. You're Roman, through and through.'

Then he reached up to caress and squeeze her pouting nipples, and she felt the hard pleasure-pain engulf her.

Suddenly going very still, she gazed down at him, her green eyes glinting. She could feel the weight of her silver amulet around her neck, could feel it chafing between her breasts, and somehow it was filling her with renewed power and strength.

'Alexius,' she said.

'Mm?'

'Did you really think that the arrival of the thunder was just an accident?'

'Why, of course.' He laughed. 'What else?'

Smiling to herself, she lifted herself almost to the extremity of his beautifully long, thick shaft, glancing down to see how it was glistening with her body's secret juices. Then she slid back on him very slowly, squeezing her rippling inner muscles around his hardened flesh, hearing him cry out in sudden need as she engulfed him once more.

'I'm still one of the tribespeople, Alexius,' she said softly. 'You'd best remember that. Don't underestimate me.'

She saw his blue eyes open wide in sudden surprise, and, smiling wickedly, she started to speed up. She reached down at the same time to play with herself, feeling how the nectar of her own body had made her voluptuous flesh-folds slick and juicy, while her hot, tiny kernel of desire was plump and quivering, and ready to explode with just one touch.

She could see the base of Alexius' beautiful penis, thrusting so strongly from its cradle of dark hair before it became buried in her silken vulva. Silently, licking her lips, she gazed down at the beautiful, muscular power of his bronzed, battle-scarred body, and saw the first faint glimmer of unease in his hard-boned face.

'Fill me, Roman,' she said softly, still gazing into his eyes. 'Drive your hard penis deep inside me. I want to hear you gasp out my name. I want you to beg me for mercy. You say I am Roman, but I still have the power, the power of the old ones of the tribe, and you would do well to remember it.'

He was panting now, and there was a glimmer of sweat on his forehead as she rose and fell so sinuously above him, taking in all of him, every delicious inch, only to slide up from him again, feeling the velvety, rounded tip straining desperately to dive deep within her again as she tormented him. Suddenly, crying out in harsh need, she started to pound up and down rapidly on him, clenching his beautiful, solid shaft with all her inner strength. Rubbing her fingers hard against her soaking clitoris, she soared into mind-shattering waves of rapture as she shuddered and gasped above his tormented body.

Then, without warning, she pulled herself off him, and

he groaned in despair, his massive penis jerking and quivering in frustrated anger.

'Oh, Alexius. Sexual indulgence is a fatal weakness – remember?' she whispered gently, crouching down by his hips and caressing his full, aching testicles with wicked darts of her pink tongue.

'Catrina,' he moaned, trying to reach for her head, to pull her down on him. 'Catrina, you witch – '

'Beg, Alexius. Beg me for mercy.'

Shuddering with need, he clenched his fists and grated, 'Please. Whatever you want, Catrina, anything. Only take me now – take me in your mouth, I beg you – '

With a mischievous smile, she dipped her head and formed her lips into a perfect circle. Then she wrapped her tongue round his throbbing glans, licking and stroking round the trembling rim and feeling the tiny eye at the tip where the clear liquid already oozed. At last she closed her eyes and drove her head down as far as she could to suck sweetly at his hot shaft, taking as much of its sturdy length into her mouth as possible. Almost immediately, she felt his hips clench beneath her. Reaching to stroke at the velvety sac of his straining balls with her fingers, she shivered with delight as she felt his warm, salty seed shoot fiercely into her mouth, while his powerful body spasmed and convulsed helplessly beneath her velvety lips.

At last, when she'd licked the very last drop from his softening phallus and he lay back utterly exhausted, she leaned across his body to kiss his closed eyes, letting her nipples trail across his sweat-sheened chest.

'Look at me, Alexius,' she whispered huskily. 'Look at me. And prepare to pay homage to your priestess.'

Visit the Black Lace website at
www.blacklace-books.co.uk